# homefree

## by bobbi loney

ONION RIVER PRESS

Burlington, Vermont

Onion River Press
89 Church Street
Burlington, VT 05401
info@onionriverpress.com
www.onionriverpress.com

ISBN: 978-1-957184-88-3

Library of Congress Control Number: 2024922461

*for Gerry*

# PART ONE

*WHITE PLAINS JOURNAL, June 12*

*Possible DWI with Injuries*

*White Plains, New York — Two passengers in critical condition were taken to White Plains Hospital yesterday evening following a one-car crash on Bronx River Parkway. According to New York State Police, the accident occurred about 8 p.m., when the vehicle struck a concrete barrier. Alcohol appeared to be a factor. The driver, Alice Wangera, 29, a Brandt University adjunct professor from New York City, was uninjured, and is being held at Westchester County Jail pending possible DWI and other charges. The passengers were her daughter, Makena Wangera, 7, and Adam St. John, 21, a Brandt University student from Farleys' Dock, New York. All were wearing seatbelts.*

# Chapter 1

## Alice

Kena slid her MedicAlert band over her hand and set it on top of her spelling list in the bin on the conveyer belt. Everything else was in the locker in the waiting room: her watch and charm and her beloved pink jacket. There was a rule: no metal. No buckles. No zippers.

No butterfly barrettes.

Patrice, her foster mother, wore the canvas slip-ons she used for jail, and Kena had on her loathsome rubber rain boots. It was their routine and, even though she was barely eight, Kena had it down. She stepped through the portal, the buzzer buzzed, and she held her arms out in what she'd named the Jesus pose.

Patrice had found that little item out when her teacher called to report that Kena had invented a jail-visiting game at recess. Patrice didn't tell Ms. Chau she thought it was funny. Or how glad she was that Kena wasn't ashamed, like too many of her foster kids had been over the years, to have a parent in jail.

The CO, short for Correctional Officer—not to be called a guard, the lady CO told Kena that first time, like a reprimand—passed the wand down Kena's small frame from head to toe, even though they all knew what had caused the buzzing. Kena turned around for the CO to scan her backside, standing stiff as a board, her left arm with its shiny scars trembling from the task of keeping itself straight. Finally, as if it needed to sneak up on the culprit, the wand got to her left elbow and the pins inside holding it together.

BZZZ.

Kena Wangera and Patrice Washington were Black, like most of the visitors. Most of the COs were white, and Kena's friend Toby told her it was because of "white privilege." But Kena didn't think it was much of a privilege to be suspicious all the time, and she didn't think being any particular color had a thing to do with how the COs didn't meet her eyes like she'd done something wrong, or was about to. Kena was used to living in two worlds, one Black and one White, but she hadn't been able to break into this one with her "How are you today" or smile.

Obeying the rules, capital R, didn't make things friendlier, either. And if she broke one, she might not get to see her mother. It had happened that one time, when they hadn't known that her new-at-Goodwill back-to-school dress's shiny buttons contained real metal.

Patrice had had foster kids before—kids who had a mother or father, or both, in prison upstate or in jail, like Kena's mother, Alice Wangera, and she prided herself on not judging. But she'd judged Alice before she'd even met her. That a no-nothin' white girl had been allowed to adopt a Black child from Africa was just plain wrong, no matter how many fancy degrees she'd collected.

But then, coming up week after week on the Metro, sitting to the side of the visiting room and sneaking looks at them—at Kena on her knees on the stool to reach Alice's hand over the two foot barrier— she saw Kena's unwavering faith in her white mother, and that white mother's valiant efforts not to let that faith down. The stools and table were hard plastic; the only softness came and left with the people, and most didn't dare show their tender patchworked parts. But Kena did. And Alice tried, for Kena. They couldn't look more different, tiny, dark Kena with her bright beads flashing with every move of her head, and she moved it a lot. And pale, freckled Alice with practically no hair at all, and what there was, red fuzz. Every week the circles under her eyes were darker and her tall, bony frame skinnier. Patrice was beginning to think that Alice needed a mother as much as any of the children who'd slept under her roof.

◊

"Then Wanjiru shut her eyes tight and counted, moja, mbili..." Alice said softly.

Kena finished: "Saba, nana, tisa, kumi!" Ten.

It was always the same, and that's how Kena liked it. First "catching up," then a story, and lastly, spelling.

Alice continued. "And then she heard them, with their warbles and pips, their gentle coos and their rude squawks, singing, singing for *her* where she perched in Mugumo, the great fig tree. And even though Sparrow Lark..." she paused. "and Scaly Babbler..."

Kena covered her mouth and giggled.

"...and little Flycatcher and Golden Weaver didn't sing in words, Wanjiru knew them in her heart. She opened her eyes, and what do you think she saw?"

Kena opened her eyes. "A sunbeam!"

"A sunbeam that had found a path between the leaves and was loving the water drops left over from the storm. And they'd given birth to..."

"A rainbow!"

"And who is that rainbow bird?"

"Me!"

Alice nested Kena's fingers in hers and sang under her breath.

"Little bird, our soft and downy bird, singing in the tree, in the tall tree, sing, sing free, ina' amaazo, banajaanh." Kena joined in, whisper-singing too.

"Little bird, our rising rainbow bird, rising to the moon, to the moon sky, fly, fly free, babaamise, banajaanh." The babel of visiting room voices softened, even the baby's.

The two COs, arms crossed, studied the ceiling, careful not to look at each other. There was a rule against singing.

Kena's hand stirred, but Alice hung on. She had 50 minutes a week to touch her daughter, and it was the only time she truly knew Kena was safe. Alice ached to hold her, but she was stuck fast to the unforgiving stool. Had someone made a decree: design a room that punishes not just a body, but its soul, too? She looked over at Patrice, sitting on the other side of the room, reading.

Patrice had told her Kena jabbered nonstop all the way there, and Alice had been stabbed with jealousy. But then Patrice had said Kena was quiet all the way back. Did Patrice hold her hand? Did she pull her over onto her lap? It seemed rude to ask. Of course she would!

But did she?

Alice pressed her free hand against her stomach, as if she'd carried Kena inside like other mothers.

"Oliver sang me that song! Right, Mama? He sang me to sleep when I was a baby and crawled to the door, in case I was looking. Right, Mama?"

"Yes." Alice's guilt sat like a stone in her belly.

Kena pried her spelling list oh-so-slowly out of her pocket, as if dragging it out might drag out their time together too. When she'd brought her first list in October, they hadn't let her bring it in. Kena had wondered if it was the words. Was it "ghost"? Or "witch"? Those were not good words to some people, she'd told Patrice. But the next week, after Alice asked for permission, she was allowed to bring the list. And ghost was still on it, because Kena had forgotten the silent h on her test. Silent like a ghost, her teacher said, to help her remember. But Kena knew ghosts weren't always silent.

"It's holiday words," Kena said. She slipped the paper over the barricade like she was mailing a letter. "I only need to do the ones that are circled. I know the rest."

Alice looked over the list. The words were from Christmas, Hanukkah, Kwanzaa, and the winter solstice. Christmas was all about Santa Claus and decorations. Jesus and the shepherds and angels weren't there. It's just a story about a baby, Alice thought. The politics came later, at Easter.

"First word. Wreath. We put the wreath on the door."

"R-e…no, I mean…" Kena frowned. "W! W-r-e-a-t-h. Wreath." She raised her finger over her head to mark an invisible scoreboard, but she didn't shout. Keep it down, stick to your side of the table, and be good. Kena tried.

"I promise, Mama! I'll be so good! The best girl! So good you won't even believe it!" The words had torn at Alice's heart. She'd thought of her First Communion, when not being "a good girl" had suddenly become a sin she was supposed to confess to a priest.

"Peter and Jackie's aunt gave us a wreath and Patrice put it on our door," Kena said.

*Us. Our.* To squash her jealousy, Alice asked, "What about a tree?"

"Not 'til Christmas Eve. That's what they do, Patrice and her sister Niah. The same name as Nia, Mama, but she spells it different. And she doesn't know anything about Kenya. Toby helped me make Nia's birthday card and Patrice mailed it. She used *four* stamps!"

"Kenya's far away."

"I drew an elephant. I was going to draw a cake, but Toby said it was *ordinary.* Draw something *Africa.* Mama! Can Nia go to the elephant orphanage with Oliver and us now she's five?"

"We'll have to wait and see. Your next word is Santa Claus." Alice sang around the lump in her throat. "Here Comes Santa Claus, here comes Santa Claus, right down Santa Claus lane." Would they ever get back to Kenya?

"S-a-n-t-a-c-l-a-w-s! Get it? Santa *Claws*, like Santa *cat*! In my Santa letter I asked for only one thing."

Alice's heart took a dive. An American Girl doll had been on Kena's list for two years.

"I asked for us to go home," Kena said proudly.

Alice felt her face go stiff. For a second, she watched herself wondering too. Maybe Santa—"Kena, that's not—"

Kena narrowed her eyes. "That's what Keisha said! She said it was stupid! I said *she* was stupid. If you don't even ask, you can never get it!"

Oh, baby. Oh, bineshii. But she couldn't get into it again, *couldn't*, so close to the end of their hour.

"Kena, if someone calls you stupid, don't call them stupid back— *especially* if it's the person who shares your room! That's not smart; it just gets a fight going." Alice saw it every day in jail and had learned to put her head down and not meet anyone's eyes. "Just one more word. Jingle. 'Jingle bells, jingle bells, jingle all the way.'" She was a playlist of holiday hits.

"J-i-n-g-l-e! Jingle bells, Batman smells, Robin lays an egg!" Kena's voice rose, and as it did, she rose too, until she was sprawled halfway across the barricade.

"Kena, stop!" Alice whispered.

"That's what Toby sings! It's funny!"

"You need to sit down." Alice cut her eyes at the CO in the back of the room. Kena began pulling on her hair.

"Don't sing that at school."

"I know! I'm not '*stupid*'!"

Alice peeked again at the CO and was relieved to see she wasn't looking at them. It was all so—*stupid*! How did they expect kids to sit and be quiet on a hard stool for 50 minutes?

But a lot of people inside didn't even have that.

Alice leaned and stretched her arm and plucked Kena's hand off her head. "Patrice did a good job with your hair."

"For the concert, except I'll have butterflies. Mama, are you gonna come see me?" But Kena knew the answer and was abruptly on the verge of tears.

"Patrice will take pictures and you can show me," Alice said, making her voice matter-of-fact like she would for Kena's blood tests, as if every little girl got poked with needles all of her life.

"You won't be there for the tree!" Kena wailed. "Will you have one? I want to see your room!"

They'd been over it a hundred times. And thank God Kena couldn't see her "room." Wanting Kena to picture it as a cozy place, she'd made the mistake of saying it was like the little room on the train to Wisconsin the one time they went. How they'd loved the little sink and hidden toilet and seat that became a bed. Like playing house.

"It's a rule so the people I live with have privacy."

"I hate rules!"

"Five minutes," a CO called out, and Kena went into fast forward.

"I forgot to say! Toby had his birthday too. He's 12! Patrice made M&M cupcakes. Keisha picked out all the green ones. She said they taste like puke! That's rude! And they taste all the same anyway, because Oliver and me did that test with our eyes closed, remember, Mama? I made Toby a card with a horse but Keisha said it was a giraffe because of the spots, but it was a paloosa. Toby might can go home for vacation but they didn't say yet. Ms. Chau let us make snowmen with balls and toothpicks. Omar poked his with his pencil and little beads stuck all over and Ms. Chau said it was a Holy Mess!" Kena stopped for a breath.

"Ms. Chau folded paper and stapled them to be books and cut them to be shapes; I chose tree," she went on. "Mama, I told them not to cut angels, how it was disrepec-*spec*-ful. An angel might be somebody from your family! Are angels and ghosts the same?"

Alice had wondered the same thing when she was little. Sometimes she still did. "I don't know."

"I think first you're a ghost and then an angel, unless you want to stay a ghost so you can visit your people. Angels only Watch Over. Can I go to a movie with Toby? He can go with a friend now he's 12, and I'm probably his best friend." Kena darted a look at Patrice. "Patrice said I can't go see Adam. But Mama, kids visit hospitals. Toby visited his grandma!" Kena stopped, her eyes welling up. "I miss Adam!" she wailed.

Alice wanted to raise her own head up and howl too. She'd be in line going to Rec and be suddenly flooded with terror; Adam could die! When I get to that window, when I go one more step, after my next breath. He might have died a minute ago. And she would lurch.

In her mind she'd be falling, falling headlong, head over heels, tumbling in slow motion and landing in a heap. In a *heap*. She *saw* the word, like it was The End at the end of it all. Like a mess of parts, her arms and legs and elbows tangled in a pile, a pile of worthless rags of a person to be swept up and thrown out with the trash. But there was Kena.

There was *Kena*, so she would put her hand on the wall like a blind person and carefully take the next step.

"I miss Adam," Kena whispered, tears trickling down her cheeks, her eyes begging Alice.

"Time!" the CO called out.

Voices rose as people hurried to say their last things and do their goodbye hugs. The baby started crying. Kena ran around the table and flung her arms around Alice. Alice bent and breathed her in.

"Okay, people!"

Alice wiped Kena's cheeks with her palms and kissed her on her forehead and the tip of her nose. She took the scrap of paper out of the pocket of her jumpsuit and tucked it into Kena's pocket. "Remember to find one good thing a day to tell me." Patrice was there.

Kena wrapped back around Alice and dug her fingers into her back, hard. Alice felt mumbles against her belly. "What?" she whispered.

"I *said* you didn't *tell* me if I can go to the *movie!*" Kena answered, punching her head into Alice's stomach. The baby cried louder.

Kena was sobbing. She *needed* to cry. Alice worried that Kena, like her, didn't cry *enough*.

"Wangera!"

Kena had to stop. Had to, had to. Patrice reached out. Alice sang into Kena's ear. "Jingle bells, Batman smells, Robin laid an egg, the Batmobile lost a wheel, and the Joker got away." Kena looked up in astonishment.

Alice smiled. She made herself peel Kena off and pulled the tissue from her pocket. She wiped Kena's cheeks again, and then her nose. Kena shuddered, making an effort. The baby was quiet, thank God. Alice placed Kena's hand into Patrice's. "Thank you. I can never—"

Patrice stopped her. "I left that book you asked about, by Anne Lamott."

"You found it?"

"At the nursing home, of all places. One of my ladies had it from her pastor." Patrice held up Alice's last book. "Maybe I'll read this one."

"Oh! I hope you like it!"

"You take it easy, honey." Patrice touched Alice's hand and turned for the door. As usual, they would be the last through while every-one watched.

"Mama! My words!"

Another rule: Don't leave *anything* in the visiting room, not even an innocent piece of primary school paper. As Alice picked it up she had a crazy desire to bite the corner off and swallow it—a piece of Kena, like Holy Communion.

But when Kena ran back and grabbed it, Alice held it out and stepped away. No more tears. She blew Kena a kiss when she looked back as the door closed behind her. The window was almost over her head, and Alice saw her hand waving the white paper like a flag. The other hand was twisting, pulling her hair. And then she was gone.

Every Sunday, Alice woke up to joy. She pulled on her ugly orange jumpsuit in joy. She waited in line for the limp pancakes and ate them in joy, and then: "Wangera! Visitor!" Fifty minutes.

"Let's go, Wangera."

How was she supposed to do this?

◊

Kena always saved her poem until the train was by the river. She took it out of her pocket.

> *The same stars*
> *The same moon*
> *The same sun*
> *Look up, and I am too*
> *And we are home*

She closed her fist around it. She pulled her hood over her head and pressed her forehead against the cold window. The water was flat and gray like the sky. You wouldn't be able to tell where one left off and the other started if it wasn't for the brown hills in between.

Patrice held her place with a finger to put her other hand on Kena's head. She rested it there as she returned to the book: *Grace. (Eventually)*

# Chapter 2

## Oliver

"All the animals chanted together, the most squabbly and the most picky-picky and even the most shy. No one wanted to pass up an opportunity to see the others make fools of themselves: 'Kana ka Nikora'…do you know it, Jaafar? Kana ka Nikora kona kora kora."

Oliver sang the tongue twister faster and faster until kora became kona and kana became nana or something else entirely. He knew he couldn't carry a tune, so he exaggerated his wrong notes to make it even funnier. "Then Nicole's child sees a frog and runs, and when the frog sees Nicole's child, it runs too. Aaah!"

When he got to where the frog sees Nicole's child, Oliver bugged his eyes and tongue out and waved his long, spidery arms up in fright until Jaafar pulled his T-shirt up over his mouth to hide his smile. Oliver leaned his head back against the cool wall of the main house and indicated the space on the bench next to him for Jaafar to sit. He checked his watch. He was leaving in two hours for Nairobi and still had to say his goodbyes.

But first, this.

"Did Tata Wanja tell you why she wanted you to see me?" he asked.

Jaafar swung his bare feet and frowned at the red clay beneath them, so different from his home by the sea. "Yes, Anka."

"So?"

"I would not do the lessons."

"All of the children begin at your age, Jaafar. Yet you refused?"

"Yes, Anka, that is true." He risked a glance at Oliver's face.

"And you wouldn't say why."

The little boy folded his arms across his thin chest and stuck his lip out.

"Ah, I see," Oliver nodded. "You are showing me how you refused. *Asante.* Thank you. Now, can you show me *why*? That would be helpful."

Jaafar jumped to the ground. He had to think. When he was given over to Mr. Wangera in his village, he was frightened because the man was so very tall. But on their long journey Mr. Wangera gave Jaafar his own money to buy a Coca-Cola.

Jaafar walked away, looking back and waving goodbye until he came to where the girls' skirts hung between two papaya trees.

"I understand," Oliver called out.

Jaafar ran back. Uncle sounded sad.

Jaafar hopped in a circle. The packed dirt was damp and cool. His feet made small impressions. *Kona kora kora.* He had shown he wanted to go home, but still there were angry flies buzzing in his stomach. He hopped harder.

"Wait here," Oliver said, and in a few long strides he leaped up the steps, crossed the verandah, and went inside. He returned swinging a cloth bag from his hand. "Look inside."

Jaafar saw something wrapped in a bright red kanga. Oliver pulled back the cloth and took out a laptop. When he opened it, the screen lit up. Oliver touched it.

Jaafar held his breath. It was like Anka had a magic finger. Every time he touched the screen, a new picture came. Jaafar saw the teacher Tata Wanja, Mr. Wangera's sister. And there were the children behind the long desks, clapping. There were boys playing football. And there were his age-mates setting the tables. Jaafar wasn't there. He saw little children on grass and then a baby on a scale like at the market, and the baby ladies smiling. And one more. Everyone together. Two boys in the back held up a banner. He looked but he was not there, he knew.

"What does it say?" Jaafar asked.

"Kirinyaga's Children's Home. 'Where God lives.' Here, on the slopes of Mount Kenya. A good place. And *always*, when boys and girls go away to school or university or to learn a trade, at New Year's they'll tell their friends they are going home to Kirinyaga, and their return will be celebrated. Babies come, and young children and older, and all are welcomed when they first come and, later, welcomed back home."

Jaafar hopped in a circle to keep away from his thoughts. He hopped faster. He ran to the furthest papaya tree and pulled roughly on the skirt hanging next to it. He didn't mean for it to fall and quickly grabbed it up. He turned away and rubbed and rubbed the skirt, but the dirt just spread.

Oliver went to Jaafar. He took the skirt gently from his hands. "It doesn't matter. It will wash." He placed his big hand on Jaafar's back. Finally he felt the shudder of Jaafar's grief begin to rise. The little boy had been at Kirinyaga for five days. He'd been put with a neighbor who didn't want him a month before that. He'd lost his mother a week before that.

Six weeks holding such devastation.

He picked Jaafar up. He walked up and down with the little boy's arms and legs wrapped around him. He walked and rocked, like walking a baby—like walking Kena—until Jaafar's sobs wound down and Jaafar rested his head on Oliver's shoulder. Oliver could hear the singing from the school on the hill, from Sunday church service—words he knew by heart, though he no longer believed them. "Ve Umwe Yu—there is One above."

They returned to the bench, and Oliver handed Jaafar a handkerchief.

"Blow."

Jaafar blew. He sighed.

"I will live here." He leaned against the tall uncle in surrender.

"Yes, ii," Oliver said, and sighed himself. "This is a good place, you'll see." He patted the laptop. "I'm taking these pictures to America, where I'm going to ask them to give things to Kirinyaga."

"Presents?"

"Medicine."

"Medicine is not a proper present."

"Ii. I agree. I'll ask for a building, then."

"It's too big!"

"You're right again! I'll ask for money and we can build it ourselves. Will you help?"

"Ii!"

"Good. If you did get a present, what would it be?"

Jaafar swung his legs. "A book."

"Will the book have pictures?"

"And words."

"So, and what will they say, I wonder?"

"They will say about elephants."

"I think a person who gives a boy a book about elephants would like to see what he looks like, don't you?" Oliver pulled out his phone. Jaafar puzzled it out and then nodded, his eyes wide.

"Where will you stand for your photograph?"

Jaafar jumped down. He tucked his shirt into his shorts. He frowned to show he was a thinking person. Oliver clicked. He pulled out a short cord and attached his phone to the computer. Jaafar ran over, and there he was on the screen!

"Now turn away while I fix a surprise." Jaafar turned. "Come see." It was the picture with the banner. "Look carefully."

Jaafar looked carefully. Then he squealed. "Me! It's me!"

"If you go to school, you'll learn how to use a computer and other important things. So now you will participate with the other children?"

"Yes, Anka."

"Good. That's the second good thing to do."

Jaafar was confused. "What is the first thing?"

"Apologize to Tata Wanja. Why, Jaafar, do you need to apologize?"

"For refusing to do lessons!"

"For refusing to tell her your *reason*. Do you understand? It is permitted to have your strong feelings, Jaafar. It's even important. But it is not helpful to keep silent about them. You see?"

Jaafar nodded.

"Now go play."

"Asante!" Jaafar called out as he ran toward the path that wound up the hill.

"You're welcome," Oliver responded, and sighed, getting up to go inside. An hour later, he leaned back and stretched his arms toward the ceiling. Lillian's latest numbers were off to Washington, DC. He closed his eyes and listened to the children laughing in the kitchen. He wished he could scoop up the sound for when his lonesomeness hollowed his heart.

He heard the cluck-clucking of a chicken and opened his eyes. Aunt Njoki had flown up to the windowsill and was telling him something, probably about Nia. Because if the hen was here, five-year-old Nia was nearby.

"Hodi!" He heard her gruff little voice, and her head popped up in the window. Aunt Njoki stuck her beak into Nia's hair, looking for a seed that Nia would hide there as a treat. As far as the hen was concerned, her job was to take care of Nia, and that included grooming her. Everyone agreed that the chick born so soon after old Njoki's death had to be Njoki herself, come back to continue caring for her orphaned grand-niece. How else to explain the extraordinary bond? And didn't Njoki fly up to gossip with the other spirit ancestors in the mugumo tree?

Nia and Aunt Njoki abruptly disappeared, followed by furious buck-buck-bucking and wailing. Oliver leaned out. Nia's bucket perch was rolling down the incline. Aunt Njoki was flapping and scolding her charge, who was wailing at the top of her lungs—not so much from being hurt, Oliver thought, as from being betrayed by the bucket.

He ducked through the doorway and across the verandah, jumped down, and went around the corner. Nia held up her arms. He felt a sense of satisfaction at the volume of her wails and the solid heft of her, compared to when he'd been there in July. He returned to the verandah and backed into a chair. Aunt Njoki settled herself on the cement floor, which had been washed down that morning and was still damp. A current of air lifted the shirts hanging from post to post. The first Aunt Njoki had been fat and appreciated a cool floor and a breeze. Nia pinched Oliver's chin between fingers that were sticky with pineapple.

"Are you leaving today?"

"Yes."

"To Abbabadda?" Addis Ababa. He didn't correct her, allowing himself this small enjoyment.

"I'm going to America."

"New Yok! Cucu Lillian's grandson went there. Yakee ball!"

Yankee ball? "I'm going to Washington, DC. And to a place

called New Jersey."

"Why? Are you going on holiday?"

He wondered what "'going on holiday" meant to her, who'd never been on one.

"Not on holiday."

"Why?"

Why. It was her latest, to be inserted randomly, to keep him there.

"To get help for Kirinyaga."

"Why?"

She plucked the pen out of his pocket and pushed the end of it. Click, click, click.

"Because there are people in America who like to help children." At least some of them, he thought. "I hope one or two of them will come here and help with the school and the babies."

"Who?"

"I haven't met them yet."

She drew her eyebrows together.

"Tata Wanja has too many to teach. And you children need to learn to write fluent English before secondary school."

"What is that floont English?"

"Flu-ent. Flowing like the streams during the rains. And before you ask why, it's because it will be good for your future."

"I'm going to be a matutu driver." She'd recently had a thrilling ride in one of the colorful minibuses, hiphop blasting from the speakers as they careened around corners and stopped suddenly for animals in the road.

"Does Zari know where you are?" he asked.

"Oh! I'm to tell you there's a surprise!" She ran down the steps. Aunt Njoki shook out her feathers and hurried after her. "Come on!"

Oliver followed them down the hill through the fragrant tunnel of purple passion fruit. He could hear the high voices of the little ones, punctuated by Nia yelling, "He's coming! He's coming!"

When he arrived at the clearing, the nursery teacher called over, grinning. "It's a goodbye present. They're so excited!" She was herding the toddlers and preschoolers into a circle.

Oliver's mother, Zari, and the director, Lillian, were sitting on stools holding sleeping babies. His mother's ample lap held two. He stooped to kiss her cheeks, pushed on an adjacent stool to anchor it, and sat down. His mother handed him a baby. He laid the moist bundle on his legs and straightened her white dress and sunhat. Her eyes flickered behind their lids.

"We're giving up on those Earth balls you brought." Zari pointed. The land was terraced so that the roof of the baby house was below where they sat. And there on the corrugated roof were the blue and green balls, living up to their name. They were truly beached.

"Maybe Wanja can use them for a map project," Oliver said, smiling. Wanja was resourceful. "But somebody better get them off there before they melt."

Lillian clapped her hands. They were ready. The children clasped hands and sang.

"Muti muhande rui-ine, a tree planted on the river, look at its leaves, playing with the wind." They swung their hands, like a gentle breeze.

"Even us, let's play with the wind." They began to move in a slow circle. Then faster. And faster. Two-year-old Mugo looked both thrilled and terrified, his feet barely touching the ground. "Even us, let's play with the wind. Even us, let's play with the wind." Faster and faster, until they all fell down, screaming and laughing and rolling into each other. Aunt Njoki fluttered around them, scolding, and they laughed harder.

Oliver clapped. "Ni Wega! Asante! Thank you!"

Lillian plucked the baby from him as children crowded around to be kissed and patted by the big Uncle who'd come to visit. He breathed them in…pineapple and mango and ugali, eucalyptus and dirt…the smells of home.

"We're so grateful, Oliver. Ni Wega," Lillian said, putting her hand on his arm.

"I'll try to get them to see."

"I know they will, with you as our ambassador." But her forehead was creased. Lillian was an excellent administrator. And wonderful with the children. But she was a worrier.

His mother, still holding a baby, walked partway back with him. "I've been deciding about speaking to you."

He stiffened. He wanted to cover his ears like when he was a child.

"I want you to go to New York and see Alice and Makena. I looked at a map. That place with the medicines in New Jairsay is just across a river from New York City."

He took satisfaction from her mispronunciation, and felt ashamed. As if that gave him permission to dismiss her opinion! They'd reached the path to the boys' house, where he'd slept the last two nights.

"You need to tell Alice how you feel! It isn't fair to keep your feelings a secret."

He thought of Jaafar.

"If your father were alive, he'd say the same thing." Her eyes filled with tears.

But if his taciturn father had been accustomed to talking about feelings, he may have gotten treatment in time.

"I miss him too, Mama."

The baby began to cry. Oliver took him and, with one big hand underneath his head and the other beneath his padded bottom, swung him up and back gently. Surprised, the baby stopped crying and stared at Oliver.

"There you go." He handed him back. "I'll think about it, Mama."

"Makena is going to forget us. We are her *family*! No matter what Alice decided." She went up on her tiptoes and kissed him on both cheeks. "You tell her that!" She turned to walk back, the baby nodding over her shoulder as if he agreed with every word.

New Jairsay to New Yok. Just over the George Washington Bridge. Oliver ducked through the doorway and groped his way in the sudden twilight toward the cot he'd borrowed.

"Hodi!" Wanja called from outside. He grabbed his carryall and joined her on the path.

"They said at church that Thika Road is one lane from the flooding," she said, taking his arm.

"My flight isn't until after midnight. I'll see the boys, and then I just need to stop at my place to pick up a few things."

"Will it be very cold in Washington?" She wrapped her bare arms around herself.

"It will be so cold my toes and fingers will freeze. My nose, also. When I return, you'll see they are all shorter from the frozen bits falling off."

She shoved him.

"I worry. And Maitu worries worse, and it's my job to reassure her. Did she talk about Alice and Kena?"

He sighed. "Ii."

Wanja's silence was as pointed as their mother's words. But it wasn't his fault. Njesu! Not this time.

As they rounded the corner, he saw that most of the older children were there, still dressed in their church best. Many of the neighbors were there too, gossiping in the shade of the verandah. A few boys were wrangling the donkey into a makeshift bridle.

"I should have warned you, standard eight are planning to accompany you to the road. I forbid the rest of them, or you'd have all 38.

And Oliver…" She put her hand on his arm. "Thank you for seeing Jaafar. I knew it wouldn't be easy to fit him in this morning."

"Uncle! You can put everything in the cart!"

Two boys had wheeled the cart behind the donkey. The girls were tucking white poinsettia blossoms under his bridle and into each other's hair. Someone took Oliver's carryall and placed it tenderly in the cart.

He went inside. The youngest of the school children were setting the tables for first lunch, a task they instantly abandoned.

"Tata Wanja said you're going to America!"

"Will you take pictures?"

"How far away is America?"

"Twelve thousand kilometers, she said! You don't listen!"

"And when it's tomorrow night, it will be daytime there!"

"Anka, is that true?"

Surrounded by their curiosity and exuberance, Oliver was filled with gratitude. There wasn't, at least at this moment on this day in this month, one actively sick child among them. May it remain so.

"How many airplanes will you be on?"

"Two. It will take 21 hours."

"That will be tomorrow!"

Just like that, he was aware of his middle. He'd flown many times on planes large and small, and each time felt he had to help keep the airplane aloft with his unwavering attention to every noise and dip. And this time he had an added up-in-the-air feeling, as every hour would bring him closer to Alice and his promise to "think about it."

He grabbed the photograph of Kena at the elephant sanctuary off the desk and tucked it next to his laptop in its bag. When he took the picture, had Alice already decided they wouldn't return this year?

He kissed cheeks all around: the cook and kitchen boys, the old gardener, and Wanja. The children had put two baskets of fruit in the cart for him to bring to the boys at their boarding school.

"Tuthii!" he called to the children waiting at the head of the path. Just one tug was needed; the donkey liked going downhill and knew he'd get a snack at the bottom. He didn't remember about coming back up.

"Kwaheri, Oliver!"

"Kwaherini!"

"Goodbye, Uncle! Come back soon!"

"God go with you!"

"I'll see you when you see me!"

His favorite, the traditional farewell from his childhood.

The path was steep at times, and the boys in the lead enjoyed pretending to almost fall to make the girls laugh. Oliver walked at a more sedate pace in the rear. The children were barefoot, but he wore flip-flops and they pressed between his toes. The midday sun beat down.

"Mr. Wangera, do you think someday I can go to America?"

"If that's what you want to do, Kanyi."

"Is it true the medicines we take were invented there?"

"Yes, that's true." He had a swift impulse to do a little educating, which really meant ranting about how some medicines were withheld unless someone paid hundreds of dollars for just one pill.

The anger he carried wouldn't help as he entered the belly of the beast with his hand out. He could hear his father's words: *He that has no trouble in this world must not be born in it.* But Americans were different; they thought trouble was a fault.

"That's what I'm going to do," Kanyi said. "And I'll invent a medicine that makes it so no one ever dies from AIDS."

"That's a very worthy goal," Oliver said, moved. They'd come to where the path twisted, roots crisscrossing, and everyone slowed down.

"Nyoka!" Snake! Someone up ahead called out.

They stopped and waited, Oliver pulling back on the cart while the boys leaned on the trembling donkey.

"Sawa sawa! Imeenda! Okay! It's gone!"

They proceeded on to where the path leveled off, and soon came to the road. Nothing moved in the heavy heat; no voice could be heard, nor could a flicker of movement be seen in either direction. Lillian had had a shelter built for people to wait in during the long rain, with a bench along the back. One of the girls found an oleander leaf and brushed the dust from the bench. They all waited politely for Oliver to sit and he did, despite the fact that he would prefer standing while he still could.

Everyone was quiet, some imagining an airplane crossing an ocean and wishing they could be on it, and others grateful that they got to go back up the hill for lunch and a free afternoon. The only sound was the donkey's big teeth crunching on kale. Then they heard the sound of a motor and the heavy beat of pop music.

"Out of the road, now," Oliver warned.

The matatu, a loudspeaker tied to its roof, rumbled around the curve and stopped. There were only two other passengers, teenagers. Most people were in church or at home enjoying their day off.

"You two hop in the back and let the gentleman sit there," the driver said.

Oliver bent his long frame onto the seat, his carryall at his feet, with the bag holding his laptop perched on his knees. The children tucked the baskets of fruit under the seat where they'd be out of the sun. Oliver turned to wave as they jerked forward, and the speaker abruptly blared again.

"Goodbye, Anka! Come back to see us!"

"I'll see you when you see me!" They wouldn't have heard, though, above the music. But of course they knew. Kirinyaga was the home of his heart, and he always came home for New Year's.

# Chapter 3

## Alice

Alice flung herself back into her dream, trying to grab onto Oliver.

*It was the sleeve of a CO.*

*"Have you seen my little girl? Have you seen my little girl?" The woman looked through her as if trying to figure out who, or what, was making such a fuss.*

*"Kena!"*

*"Alice! She's right here!" It was Oliver's voice.*

*"Mama! I forgot my words!"*

*Kena's Lemmy was at her feet. Alice stooped and picked him up.*

*She was in handcuffs.*

*"Don't be stupid." It was Aunt Lena, oxygen lines snaking into her nose. She grabbed the lemur's long tail and tossed him, yelling, "Filthy beast!"*

*But it was Adam tossing Lemmy across a carpet of green grass and directly into Kena's arms. He marked a line in the air and sang, "Jingle bells, Batman smells, Robin laid an egg."*

*"Mama! Hurry!"*

*People were dancing the Looby Loo, kicking out their feet. Adam pulled Alice into the line. "You put your right foot out." Adam flapped his arms, rose up, and was gone.*

*I'll fly away.*

*Kena hid her face in Oliver's neck, Lemmy dangling from her hand, as they disappeared into an airplane.*

*"Oliver!"*

Alice fell awake. Sparks blinked above her in the dark like distant stars. Her mother said that stars were holes in the sky-world that her ancestors poked to watch the people they loved below. Was her mother watching now?

"I'm sorry, Mama." She covered her face with her pillow to shut out the night groans and crying-outs, the crackle of walkie talkies, and the stink of industrial cleaner mixed with tomato sauce and sweat. Her hands clutched each other as if they wanted to pray.

But she couldn't. She couldn't pray to someone who didn't, didn't—*didn't*—stop her from driving the car. And she *wouldn't* pray to someone who'd taken her mother and father away and left her behind.

She'd been eight, Kena's age, and now she'd left Kena.

Oliver said God couldn't stop bad things; he, or she—they—could only keep us company when they happen. What good was *that*? Did God at least cry? She'd been like the *Catcher in the Rye*, on the alert to keep Kena away from the edge of her world, but she'd looked away. Was God looking away too?

*Adam.*

Her stomach clenched, and she sprang to the toilet and heaved up the spaghetti she'd forced down a few hours ago.

"Come on!" It was Violet. "Every fucking night?"

"I'm sorry," Alice whispered. She crawled back to her cot, shivering.

Hamlet had called midnight to 3 a.m. the "very witching time of night," when ghosts appeared to do their ghastly worst. It was when she was most a prisoner, waking out of dreams of loss and losing, no refuge in reach. She couldn't even write in her cell because some desperate person had stabbed their eardrum with a pencil once upon a time.

She couldn't kneel in front of her bookcase to finger the books from her childhood that she'd carted from place to place to retreat into, their covers finger-worn to softness. She couldn't tiptoe into Kena's room and pick up Lemmy to tuck him back in and watch Kena wrap her fingers around his skinny tail where she'd rubbed the fur away, and curl up on Kena's "flowerdy" rug and breathe with her. She was locked in her mind, and it had turned on her.

When she was a child and had been teased about her hair and freckles—*forget to wash your face, Brillohead?*—she would think, *but I'm smart. And I have words. Wonderful, wonderful words.*

When they called her half-breed, and worse, she'd picture her mother's flowing hair, a dark blanket keeping her safe. And she'd think about Mary, who had grace inside. *Hail Mary, full of grace, the Lord is with thee, blessed art thou amongst women.*

When her father's sister, Aunt Lena, "took her in"—*You're not going to those prairie-squatters!*—she had to go to mass every week and afterwards hear all the things she'd done wrong. "Don't blame me if you end up in Purgatory like your mother." Even Aunt Lena didn't dare go as far as Hell. But Alice would go anywhere to see her mother again.

She would stare up at Mary looking down at her, imagining that's how her mother would look, *was,* at that very moment, looking down from the sky world and loving her. No matter that she scratched her mosquito bites under her Sunday dress until they bled, no matter that she chewed on her fingers, no matter that she forgot not to pump her feet and, that one time, wet her pants.

No matter her mean thoughts.

Hail Mama, full of grace, the lord is with thee, blessed art thou amongst women, and blessed is the fruit of thy room. And Alice imagined herself as the little girl in *Mr. Rabbit and the Lovely Present*, wearing the hat with the ribbon and the pink coat, collecting the apples and bananas, the pears and blueberries for her mother's birthday, which had been in September, the same month as her own.

Then one day she asked her aunt what Mary's fruit was.

"What are you talking about *now*?"

"Mary's fruit. The fruit of thy room. *Mary's*. You know. Blessed is the fruit—"

"Are you making fun of the Church? Oh, you're just like your mother!"

But her mother was like Mary, Alice thought. And now she was in jail; she was in Purgatory, and her mother wasn't there.

She'd learned to escape into her imagination after her parents died. Her thoughts were like secret balloons, tied to her but above her real life, safe from the bullies and Aunt Lena. But now she wasn't tied to anything; she was helpless and untethered and her mind spun around and around and around: Kena sick. Kena sick; Kena crying and crying.

Kena screaming, screaming, screaming, screaming—*Mama!*

Blood streaming down the windshield like rain.

Alice's empty stomach spasmed.

Lights flashing. Off, on, off, on, off, on—

*Mama!* Kena crying, crying, crying.

Glass. And blood that was Adam's all along.

Mama! Ninaamaa! I'm sorry, I'm sorry!

Adam, please. Please, God. Adam, please. Live.

Please live.

Terrified, she pressed against the unforgiving mattress to feel herself somewhere.

Help me, help me, please. Please. Please, please help me.

Help me!

It wasn't even a whisper, but it was a cry from her soul. And suddenly she was in a waiting room. Then, as if her name had been called, she stood up and walked to a door and opened it. The room was filled with light; the room *was* light, and she was dazzled by it, *flooded* with it. *Of* it. *Peace beyond all understanding.* And then, abruptly, she was back in her cell. She curled into a ball facing the wall, and pulled the rough blanket over her head. She touched her finger to her thumb and rubbed, like rubbing a bead on a rosary. Then a finger, and another and another, one for each of them, whispering the loving-kindness prayer.

"May you be at peace, may your heart remain open, may you know the beauty of your own nature, may you be healed…"

Kena.

Adam.

Lily.

Enoch.

And one more. Her thumb slipped.

Oliver.

Alice put her hands over her face and wept.

Like a blessing.

Like the blessing of the rain in Kenya.

*Oliver.*

# Chapter 4

## Lily

"In our sleep, pain which cannot forget falls, drop by drop, upon the heart until, in our own despair, against our will, comes wisdom through the awful grace of God."

Lily handed the sticky note to Clare for her to read. "Aeschylus said it. He wrote the first tragedies. I remember learning about him in English class, but I don't remember this. But why would I have? I didn't have an inkling about tragedy. Anyway, I watched this thing about Robert Kennedy last night? He quoted it to a crowd the day Martin Luther King was killed." Lily's fingers worked her half-eaten muffin into a ball.

"When he told them, it was like everybody got hit…punched. People screamed and sobbed and…and keened. And oh God, Clare, watching, it was *comforting* to me! Like, look, it happened to other people too; it happened to a whole *country*. And I wasn't alone." She watched Clare's face. "I felt so guilty! I mean, it was Martin Luther King!"

"Oh, honey."

The cafe was filling up for lunch. Lily ducked down in the booth so no one would see her whenever the bell over the door jingled. An angel getting her wings. Or his.

Stop.

"The awful grace of God," Clare said softly. She handed back the sticky note. "Our teacher cried in front of us when King died," she said. "I was more shocked by that than what had happened, I think. I didn't know enough."

Lily had been at the library when it happened. Someone had burst in, calling out, "King was shot!" The grownups had gathered around a radio in the room behind the checkout desk. She was just seven and thought a king had been shot. When she returned her books the following week, she discovered they hadn't been stamped.

"After he said that—Kennedy—about the awful grace of God…" Lily peered into her cup as if grace—or God—might be waiting at the bottom of it. "Just a few weeks later *he* was shot. God, Clare! Did his mother remember those words? Grace. Where was grace *then*?"

The waitress came up to the table with two coffee pots. "Want a refill?"

"No, thanks, Morgan, I have to get back to school," Clare said.

"Bet the kids are excited for vacation!"

"They're like jumping beans at rehearsals."

"I heard your daughter's back."

Lily watched joy wash over Clare's face. Then Clare said, as if it were nothing much, "Yup, last week."

"Just in time for Yule," Morgan said. She lifted the coffee higher. "Ms. J?"

Lily pulled her travel cup out of her bag. "Half decaf, I guess."

"Living on the edge." Morgan started pouring and stopped. "Oh, God, I'm sorry! I can't believe I said that!"

"It's okay. Please. Don't give it a thought," Lily said. Then, to change the subject, "I heard there's snow coming."

"Just not Thursday!" Clare said, helping out. "With the concert."

"And we don't have snow tires on. We're giving them to ourselves for Christmas," Morgan said. She took the check from her pocket, put it on the table, and walked away.

Lily screwed the lid onto her cup. "I looked up 'grace.'"

"Of course you did."

"There were *13* definitions. One was goddesses."

"You're wasted on kindergarteners." Clare grinned.

"We do dictionaries!"

"A is for apple."

"No. Don't you remember when Ian Carmichael said alimony?"

"Oh, right," Clare laughed.

"So listen. Grace comes from gratia and it means favor."

"'Ars gratia artis.' Art for art's sake. Like grace notes."

"Grace notes?"

"They're extra notes in music. They aren't needed for the melody; they're embellishments."

Lily folded the sticky note once, and again. "This morning the swing tree, the maple…" She pressed the creases hard. "The tips of the top branches looked like they were on fire. From the sunrise." She leaned forward as if she had a secret and whispered. "Does Adam *not* seeing mean I see *more*? Is that the 'awful grace'? I can't even tell him. Except I do. Is that weird?" Her eyes begged Clare.

"Oh, honey," Clare said. "It's not weird at all."

"It feels like my eyes are thirsty. For the sun, and for…well, for beauty. Is it from crying?"

"I don't know, but I'm grateful you can find some." Clare's phone chimed. "Gotta go. They'll be lining up."

"Oh, Clare, the concert! I forgot! I'm sorry!"

Clare stood up. "Lily, don't be sorry, okay? With everything that's happened, and still will, give yourself some clemency."

"I'm better when I'm at the hospital. You said you have a

conference later?"

"The Fords each want a different instrument for Joel. And they're coming together."

"Good luck with that!"

Clare pulled her coat on. "Keep an eye out for grace notes."

"Clare."

"What?"

"You're my best friend. It's okay to be happy in front of me. I'm glad, too, that Mari's home from China."

Clare leaned over and hugged Lily, then left, the bell ringing as she went out the door.

Lily put down two $20 bills and slid out.

Morgan paused on her way to the next booth.

"Thanks, Ms. J! This will help Santa out! Steffi's so excited. She told Santa she wants a princess doll. Except she says 'pinkess.' I don't know where she gets all that princess stuff. From Warm World, I guess."

When Adam was little, he thought the preschool was Worm World.

"She starts kindergarten next year. I hope you'll be back then." Morgan covered her mouth. "Oh!"

"It's okay, Morgan." Lily touched her arm. "Enjoy your little pinkess."

Outside, she zipped up Adam's fleece and stood on the sidewalk, adrift. Every other December she'd be in the thick of things at school. Helping her "jumping beans" practice their song and make Yule decorations. It was Adam's favorite holiday, and she didn't think she could bear it.

She was living in a place without gravity. The earth turned, with its days and nights ticking along, but she wasn't part of the design. No matter what she was doing—having coffee with Clare, walking Homer—she was really with Adam. It was easier when she'd been at the hospital full time, watching him breathe.

But the sun still rose every day and even bathed her eyes with hope, despite the night she'd just endured. The geese still flew from one horizon to the other, taking turns in the lee of the flock, calling and calling to each other and maybe to the sky itself: we can do this, we can do this. And for a moment, she'd think, "We can too."

Her phone began its song—"Imagine"—and she fumbled for it frantically. Adam had put the song there. She couldn't bear to change it, and she couldn't bear to hear it. "Clare?"

"Want me to come over after school?"

"Are you playing hooky?"

"They postponed."

"Yes! I have some errands, and I need to take Homer for a walk. He's been going to the river if he goes out alone, and I get nervous." She tried to laugh. "He's my boon companion, after all." Over the phone she heard the high voices of children singing "Deck the Halls" and recalled last year's heated discussion about whether the song was ecumenical enough for the school board after they'd banned Christmas carols.

"—fa la la la la, la la la la!" The kids were shouting every other "la" as if they were part of a Christmas cheer. Oops. *Holiday.* Holiday cheer.

"I'll pick up some wine," Clare said, and she was gone in her usual abrupt fashion.

Planted on the sidewalk, Lily was pierced with longing. Her kindergarten babies were shuffling into the auditorium. They'd forget to sing the second they saw the stars floating above the stage. Being initiated into the magic without her. When it was their turn, they would march up the stairs to sing "Little Suzy Snowflake," a tradition that had hung on since before she started teaching. During the actual performance, they'd interrupt their hand and arm dancing to wave to their moms and dads.

Grace notes.

Did someone make sure Walter Smits went to the bathroom?

She zipped the phone into Adam's pocket. Hunched against the cold, she minced from dry spot to dry spot to the car. She saw that the inn's scarecrow family had finally changed into their winter coats and hats. She opened the car door, stuck her coffee into the cup holder, and pulled out her book bag. All she could read these days were books with no surprises, and books from her childhood were the safest.

She slid the four *Anne of Green Gables* volumes through the slot next to the door to avoid Molly Mulligan's compassion. Sneaking away, she felt guilty and began to rattle things off to the librarian in her head. "I unpacked the clothes that Gideon dropped off. Did you ever see that jacket I got Adam for Belize, some miracle fabric that dries in a minute? I can't give it to Gideon because he'll think I've given up, although I know Adam would want me to."

One of the jacket pockets had contained a baggie with two torn cigarettes in it, and she'd realized with a shock that they were marijuana. It wasn't that she didn't know. She'd smoked it herself at his age. But still, that he would risk crossing a border! The baggie, the joints still inside, was in the Tibetan bowl on her dresser because she couldn't throw away something of Adam's, not even that.

She stopped walking; did he drive when he was stoned? Enoch did before they had Adam, and that one time after when he drove Homer to the vet and asked if the vet knew why they were there. DUI. Driving under the influence. DWI. Driving while intoxicated. It wasn't just alcohol. It was drugs too. She swung around and saw herself in Halvorsen's window, a round hologram floating over red shovels and blue plastic sleds.

She was nothing like a lily. She wasn't pretty or tall. Sturdy, her mother said, but Lily, even at age six, knew that wasn't good for a girl to be. Then one day in second grade her teacher said, "I love your name. 'Consider the lilies of the field, how they grow; they neither toil nor spin.' A great teacher said that."

"What is 'toil'?" she'd asked, wondering, toilet?

"It means work, the kind that isn't any fun at all."

No one wanted to clean a toilet, Lily knew.

"I like to spin," she'd said, lifting her arms up.

"I used to, but now I get dizzy. But he was talking about spinning wool to make thread for cloth. And he was saying that lilies are perfect just as they are. Like you."

That was when she first thought of being a teacher, Lily thought, and walked on. There was a new display at the shoe store, high-tops hanging by their shoelaces along a clothesline. Funny how they'd come back. But better: purple or pink. *Plaid.* Hers hadn't been Converse; what were they?

Entering the drugstore, she quickly scanned it. Some days were worse than others. How *are* you? How is Adam? Any change? Or someone looking away, tongue-tied, and ducking into another aisle.

"Hi, Ms. J." The young woman at the counter began to leaf through the bin for her prescription. Lily grappled for her name. Her brother had been in Lily's class first, a shy boy who lisped like Winthrop in *The Music Man.*

"Got it!" The woman—really, just a girl—held up the bottle of pills and pushed up her glasses, and Lily remembered. Her brother's name was Jason. And this was Julie. Julie West. No, Ferguson. She'd gotten married and pregnant, or the other way around.

"Thanks, Julie. How's the baby?" She couldn't remember—boy or girl?

Julie beamed. "Jackson. He's walking! He'll be 1 in a month. January 12th." She held out a pen. "You need to sign."

Lily signed, embarrassed that she was using sleeping pills.

"He's got a red snowsuit for Yule. And a hat with pointy ears. So cute!"

A Santa bunny? Lily dreaded Yule.

"Do you know if they're still doing the bonfire?" Julie asked. "Oh, you might not…with Adam. I mean—how are you doing, anyway?"

"I'm…" Sometimes she blurted out the truth. Sometimes she said "I'm fine!" and felt like she'd betrayed herself. "I'm hanging in there."

"Well, I'm praying for Adam and you."

Lily was embarrassed when people said that. But they meant it. A lot of people actually prayed, she'd found out, for "those in need." Well, she and Adam certainly fit the bill, and Enoch and Gideon and Homer too. They needed a miracle. She turned to leave.

"Ms. J? Don't forget your pills."

Flustered, Lily took the small white bag. "Thank you. And I hope Jack enjoys his first Yule. And I happen to know: the bonfire's still happening."

Outside, she smacked her forehead: Jackson! Not Jack. And just because some fool boys set the dock on fire shooting lit arrows into the lake, pretending to be Vikings, was no reason to stop the bonfire. Adam would think it was funny. It *was* funny, but she hoped it wasn't anybody she'd had in class.

Every September she'd lead her kindergarteners around town and the shopkeepers would give them treats, like a rehearsal for Halloween trick-or-treat. They'd be given frosted cupcakes at The Lake House, which had once been home to the Farley family. Lily ended the tour at the dock, making sure her students knew the town of Farleys' Dock was named after the real thing.

Driving past the school, Lily remembered a game they'd played when she was in sixth grade. Home base was at one end of the playground, and everyone would line up at the other end. Whoever was

It roved around—the rule was twenty feet away from home base—and called people home.

"Come home if you ever got stitches! Come home if you have a sister! Come home if you've been to another country! Come home if you have a dog!" One at a time, and if it was true for you, you ran for home, and It would try to tag you and anyone else who ran.

"If you've ever been kissed on the lips, *not* by your mother." It was a girls' game. Sometimes someone called out something no one knew about you yet, and you got to decide to run or not. There were surprises. Who knew that Vicky Murphy had a ferret? Sometimes you'd find out something was true for someone else too. BFF—Best Friends Forever—for that day. And best of all, when she was the only one left, everyone would yell "home free!" And she could just walk home, no matter what she'd done or hadn't done or been or might be or have or not have. No shoulds or buts, no strings attached. Home free.

PF Flyers! *That's* what the high-tops were. She turned onto their road.

She and Enoch had their first real fight after they'd decided to buy a house. She'd grown up in town and wanted their children to walk to school and the library and play neighborhood games. Enoch had grown up in the country and even raised chickens. He'd imagined their kids exploring woods and a stream, with at least one dog following them around. Preferably two—and big ones. Big dirty ones, she'd thought, from those woods and the stream. With ticks.

But in the end, it was a chicken coop that sold her. It had tiny windows and roosting boxes that could be accessed from inside or out. And, when she lifted the lid of one box, she found a set of tin doll dishes with faded pink roses around their rims. Another box held a jumble of nibbled seed packets. Ducking her head inside the coop, she saw an upside-down apple box. She squeezed in and sat down. She sneezed.

She loved it.

Enoch said there were bound to be mice, but she didn't mind, picturing Beatrix Potter's Hecca and Becca putting out the dishes and serving seeds to their families.

So they'd bought it, a farm that had stopped being a farm a generation before, its barn a graveyard for rusty machine parts and bald tires. There were four bedrooms and the required woods and stream nearby.

Half the cellar flooded that first spring. The mice in the corner kitchen cupboard were not wearing aprons and mobcaps. They got a kitten and named her Pooky because she puked if they fed her too much. Eventually, she did catch mice and brought them to Lily as if she were supposed to fry them up for supper. When Pooky disappeared— the victim of a fisher, Enoch suspected—they got Pooky Two, soon to be Too, who was a He and seemed to think mice were fellow pets. Squirrels used the attic, and groundhogs the foundation, as nurseries. The sprawling wood-framed house was insulated with bricks and straw, as if it had been built by the three little pigs. The hand-crafted kitchen cabinets had been covered in lead paint.

But the lilacs' perfume drifted into the living room in the spring, and the groundhogs' babies came out to explore under the bay window. They put up a bird feeder, and Enoch's battle to keep the squirrels out of it began. He hung one of the bald tires from a maple tree, and Lily found an old porch swing at a lawn sale and painted it bright blue. Robins nested in the rafters in the corner of the porch, making it off-limits for a few weeks every April.

So many babies, and finally it was her turn. Adam came, and her real life began.

By the time he was three, the chicken house had become his playhouse, where he made beds for his stuffed animals in the roosting boxes. A poster of a pyramid went up alongside one of hieroglyphics when he was five. Soon after that, jar lids disappeared from Lily's kitchen to become Petri dishes, and Adam and his best friend Gideon jury-rigged shelves for their potions. Maps were tacked up: Mount Mansfield. Acadia. The Catamount Trail. The Adirondack Trail. The Long Trail.

Bones and skulls and "scat," sorted and labeled, came next. The maps were replaced by drawings of dissections, and when Adam turned 13 he began to write down his thoughts in notebooks kept in a trunk he'd bought at the Rotary auction for "first dollar gets it." Now and again, Lily went in and sat in the bean bag chair that the mice thought was a feedbag and read, feeling sneaky and guilty, until the day Adam brought home a pine box he'd made in shop. It had a padlock. They never talked about it.

She'd moved to the country because of a chicken house and the dream of a life that was like playing house: children swinging and putting on plays in the barn, planting a garden and eating from it when they wanted a snack, jumping in leaf piles, coming in for cocoa after making a snow fort. A happy *Good Housekeeping* family.

Enoch wanted that, too, and maybe if he'd never met Khai they would have kept on doing the best they could, struggling to be that couple—that impossible couple, as it turned out. Maybe if she'd been able to have more children.

But it was only Adam who brought home babies, nestless birds and bunnies and, once, a half-mowed milk snake that survived after he stitched it up. Was that snake still alive somewhere? She took the turn for her driveway, unconsciously curling her toes. She looked toward the house, already lonely. At least Homer would be there. He was even lonelier than she was.

# Chapter 5

## Oliver

After landing at Dulles Airport, despite moving like a contortionist in the tiny airplane toilet to shave and twist a tie around his neck so he'd look respectable, Oliver was asked to wait while they decided he wasn't a terrorist.

As a very tall, very black man, he'd had enough experience living in New York to be polite while he was treated unpolitely. But handing each item of his clothing over the door of a cubicle that stunk of sweat, and worse, so the United States Bureau of Customs and Border Protection could feel confident that they'd secured their homeland, was a supreme test.

They asked if he would be amenable to turning on his laptop for them to examine. Except it wasn't a request. What would they do if he wasn't "amenable"? The photographs he'd enjoyed showing Jaafar summoned a superior officer to pass judgment on little naked Kamani being weighed.

Oliver handed them one of the cards Lillian had gotten printed. "Kirinyaga's Children's Home, in the hills and in our hearts" danced along the tops of two green triangles, an umbrella tree nestled between them. The officers might at least feel poked a little, made to think about what was under people's skin.

The exit felt like miles away. Other travelers didn't look at him or each other, as if they were still off in different time zones. It was freezing outside, and his flimsy anorak was futile against the wind. A taxicab pulled up. Oliver tossed in his bags and ducked gratefully inside. The cab took off with a jerk, swerved across several empty lanes, and went up a ramp. The driver began to sing.

"'Soar we now where Christ has led'—where to?"

It took Oliver a moment to realize "where to" wasn't part of the hymn.

And where *had* Jesus led?

"Uh…" He'd memorized the address for this precise moment, so he could rattle it off as if he'd been there before to prevent being overcharged. When he recited it, the driver laughed a deep laugh, followed by "bad, bad, he wouldn't wish that neighborhood on a dog's flea!"

The driver shifted roughly into a higher gear, and Oliver smacked against the barrier between the front and back seats. He was the prisoner of a hymn-singing racecar driver wannabe on the other side of the world. And was there any heat at all? It seemed reckless to ask.

"Open my eyes, that I may see glimpses of truth thou hast for me," the driver sang. Oliver found a lever. A blast of cold air blew over his feet.

"'Place in my hands the wonderful key'—want to hear my business idea?" The driver reached back and opened the divider all the way. Blessed warm air flowed through.

Want to hear my business idea? Was it a riddle? *Knock knock, who's there, want to hear my business idea?*

"Aii. Yes!" Oliver ventured.

"Take that jacket you're wearing. It's okay where you come from—Africa, right? But here?" He adjusted his rear-view mirror to look at

Oliver. "So how's about a place at the airport where you could rent a winter one? Ten dollars. There'd hafta be a deposit, human nature being what it is, but everybody uses a credit card nowadays. And I'd sell those one-size-fits-all gloves you get at the dollar store. Where you from, if you don't mind my asking?"

"Kenya."

"What's your business, then?"

"I work for UNICEF, but I'm here to solicit donations for an orphanage."

"An orphanage! You mean with real orphans?"

"59 real orphans."

"Was it war, then?"

"Their parents died of AIDS."

"Fuck me," the driver said softly. "Are the *kids* sick?"

"They're infected, but only about a third have AIDS."

"Poor little buggers. No mom and dad and then sick on top of that. Can they play and stuff? You know, go to school, play ball, get up to stuff?"

*Poor little buggers.* Oliver wanted to protest, to defend them—Mugo, Jaafar…*Africa.* "They take medication," he finally said. "Do you have children?"

"Four girls! And three grandbabies! More girls! And they are definitely the boss of me!" Oliver heard that deep laugh again. "Do you have kiddies of your own?"

59. Or what if he said hundreds? Thousands. All over Africa.

And one more in New York City.

The taxi plunged down a ramp and jerked to a stop. They turned and turned. Was that the White House? A gigantic Christmas tree came into view.

"Thought you might like to see the national tree. We used to bring our girls to the tree lighting, but now there's so much security, it's better on TV."

More turns and another ramp, this time going up. Oliver found himself looking into windows that seemed to be a few feet away. A small boy was looking out of one and waved to him. He waved back, but they'd already gone by. They careened down another ramp and bumped across a potholed intersection where a group of men huddled over burn barrels. They'd gone from an opulent Christmas tree with thousands of lights and bows to the third world. If it weren't so cold, he might feel at home. They jerked to the curb.

"Home sweet home." A neon sign flickered over the door of his "wouldn't wish it on a dog's flea" hotel.

"Is it okay if I put your kiddies on our prayer list at church?"

And Oliver remembered another side of Americans...their generosity.

A hydrant was in the way, so Oliver slid to the street side and staggered out. He could see his driver's face clearly for the first time and saw deep smile lines on skin as dark as his own. He put his bags down and reached for his wallet.

"Five will do it."

"Five?" Lillian's budget had allowed $40.

"For the kiddies."

"I'm Oliver Wangera." He held his hand out.

"Leroy Jeffers. So—does your orphanage have a name?"

"Kirinyaga's Children's Home. After Mount Kenya—'Where God lives.'" Someone who sang hymns might like to know that. Oliver handed the driver one of Lillian's cards and a $10 bill.

"Are they gonna die?" Leroy Jeffers asked the card.

"Not if they get the medicines they need. That's why I'm here. To get them."

Leroy stuck the card in the visor. "What else do the kiddies need?"

"Whatever your granddaughters need—clothes, games, books.

No winter coats, though."

"We'll get started." Leroy shoved something out the window into Oliver's hand. The window rolled up.

Oliver watched the red taillights detour around the men and their makeshift heater and turn the corner. He looked at what he was holding. It was a pair of black gloves. And the $10 bill.

"Help a brother?"

The voice came from a bundle of clothes on the sidewalk. Oliver tucked the money into a glove, folded the gloves into a ball, and put them into the bare hand reaching out. "There you go."

# Chapter 6

## Lily

Lily saw Homer disappear from his lookout at the front window. He broke her heart every time. When she opened the door he was there, looking past her for Adam. He circled twice and grabbed his duck to set at her feet, but it was ceremonial rather than heartfelt. They were the wrong feet.

"Homer! Sweetie."

She put her cup and purse on the table, knelt, and rubbed his bony head. She threw the duck out the open door. He shuffled slowly out, and she followed him to sit on the swing. The trees were empty; their exposed skeletons seemed vulnerable to her. Did they mourn the loss of their leaves? she wondered. Did it hurt when they fell? Did they wail in secret tree language as the bitter December wind tore them off?

Homer plodded over and dropped his soggy duck into her lap. She tossed it over the railing onto the brown grass. He crossed the porch and tottered down the steps, his backend swaying like a caboose. But he walked past his duck and went to the playhouse to sniff around the door. Trying to find Adam. She blinked at the sky, at the maple tree, at the sky, at the tree.

Grief swelled into her chest and then, rising, into her throat, and then, despite her fiercest blinking, spilled down her cheeks, and she howled. It hurt. Oh! It hurt!

She staggered to her feet and into the house. She kicked her boots off against the wall, hard, but it didn't help. She grabbed a fistful of tissues and reeled into the living room, through the dining room and to the kitchen, sobbing and blowing, wailing and wiping. Too poured himself out of the empty fruit bowl and fled. She made a circle in front of the sink, and another one, like Homer. She sank into a chair and sobbed and rocked, holding herself. Oh, it hurt!

The message machine was blinking. She pushed the button. "This is Dr. Sanjay's service. Please give us a call." The nurse began to recite the phone number. Lily leaped to her feet, searching frantically for a pen. Too fast! She felt a burst of intense anger: at the nurse, at the machine. At Enoch for getting such a stupid machine. At Adam.

At Adam. At Adam. *Why, why, why* did he get in that car? He wasn't a child!

At *her*, Alice Wangera.

Don't, don't. Just—don't.

The pen was right there on the table, had been there all along. She pressed the button again, poised. "212-466-" Too fast!

Stupid! She had the number on speed dial.

Ringing, ringing, that horrible singsong voice. "We're sorry, but we're not able to take your call right now. Please leave your name and a number and we'll get back to you soon." If that woman ever dared speak in the real world she'd be torn to pieces.

"This is…" Beeeep. "This is Lily St. John, and you can reach me here at home or on my cellphone. It's about my son, Adam. St. John. Adam St.—" She was cut off.

Her cellphone! She went to the hallway. Her purse was on the table. She grabbed for it and bumped her travel cup. When the cup hit the floor, the lid flew off and coffee splashed out. She reached for the tissues in her pocket.

Her pocket! She pulled out her phone and pressed 2 for Adam's unit at the hospital.

"ICU."

Thank God. It was Ellie. "It's Lily."

She walked out the open door and perched on the edge of the swing, dizzy with tension.

"Meow!" Too protested and sprang off.

"Lily! Uh, just a second. Listen, we're doing an intake. Can I call you back? Ten minutes, max. I promise. Sanjay's not on the unit, but I'll page him. Be right back. Really. I promise."

"I just need to know—" But Ellie was gone.

Oh God, oh God, oh God.

The landline, what if Ellie called it!

She ran inside and grabbed the receiver and stood there, a phone in each hand. Could it ring if she was holding it? She hastily put it back, then picked it up.

Homer hadn't come back in. Carrying both phones, she stepped outside, to the edge of the porch. "Ho-mer! Here, sweetie!" Gideon thought Homer was losing his hearing. She went down the steps. The ground was bumpy and hard under her socks. She peered into the playhouse. Nothing. Damn!

She headed for the river path. "Homer! Ho-mer!"

Stepping in a muddy spot, she skidded, and held the phones up high. She put the cellphone in her pocket. Her socks were soaked.

"Here, sweetie!"

She came to the dip in the path into which Adam and Gideon had wrestled two flat rocks to be stepping stones. She looked down, her footing tenuous. Oh God, a snake! She leaped, running forward several feet. She looked back, embarrassed. Could it have been

Adam's snake?

"Sorry! I'm sorry!"

God, she'd have to come back this way too. It was December! Didn't snakes hibernate? She got to the rise for the railroad track and looked both ways, even though it hadn't been in use since Adam was six. When he'd gotten older, he'd teased her. "There might be a *very* late train, Mom, you know Amtrak! Stop and look both ways!" The path became soft with pine needles that stuck to her socks. Every year she had her kindergarteners walk in the school woods in wet cotton socks to see what seeds would stick to them. Then they planted the socks.

The path curved downhill and there was Homer, sitting and watching the water drift by. He thumped his tail as if to say, "What took you so long? Have a seat." So she did.

She placed the house phone carefully next to her on the ground and put her arm over his soft smelly body and leaned in. It was always so, that Homer's big warm body next to hers gave her respite, as if he absorbed her feelings. She knew he would if he could. He thumped again and turned to nose her cheek, then went back to watching the river. For his boy.

"Oh, Homer."

Something brushed against her back and she jerked, and then saw that Too had followed her. Suddenly her pocket began to sing and Too jumped straight up in the air like a cartoon cat. Lily fished out the phone with fingers stiff with cold.

"Hello?"

"Lily. It's Ellie. Adam is having grand mal seizures. Dr. Sanjay will meet you at four, if you can make it."

Lily stood up, thinking ahead furiously. Get Homer inside and feed him, check Too's dishes, call Clare, call Enoch—she could do that from the car. "I'll be there."

It would be rush hour, but at least she'd be going into the city, not out.

"Okay, and I'll be here when you come." Ellie's voice softened. "Take care."

"See you soon." Lily hung up. "Come on, Homer. Home. Supper!"

Something about the light told Homer that wasn't right, but he never turned down a meal. He turned to go home. Too sprang out from somewhere and took the lead, with Lily in the rear, calling Clare on her cellphone.

"Did you change your mind?" Clare asked. "Just a sec. Sophie, that's teasing. She asked you twice to stop."

"I'm going into the city. Adam's having seizures."

"I'll pick you up. Give me 15 minutes." Clare hung up.

Lily followed Homer and Too. Don't think. *Don't think.* She'd completely forgotten the snake. And the house phone, on the bank by the river.

◊

Clare dropped Lily off at the hospital entrance before circling around to the parking garage. Lily hadn't reached Enoch, and her cellphone hadn't rung. She'd held it in her hand for the entire drive while Clare told a story she'd just heard, a true one, because she knew that was the only kind Lily could bear right now. It was about severely autistic kids who couldn't bring themselves to venture out into their schoolroom. So the teachers tied ropes across and, little by little, the kids stepped out, holding onto a rope.

"Once they got used to walking in the room the teachers lowered the rope, so they could do floor activities still holding on. But here's the best part. After a while, they just gave them a piece of rope to hold, not attached at all."

Her cellphone was her piece of rope, Lily thought, clutching it as she followed the familiar blue line to the E wing elevators, trying to close her nose to the odors of pizza and disinfectant and avoid collisions with the bustling foot, wheelchair, and cart traffic. Many people were gazing at their phones as if they were following Google Maps. When someone actually looked at her, she tried to reward them with a smile.

There was nothing sadder than a hospital at Christmas, with its brave garlands and Santa Claus stencils and holly, and the pink-flocked tree in the gift shop window, its white lights blinking. The usual bouquet of get-well balloons included one shaped like a physically challenged reindeer.

The elevator emptied and filled while she leaned against its back wall until it was her turn to say "Excuse me, excuse me." Then the seemingly endless hallway, people coming and going from side tributaries but no one bumping into anyone else, as if their beeps, buzzes, squawks, and voices were sonar.

Entering the ICU was like ducking underwater or entering an alien spaceship, the nurse's station the hub of a wheel with the patients' rooms its spokes. The beds were themselves hubs for machines that bubbled and burbled and hummed, umbilical cords feeding nutrients and oxygen and drugs and other tubes taking away the waste. Enoch had remarked at the beginning that they should call it Limbo, where souls waited for their final push. He looked so bleak she couldn't get mad.

The shade in Adam's window to the hallway was down. She opened the door and slipped into twilight. The lotion for his feet, a box of tissue, and a foot-tall plastic Christmas tree stood like shadows of themselves on the bed table he'd never used. Adam lay as still as always, but when she touched him the tension she always carried let go a little.

She kissed his cheek, practiced at not bumping a tube or wire.

Now that she was taking turns with Enoch and Gideon, she noticed how much thinner, how much less, he was becoming. His skin was loosening and drying up like an old person's.

Small talismans hung between the bars of the bedrail: an origami frog, the leather MOM bracelet he'd made for her at camp one year, the prism that had hung in the dining room window, a plastic starfish they'd gotten on Cape Cod, a clothespin angel, a blobby dog from a Crackerjack box that spun slowly from the vibration of the machines. It was Ellie who'd made the angel.

Grace notes?

She squeezed Adam's hand. "Hi, sweetie," she said softly.

She tried to believe them, that Adam, even if he woke up, would be—someone had actually said the word back in August, and she hadn't touched vegetables for weeks afterward; root vegetables were particularly grotesque.

"Lily."

It was the softest whisper, but she jerked and had to grab the railing to keep from falling on top of Adam. For a second it had been his voice.

Enoch stood just inside the door. He pointed and slipped back out.

Lily's heart was pounding. God!

But she hugged Enoch hard.

"Did you just get here?" she asked. "Is Khai here?"

He shook his head, checking his watch. "I've been here an hour or so. I got the call about when you did, I suppose, and came right down. I tried calling you, but the phone kept being busy."

"Why didn't you call my cell?"

"I don't know. I went on automatic, like I still lived there, and… anyway, you're here. Khai's in court, probably 'til four. I made Gideon go down for some food. He's been here since early this morning."

"Have you seen Sanjay?"

"All I know is from Ellie." Enoch winced. "Lily, she said…Ellie said…" He couldn't say it, but it didn't matter. She knew.

"Mrs. St. John. Mr. St. John."

They'd stopped asking him to call them Lily and Enoch months ago. As usual, Dr. Sanjay was wearing an immaculate white coat and a colorful bowtie; today's was candy-cane red and white, like a clown's. But no one could be further from being a clown, even a sad one, than Dr. Sanjay.

"Let's go to my office," he said, speaking over his shoulder, already walking.

There were no personal touches in the office, not one photograph, just framed certificates on the back wall. Ellie had told them Dr. Sanjay's parents had died in the tsunami back in 2004. Lily was ashamed that knowing he'd lost someone made her feel better. She wished, for his sake, that he kept a photograph or two on his bare desk.

Now he walked around it and sat down, folding his hands on the top. Lily took the chair opposite, next to Enoch, stupidly flashing back on the time they'd sat in the middle school principal's office to find out Adam's punishment—"consequence"—for the April Fool's soap-in-the-dispenser-cups joke he and Gideon had thought was a good idea.

Adam was being punished now for someone else's crime.

Oh, stop!

Sanjay made a steeple with his fingers. "Adam had four seizures this morning. We increased the sedative and the neuroleptic imme-diately, and while we were monitoring the effects, he had another major one. We added a neuromuscular block, for a kind of induced paralysis. And that's where he is now, but…" He hesitated. "If he can't breathe on his own when we take him out of it, we could put him on a ventilator." He met Lily's eyes, then Enoch's. "But it's like a forest fire. One area gets put out and another flares up. There's just so much damage. I know you tentatively decided not to subject him to a ventilator. Now it's real."

Lily felt Enoch's hand cover hers where it was a fist on her thigh. She wanted to fling it off. She sat, wooden, as if she could stop time if she never moved again. Then Enoch's hand became just as still. They were like dolls waiting for someone to speak for them, so they didn't have to say it themselves.

"It's come to having to make the decision about whether to with-hold care. I know you hoped for Adam to just slip away. These things are especially difficult in the absence of a living will. I'm so sorry. I'll leave you alone to talk." Dr. Sanjay stood up. He patted Enoch's shoulder as he went to the door.

"Adam isn't feeling any pain—remember that," Lily heard him say, as if it were easier to say it to their backs, she thought. She felt the air from the door opening and closing on the back of her neck. She slipped her hand out from under Enoch's.

Her next breath. The one after that. Words popped into her head as if another part of her was trying to help. *You could tear your clothes. You could scream.* "As if 21-year-olds are making living wills!" she said through clenched teeth. "As if they can know he's not in pain!"

"Lily, don't. Just don't."

"So we just *sit,* and *wait,* and *watch* as the rest of his brain *implodes!* Until—what? Until he stops breathing? And how long will *that* take? While he lies there, *paralyzed?* Why don't we just put a pillow over his face! How exactly does this *work,* Enoch?"

She was being cruel and made herself stop. "How are we supposed to do this?" she whispered.

The door whooshed open behind them, and they turned to see Ellie, Dr. Sanjay behind her.

Ellie told Lily later that it broke her heart, how they both looked up at her and Dr. Sanjay as if they might be bringing good news. And that she'd realized that in a horrible way, they were.

"I'm so sorry. Adam's gone. He's stopped breathing," Dr. Sanjay said.

Ellie stooped between them, as if they were her children. Their world was making a terrible wrenching shift. "Gideon was with him. He wasn't alone."

Lily's heart protested. *Gideon*! Not her! She became aware of Enoch shaking. Lily put her hand on his arm. He was weeping, totally silent. She leaned over and wrapped her arms around him and put her cheek against his, and felt his tears going down her neck. Then Enoch gasped and began to sob. He hadn't cried since that one time at the beginning, at least with her. Maybe with Khai. She hoped with Khai.

But she was in an isolation booth, and Enoch was outside of it. She didn't feel a thing. She observed Enoch as if she were watching a play. That's what Wracked with Grief looks like. She thought, why am I not Wracked? She thought, Where is Adam? He didn't wait for her.

She sat perfectly still, holding Enoch. She had to make an act of intention, a conscious decision to open her heart. Because she knew that when she did, it would be broken forever. Shards.

# Chapter 7

## Oliver

The neighborhood where the LuluWells Foundation lived couldn't be less like home. Or less like the place Oliver had just spent the rest of the night, with cars blasting music and what sounded like a party down the block. It would have reminded him of Nairobi if it wasn't so cold.

He looked up at the tall brick townhouse standing smugly behind an ornate security fence. It seemed to be looking down on him, deciding if he measured up. Feeling like he suddenly had two left feet, Oliver mentally pushed himself from behind and unlatched the gate.

Walking to the subway that morning he'd been acutely aware that his feet were on the same ground as Alice's and Kena's, and he kept going over what they would be doing: having breakfast, waiting for the shuttle to that fancy school that Kena didn't like. If he took the subway to Union Station, he could take the train and be in New York City to greet Kena when she got home.

The slate sidewalk leading to the townhouse was slippery with frost, and the steps were downright icy. As he reached for the knocker, the door opened. Surprised, he stepped back into space, grabbed the railing, and slipped to one knee.

Not the dignified entrance he'd planned.

"Oh my God! Are you okay?"

She looked to be about 13, playing dress-up in high heels and a gray trouser suit, her hands over her heart. He got himself upright and stepped inside.

"I saw you go by, and I thought it was you! You *are* Mr. Wangera?"

Before he could answer, she went on.

"Did I say it wrong? I asked Dr. Davies, but—"

"No, Wangera. You said it just right."

"Oh, good! Well, I'm Dinah, and I'll be your assistant today!" She shook his hand in satisfaction.

She led him to a closet the size of his digs at home in Nairobi. He slipped his anorak onto a hanger, whispering to it. "You're rubbing elbows with the swells, so behave yourself."

He followed Dinah up a broad staircase and down a hallway lined with photographs that he would have stopped to look at any other time. His pinching, going-to-church shoes sank into an emerald green carpet. He felt far away from home and shifted his bag from one hand to the other to dispel some of his nervousness.

"That's a wicked cool bag," Dinah said, pointing.

"My grandmother made it for me."

She stopped walking. "No way! She *made* it? They cost a fortune here! She could *sell* them!" She slapped her hand over her mouth. "Dinah, shut *up*!" She put her hand on Oliver's arm for a moment. "I'm kind of a blurter. It's one of my goals."

They entered a room walled with bookshelves that were interrupted by three floor-to-ceiling windows along the back. A gleaming oval table surrounded by red padded chairs took up most of the space. A smaller table was shoved up against the bigger one, like the children's table at the one Thanksgiving dinner he'd been to. He remembered Kena banging her spoon, thrilled to be with bigger kids.

"Will this room be adequate?" Dinah asked.

He had to laugh. "Quite adequate."

Suddenly she grinned. "I *know*. And there's more! Watch this." She picked up a remote. A screen slowly rolled down over a bookcase. "There's even more," she said, pressing again. Green shades descended over the windows. She raised everything back up. "Isn't that cool?"

"Very cool," he said.

"I read everything about the orphanage. I think what they're doing is awesome."

"Are you a member of the board?" he asked, smiling.

"What? Oh, you're joking! I'm the lowest of the low—an intern. I'll be a freshman at Spelman College in Atlanta, but I'm taking a gap year."

"Then I came at the right time."

"I'll be right back!" Dinah said. "The little table is for you."

He took out his laptop and hand-outs, and after searching along the wall, found an outlet on the floor behind him. He lowered the screen, then picked up the remote, and after a few false starts, connected it to the computer.

Dinah returned pushing a cart. There were baskets of biscuits and buns, bowls of cherries, pitchers of water and bottles of juice, carafes of coffee and hot water, and an assortment of teas. There was a tray of cups embellished with pink roses and gold rims and a stack of porcelain plates. Paper napkins were piled next to them like poor relations.

"Everyone loves a presentation because of the goodies," Dinah said. "Help yourself." Oliver poured himself a glass of water and took a croissant. It was warm. He took a bite and wrapped it in a napkin.

Her hand flew to her mouth. "Oh, I didn't mean they won't like *you!*"

He smiled. "No worries." Dinah reminded him of Wanja's girls at Kirinyaga.

People began to drift in. They clearly knew each other well, with talk about a new puppy, a search for a *Toy Story* toy, a Christmas concert in which someone's daughter had a solo. Was Kena in a concert like last year? Her small dark face had stood out in the rows of white girls in the photo Alice sent. She hadn't looked happy.

There was a crush to stock up provisions. Oliver had been told the founder wouldn't be there but "took an interest." He wondered who the important people were.

A heavyset Black man rushed through the door and approached him.

"I'm so sorry I wasn't here to welcome you! I'm Hugo Davies." He shook Oliver's hand vigorously. President of the Board. An important one. And just like that, he picked up Oliver's pen and tapped it on Oliver's water glass.

"Thank you all for coming! As you will have ascertained, this is Oliver Wangera, from Kenya! Welcome, Mr. Wangera!"

"I am very pleased to be here."

"Our pleasure, also." Dr. Davies turned to the room. "Mr. Wangera works for UNICEF for the Unite Against AIDS campaign, documenting children with HIV in East Africa. So before we give our attention to one particular group of kids, I'd like to acknowledge him for his work, which must come with a heavy burden of heartbreak and frustration." Dr. Davies began to clap, and everyone followed. Oliver was disconcerted.

"And now…we're all yours!"

They'd given him an hour and a half for the presentation, and he'd tried to time it on the plane, but his mind kept jerking to "What was that sound?" and "Should I call Alice?" Finally he was so wrought up that he'd quit.

He smoothed his tie. Kenya's colors, a gift from Alice seven years ago.

"I'm grateful for this opportunity to tell you about Kirinyaga's

Children's Home. Ancient Kikuyu tradition has it that Kirinyaga—Mount Kenya—is God's resting place. I grew up in its hills, imagining the Kikuyu god Ngai sleeping above, and my spirit ancestors keeping their eyes on me from the branches of the mugumo tree. When my father passed, we gave our homestead over to a small orphanage in the town nearby, where my sister was on staff. Our farm had been home for three generations, given to my grandfather by the British as reparation. We grew coffee, and then tea." He paused. "But now it is children who are growing there."

Some smiled, as he'd hoped they would.

"Kirinyaga's Children's Home began as a sanctuary for seven siblings and cousins orphaned by AIDS. It now cares for 59 children, from infants to age 16, including five teenagers at secondary school in Nairobi. That the number is still growing is stark evidence that AIDS is still prevalent in Africa, despite the progress made in the last decade. Kirinyaga's children either have AIDS, are HIV positive without active disease, or are siblings, and *all* of them lost one or both parents to AIDS."

Wanja had said, "Let the facts soak in. Give them time." Oliver took a gulp of water. He coughed. "Sorry," he croaked.

"Drink some water," someone suggested.

"That is how I got into this predicament at the first," he squeaked. He held up his finger and coughed. "Sawa sawa. Okay." Where had he left them? Oh! He clicked to get Lillian's numbers on the screen.

He'd forgotten the shades. Dinah scooted over. "No worries," she whispered, as the shades went down.

"So. Medicine. Most East African countries purchase generic HIV medications from India at the cost of about $150 a year per child. But over time children develop resistance and require new drugs. The newer meds average $4,000 for a year's supply—untenable, of course."

He clicked to the next section: Funding.

"The biggest contributor to HIV/AIDS funding in Africa is your PEPFAR—President's Emergency Plan for Aids Relief. It has, conservatively speaking, saved over 25 million lives. It's up for renewal every five years by your congress, and will be next year. Second to that is the Global Fund, with $100 million, started by Kofi Annan to treat AIDS, malaria, and TB. The Kenyan government has pledged to contribute $35 million annually."

It sounded like an enormous fortune. Did they know how little it really was? They had to; funding was their job.

"These funds must cover testing, prevention, treatment, and education…including the education of desperately-needed doctors and nurses. The doctor-patient ratio in Kenya is one to sixteen thousand." Someone gasped. Good.

"There are many women who are *known* to have AIDS/HIV who are not receiving prenatal ARVs—antiretroviral meds—to protect their babies. More than two and a half million children are orphans in Kenya, half of them because their parents couldn't get treatment or weren't aware they needed it."

No one was eating.

Oliver knew the numbers were painful to hear. It hurt to say them. He glanced at Dinah. She looked like a deer in headlights.

Like the duiker.

"That each of you is here is a testament to your dedication to your…" Desperation? Devastation?

He felt, abruptly, spent, as if he'd come to a finish line. He felt done in.

He'd been *numbering* them, *columns* of numbers, *pages* of columns of numbers, *books* of pages of columns of numbers: age…weight… height…BMI and blood levels and side infections. Leaving them behind while he moved on to the next devastation, and leaving that behind, and the next, and the next. How many thousands of children had he walked away from? Left to fend for themselves or with inadequate care? His hands started to shake as if to show they couldn't write another number; they were done too. He pressed them against the table. *Njesu!*

"Mr. Wangera?" Dinah asked softly. He looked at her worried face. Worried for him. It wasn't her fault.

Hugo Davies stood up. "Let's take a five-minute break."

Oliver took a breath and then another, deeper one. He unwrapped his croissant and flakes fell down his front. He lifted his tie and carefully shook them onto the napkin, but couldn't stop the trembling of his hands. He had no appetite anyway.

Kena had begged them to save the duiker, begged and begged and begged, crying. Couldn't they put it in the truck? She'd hold it in her lap! Couldn't they take it to a doctor? The tiny duiker's eye rolled, and it tried to lift its head. Kena flung her arms around its neck. Blood smeared her overalls. He met Alice's eyes, and Alice picked her up and walked away, far down the road so she wouldn't see him do it. Oliver walked out in all directions, making a circle, in case the baby's mother was watching, and even called softly, in case she could understand in some miraculous maternal way what he had to do. Had to, and all he had was his hands and a tire iron.

"He died, Kena. He died. He was too hurt. But it's better he did. He was too hurt."

"You made him die! I would have taken care of him! I would have brought him to Martin at the elephant place!"

Sobbing. Refusing to take his hand.

When he'd gone to fetch him from his village, Jaafar wouldn't take his hand either. He needed to find a book about elephants.

This time he was the one to tap on his water glass, but empty, it didn't have the same authority. "Let's move on to the children of

Kirinyaga."

The wall of growth charts came up on the screen. "Most of the children receive antiretroviral treatment, and many take an antibiotic prophylactically. Each child's viral load requires monitoring, anywhere from every fortnight to every six months, in Nairobi, 120 kilometers round-trip. The virus makes them vulnerable to pneumonia, respiratory infections, thrush, diarrhea, dermatitis, and infections from cuts, requiring additional trips and sometimes hospitalization. These charts show the results of their bimonthly weigh-ins at the orphanage. The stickers are for gains in weight and height."

"Here we have charts and stickers for summer reading programs," a woman said softly.

Oliver nodded. "The kids strut around like Geoffrey Kirui when they get those stickers." Everyone stared at him blankly. "Sorry. He's a marathon runner." He pumped his arms overhead in victory, getting Dinah to smile.

He smiled at the next image, the bird's-eye map that Wanja had standard three draw as a geometry project. "The weigh-ins take place in the main building, represented by the red rectangle, where everyone eats meals. The dining room serves as the playroom too, with drawing materials, board games, books, and puzzles shoved onto shelves along the walls. Cooking and washing-up are done out back where the polka-dotted oval is. The land is steep and terraced, and the orphanage receives a percentage of profits from the tea grown by a local cooperative. The school—that rainbow-colored hexagon— also serves as the neighborhood church. There are 38 children in standards one through eight—first through eighth grade in your system—with one teacher. They're hoping to get a volunteer from the U.S to help."

Sensing a reaction, Oliver explained: "That ratio is not unusual in rural Kenyan schools. When I was a boy, I read a book from here that took place in your olden times, and the school reminded me of mine—everyone in one room."

"*Little House in the Big Woods?*" a woman offered. "I'm reading it to my son."

"There was a snowstorm—fascinating to me. The father went missing?" Oliver asked.

"Pa dug a cave in the snow and ate the Christmas candy," the woman said.

"No, Mr. Edwards brought the Christmas candy," someone else said.

"Pa tied a rope to the barn so he wouldn't get lost in the blizzard."

"That was Ma."

Oliver was taken aback. It was as if they were talking about their own family.

"Kirinyaga is like a big family." He pointed. "Those yellow squares house the younger children and babies, and the blue triangle represents the new escape-proof henhouse. The chickens had been laying their eggs in the bush. It had become a sought-after chore to round them up for the night."

He pointed again. "The green circle is called a kithunu. It's traditional for young single males to live apart, and Kirinyaga's boys stay there when they're home from boarding school. I myself lived there with my cousins when I was a teenager, before there was the orphanage. We didn't get up to *too* much mischief." He grinned.

"And finally...here are the children."

Bright color burst onto the screen. There was an audible response, and he imagined Lillian's satisfaction. First the facts, Oliver. *Then* the children.

There they were, arms flung around one another or holding babies. The oldest boys, home for their holiday, held the banner high. A few children wore their green and white school uniforms, but most had dressed up in colorful printed dresses and cherished shirts. Getting their picture taken was an Event.

There was one solemn face. Jaafar. Oliver cleared his throat around a flood of feeling.

"Does that T-shirt say I Love New York?"

New Yok.

Njoki stood at Nia's feet.

He went to the next picture.

"They've cleared a place for football—soccer—and rigged up a fence to keep balls from going downhill. They've been encouraging the girls to play, but I don't believe they've had much success."

"They should get a female soccer player for their teacher's aide."

"Dinah, do you play?" someone asked.

Dinah, startled, jumped away from the wall. "Uh…no, not really." She looked apologetic. Oliver rescued her with the next picture. They laughed at the hens sitting along the peak of their house like spectators.

"The children gather a couple of dozen eggs every day. They start chores at age seven, caring for the animals, gardening, cooking, setting tables, washing-up and laundry, and helping with the babies. Kenya's national motto is 'Let's all pull together. Harambee!'" Oliver said. And instantly felt ashamed.

Like a bloody tourist guide, putting a good face on things. Let's all pull together while AIDS tears families apart. Anger at their American innocence, at their wealth and medical care, surged through him. As if it were their fault.

He didn't speak as he showed Shani milking the cow, children doing sums at the blackboard, and a boy holding a too-skinny baby carefully against his too-skinny chest.

"Subjects taught in Kenyan elementary schools are GHC—geography, history, and civics—maths, cultures, and health, which, for standards six through eight, includes prevention of HIV, though there aren't enough trained people to do a proper job of it."

He hesitated, then plunged ahead. "The teacher at the orphanage, Wanja Mithamo, lost her husband to AIDS and is herself HIV positive. She's been a role model as well as a confidante for the older girls. They want the children to think of HIV like any other chronic condition that requires monitoring and medicine, such as asthma or diabetes, and not something to be ashamed of. Attitudes are slowly changing in Kenya, but people continue to be secretive."

Click. The boys, smiling broadly, at the entrance to their school in Nairobi.

"The orphanage pays the boarding fees, and the Kenyan government pays the tuition for the boys' secondary education, but funds for university or training courses will need to be found. Next year two of the girls will be going to secondary school, and as I was leaving, one of them told me she intends to invent a vaccine to prevent AIDS." Oliver stopped to find the right words.

"Kirinyaga is as committed to these children as birth parents are. This is important to remember. They're determined to keep the promise of a forever home."

"Are most secondary schools boarding schools?"

"There are many more proportionally than here in the U.S., and for all socioeconomic levels. I myself went to a boarding school."

"And you lived in that teenager house, you said?"

"When I was home."

"Sign my two up! They're driving us crazy!" Everyone laughed.

"Do they play soccer?" Someone asked. More laughter.

They were like children in need of recess, Oliver thought.

"The best for the last," he said, and clicked on the photo of the babies piled in the donkey cart.

There was a chorus of "Ohhhhs."

Click. The picture that almost got him detained—Lillian weighing the baby at the airport. Click. The toddlers doing their versions of somersaults, Mugo looking between his fat little legs. And last, Jaafar.

The oohs and aahs stopped.

"This is Jaafar, seven years old, a new arrival. I told him I was going to America to get things for Kirinyaga's Children's Home. 'Presents?' he asked. I asked him what a good present would be. A book, he decided. A book about elephants."

"What happened to his face?"

"It's a viral skin infection common with HIV."

"Does it hurt?"

"He'll be receiving better care now." It wouldn't hurt to ask. "A book about elephants could help too." He brought the shades up, and Dinah raised the lights, and everyone sat blinking.

"So." He held up Lillian's proposal. "The details of the project are in the papers you're about to receive, down to the price of nails and cement. A copy was also sent to you online with the most up-to-date numbers. Dinah? Could you pass these out?" He waited until everyone had a copy.

"The Kenyan government has guaranteed testing for everyone, free ARVs for all pregnant women, and immunizations and primary care for children under six. But there is a problem. There aren't nearly enough facilities to provide the services they are promising. The clinic the orphanage wants to build will provide HIV/AIDS education, testing, contraceptive services, prenatal care, and regular medical care for children up to age 12, not just at Kirinyaga but for the district. And the clinic will not only help with medical needs, it will be a place for people to gather and share problems and help each other, as the church services are now. It will be a model for other districts to emulate."

Oliver looked at their earnest faces. "I hope I've balanced the overwhelming needs—and sadness—with the real children enjoying their lives. Even in an AIDS orphanage, children have a talent for finding happiness, something we adults can learn from. Imagine the children you just saw receiving the best health care and more teachers…and books about elephants. Just imagining such a future renews my hope, as it has been renewed telling you about it. Thank you."

One by one, then in twos, then as a body, they stood up. They were clapping. Heat rose into his face. Dinah beamed at him as if he were her big brother.

# Chapter 8

## Alice

By the fifth week of class Alice began to think it might work.

It had started with Sylvie, in the cell next to hers.

Alice had been keeping to herself, trying not to stand out or make a mistake, terrified of becoming a target like she'd witnessed, and like she'd been growing up. Then one day, Sylvie said it right out. "Girl, I know you're scared to death. So quit walkin' around like you think your stuff don't stink."

"No, I do!" Alice blurted, and Sylvie laughed and laughed.

It was Sylvie's idea that Alice teach a class, after she found out.

"You teach poems? They *teach* that stuff? In college? You get paid? You can't be much older than the kids you teach!"

And people came. Alice began with a poem and written responses, like she would at the university. She had to use *Best Loved American Poems*, the one poetry book on the unit, while her request for books went up the requisite ladder to God or someone. When the others arrived, she held one of the books to her nose before handing it to the CO, who would hold them until the next class. She would have sniffed each book like a dog if he hadn't been staring at her like she was crazy.

Today she asked the remaining three to take turns reading the lines of the poem Sylvie had picked out. Keresha mumbled through her turn, but Cricket refused altogether.

"I'm no good with this stuff."

"What's something you're good at?" Alice asked, nervous Cricket would say "nothing."

Cricket suspected a trap, but she wanted them to know. "Cooking," she said, sliding her eyes to the others.

"Cooking! Good! So. Cooking. You have a recipe, right? Poems are like that. The words are the ingredients, and—"

"I never follow some recipe! Just throw whatever's around together and taste along." Cricket shook her head and put up her hand for Keresha to high-five.

"Cricket's leftovers list!" Keresha teased.

They all laughed except Alice, even Cricket. So Alice laughed too.

They stopped and looked at her. She froze. They burst out laughing again.

"What?" she said.

"We're just foolin' with you," Keresha said and held up her hand.

Alice met Keresha's palm with her own as if she'd done it before, and nobody laughed.

"Cricket, how come you read your own stuff and not this?" Sylvie held the book up.

"My stuff isn't reading! It's just sayin'." Cricket pointed. "Somebody else said *that*."

It made a kind of sense.

There was a hush after Sylvie read the last part of Thomas Smith's "Housewarming."

> "On Christmas Eve, I prepared a warm
>     place for my mother and father, sister

and brothers, grandparents, all my relatives,
none dead, none missing, none angry with another,
all coming through the woods."

They waited, pencils poised, for the topic. Christmas?

"Home," Sylvie said.

And everyone from this remnant of the original eight started to write. It had shaken Alice, the dropping out. Sylvie said most of them came just to get out of the unit, then they saw there was work involved. But Alice thought, even so, didn't they want a voice? Didn't everyone? But last week, down to five women, when she'd said the topic—dreams, from Langston Hughes—it was as if she'd opened a jar of hornets.

Now there was only the whisper of pencils on paper.

She wrote: Home.

◊

"Wangera."

The CO pointed to the clock. Alice rushed to get down one more sentence, the words suddenly popping out and writing themselves down, the way they would sometimes. *Maybe telling you will help keep me whole if it happens.* Because the CO, who'd been so suspicious at first, as if they might attack each other with the pencils, had made sure they had time to read.

"Who wants to go?" Alice asked.

Sylvie raised her hand and then lowered it sheepishly. They didn't need permission here.

*"That poem's how it used to be for me. But if anybody in my famly was going to talk about home now, I'd be the one who's missing. I'd be the one who everbody's angry about. I could about be the one who's dead too. But nobody would be talking about home because we don't have one anymore; we*

*got scattered like leaves to a wind. When I was coming up, my Grandmom's house was the place you go if you got in trouble, the place you go to be made a lot of, like you're the best girl in the world. My Grandmom gave the neighbor kids Tootsie Rolls on Halloween, but we got Tootsie Pops. And she had everbody for Christmas. Us kids sat on the floor, but it would be set proper with a tablecloth and real dishes, not paper plates. And did we eat. There'd be no leftovers for Cricket to use."*

Cricket ducked her head, proud to be in Sylvie's story.

*"There must've been 10 diffrent pies. My favorite was lemon with that sticky sweet stuff on top."*

"Meringue," Cricket instructed.

"Don't interrupt," Keresha said.

*"Ever child got a present. I don't know how they did that, nobody had two nickels to rub together, but we all got something, and special too. One year I got a little book with a key to write my private thoughts. I wrote everday that whole year."*

"A diary!" Keresha said.

"Don't interrupt; you said it yourself," Cricket said.

Sylvie gave them a look.

*"And we sang, the old songs.* 'There is a balm in Gilead, to make the wounded whole. There is a balm in Gilead, to heal the sin-sick soul. Sometimes I feel discouraged, and think my life's in vain, but then the Holy Spirit revives my soul again.'"

Alice sat very still, not to miss any part of it, stunned by the beauty of Sylvie's voice.

And *was* there? *Was* there something to heal the "sin-sick soul"? She made her eyes wide so as not to spill a drop of her sudden tears.

*"My Grandmom when she sang would cry and be smilin' at the same time. Uncle Roy said, 'Here come the waterworks, batten down the hatches.'"*

Sylvie put her paper down. Her voice went quiet. "It's hard to remember all this." She stole a glance at Alice. "But good hard."

Keresha and Cricket began clapping.

Alice had been alarmed the first time it happened; it would never have happened—or been allowed—at the university. But now she clapped right along with the others, blinking and blinking. Here come the waterworks.

"Keresha, your turn," Sylvie said.

"Okay. Okay." Keresha cleared her throat. "Okay, here goes. *Home. When I get out, my mom and pop will make a party. Mom will invite her ladies*—she does hair—*and my cousins and my aunt*—my uncle died, he just dropped dead right there in CVS getting Aunt May's blood medicine Christmas Day. His heart."

Keresha saw that Cricket was about to say something.

"Okay, okay! *Pop will make his ribs, and Aunt May will make her three-cheese macaroni, and my mom will make her five-layer salad with bacon bits, my favorite. And she'll clean, even wash the curtains, and make Pop wash the front window. They'll go to Klingman's for the cake.* That's the bakery."

Cricket couldn't stand it. "Keresha, you interrupted yourself three times!"

"I think of more! Besides, it's my turn. Just pretend I wrote it! *It will have pink buttercream frosting and my name on it. That's what we did when Kenny came home from Iraq, except for he had chocolate.*"

She stopped. They waited.

"I'm done!"

She held her paper up to her face while they clapped.

"You never said your brother was in Iraq. Did he get shot at?" Cricket asked.

"He got that PSD."

"P*T*SD," Sylvie corrected. "Traumatic."

"He takes stuff for those flashback things. Once he punched a hole in the wall right next to my head." Keresha shrugged. "I about sh—." She looked at the CO and stopped.

Those flashback things, Alice thought. She wished she had "stuff" to stop them.

"Your turn, Cricket," Keresha said.

"Don't you say anything; it's a list."

"Poems are lists," Sylvie said.

"She's a poet and don't know it," Keresha said.

"I'm gonna read now!

> Home
> 1425 Western Apartment D
> Albany, New York
> United States
> Earth
> Universe
> Tanya
> Ceiling stars
> 'Daniel Tiger's Neighborhood'
> 'The eggplant that ate Chicago'
> St. Mary's
> Rolling skirts
> Tutu
> Cristina"

Cricket folded her paper one way and then the other, like a fan, while they clapped.

"That's short!" Keresha said.

"It's like clues," Sylvie said. "What's rolling skirts?"

"You know, Catholic school. UgLY! The nuns would make us kneel, and if your skirt didn't touch the floor you had to go to the priest. But after school we rolled the waistband to make it short."

"I did the same thing," Alice said softly.

"You *did*?" Cricket grinned.

"What's 'the eggplant that ate Chicago'?" Sylvie asked.

"'You better watch out for the eggplant that ate Chicago, for he may eat your city soon, wacka-do wacka-do,'" Cricket sang off-key. "My gram sang it when I got dropped off by my mom."

"What? Why?" Keresha asked.

"So I didn't cry and upset my mom."

"You had a tutu, Cricket?" Sylvie asked.

"I *peed* in it at a dance show! The teacher said nobody knew, but this other girl laughed." They stared at her. "Come on, everybody's peed their pants sometime! Raise your hand if you never did!"

No one raised her hand.

"My mom saved it for Tanya."

"Ew!" Keresha said. "That's disgusting."

"Get over yourself! It's been washed like a million times!" Cricket looked at Alice. "You going?"

Alice was nervous, even though she'd read the other times they'd met, as an example. But this one was more personal.

*"When I was a kid, home was where they had to take me in, but they didn't like it. My parents died when I was little, and most of my memories of my mother come from my aunt's stories, told to me as lessons about how not to be. I imagined being in happy families like in the books I read. There was a house down the block that was like one in a picture book I had. It had a white picket fence and flowers inside a circle made of painted rocks. I would jump rope on the sidewalk in front and pretend I lived there."*

She stopped to catch her breath.

*"But when I grew up and went to Kenya and met Oliver, that all changed. It's like I finally got home. I thought he was the reason."*

She almost copied Keresha, to stop to describe Oliver.

*"When I adopted Kena, I tried to make Oliver be the daddy part, but he grew up in a place where there wasn't just a mommy and daddy; there were lots of relatives to help, even ancestor and tree and animal relatives. It was too hard*

*for him here, just us, and he went back to Kenya, thinking I'd come too. But I was so hurt too that I didn't. We visit every summer, though, and Kena feels like a part of her Kikuyu family. I am too, she says. She takes people into her heart; they become part of her family easily, and she assumes I do too. There's something in the Bible about my people shall be your people, and a child shall lead. That's Kena and me."* Breathe.

*"But now she's living in a place I've never seen, and I lied to Oliver about why we couldn't visit last summer. He doesn't know what happened or about me being in jail. I hope he and Kena are right, and our spirit ancestors help us, because we need help and Kena needs a family, and they're the only ones available to her right now. I feel like I'll break into pieces if she goes to Oliver in Kenya, but I have to tell him."*

The last sentence. *"Maybe telling you will help keep me whole if it happens."* She glanced at their waiting faces. Sylvie nodded. Cricket had tears on her cheeks. Alice pressed her palms against her forehead. No crying, like crocodile tears.

The CO called over. "I'm sorry, ladies, but time's up."

Alice collected the pencils without meeting anyone's eyes and handed the precious crate of books to the CO. When she turned around, they were still there, waiting for her. They began to clap. A hot flush rose up her chest and into her neck and face, turning her an ugly red.

"Glad I ain't white!" Keresha said.

Just foolin'. Like a friend.

◊

They arrived on the unit along with the lunch trays.

"Wangera, you had a phone call!"

Scared, Alice took the message slip. But it wasn't Patrice; Kena was okay. She went to the bank of phones and punched in her phone card number and the number on the paper.

"Westchester County Public Defender's Office. If you know your party's extension, you may dial it at any time. Please listen to the following options." Her stomach took a nosedive. She leaned on the wall to keep her balance. She pressed her ear to the receiver and covered the other one with her hand to hear above the clamor of trays and voices as names and extensions were rolled out. She heard "Abbott—nine." Her hand shook so much she had trouble aiming her finger at the nine.

"You have reached the office of Brian Abbott. Leave a message." BEEP.

Alice gulped. "It's Alice Wan—"

"Ms. Wangera! I was just leaving, and heard the machine. I should have told them you should call my cell. You have that number, right? Anyway…" He cleared his throat.

And Alice knew for sure.

He cleared his throat a second time. "I was informed this morning that Adam St. John died yesterday. I'm so sorry."

The floor sank like an elevator beneath her feet.

"It's not unexpected, but it's nonetheless painful to hear, I know. I would have come in person to tell you, but I'm due in Plattsburgh."

"How—" But it was a squeak.

"I don't know the details. I'll be checking in with the DA's office, and I'll drive up to see you when we have more information about what they plan to do. I wish it could be this week, but more likely it will be after the holidays, since the DA will want to meet with the family before making any decision."

The family. Were they there? Enoch. Khai. *Lily.*

Oh, please, were they *there*—

*Kena.* Oh, God. She broke into a sweat, dizzy, and slid down the wall.

"I'm very sorry to be giving you this news."

*She* needed to tell Kena, no one else.

"I'll call as soon as I know more. Will you be okay?"

"Okay," she echoed.

"What a stupid thing to ask! I'm sorry. I just wish…well. I do have to go. You take care."

She needed to call Patrice.

Patrice was at work.

She fumbled to replace the receiver. She left it hanging. She needed to get to her cell. She just needed to get to her cell.

She needed to call Patrice. *She* needed to tell Kena. Not Patrice.

"Wangera! Get in line!"

It didn't make any difference, what she needed.

She took a step forward. Another. She reached the lunch cart, groping for the edge, and clung to it, the cold metal biting into her fingers. She shivered. Goosebumps. What a funny word.

She slid a tray out. She watched a fruit cup slide to the floor and burst open. She watched a bright red cherry roll under the cart.

She watched a hand take the tray.

"Alice, what's wrong?" Sylvie.

*Adam.*

"Alice?"

"Adam."

"Oh, Alice!" Sylvie put her hand on Alice's arm.

Alice reeled back. *Don't touch me. Don't touch me or I'll break into pieces.* She stared across the cart at forever.

# Chapter 9

## Oliver

Oliver checked his watch. He'd taken an hour and fifteen minutes of their time. A young man approached him and held out his hand.

"Mr. Wangera, I'm Wally Robinson. You've given us a lot to absorb."

"Please call me Oliver. And yes, it's a lot. And I get sidetracked."

"Well, if Geoffrey Kirui was a sidetrack, I wanted to tell you I saw him in the Boston Marathon in 2017."

"You were *there*?"

"I was in high school. We were ostensibly there on a history field trip, but I ran track back at home, and I snuck away to see the finish. I'm from Atlanta."

Oliver noticed Dinah watching them and motioned her over. "Dinah will be in Atlanta next year at Spelman."

Wally grinned and pointed at himself. "Morehouse, class of '22." He turned back to Oliver. "I have a question. The first proposal we received included funding for medications. Why was that dropped?"

"The director of the orphanage got me an appointment at the pharmaceutical company tomorrow to discuss a contribution. I'm going to ask them for the drugs for free." Oliver raised an eyebrow.

"I'll appeal to their best principles."

Wally grinned. "Good luck with *that*. I didn't realize that the school is home to a church. I hope you don't run into the foundation's bylaws with that. The board might not allow funding if the orphanage supports a particular religion. I wouldn't mention it to that pharmaceutical company."

Oliver had never thought about it. What could he say?

"I must confess it never entered my mind. Church attendance isn't mandatory, but most of the children go, I believe. Many remember attending church with family members. All of the children have *lost* a family member, parents of course, and more, to AIDS. Many loved another child, a brother or sister or cousin. Being embraced by a faith community that has beliefs and rituals surrounding death is not a small thing."

He felt bad. What could he say to restore Dinah's smile? "Also, they like dressing up."

She laughed. "Me too."

"They have just a school uniform, one set of play clothes, and one special shirt or dress."

He'd done it again.

Dinah looked down at her pantsuit. "Can I send clothes there? I have enough for five of me!"

Oliver thought of Wanja's girls. "Aii. Yes, that would be wonderful."

"Okay! But now I better do my job."

Wally watched her walk away before he turned back to Oliver. "I was wondering about adoption. I mean, I can see that it might be harder, because of HIV/AIDS, but…"

Oliver sighed. "Yes, of course. However, out of the two million Kenyan orphans, only about two hundred have the necessary documentation for adoption. At Kirinyaga they have only three eligible children at this time. It's very difficult if there's no family to approve."

He looked at Wally's shocked face.

"Over 140 million children in the world are orphans, 168 million are child laborers, 124 million are out of school, 64 million suffer from acute malnutrition, and half of child deaths are linked just to that. Not even counting AIDS, malaria, diarrhea…" He held out his hands. His empty hands. "I often feel paralyzed."

He stopped. Shame washed over him. "I must apologize. You know all of this. Of course you do; that's why you work here. And I give you a lecture." He tried to smile above the fury of feelings in his chest. Shame, yes, but grief and overwhelming helplessness too. And anger. And he suddenly realized: he was jealous. He was tallying up the victims, but Wally got to help them.

"Is there anything I can do? Not clothes, but something else?"

*Your lap. Reading a book about elephants to a little boy.*

"Aii. Yes. Books and art supplies are in short supply. Laptops! Toys that can be shared. Stuffed animals, called stuffies here, I believe. Footballs. I mean soccer balls."

"They make them in pink! That might get some girls to play."

Pink was Kena's favorite color. She'd turned eight in August, her first birthday without him. He'd sent a pink hoodie. Eight years old and healthy, thanks to American food and medical care. And she had an American library card, an overflowing bookshelf, and a closetful of clothes.

◊

The room had emptied quickly. Dinah had finished the clearing-up, just cherry pits left, the baskets empty. So that's why the napkins were paper, Oliver realized, to wrap up the leftovers to take with them.

Wally Robinson hovered in the doorway. "Well, good luck! I hope they take you up," he said.

"You're not included in the decision?"

"Nope. That'll be the board. And Maggie Wells will weigh in."

"How many then, of the people that were here?"

Wally scanned the empty table. "About half. But if it's a go, we worker bees will be involved. I'd like to be. Listen, what are you two doing for lunch?" he asked, looking at Dinah. She was stacking the baskets, and one jumped out of her hand and fell to the floor. "There's this vegetarian place a couple blocks from here. Have you been to Annie's Garden, Dinah? On me." Wally scooped up the basket and put it on the cart.

"No. I mean, I never went…I mean, yes, I'd like to."

"I'm game," Oliver said.

Wally wheeled the cart into the hall, and Dinah took it from him and pushed it down the hall to the elevator. "I'll be right back!"

As she entered the elevator, Dr. Davies exited.

"Mr. Wangera! Mrs. Wells has invited you up. I hope you don't have to run off."

Wally grinned at Oliver. "The inner sanctum."

But Oliver stood there, feeling uncertain.

"She's on the top floor," Mr. Davies said, and he walked away as if he was sure Oliver would get on the elevator in the next minute or so.

"Listen man, if Maggie Wells gives the okay, you're in!"

"Will you still go with Dinah?"

"She's pretty cute, isn't she?"

"She can't be older than 18 or 19."

"I'm 23. But everyone knows girls mature faster than boys, so that makes us even."

Oliver laughed. He put out his hand. "I hope we meet again."

"So do I," Wally said.

The elevator doors opened again, and Dinah walked out wearing a brown fleece hat with ears. She looked about 10 years old.

◊

Oliver stepped into the elevator and pushed the top button. The elevator shook on its way up. It opened to a small hall with one door, a bell next to it. There was a window opposite. He looked out and saw Dinah and Wally on the sidewalk below. He felt like a kid whose friends were going off to play while he had to face the head teacher.

He pushed the bell. He waited. He knocked softly. And waited. Maybe there was a misunderstanding. Maybe he could turn around, descend to the relatively known world below, and chase down Wally and Dinah at Somebody's Garden.

The door opened. A woman stood there, breathing hard. Her dress draped off her bony shoulders as if it was on a hanger. A plastic butterfly held a tuft of purple hair on top of her head. She was leaning on two canes.

"I'm Oliver Wangera."

She began to turn around. "Of course you are, with that accent! Call me Maggie." She began to walk, one bare foot forward, the opposite cane, the other bare foot forward, the scent of eucalyptus in her wake. "Take your shoes off," she ordered over her shoulder.

His big toe stuck out of a hole in his left sock.

At the end of a narrow hallway, he stopped in amazement. The room must go across the entire back of the house. The back wall was glass, and an enormous white paper dove hung between two ceiling fans, drifting in their breezes. White poinsettias, like the ones the girls had tucked in the donkey's bridle, bloomed all along the windowsill, glowing against a threatening sky. Dinah and Wally were about to get wet.

A tree, hung with green and yellow balls, grew out of an enormous glazed pot. No, they were lemons! She had lemons. In Washington,

DC. In December.

"Don't just stand there gawking. Come in."

His feet sank into the green velvet-soft carpet. Two purple sofas and two white armchairs were squared around a low table piled with magazines and books, scraps of paper sticking out of them. Perched on top of the stacks were an open laptop, several cups and glasses, a plate holding a fork and a hairbrush, and a carved wooden box.

Mrs. Wells—Maggie—fell back into a chair, wheezing. Oliver put his bag down and looked away, feeling like an intruder as she recovered from the walk that would have taken him a few strides if he hadn't been following her.

Dozens of photographs covered another wall.

"They're my granddaughter's. Lulu's."

LuluWells Foundation. He'd been told it was named after someone who died. So that someone was her granddaughter.

It was a gallery of children.

"Lulu was a photojournalist. Her work focused on refugee children. Go ahead, look."

He stepped closer. The photographs, ranging from large poster-sized to small postcard-sized, were all matted in the same buttery yellow inside plain black frames. He saw a small child who, he was sure, suffered from malnutrition, gazing up at iridescent bubbles in wonder, her dark eyes like deep pools. Then he realized that the photo was black and white and there weren't really any rainbows. But for a second, he'd seen with the child's eyes.

There was a photograph of three girls, their skirts hiked up to sit between each other's legs. Each girl's slender fingers were busy with the hair of the girl in front of her. Like girls he saw all over East Africa, they were grooming and chattering as if destruction wasn't simmering under them. He could almost hear their high voices.

There was a photograph of a potbellied baby boy waving his

hands, dark against a torn, striped T-shirt on a dirt floor. Another child's hand and wrist extended into the picture, dangling a scrap of cloth from a stick.

There was a photograph of a toddler in a diaper printed with a Sesame Street character…Oscar or the Cookie Monster, he never got them straight. She was propped up against a stained, striped pillow, and the diaper went up to her armpits. Her left arm stuck out in a small cast. He realized with a jolt that her other arm ended at the elbow. The cast was covered with crude drawings of birds. The little girl was laughing at the camera, as if she lived in the best of all possible worlds.

"Lulu was determined to bring a smile to every child she photographed. Most of the time it wasn't the one that was published. Tragedy sells. But Lulu said a little happiness was payment for using their suffering to tell the story. She gave them a copy of the happier picture when she could. But of course the suffering's in those too."

Maggie plucked the carved box off the stack of *Smithsonian* magazines and set it on her lap. When she lifted the lid, colored foam balls spilled out and rolled to the side of the chair. She swiftly scooped them up, squishing them into her fists. She placed two on the table, pushed against the arms of the chair with her knuckles for leverage, and got slowly to her feet. She held her head up and began to juggle. The empty skin under her arms swayed in rhythm with the balls. She swooped up a fourth, and then the fifth. Red, blue, green, yellow, and purple. Oliver watched, enthralled.

Someone had given Kena a book. Alice said it was too Christian, but Kena had loved it. *The Clown of God*. And here was Maggie Wells, juggling a rainbow just like the clown. She fell back into her chair, letting the balls fall and roll. She reached down next to the cushion, pulled out a handkerchief, and mopped her face.

Oliver scrambled to collect the balls and squeezed them into their box. He saw that the carvings on its lid were animals. One might be a rhino. Or a unicorn.

"A boy in a camp in Nigeria made that for her after she made a ball disappear and pop out of his ear in another color. I was always on the lookout for small toys, like little animals and cars, for her to give away. Once I scored fifty miniature bubble bottles, favors left over from a wedding."

Oliver smiled at "scored."

"And beachballs; they pack easily."

He laughed out loud.

"And she'd sing. Lulu said it could be anything—the Beatles, 'Itsy Bitsy Spider'—and it didn't matter if they didn't understand, she made up hand motions."

Alice had sung that to Kena, except it was "Eensy Weensy Spider." He turned back to the wall of children. Their capacity for happiness.

"Lulu grew up in this house. She lost her parents—our only child, Madeline—in a plane crash in Alaska when she was six. By a miracle, Lulu had been left with friends back in Anchorage because she had a cold."

He didn't know what to say.

"It was a lot to bear. But what else was there to do? We might feel like life is over, or want it to be, but it just marches on. The earth keeps spinning, bringing another day, even when life hurts so much a person can't believe the sun dares to show its face. But there was Lulu, and she needed us."

Maggie Wells suddenly smiled. "She became the light of our life. Every year we took a trip: the Galapagos for the turtles, Nova Scotia for *Anne of Green Gables*, India and Thailand and Alaska. Even your Kenya for the elephants in Masai Mara Reserve. We went all over, and Lulu took pictures. She went into the Peace Corps, and after that she got her first photo assignment, and then one thing led to another and another and another. She'd come home and dump out her anger at the latest horror and go off again, bearing gifts. After Henry died—my husband—she came home more often."

She picked up the box and ran her fingers over what he now knew must be a rhino.

"It would be easier if she'd died in some godforsaken place. So many died. She'd be with the others, people she already gave her life to." She put the box back on the table. "But the way she died was so… careless. In Africa, or the Middle East, she would have been paying attention. But here? She got hit by a mail truck. A mail truck! It's so… random! It wasn't his fault, either. She was crossing against the light. She was always rushing, as if the days didn't give her enough hours to live in. And they didn't, did they? The foundation is her legacy."

Maggie leaned abruptly forward. "Your turn. What happened to you that got you mixed up in all this?"

He stared at the wall. The eyes of a little girl stared back. The shoulders of her too-big dress were at her elbows. She had a string of white beads around her neck and held one between her tiny finger and thumb as if she were showing it to the photographer. To Lulu Wells. She had the fat wrist of a toddler. She wasn't smiling. She was looking right at him. Asking, "Are you going to let me down, too?"

It must just be that he was over-tired from the time change. From too little sleep. From the tension of the morning. It was being over-tired that made him need to cry.

The little girl's eyes were old from seeing too much.

Maggie Wells had lost every person she'd loved.

He walked over and sat down. The chair was too low for his long frame, and he wrapped his arms around his knees like a kid.

"I wasn't surprised when you said you feel paralyzed," she said. "I know how that can happen."

He was nonplussed.

"Oh, I watched the whole thing." She pointed to the laptop. She folded her hands on her small, Buddha-like bump of a stomach. A Buddha with purple nail polish. "How did you get from a tea farm in Kenya to here?" She pinned him down with her eyes. "And I don't want an abbreviated version."

He sighed. "I guess it starts with…when I graduated University I volunteered to help students from here—the U.S.—who were collecting the old stories and riddles from the elders where I grew up."

He'd heard Alice's laugh before he saw her. He'd come through the gap in the wall, and she was in the courtyard playing the pebble game with a little girl and looked up at him from under her halo of fiery hair.

"One of them was Alice, from New York. She was staying with a family in the Ngong Hills and needed a translator for an elderly Kikuyun couple." Oliver looked into the distance, flooded with memories.

"For both of us, it was like…" He leaned forward. "I'd never felt such happiness. We were married just two months later. If my family ever had mis-thoughts, I didn't hear them. She was their daughter and granddaughter and niece and sister and cousin. *Is* her daughter still, my mother insists. And Alice found a home, something she hadn't really had most of her life."

Guilt poked at him, but he was practiced at ignoring it.

"Then a daughter of Alice's former host family died from AIDS, leaving an HIV-positive baby girl. I'd seen how AIDS had affected family after family when I was traveling around the district with the American students. Before that, I'd thought its victims were careless people who deserved it because of their lifestyle. I held those stereotypes back then. At that time, it was a death sentence for poor rural families. Treatment for just that first year would cost more than Kena's birthmother's entire extended family's income."

"Kena?"

"Oh! The baby. Makena. Her birthmother named her. It means happy one."

"And her father?"

"He'd died before she was born. The custom is for a wife, and of course her children, to become part of her husband's family. But when Kena tested positive, they didn't want her."

"Oh, no!"

"Alice became obsessed, traveling to Nairobi to see doctors and writing to people here. And that's where we found a solution. If she adopted the baby, her university insurance would cover Kena's treatment. And it worked. She didn't have any intention of taking Kena from her mother's family."

They'd had such optimism, born out of their own happiness.

"Alice had two semesters to complete her graduate degree, so she and I flew to New York with the plan to return to Kenya when she finished." He frowned. "This is becoming a long story."

"You can't stop in the middle of it!"

"I found work at the UN with the Kenyan delegation." The relief he'd felt being with people who looked and spoke like him!

"Every few weeks we'd get a letter from Kena's aunt: all happy, all good, Makena is rolling over, she has another tooth, she loves unga…maize…she sleeps with the stuffed animal we sent, a lemur that Alice bought at a fancy New York toy store, thinking lemurs lived in Kenya." He smiled. "She still has it. Lemmy. We studied the insurance statements for reassurance; she was getting the immunizations she needed, the blood draws, the meds."

Oliver became aware that he was drumming his fingers almost frantically on his leg and made a fist.

"Then an antibiotic showed up, and another one, and more frequent checkups, and a change in medication. Things no longer felt 'all happy, all good.' We'd been saving up for our return, but Alice took the money and bought a round-trip ticket to see for herself." He'd been almost angry with jealousy. How he'd longed to see home!

"When she returned, she had Kena with her. She was tiny…too tiny. There were sores on her scalp and in her mouth. But when I spoke to her in Kikuyu, she held her arms out to be taken. And when I did, she pushed her head into my neck." He cleared his throat. "Maybe I sounded like home."

"How old?"

"Nine months, but not even sitting up yet. Sucking and chewing hurt, so we used a dropper, and it took a while, but by Alice's graduation at the end of summer term, we knew Kena had evaded AIDS, and she'd begun to crawl. *Time to go home*, I thought."

He slapped his hands down on his thighs. "But no. To Alice, she'd 'rescued' Kena from my home. Kena needed *American* medical care, American food, American everything. Kenya had killed Kena's mother, and she wouldn't let it have her baby too."

Oliver grimaced. "I was just as stubborn. Kena needed her Kenyan family. Her Kenyan roots." He gazed into the past. "I was used to a big extended family helping out, but Alice…she didn't even have *one* parent. She was scared and overwhelmed, and it was all on me, unless we went back." He met her gaze again and saw only sympathy.

"I stuck it out through another winter, but then I returned to Kenya alone."

"Oh, no. Oh, no," Maggie mourned. "The baby?"

He shook his head.

Kena was still asleep the morning he left. She was too little to say goodbye to, but she'd look for him later. He'd longed to wake her up one last time. She'd pull herself up and bounce with joy at seeing him; every morning he was a thrilling surprise. He'd sung their goodnight song alone the night before because Alice was in the bathroom with the shower on, crying.

Oliver met Maggie's eyes but had to look away. Too much compassion.

"How do you feel about working for UNICEF? And for the orphanage?" she asked.

"It's a lot of traveling. I'm tired, but it's fine," he lied. "As for the orphanage, that's family."

"It seems to me you're more than tired; you have a touch of soul sickness."

"And what does one take for that?"

"I've been selfish," Maggie said abruptly. "The kitchen's down the hall. There's stew in the crockpot and fresh bread. Take whatever you'd like to drink."

"What can I bring you?"

"Oh, I eat like a bird. Nothing for now."

There was a tray on the kitchen counter waiting for his bowl and bread and, after some indecision, a bottle of beer. When he returned with his meal, she'd cleared him a space and was looking through an album on her lap.

The gingery stew had carrots and kale and chunks of chicken in it. He discovered he was ravenous.

Finally, he wiped his mouth and sat back.

"That was wonderful."

"I can't take credit. It's my husband's recipe."

They were silent then.

"How is Kena now?"

"I believe she's fine, but I don't know for sure."

"You don't *know*?"

"I haven't seen them for a year and a half. They always came in August to see Kena's family and mine, and for her birthday, but..."

"But?"

"Alice wrote to say they weren't coming. That she didn't want to keep up our 'connection'." He couldn't keep the hurt out of his voice.

"Did you tell her you were coming? To the U.S.?"

He stared at the window. It had begun to drizzle. He shook his head.

"Oh no, no, no. You can't do that. You have to see them."

He'd thought, each summer when they came to Kenya, *this time*— *this time* they'd talk, really talk it out. Wanja told him to start by saying he was sorry. But Alice knew that, how could she not? Wanja said he had to *say*. And what about Alice? Was *she* sorry?

"Oliver," Maggie said. "You're living with a big part of yourself tucked away like it's hiding. You have to see them, at least try. At least Alice. Do you see that?"

He abruptly picked up the tray and carried it to the kitchen. He washed the bowl and plate and put them upside down on a dish towel. He poured out the rest of the beer and rinsed the bottle, leaving it in the sink. But then he'd run out of things to do. He stood in the dim kitchen, swallowing to keep from bawling like a little kid.

He could just leave. Run away.

Finally he walked back but faltered at the doorway. The children on the wall were weeping. Then he realized: rain was flowing down the big windows, and rain shadows were streaming down their faces.

"Come here," Maggie said. She tilted the album for him to see.

The photograph was of a young woman sitting cross-legged on top of a big rock, a child on her lap, squinting against the sun. The little girl was Asian…Vietnamese or Cambodian. The woman had Maggie Wells's smile. It must be Lulu holding a refugee.

"Imagine me scrambling around on rocks! And that little munchkin, of course, is my Lulu."

"What?"

"Oliver Wangera! You—of all people—surely Kena has shown you that it isn't blood that makes a family!"

# Chapter 10

## Kena

When Kena first typed Adam's name on the library computer in September, a creepy picture came up. Toby said it was Adam and Eve, and the snake was the Devil. Her mother had told her there was no such thing as the Devil, but still, she was embarrassed to see naked people in front of Toby. He said he'd seen it all before. So she told him about the picture those girls showed her in a magazine at her old school. The ladies in the picture were nursing babies and had no clothes on top and one girl said, "There's you and your mother."

Toby said, "Forget about those losers." She hadn't, but when she came to Patrice's, she got to go to a school where almost everyone looked like her. Every Tuesday the after-school group went to the library, and Kena would sneak away to the computer room and wait for Toby, who was in middle school and could get an internet pass. And every week they read Adam's friend Gideon's blog to see if Adam was better, but he never was.

Sometimes Gideon wrote about when he and Adam were kids, like the time they lay in snow with no clothes to be Spartan boys. It was a test. Adam's dog, Homer, squeezed in between them and smelled bad, but they let him stay. And Gideon wrote about Adam's hospital visitors. Adam's mother brought peanut butter cookies for him to smell, and his father played the flute. Lily and Enoch. And Khai, Adam's other father, read to him. *Jayber Crow.* Which must be about crows, which was good because Adam loved birds. Someone else brought fuzzy socks and lullaby music. But Adam didn't wake up.

Today, after logging on, Toby left to look at that week's *Explorer* magazine. One day he'd discover a place nobody had ever seen. She could come too, but she'd have to be like a Spartan.

"Not naked!"

"Fine. But only because you're a girl."

When the blog opened, though, it was the same one from the week before. She clicked to go back and saw two new posts with Adam's name. She picked one, and her mother's university ID picture leapt out at her. She huddled close: "St. John Dies of Injuries." *Mama!*

*Whoosh.*

She was looking down at herself like after the car crashed.

She slammed back down, her heart hammering.

*White Plains News Journal, December 13*

*Adam St. John, 21, died Monday, December 12 at New York—* some-thing—*Hospital of injuries sus-tain-ed in a June single car accident in White Plains. Alice Wangera, the driver of the car, is currently serving a one-year sentence for ag-gra-va-ted DWI at Westchester County Correctional Facility for injuries to her seven-year-old daughter, who was also a passenger.*

Kena grabbed onto her hair.

*Further charges have been pending on the outcome of St. John's injuries. Robin Barker, Westchester County Assistant District Attorney, indicated she is considering—something—mans-laughter or veh-? ho-mi-cide. Either could bring a prison term of up to fifteen years.*

Kena gasped.

*Wangera's daughter is in foster care, and it is likely that Child Protective Services will now ask for a custody hearing. Wangera, a published poet, was an adjunct professor at Brandt University in New York City at the time of the accident.*

Kena jumped up and tore into the hall, barely making it to the bathroom. She heaved up egg salad and blueberry yogurt, chunks clinging to her face. She swiped her sleeve across her nose and chin. She began to sob, gripping the edge of the sink. She turned the faucet on and stuck her head under the water.

Toby.

She spun and shoved the door open and ran down the hall to the main room. She saw the top of his Yankees cap and rushed over.

"Kena? You're all wet!" He made a face. "You stink!"

"He died!" she wailed, and she began to sob again.

Toby dropped his magazine, grabbed his backpack, and pushed Kena toward the doorway. "Come on."

Out in the hall, Kena flung herself at him. "He died!"

His shirt was getting wet, but he didn't push her away until she wound down. He looked down at himself. It wasn't just tears. It was snot. It was throw-up. "Yuck! Kena, look what you did!"

"I couldn't help it."

"It's gross!"

He pulled her in the direction of the bathrooms. "What happened?"

"I told you," she said, her voice tiny.

"Was it on Gideon's blog?"

She shook her head and, remembering her mother's face, her eyes welled up and spilled over. "It said 15! Fifteen years, Toby!"

"Kena, we need to clean up," Toby said. "I'll meet you in the computer room."

Kena grabbed his hand. "No! You have to wait here!"

"Okay, okay." After she'd pushed into the bathroom, he went into the men's room. When he came out, the front of his shirt soaked, she was there and grabbed his hand with cold, slippery fingers.

"I'd left the faucet on and the drain got plugged and there's water on the floor."

"Is it off now?"

She nodded.

He hesitated. It was a *girls'* bathroom; what if someone came in? "Somebody will take care of it. Show me what you saw on the computer."

Toby rolled the chair close and read the article. It was bad.

"What does mans laughter mean?" Kena asked. "See—here."

"It's 'slaughter.' Kena, did the car hit an animal?"

"I don't think so." She reached for her hair.

"Don't." Toby pulled her hand down.

"What does it mean, man-slaughter?"

"I don't know."

"Toby, I have to know!" she pleaded.

He clicked on the word. "The unlawful killing of a human being by another without mali…mal-ice aforethought."

Kena started to shake.

*Killing.*

"Manslaughter and all this stuff," Toby said. "Somebody dies. And vehicu- that's a car accident, like what happened." But the next word was homicide, like his father.

"It's lies," she whispered. Her mother would never *ever* kill somebody. It was a *accident.* And the other part was wrong too. She was *eight.* It was all lies, like when Susannah Bush-Talbot told everyone they'd die if they held Kena's hand. She'd felt ashamed, but her mother said when someone lies you have a right to be angry, Kena, and stand up for yourself.

But there was more. She put her finger on the word. Custody.

"Custody? Well, it's like…first my pop and mom had custody of me. They took turns. Then my grandma. Now I'm with Patrice. Custody is like owning, who owns kids."

"Like slavery?"

"No! Like…like parents, or Patrice, like foster parents. Or when somebody gets adopted."

"I don't wanna be adopted! I already am!"

It said prison. Toby's dad was in prison. He wouldn't get out until after Toby grew up. Toby had told her jail was shorter, but already her mother couldn't come home until she was in third grade. It said 15 years! She'd be a grownup!

"Who decides?"

"Sometimes the kid gets to say. And the social worker. And sometimes the mom or dad. Or other relatives might."

"No! *Prison!* Your father, Toby. Who decided?"

Toby looked at the floor. He didn't like to think about that time.

"Toby! It's important!"

"Okay! Okay. The man my pop kill—shot—a judge decided after his wife said what she wanted to happen."

"Why the judge's wife?"

"Not *her*! The man my father *shot. His* wife."

Kena grabbed the mouse and clicked on the other new post. There was a picture of Adam wearing a tie, smiling. She touched his face with her finger.

"Toby, look, maybe they're wrong!"

"Oh, Kena," he said.

It hurt, looking at Adam, but she didn't want to ever look away. "Read it!"

"Oh, Kena."

"Read it!"

"FARLEYS' DOCK, NY: Adam Forbes St. John, 21, died at New York-Pres—Pres-by-teri-an Hospital, New York City, on December

12, from injuries sustained in an accident June 12."

Kena began to cry again, and Toby took her hand.

*"Adam grew up in Farleys' Dock, graduated from Falls Academy, and was attending Brandt University with the goal of becoming a veterinarian."*

"That's an animal doctor," Toby said.

"I know what a veterinary is!" Kena wailed.

"Veterin*arian*."

Kena pulled her hand out of Toby's.

*"Passionate about animal welfare, Adam volunteered at the Humane Society and worked at Kat-o-nah Veterinary Clinic during vacations. He was also a* ment-or *with the Big Brother-Big Sister Program at Brandt.* That's you!"

Kena gulped. She took his hand.

*"He enjoyed hiking, and walked one quarter of the Ap, Ap-palachian Trail* I know about that," Toby said. "I read a book where this kid's plane—"

"Toby!"

"Okay!…*with his father, Enoch St. John, and his best friend, Gideon Wainwright. He also shared many adventures with his beloved dog, Homer, in the woods near their home."*

"Homer!" Kena began to cry again. "Oh, Homer."

*"Adam was pred—pre-de-ceased by his matern-al grandparents, Thomas and Lillian Forbes. He leaves his parents, Lily St. John of Farleys' Dock and Enoch St. John and Khai Nguyen of White Plains; his patern-al grandpar-ents, Lois and Bernard St. John of Plattsburgh; his lifelong friend, Gideon Wainwright; Homer; his cat Too; and many others."*

"They put a capital T in front of too. They made a mistake," Toby said, feeling better about his reading difficulties.

Kena wiped at her cheeks. "That's his cat's name. Too." Why wasn't *her* name there? She was his Little Sister! They made her be Many Others.

"His name?"

"Just read!"

*"The St. John family express their heartfelt gratitude to the staff of New York-Pres—Presbyterian for their support and many acts of kindness through a pro-long-ed and difficult time.*

*"An inform-al gathering of friends and family will be held at The Lake House, Farleys' Dock, New York, from 7-9 PM, Friday, December 16.*

*"A Quaker Worship Service of Thanksgiving for the Grace of God in Adam's Life will be held Saturday, December 17 at 11 AM at Falls Meeting House in Farleys' Dock, followed by light refreshments at Lily St. John's home. All are welcome and guests are asked to bring an ornament to hang on an evergreen tree that will be planted next spring at the library.*

*"Contributions may be made in Adam's memory to the Westchester Humane Society."*

"That's the funeral, that 'worship service'. They didn't call it a funeral at my grandma's either. They don't use those words anymore," Toby said.

"I have to go!"

"What? You can't; you're too little."

"*You* can take me."

"No, I can't!"

"Why? Toby, I have to go!"

"Kena! You don't get it! We have to follow the rules. That's how we get to go home."

"I do *so* get it! I know a lot more rules than you, I bet!" She stuck her face in his. "She needs to know it was a accident! I need to tell her!"

"What are you talking about?"

"His mother! She needs to tell the judge. So my mother doesn't go to prison!" She grabbed her hair. "It was a accident," she whispered. Not that slaughter thing.

Toby pulled Kena's hand down. "Don't you have that thing to hold?"

"And she's sad! She's so sad, Toby!" She pulled her ostrich charm out from under her shirt and rubbed it with her thumb. "It said *friends*. All are *welcome!*"

"Kena. Patrice—"

"No! Patrice can't know. She said 'You can't have anything to do with that family.' And I was only wanting to make them a *card*. *Please*, Toby. It's not far away; Adam said it was just a hour. I have to *try*. *You* would if it was *your* mother!"

Toby painstakingly typed out "New York Metro North." A few clicks and he had it, and she followed his finger to the words "Farleys' Dock," and down from there to Grand Central Station. "I go on the train every week. I can show you what to do."

"I *know* how to go on the Metro, Kena."

"*Please*, Toby! How long is it?"

"An hour," he admitted.

She sank her fingers into his arm. "Please, Toby!"

"Okay! Okay. We'll say we're coming here. Patrice likes the library. An hour there, an hour for the thing, and an hour back. Plus getting to the station and back. Four hours. Maybe five. But you have to do everything I say, Kena. And I mean it."

She nodded her head vigorously.

"And you need to wear a black dress."

She wanted to wear her Big Apple Circus T-shirt. She'd tell Adam's mother about the magician putting fire in his mouth. Real fire, and then he closed it. She'd tell Adam's mother *everything*. "There's the light refreshments, I have to go to that!"

"No, Kena!" He pried her fingers off his arm. "We'd be gone too long. The library closes at 4:30 on Saturday. If we're not home by 5:00, Patrice will get worried. She might even call the police."

She ran right over Patrice to the heart of things. "I need to see Adam's room. And Homer."

"Do you think the raft is still by the river?" Toby wondered.

The raft Gideon described in the blog. Kena's heart lifted. He'd do it! "You can go to the river! I have train money. From Tam. And a credit card." For a DIRE emergency, Tam had said. "This is an emergency, Toby."

Toby blinked as if he'd been dreaming. And watching him, she saw it all sinking away: the raft, Homer, Adam's room. Light refreshments. Her heart sank too.

"Kena, I said I'd go to the funeral thing with you, and I will. But not the other thing." He said the hateful words. "It's out of the question."

Her watch beeped.

"You hafta go to the shuttle."

He helped her with her jacket and lifted her backpack over her shoulders. "I'll get a prepaid phone for the trip just in case we need it. Tell Patrice I'll be home by suppertime."

"You just want a phone," she teased. He'd wanted one for his birthday.

She stood there, needing something more. He half-hugged, half-pushed her away. "The credit card! For the phone! It's in the side pocket." She turned so he could pull it out. He pulled out Adam's book. She grabbed it.

"I wasn't gonna keep it." His fingers found the credit card. *Tamara Jacobsen.*

"I don't have a black dress!" She fought against more tears.

"It doesn't have to be black." He looked at her jacket and backpack. "Not pink, though."

She raised her chin and walked to the door, clutching the book against her chest. Her stiff back showed that she was angry, but Toby didn't say anything more. Mad was better than crying if you had to go on a bus.

# Chapter 11

## Oliver

The pharmaceutical application sat on his lap, unreviewed, on the hour-long flight to Newark, as he imagined huddling under Lindstrom Bakery's striped awning across the street from Alice's apartment to catch a glimpse of her and Kena. How many times had he held Kena up to choose a gingerbread person from the broken or flawed ones Mrs. Lindstrom gave away to the neighborhood children? She'd press her face into his neck and peek when the baker asked her what icing she wanted and whisper the answer into Oliver's collar. "Strawberry." Because it was pink.

The car rental guy seemed happy to offer a free upgrade when the economy car Lillian had booked wasn't available. It was like popcorn at the movies, cheaper to get the bucket size. But when he felt the soft leather embrace him, and the spaciousness, he sighed. He'd never driven a car big enough for his long legs. The engine was so quiet he wasn't sure he'd turned it on.

"Hello. My name is Nigel. What is your destination?"

Oliver's head would've hit the roof in an economy car. He whirled around to see who was talking.

"Hello. My name is Nigel." The voice was coming from the

dashboard. "What is your destination?" It was pure science fiction.

"Uh...Ridgefield Park, New Jersey." Was there a microphone, or telephone, or something he should push? "Uh...Kingdom Pharmaceuticals."

"One moment, please. Four six zero Juniper Lane, Ridgefield Park, New Jersey. Is that correct?" Oliver pulled his bag onto his lap.

"Four six zero Juniper Lane," Nigel began repeating.

"I'm looking—uh—one moment, please." He'd adopted Nigel's manners. "Yes, that's it, 460 Juniper Lane." He felt self-conscious, as if an actual person named Nigel lived in the dashboard.

"Proceed to Express Road and turn right."

Between remembering to drive on the right and Nigel's directions—slight right...keep right...continue...keep left...slight left...exit to right—and cars and trucks passing—one driver maybe giving him the finger—he was sure he'd cause a pileup before he got there. Nigel should have made him practice in the carpark. But an hour later he was driving down a road divided by bare trees decorated with fairy lights that ended at a closed gate.

"You have arrived at your destination," Nigel congratulated him. After struggling to open the window, Oliver pressed a red button on the gatepost.

"Name, please," a female voice squawked.

"Oliver Wangera."

"Name, please," she squawked again. He squinted at the small print next to the button and held it down.

"Oliver Wangera."

"One moment, please." Static, then, "Proceed to Lot D." The gate opened. He drove forward.

"What is your destination?" Nigel asked.

"I'm parking."

"One moment, please."

Nigel and the squawker would make a good couple, he thought.

◊

The inside of Kingdom Pharmaceuticals looked like the lobby of an upscale hotel. Two empty escalators ran between the ground floor and a mezzanine, a tall, blue-flocked Christmas tree at their base. Empty sofas and chairs waited with open arms, listening to soft music. A bank of lifts covered a far wall, and a man in a uniform stood in front of them, staring into space. A young woman wearing a black bowtie smiled at him from behind a long reception counter. "I'm Oliver Wangera, here to see Andrew Tannager. I have a one o'clock appointnent."

"Good afternoon, sir." She punched keys on a machine and a light flashed in his face; a card whirred out. She slipped it into a plastic sleeve on a clip and handed it to him. She'd caught him with his mouth gaping like a fish. Could he ask for another take?

"Someone will be down shortly to escort you. Help yourself to snacks." She pointed to a kiosk near the lifts. "Have a good afternoon!"

There were packaged biscuits, crisps, those protein bars, and the kind of juice boxes that squirted if you pressed them. Eight coffee dispensers sat in a line, including one labeled Kenyan Extra Bold. He didn't want to be wolfing down the free provisions when his "escort" came for him, but he took a cup of coffee. Need to support the home team. He looked over his shoulder. The rent-a-cop was still gazing into space. He took three protein bars and stuffed them into his bag. Our drug money at work.

He chose a chair from which he could see both the lifts and the escalators. There were newspapers arrayed in a circle on a low table around a gold wreath that itself encircled a fat red candle that had never been lit. He pictured the people, probably immigrants, who came in every night and cleaned, even though nothing was dirty, and replaced the newspapers, even if they hadn't been read. He hoped they helped themselves. Maybe he should leave a note: "Greetings from a fellow human being."

The coffee was a credit to Kenya. He should bring a cup to Mr. Tannager as a bribe. It was already fifteen minutes past the meeting time.

Would that be taken from his "He can give you half an hour, Mr. Wangera"? He pressed his leg to stop its bouncing. He looked up. Chandeliers, and faint music that teased him to remember the tune. Somewhere in the floors above there were people in lab coats peering into microscopes, working to find cures for AIDS, malaria, Alzheimer's, Ebola. He lifted his cardboard cup in their honor, and the tune popped into his head.

"Raindrops keep falling on my head, and just like…" What was the rest? He shook his head but the words didn't fall into place.

He leaned over to scan the newspapers: *Wall Street Journal*, *The Weekly Standard*, *The Christian Science Monitor*, *The New York Times*. He picked up the *Times* and thumbed through for the New York Region section he used to read on the subway going to the UN.

His heart took a skip, and he looked more closely.

A headline below the fold read "Barker to Wangera—Manslaughter?"

There were plenty of Wangeras back home, but he'd never run across one here in the U.S. Poor bugger. He read: *Robin Barker, Westchester County Assistant DA, indicated Tuesday that she may charge Alice Wangera with involuntary manslaughter. Adam St. John, 21, of Farleys' Dock, N.Y., died Monday of injuries sustained in the June accident for which Wangera, a former Brandt University instructor, is serving a one-year sentence for Aggravated DWI for injuries sustained by her daughter.*

He lunged to his feet and read it again. And again, in disbelief. *June.* He'd gotten Alice's letter in July.

He dumped his bag and opened his laptop. Nothing. He'd need the wifi password. He stuffed everything back in and raced to the counter.

The receptionist smiled and held her hand up. "I know, I know. I'm sure it will only be—"

"May I have your wifi password?"

"What?"

"Wifi. I need to get on the internet."

"Oh! There are computers on the mezzanine. You can access the internet there using your guest pass. I'll let your escort know where you are, shall I?"

It took him four strides to get up the moving stairs. There were at least a dozen computer stations. The card didn't work twice, three times.

"Let me help you."

Oliver spun around. It was the rent-a-cop from below. He leaned over and punched in a few numbers. The screen came up.

"Thank you."

"No problem, sir." The man walked back to the lifts and put his hands behind his back. Oliver had just entered Alice's name when he heard another voice.

"Ralph! How're things? I heard you're going to see your son." A woman's voice.

"The folks at Walter Reed fixed it so he can leave for the afternoon," the rent-a-cop said.

"That's good news. You've been waiting a long time! I'm here for Mr. Wangera." His escort.

*Wangera/White Plains Journal.* Oliver clicked—and stopped breathing.

Kena. Her face was streaming with tears. His mind reared back. Was it *blood*?

"Over there."

*Makena Wangera, 7, injured in last night's accident on Bronx River Parkway, suffered cuts and contusions as well as a broken arm and a concussion. She was brought by ambulance to White Plains Hospital, where she is in stable condition. The driver of the car, her mother, Alice Wangera, is being held at Westchester County Jail pending charges, including those for a second passenger, Adam St. John, of Farleys' Dock.*

There was a second photograph, a car on its back. *Their* old car.

"Mr. Wangera, I'm here to—Oh, my God! What happened?"

*A concussion.*

"Do you know her?"

A broken arm.

"Maybe you'd like to postpone. I can ask Mr.—"

"No. No. Let's just get it over with."

It was *months* ago.

Cuts. Contusions.

"If you're sure."

Concussion.

Ralph opened the lift. Going up, Oliver remembered about his son. His dark face looked careworn.

The doors opened to a bustling corridor. There was no carpeting or soft music, or soft anything. Here it was all business, not a penny spared on appearances.

It was *months* ago. She'd be healed. But where *was* she? And Alice. Manslaughter.

His guide pointed. "It's just down this way."

He knew she was sneaking looks at him, and he tried to keep his terror from showing. She stopped at an open door and motioned him in. A desk took up most of the room. A heavyset man worked his way around it and put his hand out.

"Sorry for the wait, Mr. Wangera. Or may I call you Oliver? I'm Andy Tannager. How was your trip? I'm guessing it's a lot colder here, am I right? Please have a seat. I've just been looking over your file to refresh my memory."

A half hour. He could handle that. Had to. They wouldn't get a chance like this again. He sat down and pulled out his own file. He pretended to look through it, working for composure. "Refresh my memory" didn't sound promising.

Mr. Tannager picked up a pen and tapped it on the file.

"All right. Let's get straight to it."

But he didn't. He tapped and tapped, until Oliver realized it was he who was supposed to get straight to it.

"Mr. Tannager," he said. "Firstly—"

"Andy."

Oliver leaned forward. He felt dizzy.

"Firstly, as you know, receiving the new drugs from your company is contingent on the necessity for them when children develop resistance to their current medications. We're not asking for them for everyone." His head felt like a bobbing balloon. A blathering bobbing balloon, barely attached to his body. Hold it together. A half hour. Less.

"Secondly, the director has estimated—and I'm sure you've gone over the numbers yourselves—the costs extended out to five years, and in the worst circumstances, would be an insignificant commitment from Kingdom's Pharmaceuticals, just under 6,000 U.S. dollars a year if the drugs are sold at cost." Kena's face flashed before him. He lost track. What else did he need to say?

Tap tap tap. "Is there more you want to say?"

More. More was the strangest word Oliver had ever heard. More. Door. Snore. Hah! The balloon could rhyme!

"Mr. Wangera?"

Oliver put his hand up as if he were a crossing guard. He had to finish, but he didn't know where he was in the speech. He sagged against the back of the chair, giving up.

At least Mr. Tannager had stopped that irritating tapping. "We've given this considerable thought," he said.

Right. Thus the need to "refresh," Oliver thought.

And Mr. Tannager had more. "As you're no doubt aware, it costs millions of dollars to fund the research, testing, trials, licensing, and promoting of a new drug. The period before it becomes generic is what pays for these new treatments that are so desperately needed to fight the HIV/AIDS epidemic. And hopefully, down the road, we'll come up with a cure, something we are actively engaged in. To put it bluntly, we can't just give pills away; research and development would be stopped in its tracks."

Mr. Tannager smiled at Oliver and held up the file.

Oliver felt sick to his stomach.

"In addition, we are required to honor protocols and agreements with many constituencies…other pharmaceutical companies, insurance companies, medical facilities, pharmacies, and governments—ours and others'—and that's the short list."

Fuck them. He had to get out of there.

Mr. Tannager spread his hands out expansively. "We really can't afford to just—"

*Fuck you.*

"Can't *afford*?" Oliver burst out. "Let me be sure I understand. Kingdom's Pharmaceuticals can't *afford* to give 59 *orphans* $6,000 worth of drugs a year?"

"I thought there were more youngsters."

It sounded to Oliver like an accusation…or a justification. *We were thinking of giving you the prize, but if you falsify your numbers, well… what can we do?*

"No, it's your lucky day, *Andy*. We're having a sale…just 59 *youngsters* if you act now!" Oliver knew he'd lost perspective, but he didn't care.

He got to his feet and smacked his hands down on the desk.

"And here's a suggestion. Sell a couple of those empty sofas down in your empty lobby on that Greg's List…and stick the money in one of the banks over here that your government bailed out, and you can use the interest for our little request—how about *that*?"

"There's no need for sarcasm, Mr. Wangera. Please sit down. We're all doing our best with the painful realities of HIV/AIDS."

Oliver boiled over.

"Except the 'painful realities' aren't the same for you, are they? Because *your* reality means you would never be faced with the choice of buying your child's medication or paying school fees. Your reality gives your family all the health care they need. With trimmings. You even get to shop around. You're so used to having the best—you expect it, as your *right*—you don't even try to imagine what it's like to spend every day keeping a sentence of death away from people you love."

He lifted his hands from the desk and slapped them down again.

"Mr. Wangera—"

"We have *no safety net*…our continent doesn't, our country doesn't, our children—there are children, too many to count, although I've been counting, too many to take care of—so many." He had to stop before he burst into tears.

"Mr. Wangera—"

"Kirinyaga's children…Kirinyaga means God's resting place, did you know that? They just have to hope, *hope* that the medicine they take one, two, three times a day will keep them from dying like their mothers or fathers. Or sisters or brothers. For some, fucking God's resting place will be a *cemetery*. I don't bet that would be a popular reality show, would it? Who's going to be sickest this week? You'd better stick to *The Biggest Loser*."

Oliver was shaking. Stop. It's over.

Andy Tannager got up, walked around the desk and past Oliver, and left the room. Oliver sat down and put his head in his hands. *Holy fucking hell.* Mr. Tannager returned with a bottle of water.

"Drink it."

Oliver gulped it down.

"Better?" And the man had the nerve to smile.

And Oliver had one last bitter pill to spew up.

"There's another thing. It's not doing the best you can to make me wait 30 minutes, after I fly up here from Washington and drive from the airport on the wrong bloody side of the road, to give me a lecture like I'm some fool from some inferior place who doesn't know better. And now I've acted like one, too, so you can feel completely justified."

Oliver stood up. He put out his hand. "I'll say goodbye."

"Sit back down, young man. You are acting a little like a fool, but fortunately the committee that's granting your request isn't here, and I won't tell." *Granting my request?* Oliver fell back into the chair, bewildered.

"I don't fault you for anything you said, especially your passion," Tannager continued. "Except the crack about *The Biggest Loser.* That seems like a low blow." He patted his midsection.

Oliver thought he'd never been so confused.

"They added some equipment to your request: an autoclave, centrifuge, microscope, hemocytometer, blood analyzer. A consultant—on our dime—will help Kirinyaga's director decide what will work best for her situation." Mr. Tannager cleared his throat. "I've cleared another hour, but before we go into the details, let's agree on a fundamental fact. I've been an insensitive prick. You're absolutely correct. I can't imagine the realities those of you in the frontlines face. Or the children. So please don't regret your words. I needed to hear them."

Oliver was mute.

"I apologize," Mr. Tannager went on. "When I feel uncomfortable I tend to do exactly what I did today. Instead of just saying we'll give you what you need, I had to list all the reasons why it's bad for us to do it, so you'd see just how generous and wonderful we are and that we're not the money-grubbing, pompous jerks the world thinks we are. Everything you said is true. You're doing real work with real kids. You're right there in the trenches. And I *am* insulated and spoiled. And I feel guilty."

They stared at each other, each confronting his own stereotype.

His was how he'd justified leaving Alice—making her out to be a spoiled American.

It was *blood* on Kena's face.

"Mr...Andy. I have to ask...I found out that a good friend is in serious trouble. Is it possible to meet later? I have an open return for home...perhaps next week?"

"But of course. We can try to get through everything so you can get home for Christmas."

"I expect my friend's trouble will keep me here. If I could get online with my laptop, I'd be grateful."

"Of course. If you weren't needing to help your friend, I'd invite you home for dinner."

Oliver felt a rush of feeling. "And I would accept your invitation."

"I'll get you the wifi password and a place to work. Do you need directions anywhere?"

"Oh!" Oliver said. "No worries. I have Nigel."

*Friday, December 16th*

# Chapter 12

## Kena

Heart pounding, Kena squeezed between the iron posts at the corner of the playground and ran down the block to the phone booth. Pee-ew! It stunk like pee! She pulled out the number she'd copied from the list Patrice kept by the phone. The same phone that rang yesterday that was Toby's mother saying he could come for vacation and she'd pick him up after school today, and Kena had to pretend to be happy for him.

She stretched to reach the coin slot and put in the two quarters.

"This is the absentee line for Rosa Parks Elementary School. State your name, the name of the student, the date, time, and reason for the absence, after the beep."

BEEP.

She squeezed her nose and lowered her voice. "This is Patrice Washington. Kena…I mean *Ma*kena Wangera will leave after noon recess for the dentist Friday…" She didn't know the date! "Today." She reached to put the receiver back and missed. It swung from the cord, but she could hear a buzz, so she left it like that. Ms. Chau would be asking everybody where she was.

Where she was, was skipping school, practically the baddest

thing you could do.

She kept her eyes on the sidewalk as she walked the six blocks to Goodwill, as if nobody could see her if she didn't see them. Crossing the parking lot, she slowed down. She'd been there two times before, but she'd been with a grownup.

A lady walked around her, and as the automatic door opened, Kena skittered behind her as if they were together. Then she veered off, turning and turning, like a mouse in a maze, toward kids' clothes. She came to a rack of Christmas pajamas, Elves and reindeer and Santas. She ran her palm along the row and tripped. It was a bin of boots, a jumble of star wands on top. She waved a wand and noticed a pink cowgirl boot peeking out as if summoned by her magic. She pulled it out. There was a star on its side!

She loved it.

"Want some help?"

A white lady stood above her. She wore a green vest with a name on the pocket: Angela.

Angela went at it methodically, pairing boots in the aisle. Then she turned around, holding up the other boot like a prize. "There's a chair somewhere," she said, looking around.

"That's okay." Kena toed her rubber boot off and tried to pull the pink boot on.

"Try stamping down."

Kena stamped. If her mother was there, she'd say, "Can you wiggle your toes?"

Angela stooped and felt the toe. "Can you wiggle your toes?"

She could, but barely. "How much do they cost?" Kena rubbed the star on its side. Cloth. Not metal.

"Four dollars."

Kena stopped rubbing.

"What am I thinking! I'd forget my hair if it wasn't glued on!

Children's boots are half off for the holidays!"

Kena pulled her dollar bills out of her pocket.

"No, you pay up front. Just take the tag." Angela plucked a pen from her vest pocket, crossed out the 4, and wrote a 2. "Tell them Angela said okay. Anything else I can help you with?"

She almost told.

"No thank you. I'm just going to…browse."

"Okay, honey. You have fun browsing." Angela smiled and walked away.

Kena stamped into the other boot, held one foot out, and then the other, admiring them. She hid her old boots on the bottom of the bin. Someone might like them, maybe even love them. She had, before having to wear them in jail. She went along the size 8 racks, clothes sticking out and waving, saying "Pick me." But none of them were black.

Then she stopped. It was the dress of her dreams.

It was pink. The buttons were daisies.

She pulled it out and draped it over herself. She imagined twirling, twirling; she stumbled. There wouldn't be any twirling, or any pink. She fingered the daisies. Metal. She pushed into the forest of clothes and sat down on her backpack between two rows. She pressed her fists against her eyes until she saw stars. Her mother didn't know where she was. If she was thinking of her—and she did, all the time—she'd be thinking she was at school, having lunch.

"Mama," she whispered, like her mother said she should when she missed her. Because their hearts were always connected. Same moon.

And her birth mother's too, on Mount Kenya.

"Maitu." She burrowed her face into the dress. Velvet. Oh, how she loved it!

And that was the problem, right there. It wasn't a time for loving things. It was a time for Rules, and she was breaking them all over the place. Toby going to his mom's meant he couldn't stop her, and she'd lain awake planning the whole thing, how she'd go to that Lake House, how when she told Adam's mother everything, she'd help. She'd talk to the judge.

The silver star on her boot was like the star she and her mom put on top of their Christmas tree, made of glitter cloth glued to cardboard. She knew, really, her mother wouldn't be home at Christmas, and her chest filled up with tears.

A voice cut through her sadness. "Are you all right down there?"

Did "Angela" mean angel?

Kena hesitated. But Toby didn't know everything.

"Do you have to wear a black dress if you go to a funeral?"

Angela stood there, tapping her fingers on her chin. Her fingernails sparkled.

"Whose funeral, honey?"

"Adam. My friend."

Angela put a hand against her back, leaned over, and held up the dress.

"Well, it *is* customary for adults to wear dark colors. But as for me, I want my people to wear all the colors of the rainbow when they sing me off." She smoothed out the dress. "What do you think your friend Adam would want?"

Not black. Not black at all. He liked her Valentine party dress. Adam liked pink.

◊

Kena ducked down the passageway between the houses to the back door. Mr. Steckle, the basement tenant, worked nights and slept during the day, so she had to be quiet as a mouse. She tiptoed up the worn wooden steps, opened the storm door, and inserted her key.

She'd never been in the apartment alone. It was so quiet she could hear the kitchen clock ticking. She tugged her new boots off, bumping Sully's water bowl and getting her socks wet. She shrugged off her backpack and jacket and pulled her socks off and used them to wipe up the water. A thump came from the living room, and Sully slinked through the doorway. He went to his food dish, sniffed, and examined his water bowl. She sat down cross-legged and patted her lap, and he jumped in, rubbing up against her sweatshirt; the golden Brandt lion on its front almost matched his fur.

She stroked his ears. "I'm going away, Sully. To Adam's. He has a cat named Too, because there was another one before. But not two like the number, too like—" Sully jumped away and padded to his water bowl and looked at her. She brought the bowl to the sink, rinsed it out and filled it, and carried it carefully back. It only spilled a little. "There you go."

Kena picked up her backpack and tiptoed upstairs to the room she shared with Keisha. She reached under her bed and pulled out her box. She turned Dora, her old flashlight, on, then off. She tucked it in the bottom of her pack next to Adam's book. She took out the money Tam had sent and put it in her pocket. She picked up the picture of Oliver holding her on his shoulders. She looked at it and closed the lid on their happy faces.

She went to the dresser. *Two* pairs of underwear, just in case. Three pairs of socks; you can't have too many. Big Apple T-shirt, leggings. Her star belt that matched her new boots. Her nightie from under the pillow. Lemmy. She wound his tail around his belly so it couldn't get stuck in the zipper of the backpack. Finally, she pulled her new dress from the bag. She folded it carefully, making sure not to bend back the collar.

Her toothbrush! She put toothpaste on it and wrapped it in toilet paper, then went across the hall. Toby's bulging pillowcase was on his bed, packed for his time with his mother. He hadn't folded his clothes; he'd just stuffed them in. She dumped everything out. The phone was on the bottom. She stuck it in her pocket.

He had two forbidden Snickers bars. She took one. To pay for it, she folded the clothes—even touching Toby's underpants—put them back into the pillowcase, and tucked his pill bottles into a sock. She had to push hard to fit his sleeping bag into her backpack. She bumped the heavy pack down the stairs and dragged it into the kitchen.

They had different colored boxes for their meds, labeled with their names: TOBY, KEISHA, JACKIE, PETER, MAKENA. She'd need tonight's and tomorrow morning's and maybe tomorrow night's. Better safe than sorry!

Protein bars—two, four—better bring six, in case that Lake House didn't have food she liked. Two more for breakfast. What was "light refreshments?" She could skip her vitamins for one day. Her first aid packet was already in her backpack's front pocket.

She took a piece of paper out of recycling.

*I HAVE THE FONE.* Was there a p? *I HAVE THE PFONE AND SLEEPING BAG MERRY CHRISMAS KENA*

She went upstairs and slipped the note into Toby's pillowcase. She sighed and touched the Snickers in her pocket.

Sugar. Skipping school. Lying. Stealing. And sugar.

But there were nuts in it, and nuts were good.

She went back to the kitchen and wrote another note: *DONT WURRY I AM FINE*

As Kena was dragging her backpack through the back door, Sully streaked out. She went to grab him and the storm door slammed on her hand. She gasped and looked. There was a cut on her palm. She squeezed her hand under her arm and shoved her backpack to the edge of the porch. She went down two steps and backed into it, heaving it onto her back.

Sully had taken off somewhere, and Peter would worry.

"Sully," she whispered. But she knew he wouldn't hear, off on some important adventure. Like her. And just an hour later, she was hovering at the bottom of enormous steps and looking around in amazement.

This was Grand Central Station! Claudia and Jamie from the *The Mixed-Up Files of Mrs. Basil D. Frankweiler* had arrived just like her, carrying their music cases stuffed with clothes. There were the starry animals flying across the ceiling, and there was the island in the center with the clock on top. It was beautiful! And people: so many people, people of all colors and dressed in more colors than a rainbow. That nice Angela would love it! They were hurrying in every direction, like a kaleidoscope, and talking, she was sure, in every language in the world, some of it drifting up to her.

"Is it snowing there yet?" "They only had purple, I know you said red, but I got it anyway." "I told you he wouldn't call! Didn't I tell you?" "Feliz Navidad!" Happy Christmas.

A family passed her, going up the steps, the father and the mother and a string of girls holding hands in a chain like Red Rover. One of the girls asked about casa—something.

She knew that word! It was home in Spanish.

"I'll be on holiday. I'd love to meet up," a man said.

Kena's heart leaped at the accent. She whirled around and saw the back of him. He was taller than everyone else. A bright red scarf trailed down his back. Oliver! It was like a miracle! She ran up the steps, weaving in and out, and grabbed the scarf, filled with joy.

He turned and a stranger stared down at her. She gasped and stumbled back. He grabbed her arm. "Careful! You all right?"

Shaken, she nodded, turned around and took a step down, and then another and another, until she stepped out onto the gleaming floor where, swept up in a tide of giants, she stiffened her spine and pretended she was brave. She looked up at the big clock, looked down to avoid being stepped on, looked up, looked down, until she spotted a gap and plunged through, attaching herself to the end of a line. She gave way to a man swinging a briefcase, but she held her ground against a lady with bulging shopping bags. Then she was first. Her chin came to the edge of the counter.

"Yes?"

"A ticket to Farleys' Dock, please."

A finger came through the slot and pointed. "You need Metro-North."

Kena couldn't see anything North.

"Look for MTA." The finger swung right. "By the wall."

Yes! "Thank you."

"Next?"

Kena worked her way through the crowd and got into another line. She shuffled forward behind a puffy black coat. Then it was her turn.

"A ticket to Farleys' Dock, please."

"You need to be accompanied by someone or be over 12," the man at the window said. He looked over her head, dismissing her.

"Oh!" She thought furiously. "My grandmother! I'm with *her*."

"Then where is your *grand*-mother?"

He drew it out like she was five!

She thought. "She's in the..." *You don't say "toilet" in public.* "She had to answer a call of nature." The man looked surprised. Kena added, "All of a sudden."

The man looked at the line and sighed. "You said Farleys' Dock?"

Kena nodded, unzipping her pocket.

"One-way or round-trip?"

"What?"

"You and your grandmother coming back or staying there?"

"Oh! Coming back."

"Eighteen dollars."

Eighteen dollars! Almost all her money. Kena gave him the $20 bill from Tam.

"What's this? 'Banco de Guatemala'?"

"It's *from* there. Guatemala."

"What's this? 'Cinco Quet—'"

He'd said it like K. She corrected it like her mother would, by saying it in a sentence the right way. "It means five, *sinco*." She stretched and pointed. "That's a quetzal. They live there."

"I can't take it, even if it's an American eagle or the bluebird of happiness."

"What?"

"I can't take it."

"But it's money."

"Maybe in Gua-te-ma-la, but here it's funny money."

"But—"

"Sorry, kid, that's the rule. Got anything else?"

Kena had just two American dollar bills. Because she'd bought her dress and boots.

"A credit card."

"No credit card without your grandmother. And we got to move along here." Kena stepped out of line. A white boy stepped into her place. She looked at her watch. If she wasn't on the next train, it might be dark when she got there. Could she attach herself to a family? She could hide in the bathroom until the train got to Adam's town.

"Here."

Kena looked up. The white boy who'd been behind her was holding out a piece of paper.

"It's not mine," Kena said.

"It's a ticket." He waved it in front of her face. "A round trip ticket to Farleys' Dock. Don't worry, it's free."

Kena took it and studied it. It said Farleys' Dock. She looked at the boy. He had a school uniform under his jacket like hers at her old school.

"Where's your 'grandmother'?" he teased.

First, Kena folded the ticket and put it in her zipper pocket. Then she dug out her dollars and put them in his hand. "Thank you." She began to walk toward the trains.

"Hey, what's the matter?" He hitched his pack up and walked along next to her. He held the money out to her. "Here, my treat."

Kena kept walking. *Never take something from a stranger.* Never *talk* to a stranger, except for manners. Especially not a man. And this boy was as tall as a man. Her gratitude wrestled with the rules.

"You're going the wrong way, anyway. Come on, it's this way."

The boy pointed, and she saw the words Metro North on a sign. He turned. She turned too. "She lives in Kenya."

"Who?"

"My grandmother."

"Kenya like in Africa?"

Kena nodded.

"You come from there?"

Kena nodded. He was staring at her like she'd just come that day. His eyes moved to her scar.

"Well, here's the thing. You still need me, 'cause they won't let you ride on the train alone."

"Are you going there? To Farleys' Dock?"

"I get off a stop before, at Bedford. But it's the same train."

"How old are you?" she asked.

"Thirteen. Want to see some ID?" he joked.

"Yes." It wasn't something to joke about, going with a strange boy.

He reached into his jacket and tugged an ID card off his shirt pocket.

She examined it, looking back and forth from the photograph to him.

He mumbled, "It's a dorky picture. They tell you to smile. At least they don't hold up some stuffed monkey like when I was little."

They'd done that at her school. A parrot. *Polly wants a smile!*

She studied the card. *David Wainwright. 143 Forest Road, Farleys' Dock, New York.*

"It says Farleys' Dock, but you said another place."

"Bedford Hills. Where my dad lives. My mom lives in Farleys' Dock. I go back and forth," he said and reached for his ID.

She could tell he was embarrassed.

She held the card away from him. "Are you rich?"

"What?"

"I went to a school with uniforms. Everybody but me was rich."

"Well, I'm not. It's because Farleys' Dock doesn't have a school after sixth grade. The town pays for us to go where we want. Not that I do. Want to, I mean."

"Is your school here? In the city?"

"No, it's back home, I just came in for…anyway, what about you? Where's *your* ID?" He shook his head. "Come on." He began to walk fast.

"My best friend is your age." Toby wouldn't mind that she'd added a year. She handed the card back.

"What's your name?" he asked over his shoulder. There was a screech of metal. A garbled voice came from a loudspeaker. Suddenly he was stopped short. She'd grabbed the strap of his backpack and was holding out a card.

It was a library card. Makena Wangera.

"Make-na?" David was embarrassed. It was like trying to figure out a French word in front of everyone at school. Worse. She was a little kid.

"Ma-kay-na."

"Ma-kay-na."

"It means happy one."

He almost laughed. Nobody ever looked less happy.

"Awesome name," he said. And it was.

She took back her card, stuck it in her pocket, and took out a Snickers bar. He was surprised to see that underneath her jacket she was wearing a Brandt sweatshirt. She ripped away half the wrapper and divided the candy bar carefully. "You get to choose because I divided it, that's the rule."

"I hate rules." He took the smaller half. And she smiled.

"Me too."

# Chapter 13

## Gideon

Adam's baby book shared its pages with Piglet and Christopher Robin and others from Pooh Corner. Adam wrapped up like a burrito was tucked in under Piglet and Pooh walking hand in hand in the snow. The next page listed Adam's milestones above Eeyore's sad house: first tooth, first step, first word, "Poo." Was it Pooky, their first cat? Pooh? Or Poop!

Gideon was pretty sure there was a baby book of himself somewhere, probably here at his mom's. His dad would have taken the photographs, but his mom would have made the album. David's album was in the living room. It stopped at age six, when everything stopped.

When Khai suggested he make a slideshow, he couldn't say no, and when Enoch dropped off the album and a DVD, he'd left Adam's phone too. Gideon hadn't mustered the courage to look at it yet. He scanned one more Christmas picture from the album, Homer as a puppy with a red bow around his neck, a hint of future costumes.

After he loaded the DVD, he started to feel a little sick, seeing Adam on his laptop like a stop-action, as if he'd move if he pressed Play. Adding the days together, he'd probably spent a year out of the last three sitting in the dark escaping into selected shorts of other people's lives, detached from his own until the accident. But here, he was as attached as hell. He was in many of the photos with Adam, especially during those years when his parents were separating, "trying," separating again, trying again, until they finally gave up and got divorced.

There were the two of them at Adam's house eating waffles, Gideon carefully dipping a piece into syrup on the side. Adam's waffle was an island in a plate-sized lake of syrup. And again, posing with home-made swords drawn, each with a patch over one eye. Launching the raft. Homer had been so worried.

Adam in that porcupine costume for Halloween, biting into a Butterfinger. Lily had cut holes in an old brown sweater of Enoch's and bent pipe cleaners through them for quills. Butterfingers were Adam's favorite for years; Gideon could get two other candy bars in a trade and wasn't fussy, being more into quantity than quality.

In their caps and gowns, grinning, arms draped over each other's shoulders. Enoch and Adam, bent over a map spread over the hood of the same car that he, Gideon, had backed too close to a tree on a different hiking trip, tearing off the side mirror. He'd taken that picture. Recording their ordinary and awesome life.

Gideon sprang up and bounded up the basement steps and out the back door, making for the woods and their old fire circle. He planted himself on his rock across from Adam's and fished the Altoids tin out of his pocket. He pried it open, his left foot tapping like it wanted to go someplace else, or some other time. The ritual was calming: lining up the flakes along the paper, running his tongue along the seam, and pinching the ends. Cupping the flame to light it and suck-ing in and holding the burn, waiting for his ragged edges to dissolve. Smooth and easy.

*Smooth as a baby's butt*, Adam had said as he sanded the rocker he'd fashioned for the one-rocker rocking chair he'd rescued from the dump. Throwing out ideas: *I've been thinking about pigeons. We could send messages to each other, you know, like tied to their legs. In code.* Coming up with a plan, another scheme, a new adventure to share. *How about we run a zipline from the barn?*

Adam crying, that one time.

Gideon crying, more than once.

Missing Adam, sure. Weeks became months as he sat with Adam at the hospital, missing him. But the photographs were poking at the other missings, the other absences. From his mom. From his little brother. *His dad.* Where does a 12-year-old boy let himself feel what hurts too much? With his best friend, is where. They'd shared their first joint right here. He toed the ashes. It was the first time they'd peed the fire out, laughing so hard that Adam peed on his sneakers too.

Adam's family fell apart too, and without a little brother as a buffer. Of course, Adam had gotten Khai. As a bonus, it turned out, because Adam didn't have to pretend with Khai the way Gideon pretended that he and David were okay. Fine. They were "fine" when their mother asked, and their father didn't ask.

A bunch of people were coming up from Brandt tonight to go to The Lake House thing, staying here at his mom's. He dreaded the whole thing and figured Lily did too. He'd thought he'd be ready to deal with it when the time came; he'd known since September that Adam wouldn't be coming back. All he could do was wait and not run away. He did the blog. He shaved Adam, hating the touch of his dry skin. Then Adam stopped growing hair, like a little death.

Gideon drove up in Lily's car to take care of Homer and Too those months she slept in Adam's room, sneaking into town and not telling his mom or David he was there. He'd walk with Homer, Too shadowing them, to the river and back, and then go and lie down on Adam's bed and smoke. A few times he cried and a couple of times he wailed. Too fled, but Homer stuck it out.

Every morning he walked across the city to the hospital before sunrise, having spent the night watching movies in his dorm room. Occasionally a new idea for his film would drift by, and he'd punch it into his phone. He'd nod to other dawn-dwellers who were dropping off newspapers or washing the sidewalks and putting out signs. He'd give dollar bills to the homeless packing up their sidewalk nests and always stopped at the hole above Klingerman's to smell the bread being baked.

When he got to the hospital, the lights would still be down, the reception desk empty of the chirpy volunteers. There would be somebody slumped over in the waiting area, asleep. The coffee cart only had bitter dregs from the night, but he'd pour a cup and sip as he made his way to the elevators, then throw it out when he got to Adam's floor.

He'd pause before entering Adam's room. He couldn't keep himself from hoping. For a second he'd imagine Adam turning his head. *Hey, Gid, where've you been? You look like hell.*

But the only changes were what others made: something new hanging off the bedrail, a pale blue sheet instead of pale green, Adam's hands out instead of in, his thinning hair smoothed down in a way he would've laughed at. Gideon would pull the chair over and watch the lights from the machines flicker, as if the two of them were adrift in a space capsule and it was his turn to keep watch. It felt like there weren't any borders just before dawn, and it'd be an easy time for a soul to travel. He'd be there holding Adam's hand so he wouldn't be alone when he left.

There was a place he hadn't known about, a place of such rawness that he could only bear to live in it for seconds. People must have been walking around with such pain his whole life, and he'd never known.

He pinched out the joint and tucked it into the tin. He rested his chin on his knees; his body was too big for the little him inside. He suddenly remembered something his mom had said to his dad: we won't know it's the last time we'll carry them to bed.

When was the last time he and Adam shared a joint? A candy bar. A joke. A view. He squeezed his eyes shut.

*Hey, Gideon.*

*Hey, Gid, look. Put down the fucking camera and look.*

He shook his head, as if shaking off flies.

What the *fuck*, Adam! You just left!

Beep beep beep. I turned to look at the monitor. It wasn't even a second, and you left!

You just *left*! I didn't have any fucking camera, Adam! If I had, I could have caught you! He swiped at his eyes. What the *fuck*? He wanted a puppet master. He wanted a genie to rise out of the ashes and explain.

Because he couldn't get over it.

Because how was it that people had their lives a thousand years ago and a hundred years ago and just this week. Four days ago! And then it's gone, a whole life of everything—a whole *life*! *And it doesn't fucking matter. It's gone.* All that *living.* And then *gone.*

Sitting by a fire and smoking.

Catching ice cream dripping down our cones and fingers with our tongues. Butter pecan and strawberry. Pumping our legs to go higher.

Biting into a pear. New shoes. Snow falling silently from a night sky.

Diving into a lake in April, screaming. Crying in the dark of a movie theater. Being kissed by a dog.

Being kissed by a girl.

Somebody invented candy corn, for fuck's sake!

And what to name the baby? What to name the baby, it's a boy!

First smile, first step. First word: Poo.

Living. It was all so unbelievably brave.

If people knew, would they even volunteer?

"We were fucking *blood* brothers!"

Crows burst out of the bare trees above him. A murder of crows.

*God!*

*Lily's face.*

His head weighed a thousand pounds.

His mom would say "Try to cry, you'll feel better." *Crying gets the sad out of you.* "Free to Be You and Me." Who sang it?

*Rosey Grier.*

God! Was he now the holder of Adam's memories too?

The scene from *Little Big Man*—the old guy going to the mountaintop to die, lying down and waiting. It began to rain, but he stayed. It wouldn't be long now. It rained harder. And harder. Finally, he got up and said, "Sometimes the magic works and sometimes it doesn't."

Gideon never had an inkling of what pain really was. Or forever.

Inside the house, Gideon's cellphone played the first notes of "Goodbye Yellow Brick Road" and said to leave a message but he didn't hear it.

"Gideon, are you there? Dad said you'd be. I *really* gotta talk to you. There's this little kid on the train. It gets there in 15 minutes. I should've stayed on, but then Dad would find out I skipped. She's meeting her grandfather, but what if he's late or something? Can you go check? And then call me? Oh, she's Black, that's how you'll know, and her hair is full of beads."

Gideon shuffled back to the house and down the stairs. He took in a deep breath and turned on Adam's phone. The screensaver was a Belize photo, taken in the canopy. It was half-shadowed, and the contrasting color was brilliant. He would never get over not going along. He opened Photos. Adam and some kids spinning hula hoops. A girl's dress made a bright pink swirl. Adam was laughing, the hula hoop at his knees. Who took the shot? It was a great shot.

He put on *Abbey Road* and turned it up loud.

Upstairs, the kitchen phone had recorded a message: "Mom? Listen, Dad said it's okay, so I'm not going tonight. But Gideon, I *absolutely* need you to call me! Did you get my message? Call me!"

Oblivious to the message, Gideon had come to a photograph from Maine. Mt. Katahdin. Their last trip. Adam and him standing on the edge of the world, their arms around each other, looking back at Enoch and laughing, their faces washed in gold by the setting sun.

He turned "Maxwell's Silver Hammer" up as loud as it would go.

# Chapter 14

## Lily

Lily stood in her spotless kitchen, afraid to touch anything and leave fingerprints on Clare's gleaming surfaces. Her homey clutter of books and sticky notes and dog chews had disappeared. Even the fruit bowl was gone. Poor Too. The house was ready for tomorrow, all thanks to Clare, and Lily felt ashamed for resenting it, but she did. And the service, she resented *that* too. But Enoch wanted it.

So they'd all gathered Tuesday to plan, and she'd felt like an outlier as the others looked through their busy December calendars to find an open day. As if Adam needed to be fit in. Her calendar was empty. For seeing Adam.

For a second, she'd thought *Let's do it on Yule. Adam loved it so much; maybe he'd be watching the fireworks from somewhere.* Not that she believed in Somewhere, but if there was, wouldn't he be watching?

They'd made some decisions in June, when Adam dying had seemed imminent. Adam had checked that he wanted to be a donor on his driver's license, so they didn't have to decide about that when a woman from the hospital asked. God, she actually had a clipboard! They'd agreed on a Quaker service and that each person should bring a flower. Peonies were in bloom then, and there were still some tulips hanging on. Then Adam, hanging on too, was moved into the city and July came, with Sweet William and daisies. August brought sunflowers and roses, and then fall came with its hateful chrysanthemums. And now, even worse, poinsettias, which weren't even flowers.

Enoch said, there's holly.

Holly is sharp, Clare said.

Khai said, what about those red berries? Bayberry?

No, Clare said, weren't those berries poisonous? What about the kids?

No kids, *please* no kids, Lily thought, but she didn't say it out loud. She was a kindergarten teacher, after all. But then she knew. "We could have a Christmas tree. Everybody can bring an ornament."

"It should be alive, to plant in spring."

It was the first thing Gideon had said, Lily realized.

Clare offered to host a gathering at the inn the night before. "For the people from out of town." Lily was alarmed, imagining Adam's Brandt friends driving up the driveway on Friday while she cowered upstairs.

Khai asked Gideon to make a slideshow. No! she'd thought, shutting her eyes. But she didn't say it. Clare started a list. Wine or beer for the gathering? Don't worry, she told Lily. You won't have to do a thing except show up for a little while.

"We'll take care of everything," Khai said. Lily looked at Enoch. He opened his hands. Was it helplessness? Surrender? She said she had to go lie down, but Khai followed her into the hall.

"We need to put something in the papers. Just something about the service and this thing Friday night at the inn. A little about Adam."

"You mean an obituary. You can *say* it, Khai, for Heaven's sake! Just make sure Homer and Too are included. And Gideon," she said. "Oh, God, I'm sorry! I'm sorry I jumped on you!" When Khai went to hug her, she put her hands up. "No hugs." She hadn't seen what Khai wrote, but Clare said it was posted on the internet and was in yesterday's paper. It wasn't the kind of thing you stuck up with a refrigerator magnet.

Homer padded into the kitchen, followed by Too. They'd been shadowing her all day, as if they knew something was up. Too sauntered over to Homer's bed and began to knead it. Lily looked at the new landline Clare had screwed to the wall. There had been a message from the DA, but she hadn't called back. And she didn't have a clue what to wear to the gathering.

"Shit! I need an ornament too!" Too fled out the door. "Not you!" she called. "Not you," she whispered, kneeling to gather Homer into her arms. She needed to do something with the kids' flowers.

When the service was still going to have flowers, she'd decided to use her Tender Shepherd vase, and Enoch had worried people would think they were Born Again. Lily, holding Adam's limp hand, sang the "Tender Shepherd" song from *Peter Pan*. They'd watched the video over and over during a snowday when he was 5. He still couldn't say R. Or TH. Fwee. *Fwee in the newsewy fast asleep.* And that Christmas Adam gave her a very large and bumpy present wrapped in Santa paper and at least a roll of masking tape. He was so excited that Enoch held his hands to keep him from tearing the wrapping off himself.

It was a vase; a lurid shepherd with fluorescent yellow hair and brilliant turquoise eyes gazed down at two lambs melting against his blue robe. One of the lambs was looking up, though, and the shepherd had his hand on its head. The other hand held a staff. Adam said it was "actually" a crook. How she loved it!

When he became a teenager, Adam called it the Tender Schlock vase.

She pressed her face into Homer's neck.

Adam's hands were still warm when they returned to the room. She'd always had to work to hear his breathing under the buzz of the machines, but now they were silent and there was no breath to hear. For a second, she'd been incensed that they'd taken him off everything when she wasn't there. They should have waited for me! And then she was slammed all over again: it was Adam who didn't wait. She'd imagined screaming and pulling out every plug so many times. She'd imagined throwing herself across him to keep anyone from doing it.

*"I can do it myself!" Inside-out T-shirts. Shoes on the wrong foot.*
Dying.

"Oh, Homer." She got to her feet and scooped up the tissue paper flowers—as big as peonies—that Clare's class had made. They drooped as if they needed water, their pipe cleaner stems too thin to hold them up. She opened the junk drawer for tape and found Too's filthy, flattened, one-eared mouse. She threw it under the table where Clare might not see it, and then stiffened each blossom with tape. Her mom had called peonies "glories."

Lily lifted the Tender Shepherd vase down. She tucked Clare's flowers in and fluffed their tissue paper petals. Clare was at the airport picking up Enoch's parents because Lois and Bernie still wouldn't sleep in the same house where their son shared a bed with a man—and worse, a Vietnamese man, with Bernie having been in the war and all.

Lily always felt stiff with Lois. Her mind would go blank when they were alone, as if they didn't share a common language, or one of them was protecting a secret. Lois was unfailingly polite, but when Lily shared something about herself, she didn't return in kind. Although she was kind even when Lily was prickly and not-so-nice herself.

She still had to move herself out of her room so they could have the double bed. Clare had changed the sheets, and the ones in Adam's room too, which still smelled of him—or so she'd imagined. When she went to dig them out of the laundry basket, it was empty. She found them in the dryer and burst into tears.

She opened the door of the refrigerator. It was stuffed. Families had been sending cookies home with Clare all week. And bars. Lemon bars, date bars, nut bars, even Rice Crispy bars with sprinkles. "Light refreshments." As if they were having a party. She imagined throwing them on the shiny clean floor and smashing them with her feet. Then, as if she had, she was gripped by guilt. What if someone's mother had asked, "What would Ms. J like?"

"Ms. J loves sprinkles!"

She couldn't even *imagine* a tantrum without nipping it in the bud.

And why didn't people say funeral anymore? What was wrong with funeral? "Thanksgiving for the Grace of God." Pissed Off for the Lack of God was more like it. And why weren't there funeral planners like there were for weddings so *they* didn't have to do it? She'd explained to Clare that in a Quaker service, words would come when someone was moved to speak. But what if no one was moved? What if she cried? In front of all those people. Breaking the silence. She should line someone up, a ringer, to be on the safe side. She realized with a jolt that there *were* funeral planners. Ladies of the church knew what to do. And what to wear. But she'd dropped church for Enoch's Quakers and stayed for Adam's sake.

Maybe there was an emergency hotline.

Ellie had come and said it was time for them to take him away. A part of her threw her body over Adam's and screamed while, mute and obedient, she'd kissed his hands and folded one on top of the other and kissed his forehead, noticing from a distant part of herself that it was cool, and let Enoch lead her out. There were two young men, no older than Adam, standing next to a stretcher on wheels.

One of them met her eyes, a second of understanding. That her skin was all that was keeping her from crumbling into a pile of bones on the floor.

Adam had checked donor, but wouldn't he really have wanted to be put out in their woods, where the wildness he loved took him down to the bones? No organs would be left to give away. And she could go there and rub his bones over her like elephants did.

She tried to slam the refrigerator door, but it just closed with a sigh. A magnet and photograph fell to the floor. Adam's postcard from Belize, and the stunning gaze of a jaguar. She turned it over. "To the Maya, the jaguar was a god whose spotted coat resembled the starry night sky." Adam's scrawl filled the tiny space under the print.

*The plane trip in was awesomely terrifying—you would have hated it! But you would love this place—my spirit is having a feast, Mom, just like you said. Wish you were here. Maybe someday—love, your best kid*

She'd been so scared his little plane would crash.

An aide had asked if they wanted a photograph before they took him away. God! Like newborn babies. And she'd hesitated, as if she might hurt the aide's feelings.

She took the vase into the living room and put it on the piano, Homer at her heels. Adam would be impressed at how well he was heeling. There still were the kids' cards from school to put somewhere. Dougie's toothy sharks and Allie's butterflies drew a big jagged J on the envelope. The same thing had happened in June, except then it had been ladybugs and lopsided stars. Some of the June cards were for Adam: "I hope you get better." Tommy Ford, fresh from his parents' separation, had drawn a stick figure with red dots dripping from its head.

Had Adam really left in June? Like a butterfly leaving behind his chrysalis to keep her and Enoch company until they got used to it. After Lily's mom had died, Adam had said he wished he was an animal who didn't know about death. But they did. Animals did.

Look at the elephants.

She had to get moving; she had to at least move her nightie and some underwear out of her room. She'd developed an obsessive habit of putting on two pairs of socks and two extra blankets at bedtime and then shedding them through the night. She knew, deep down, it was about anger. Rage, if she were being honest, but she didn't know what to do about it. She hoped the shedding was her subconscious working on it because she was terrified of facing it. She had no experience with rage, not even when Enoch left.

Homer leaned on her leg. She shook him off. He looked up at her, confused.

"I'm sorry!" Homer left the room, looking back over his shoulder. She didn't blame him. If she could leave herself behind, she would in a heartbeat.

"Harvesting," they called it.

Harvesting for Thanksgiving. Thanksgiving for the Grace of God.

And someone *was* thankful. Someone's family was happy. Very happy. Breaking out the champagne happy. Because someone they loved got new eyes. Blue. Beautiful blue eyes. Did eye color get donated too? Oh God!

She staggered into the kitchen. Best Kid was on the table. She took the postcard into the living room and put it on the piano. Gideon was the only one who played it after Enoch left.

*Gideon. She* should have been there. Not Gideon.

"Not Gideon," she whispered.

She slammed her hands on the keys. *Not Gideon.* How was she supposed to do this? People hit pillows with bats. They even paid people to help them do it. They'd never had any bats, except the flying kind.

She whirled around, stumbled back to the kitchen, and got to her knees in front of the baking cabinet. She flung everything out until she found the rolling pin. She whaled on the angel food cake pan and dented it.

The couch. Lily went into the living room and took a whack. Whack, whack, whack. WHACK. She tried to scream. She tried again. AAAH and hit and hit and HIT. AAAAAH! She coughed and stopped hitting, embarrassed, as if somebody was watching. If they were, she'd only get a two out of ten. She sank down on the couch. *It's not in my skill set.*

"And what good were you?" she said to the rolling pin. She threw it, and it hit the leg of the side table. The lamp wobbled and she watched, mesmerized, as it teetered and fell off the edge to the floor.

Something was stuck to the bottom of the lamp. A scrap of paper. Christmas wrapping. A hedgehog.

She'd been so thrilled to find that paper. Hedgehogs wearing Santa hats. Adam's jacket for Belize had been wrapped in it. She got down on her hands and knees, crawled over, and carefully peeled the scrap off, but the white ball on top of Santa's hat tore off, stuck. No!

It was like childbirth. And like labor, she had no choice. She swayed and keened and sobbed and swayed. When she thought she was done, empty, another sob came up and another. And again. And again. And again. Oh, it hurt! How would she live with such pain? A part of her observed, it's like throwing up, just do it. God! She couldn't even cry 100 percent! *Monkey mind*, Adam would say. And at that, she was taken over. She wailed, cradling the scrap of Adam's last Christmas in her open hands.

*Oh, Adam. Oh, God, oh, Adam. Oh, God. Where are you?*

It hurt too much, too much. She rolled onto her side. She took a breath. She took a deep breath. Maybe her first since—since forever, she thought. She sat up and grabbed a tissue from the tissue box and blew. And another. And another, wadding them together into a ball. If only she could sleep for days, sleep through it all. She rested her cheek on her knees, and stayed there for a long time.

Finally she sighed and put the lamp back on the table. She tried the switch. Off. On. Off. Okay then. She went to the kitchen to throw away the soggy tissues and put back the baking things. She hid the injured cake pan behind the mixer. From whom? Nobody else was going to live here.

Feeling sorry for herself. Stop it.

Homer came out of the downstairs bathroom, looking guilty. He's been drinking from the toilet, she thought. Which was clean. Because of Clare. She began to laugh, sitting on the bottom step. She dug her fingers between his shoulder blades.

"Oh, Homer, what're we going to do?"

She went into the bathroom to wash her face. She looked in the mirror and pictured chopping her hair off in a rite of mourning.

Oh, get over yourself!

She went upstairs and into her room. She placed the scrap of paper between two pages of her mom's Bible. Who would find it someday? Not grandchildren. Stop it!

What to wear?

Homer came through the door and sank to the floor with a sigh.

"Homer, what would you wear?"

She scooped up socks and underwear, and Too was there suddenly, the way he could be. Lily took the aluminum ball out of the Tibetan bowl but instead of throwing it sat on the bed and scooped Too up.

"Oh, Too, how am I going to get through this?" Too nosed the aluminum ball. And Lily remembered what was inside of it.

# Chapter 15

## Alice

"Wangera, phone call!"

Alice scrambled to her feet. Brian Abbott? Her heart jumped into her throat. And the evening shift was always a little angry and might hang up if she didn't hurry. She'd tried to think charitably; a lot of the COs had kids and wished they were home. She'd worked to humanize the buzzing lights and shiny floors, the concrete walls and steel doors. She'd made up a truck driver named Bert who'd hauled the steel, whose kids asked Santa for something they saw on TV that cost too much, and who carried his lunch in a Dora the Explorer lunchbox his little girl cast aside when she moved to Hello Kitty. She made up a construction worker named Frank who sank into a sprung chair in front of the TV after work with a beer in his hand and a heating pad behind his back.

Did the workers imagine, too, as they built the jail piece by piece like a giant Lego project? Did they imagine her? Maybe one of them loved somebody who was incarcerated, a brother or sister or wife, and thought of them as he bolted the doors to the concrete.

The CO buzzed her through the door. She presented herself at the desk.

"Alice Wan—"

The CO pointed to where the receiver dangled down, not even glancing up from her *People* magazine.

"Hello?"

"Alice!"

"Patrice?"

"Alice, did Kena call you?"

"What?"

"She didn't come home on the after-school group bus."

"What? What do you mean?"

The clock over the CO's desk showed a few minutes before 5:00. The shuttle usually dropped Kena off at 4:30.

"Keisha said—you remember Keisha, Kena's roommate? When she asked about Kena at gym, the teacher said she had a dentist's appointment. Which she did *not*! But she left a note. I don't have her teacher's number, just the email."

Alice tried to follow all the she's. She heard a child's voice.

"No, it's her mama. Did you go to the bathroom like I said?"

"There's an email from her teacher?"

"No, a note on the table. Here, on the table. 'Don't worry, I am fine, Kena.' Toby's gone with his mother, and I wonder—they'll still be in the car, but she doesn't answer her cellphone."

"She might be with Toby?"

"Well, it's the first thing I thought of. I mean, they're thick as thieves, those two, and Toby's mother is pretty—well, *spontaneous*, to put it kindly, but I don't think she'd—"

A beep jarred Alice's ear.

"Lemmy's gone too."

Lemmy gone?

"Somebody's calling. It might be them."

"Patrice!" But Alice was left with the dial tone.

And inmates couldn't call out on these phones. She'd have to call back from the unit, and she'd have to explain and beg to cut in, and everyone in line would yell at her.

Alice looked at the CO. Her name tag read SANTIAGO, but Alice thought she'd heard someone call her Carla. Alice put her hands behind her back. It didn't help that she loomed over Carla Santiago like a giraffe.

"Ms. Santiago, I need your help. That was my daughter's—" She'd learned that "foster mother" meant a court order. And a court order meant a bad mother.

"My daughter is eight years old. She goes to an after-school program, and today she didn't get home afterwards, maybe didn't even go to it at all." She hadn't been in gym, in the afternoon.

The CO put down her magazine.

"I need help. Please."

The CO sat there forever, pursing her lips in and out.

"She's just eight! Please!"

"Okay." She picked up the desk phone. "This is Santiago in H wing. I need the duty officer."

Alice hugged herself. *It's some misunderstanding. She's with Toby. Or she missed the bus.*

"Santiago, H wing. An inmate has received news about her child and wants someone to come talk to her." The CO listened. "Someone called her and said she didn't come home. Her daughter. Uh huh. Wangera. Eight. Uh huh. No, she's right here. Yes, sir." She held the receiver out to Alice.

"Ms. Wangera?"

"Yes."

"This is Lieutenant Tomas, duty officer. I understand your daughter may be missing?"

*Missing.* Oh, God, what if it was real! "Her foster mother called and said she didn't get home from her after-school program. She left a note and—"

"I'm pulling your file up. Is this Patricia Washington? The foster mother?"

"Yes, Patrice, and—"

"Makena Wangera is your daughter."

"Yes, and—"

"I'll be over."

Alice wrapped her arms around herself. "He's coming. Thank you."

"It's my job."

"How far is he from here?"

"It'll probably be a few minutes."

"Do you think—do you think I should go back to my cell and get a photograph?"

The CO stood up, uncertainty on her face, and then punched her radio and spoke into her shoulder mic. "Wangera's going back for something from her cell."

A squawk, like a question.

"A photograph. The duty officer's meeting her here." She looked at Alice. "Be quick. It won't look good if you're not here waiting."

Waiting for the door to be unlocked, Alice jumped from empty school classrooms to empty playgrounds to dark, empty streets. A sick knot was forming in her belly. Then she was at her cell door, looking up at the CO. Come on, come on! Finally, the door slid open. She got on her knees to pull out her box. Her photographs were under Kena's latest drawing, a snow woman, a snow child, and a snow man. Oliver. The sky was filled with little circles, like Cheerios. There was no one Kena would run away to, except herself. Tam was off in some jungle. And Oliver—And she'd left a note!

When she got back the duty officer was waiting for her, a fat accordion folder under his arm. After a moment's hesitation, as if together they were breaking a rule, they shook hands.

"I went to get photographs."

"Ms. Santiago told me. Let's go down here where we can talk in private. You can tell me about Makena—is that right?" He led her down the hallway to the same room where she'd met with Brian Abbott. It was just big enough for the table and stools fastened to the floor. He motioned for her to sit.

"First, let's get back in touch with…" he pulled a paper from the folder. "Patricia Washington." He punched the numbers into his phone.

Patrice, she thought. It's Patrice.

"It's Makena. Kay-na," she said softly.

He held a finger up, the phone to his ear. Then he spoke into it. "Is this Patricia Washington?"

Alice heard Patrice's voice, excited.

"I'm not from the school. I'm Lieutenant Tomas at Westchester County Correctional Facility. Is this Patricia Washington?" He nodded. "Has May—kay—na come home?" He shook his head at Alice. "She's right here. I'm putting you on speaker phone." He placed the phone on the table between them.

"Alice! Teresa from after-school got back and said Kena was on the absent list. And Peter just now told me a key was in the back door when he came home. As if it wasn't important! And it's Kena's, all right, hers has the pink ribbon. Another funny thing, Sully was out, waiting at the door."

"What about the note?"

"It was under the salt shaker. 'Don't worry, I am fine, Kena.' That's all. Worry with a U. Oh, and I almost forgot, I got Toby's mother and she's not with them."

Alice's toes danced on the floor, needing to be moving, running.

"Patrice, you have to call the police. I know how some of the kids will feel, seeing them at the house, but they'll do an Amber Alert."

"I've been thinkin' the same thing. I already called my sister and she'll come take the kids. I'm worried sick."

Alice heard excited kids' voices. She stood up. Kena?

"Patrice?"

"Keisha says her nightie's gone." Her nightie, and Lemmy. Like for a sleepover. Lieutenant Tomas motioned for her to sit down. Alice heard a child's voice again. Then rustling sounds.

"Alice, there's a bag here with a sales slip from Goodwill. Two items. It's got today's date."

"Goodwill?"

But she had no picture of the Goodwill store, just a blank map. And it was blank everywhere, because she had no picture of the apartment, or Kena's school, or the library, or the park, or even the clinic where she went for her checkups.

Alice picked up the phone, turned off speaker, and whispered, "Did you check her meds?"

"I never thought!" Patrice said.

Alice heard a child wailing.

"Keisha, take Jackie and help him change. Just put the wet ones in the tub. Jackie, would you like to go to Rosie's for pizza? And a cookie?" The wailing stopped. "Alice? She took two days' worth."

Two days! Alice turned to the duty officer. "What would be faster? *You* call? *Me?* Patrice? Who'd get police there the fastest?"

"We already did. They should be there any minute." Alice stiffened. Why hadn't he told her right off?

"Patrice? The police are on their way there. Someone here called them."

"Oh, my lord! Peter's gonna freak out! I got to go. Alice, I'm sorry, but I got to get the kids out of here."

Lieutenant Tomas took the phone.

"Ms. Washington, I want you to have my office number too." He rattled off the number. "We'll keep in touch." He pocketed the phone.

"You hung up!" It burst out of her. He had no right.

He had every right, though. Of course he did.

*She* was the one who had no rights.

# Chapter 16

## Kena

Kena watched from the window as David walked away from the train. She'd told awful lies. She fingered her scar, imagining if it really had been an elephant tusk. She didn't make up about the blood, though, how it poured down her face so much she tasted it. And he'd been properly impressed. She pressed her cheek against the cold glass and watched the backs of lit-up houses disappear as the train sped up. People were coming home.

She crossed her legs tightly. The jiggle of the train made having to pee worse. She hated the stinky train bathrooms. But who knew how far she'd have to walk when she got there? She looked across the aisle at a girl who'd smiled at her. She pulled on her boots, wincing when they rubbed against her heels, and slid over.

"Excuse me." She leaned across and touched the girl's arm. The girl took something out of her ear.

"Hi!"

"Could you watch my backpack, please? I'll be right back."

"Of course!"

Kena grabbed the backs of seats as she went down the aisle, her arms not quite reaching from one to the next, so there was an instant between, like jumping from rock to rock in Morningside Park across from their apartment. She'd forgotten the cut on her hand, but each time it came down on a seat, she was reminded.

There was toilet paper stuck to the seat and a puddle. The paper towels were wedged behind the soap. She reached to take a few and they all fell out. She covered the toilet seat with two layers and spread the rest out on the floor with the bottom of her boot, careful not to touch anything with its pink toe. Finally, holding her sweatshirt under her armpits so it wouldn't touch the seat, she sat down and peed.

Then she did two bad things. She left all the paper towels right there, and she didn't wash her hands. She would make do with the sanitizer Patrice made them carry. Toby said Patrice was *germ-a-pho-bic*. But weren't they supposed to be?

Lurching back to her seat, she saw that people were lining up at the other end of the car.

Her backpack!

"I have it! This is Farleys' Dock. That's your stop too, right?" the girl called out. When Kena got to her, the girl helped lift the heavy pack onto her shoulders. "That's quite a load."

"Oh, I do it all the time!" Kena said and fell back onto the seat as the train suddenly came to a stop. The girl pulled her up, laughing.

"Who's meeting you?"

So Kena repeated one of her lies. And what if a grandfather *was* there, standing just below the steps of the train, a living miracle sprung from her imagination? He'd smile and open his arms, ready to catch her.

Instead, after watching the girl and her friends get into a waiting car, she trudged up the ramp, turned right onto the sidewalk, and saw the footbridge Adam had told her about. It was the shortcut to the school where Adam's mother, Lily, was a teacher, and it was real! Trip trap, trip trap. Who's that walking over my bridge?

It is I, Makena.

And there was the playground, too. She shed her backpack to sit on a swing. Adam probably sat on this very one! She pushed off and leaned back, her hood brushing the ground. The sky was pink and orange with one cotton candy cloud. She decided the cloud was a gift from Ngai. Sent by her birth mother to help her be brave.

"Loola, loola, what do I see

A cloud that looks like cotton cand-ee

Maitu, Maitu sent it to me." She stopped pumping to think.

"Loola, loola, very tast-ee."

Oliver called cotton candy cloud-on-a-stick.

Kena sang the song through again and again, pumping higher and higher and singing louder and louder against her loneliness. "Loola, loola, very tast-ee-eee!" She let the swing wind down.

"Mama," she whispered. She sat on the ground to pull on her backpack. The frozen grass crunched under her. Snowmen were taped on the school windows looking in, not out. Teachers should think about who might be outside. She went around the corner. And stopped. Adam had told her—but not like this.

The town was dressed up for Yule; its trees twinkled and dripped with white icicle lights, and the stores and houses surrounding the park—the Green, Adam called it—were decorated with all the colors of the rainbow. It was a fairyland.

Adam said the park had first been the Farley family's pasture. There had been pigs and chickens, a cow, and two horses, and the Farley children got to share beds and had a real outhouse. But Mrs. Farley yearned for—Kena had stopped Adam to ask: what is *yearn*? And it was the best word!—Mrs. Farley yearned for a real bathroom, so she set up a farmstand on their dock to get the money for it. She made a sign: "Farleys' Dock Produce and Sundries." People came in their boats and bought vegetables and other things—sundries!

Sundries were clothespin dolls and spinning tops and wooden boats that moved with rubber bands.

"What's in October?" Adam asked.

"Halloween!"

"The kids made Jack-o'-lanterns to sit at the end of the dock looking out over the lake, and people brought their children to trick-or-treat in boats."

The Farleys sold worms as bait to catch fish.

"Yuck!"

And Mrs. Farley got her bathroom.

"I'll show you everything when you come, Kena."

But she'd have to show herself; not even Toby was there to share it.

There was a round porch in the middle of the park, lights circling the roof like a merry-go-round. She went up the steps and walked all around, looking out like a princess in her tower. And there, glimmering between two houses, was the lake. Three kids were standing in front of one of the houses, staring at her. She ducked down.

She peeked and squinted. They were dressed-up sticks! She jumped down the steps and crossed the street. The littlest one's hat had fallen off, and she tucked the top of its pillowcase head into it and arranged the tassel at the side.

"There you go." He didn't have mittens for hands like the others. She didn't either, or she would have given them to him. Candles glowed in the windows in the house behind, except for one, where there was a Christmas tree. Multicolored lights wove around the railing of the porch. There was a sign above the door. This was it! The Lake House. The porch light suddenly came on. The door began to open.

Kena took off running. She swerved and ran between The Lake House and the one next door and skidded to a stop, stunned. A big white moon face hung above a cutout of black trees on the other side of the frozen lake, making a shimmering path across it. She stuck her foot out and tapped it with her heel, hard. Cracks spread out like silver snakes under the ice. She jumped away, feeling guilty, as if she'd broken the lake. She looked around. The back of The Lake House was dark. No one had seen, except the moon.

She sank down and slipped out of her pack. She tugged her boots off and poked her socks inside them. She touched her heel. Ouch! She put her finger to her mouth. No blood. She dug her sore heels into the cold, rough sand and spread out on her back like a snow angel. A sand angel.

"Mama, don't worry, I'm fine," she whispered. She stared at the moon. It stared back. There was a rush of movement and something wet and smelly was licking her face. Kena scrambled to her feet.

A fat little dog was wiggling around her, snuffling. He nosed her ankles and took a lick between her toes. She jumped back, tripped on one of her boots, and hopped to the side as the joyful dog went to sniff it. He pulled her sock out and grinned at her, tail wagging. He took a jump back, shaking the sock. A leash trailed from his collar and she lunged for it, but the dog was quicker. He twisted, running away, then back, then away, her sock hanging from his mouth like a tongue.

Kena stood stock still. The dog stood stock still. He suddenly dropped the sock and made an end-run around her and grabbed a boot.

"No!" she scolded, and she flung herself on top of him.

The dog squealed, but Kena held on. She snuck her hand up and got her fingers under his collar. Only then did she wiggle into a sitting position. And he sat too, his tail thumping the sand, all forgiven. She took his leash in her other hand. As soon as she let go of his collar, he trotted over and picked up her boot and dropped it into her lap. She laughed.

"Daisy!" a man's voice called out. "Daisy!"

The dog was a girl. Daisy. Like the buttons on her new dress. Daisy was leaping and tugging at the end of the leash. So Kena let go, and she burst down the beach to the voice, a shadow who waved at Kena, leaned down to take the leash, and melted away into the dark.

Kena shook her boots out and pulled them on, stuffing her socks into her pocket. She looked down in dismay, brushing off what she could. Her jacket was wet, and so was the front of her sweatshirt. And dirty. She couldn't meet Adam's mother like this!

The house next to The Lake House sat behind a picket fence, a sign hanging from its gate: Farleys' Dock Public Library. Monday, Wednesday, Friday 1-5:30, Saturday 10-2. A library in a house! And there were lights on. There would be a bathroom. And even though it was a house, opening the door was like dipping her face into Library, the familiar smell of books instantly comforting. She was in a hallway, and there was a big room off to each side. One was a children's room; stuffed animals sat on a window seat and snowflakes drifted from the ceiling.

*The Mole Family Christmas* was on a round table that was surrounded by four blue chairs; a teddy bear slumped down in one of them. There was a pile of striped pillows on the floor and hooks along a wall. She hung up her backpack and jacket.

"Oh!" A very large white lady stood in the doorway, her hands crossed over her heart. "I didn't know anyone was here!"

"I just came."

"It's perfectly all right." She looked more closely at Kena.

Was she staring at her scar?

"Why, you're wet! And covered in sand! You need a towel." The lady surveyed the room as if one might magically appear.

"It was a dog. A dog jumped on me. Well, actually, I jumped on *her*. But I had to. She had my boot!"

"I'll bet it was that Daisy! I don't know why Warren can't keep her under control. He thinks she's funny."

"It *was* Daisy! That's what he called her!"

"She's always getting away from him."

The lady picked up a tissue box and handed it to Kena. "There's a towel in the bathroom at the end of the hall. Just call out if you need anything."

It was a real bathroom, like for a house. There was an actual bathtub, even though paint jars and a big roll of paper were in it. There was a window with curtains. There was a cup shaped like Mrs. Santa's head on the back of the toilet and a small green towel hanging next to the sink. Kena wet a corner of it and scrubbed at her sweatshirt, but it was no good. It just smeared. Washing her hands stung. She still needed to put Neosporin on her cut.

And change her clothes and take her pills. And her heels needed Band-Aids. So much to do, and where could she do it all? "Mama," she whispered.

The curtain stirred, and the answer came to her, like magic. She raised the window and stuck her head out. Libraries were the safest places she knew, besides home. And this one was a house.

The librarian was waiting, a bag of books at her feet. Her hat had earflaps. She frowned. "Don't you have a coat?"

The lady hadn't seen it! Or her backpack. More magic.

"I'm staying at The Lake House, and I just came over." Lies *did* get easier the more you told. The librarian was examining her from head to toe. Kena put her hand over her scar.

"That's a Brandt sweatshirt. Are you here for Adam St. John's service tomorrow?" Kena nodded.

"Are you with your parents, then?"

Kena looked at her feet. "I'm with my grandfather." She was starting to picture him. He was tall like Oliver, and he wore those old people glasses. And a vest. He was mostly bald, his head like a polished brown ball.

"Come along, then." The librarian held the door open for Kena. She turned off the hall lights and picked up her bag and shut the door. She lifted an empty flower pot, picked up a key, locked the door, and returned it to its place. "Our little secret."

*Should I offer to carry her bag?* Kena struggled with the question until they were in front of the inn, where the librarian set the bag down and put her hand out.

"My name is Molly Mulligan. You should call me Molly. Not Mrs. Mulligan or Ms. Mulligan. Just plain Molly. I've known Adam his entire life. He probably read every book in the library that was even remotely about animals."

Kena thought of Adam's book in her backpack back in the library.

"And what is your name, dear? And how do—did—you know Adam? Oh, it's hard to get my heart around it!"

Kena took her hand, wanting to blurt out the whole story to this just plain Molly lady. It seemed like she would understand. "Makena."

"That's a beautiful name. Makena."

"It means happy one."

"And are you?"

No one had ever asked her that before. "No," she answered, abruptly hollowed out with sadness.

"I'm sorry for your loss, Makena," Molly said, squeezing her hand gently and letting go. Kena locked her knees to keep herself from leaning forward for a hug that would make her cry.

"You'd better get inside. You'll catch your death. I'll see you and your grandfather at the service tomorrow. I won't be attending tonight. I'm not good with small talk." She looked up at The Lake House apologetically. "It was a pleasure meeting you, Makena."

Kena waited, watching until Molly had crossed the park. Then she ran, sprinting between the library and The Lake House. Every window of the inn was lit up. People who knew Adam were inside. A necklace of lights made a circle around the lake. People had come home. Patrice had read her note.

The moon had risen. There was one star. Was Adam peeking through the hole in the sky world? She waved. "Adam, I'm here," she whispered.

But it was Oliver's voice she heard.

"Even when it's daytime, the stars are there, Kena. Just like our souls are always there when everything is so busy-busy we forget." He'd tugged gently on her hair. "And souls that love each other can always find each other."

*Oliver.*

She had to stretch to take hold of the windowsill, but she finally pulled herself up enough to shimmy through the library's bathroom window. She got tangled up with the curtain, and it fell to the floor. She hung it up, opened to the night. It was darker inside than outside, where there was the light of the moon. *Same moon.*

She ran her hand along the wall and around the sink and into the hall and groped her way to the children's room. She felt her way to her backpack and took out her flashlight and turned it on. She pulled out clean leggings and her Big Apple Circus T-shirt. Neosporin. Band-Aids. She pulled off her muddy leggings and sweatshirt and changed, then went to work on her heels. Then she'd take care of her hand.

Something brushed her leg. She let out a squeak. A ghost!

"Meowr!" A cat?

She grabbed the flashlight and beamed it around. A black cat sat on the table on top of *The Mole Family Christmas*, his eyes glowing.

"Hello." If you want to make friends with a cat, act as if it doesn't matter. She unrolled Toby's sleeping bag and placed one of the pillows at its head, her back to the cat. Then Lemmy. Then the teddy bear.

"There you go."

She went to the F bin and pawed through it with the flashlight until she found *Corduroy*. She wiggled into the sleeping bag and set the timer on her watch.

"This book is about a teddy bear who needs a home." As she began to read, the cat batted the Neosporin off the table. He jumped down and batted it again. "And a button. But don't worry. It all works out." The cat kneaded the foot of the sleeping bag and curled up to listen.

# Chapter 17

## Alice

"Tell me about Makena," Lieutenant Tomas said, pointing at the photographs.

There were five, the maximum allowed. She spread them out and picked one up. "This is from her old school, a private one. She's in a public school now, near her foster home."

How naive she'd been when she'd opened the forwarded letter taking away Kena's scholarship for this year. When she applied there for Kena's kindergarten, Alice's worry had been the health form, but the school had been "very pleased" to enroll her native Kenyan Black daughter.

They didn't have a quota to fill, however, of children in foster homes whose mothers were in jail. It wasn't the type of diversity they were looking for.

She'd cried when Kena's new teacher sent a personal note to her in jail. *I thought you'd like to know that Makena is adjusting well to school. She's a wonderful child, and I'm so glad to have her in my class.* What kindness.

"And this?" Lieutenant Tomas asked, pointing to the photo taken at the airport in Nairobi, Kena hopping with excitement, hanging off Oliver.

Tomas looked over her head. She turned around. The room was filling with state police. Her heart began to pound. Oh God, oh God, oh God! Her mind flailed. Breathe. Breathe! The part of her that knew she should stay calm floundered, sidelined. She broke into a sweat and bile stung her throat.

Oh God, oh God, oh God. *Kena.*

*Mama!*

Flashing lights, flashing, flashing red.

Mama!

My Mama!

"Hey. Hey." Alice felt a hand on her neck. "Put your head down— that's it." It was a woman's voice.

"Kena!" It came out as a croak.

"No, no…nothing's happened. We're here to help find her. Nothing's happened." A paper cup appeared in front of her. Alice took it and gulped, her hand shaking so much that she spilled half the water.

"Keep me informed." It was Lieutenant Tomas, going out the door. And there were just two of them, not a crowd. One man and one woman. New York State troopers. To help, she'd said. To *help.*

The woman slipped onto the vacant stool while the man leaned against the wall behind her.

"Ms. Wangera, I'm Officer Deidre Swenson, and this is Officer Tom Murray. I can't say I've ever seen somebody turn as white as you just did." She pulled a Kleenex from her pocket and handed it to Alice, then pulled out more to wipe water from the table and then the photographs, one at a time and with tenderness, as though she were wiping Kena's real face. She smiled when she got to the last one. Kena and Nia, fooling on the grass. A goat was watching, as if about to jump in. "Where was this taken?"

"In Kenya. We go back every summer for Kena's birthday."

Except this last one.

"Your daughter is eight?" Murray asked.

"Yes, eight last August." She swallowed around the lump in her throat.

"She's adopted?" He sounded doubtful.

"Yes." She cleared her throat. "I adopted her in Kenya. From her grandmother. I lived with the family when I was doing field work on a grant from Brandt University. With the Kikuyu. Kena's people."

"You were teaching at Brandt University at the time of your arrest, correct?" He was looking at a paper. "You seem awfully young to be teaching at a university, not to mention adopting a foreign child."

"I'm an adjunct. I'm a writer. Poetry." *Stop* it. As if she needed to prove she was fit to have Kena. Not that writing poetry did that; he'd probably think the opposite. Alice looked him in the eye and hoped he didn't see the terror hiding behind her face.

Deidre Swenson took a notebook out of her pocket. "Describe Kena."

Describe Kena? She's the most beautiful child in the world.

"She's small for her age. When I saw her Sunday, her hair was in cornrows for her school concert. Her skin is dark. Like coffee. Her eyes are dark brown, almost black. And she—" She faltered. "She has a scar on her forehead. About two inches, curving across her right eyebrow, pink. And two on her arm."

They'd said Kena had been lucky. Lucky it was "just" a concussion. Lucky her arm hadn't splintered from the impact, "just" the elbow. They'd said Kena was a plucky little girl. As if she didn't know that already.

Plucky, but not so lucky, as she got her for a mother.

"She wears a pink watch and a purple medic alert band. And a leather cord necklace with an ostrich hanging from it. Her jacket is—" Tom Murray cut her off.

"We're getting a description of what she was wearing from her foster mother."

"But when she went home she might have changed."

"Went home?" he asked.

They didn't know? "She was *there*. At the apartment. In Queens. She left a note."

Deidre Swenson interrupted. "She left a *note*?"

"Yes! 'Don't worry, I am fine. Kena.' She took her stuffed animal, a lemur. And her pills. And her nightie." Getting angry wouldn't help. Would. Not. Help.

"So she left on her own? She chose to?"

"She's only eight!"

"A medic alert? And pills? What for? Make sure they get the medical details from the foster mother," Tom Murray ordered Officer Swenson.

Alice's hackles rose. Like she'd been disqualified. But she *wanted* them to talk with Patrice! Of course she did. If they had, they'd know about the note. "Kena is HIV positive. She takes meds twice a day."

Deidre Swenson's pen stopped writing.

"She manages by herself, now she's off the syrups." Kena had been so proud.

They stared at her.

"Her watch has an alarm to remind her. She's been doing a champion job." Alice's eyes abruptly filled. A champion job.

"She's had this since—when?" Deidre Swenson asked.

Alice swiped at her cheeks. *Stop it!* "She was born with the virus. Her father died from AIDS before she was born, and her mother died when she was a month old."

"You knew this when you adopted her?"

"Yes." Alice swallowed. "Of course. That's *why* I adopted her, so she'd be able to get proper treatment."

"How old was she when you adopted her? How old were *you*?" He frowned and crossed his arms as if he wanted to stop the whole thing.

"She was two months old. I was 21." Alice crossed her arms.

"Twenty-one? What were they thinking?" Deidre Swenson stepped in. "So she's always been sick?"

"She's not sick." Didn't police come in contact with HIV all the time? "She hasn't contracted AIDS. She's had the best care. The *best*. To her, it's just a part of her life. Like asthma and allergies, things she's seen with other kids. Annoying, and she hates the blood tests. I'm not saying she doesn't ever complain, but she doesn't worry."

*Alice* worried, but she kept it hidden, how she was on high alert 100 percent of the time.

"Why would she run away?"

Alice shook her head. "*No*. She packed Lemmy and her pills. She's going *to* somewhere." But where? "But she's never done anything like this, even when things were really bad."

"Really bad?" Tom Murray straightened up, as if to say *now we're getting somewhere*.

"After the…after the accident. First the hospital, and then she didn't get to see me. For almost three months. She wanted to stay with our friend Tam while I'm here. And Tam loves Kena, don't misunderstand! But she's the last person who should be taking care of a child, especially one with special needs. And she's an archeologist; she's out of the country half the time. I finally agreed on foster care when I heard about Patrice. Because she's a nurse. And Kena could go on Medicaid."

"This Tam. Could she have gone to her?"

"She's in Guatemala. It's in Central America, below Mexico."

Alice blushed as her old neediness stuck its head out. Needing to earn a place by showing she was "smart."

"Has she complained about her foster mother or the other children? School? Has anyone hurt her?"

"She loves Patrice. And Toby, one of the kids there—she thinks he walks on water."

"How old is Toby?"

"He just turned 12."

Tom Murray looked at Deidre Swenson. "That's a big age gap. And a boy."

"No! He's—" Alice abruptly wondered. No, she'd *know*. *Wouldn't she?* Her stomach flipped. *No, Kena would say.*

"We need to talk with this boy. Has anything happened this week that could have upset her?" Tom Murray asked.

"Does she understand your situation?" Deidre asked.

*Situation.*

"She knows about my current sentence and what it's for: aggravated DWI with a child in the car. She knows…she knows she was that child. But we don't talk about what could be coming up."

"Adam St. John died Tuesday, and things are about to change," Tom Murray said. It sounded like a threat.

"She doesn't know. I want to tell her in person. And she didn't talk about Adam last night. She'd just gotten back from her school concert and was excited, talking a blue streak."

"How does she handle difficult times?"

Kena had had more than her share of "difficult times."

"She's been poked with needles all her life and has had to be pretty stoic. Books and stories are places of comfort, I think." Like her. "But after the crash—I don't know what she's not telling me, but I'm sure there are things."

"Do you trust her foster mother?"

"Yes. Absolutely. And all the kids at Patrice's are HIV positive; that's been good for Kena."

"That's a big responsibility. How many kids are in the home?"

"Five, including Kena."

"We need a list of relatives and friends."

But she didn't have any relatives and friends to give them.

"Tam sends Kena a letter every couple of weeks." She probably shouldn't mention the feathers and foreign money. "But any family of Kena's are in Kenya." She shook her head to shake away Wisconsin and Aunt Lena.

She'd sing her mother's song on the telephone most nights, ignoring the grumbling behind her. *Sing, sing free, ina' amaazo, banajaanh.*

Banajaanh. Ojibwe for nestling. Banajaanh! her mother would call. Where is my banajaanh?

But there were pieces of Kena's life that she could never make up for: the hospital, the summer before she was settled at Patrice's, going to her new school. Packing her lunch with a poem. Being at the concert to cheer for her. Holding her when she was scared, secretly looking her over for a hint of sickness.

What did he just say? Their old apartment.

"It's sublet." Kena was allowed to bring her clothes and Lemmy and her quilt. Not her art materials, not her Moomin bowl or her books, and they'd forgotten her pillow. She'd imagined Kena carrying her things in a big black garbage bag like she'd seen inmates use when they were released or moved to prison.

Prison.

"Where are *you* from?" Tom Murray asked.

"I was born in Minnesota and moved to Wisconsin when my parents died. But my aunt, she…" *Is an evil racist witch.* "She disapproved of my adopting Kena. They met only once."

"Who's in Kenya?"

"Kena's mother's family. Her grandmother, her aunts and uncles, her cousins." And Oliver's family. Her heart sank. She'd have to tell. They might contact someone there, and Patrice knew.

"Her father's family?"

Alice shook her head. "No, they didn't want her. But there is someone." She appealed to Deidre Swenson. "If he finds out I'm here, he might try to take Kena!"

Deidre Swenson leaned toward her. "Who is that? Is he violent?"

"No! God, no! No. I'm scared I'll lose her!" She picked up the photograph taken at the airport. "His name is Oliver Wangera. We were married for almost four years. He's Kikuyu, like Kena."

"Is he her adoptive father, then?"

"No. A Kenyan adoption was simple back then for an American, if the child was HIV positive. There would have been a long wait if Oliver was included, and I didn't want to wait. As soon as I adopted her, she went on my Brandt insurance." As if she needed to persuade these state police she'd done the right thing. Alice felt heat rising into her face again.

"I had to return here to finish my Master's or I'd lose my scholarship. We left her with her mother's family. When we went back to Kenya, we'd share raising her. Then she got thrush, and she was too small—failure to thrive, they call it—so we brought her here. When she got better, and it was time for us to go back to Kenya, I'd changed my mind. I decided it was better for her here. We had fights about it, but it was my decision to make." She lifted her chin as if Officer Murray would take Oliver's side.

"Where is this man now?"

Alice suddenly felt hurt, as if Oliver had lied to her instead of the other way around. "Kenya, but he travels for UNICEF all over East Africa."

"You kept his name."

"I kept Kena's name, the name I had when I adopted her. A Kenyan name." She knew the truth, though. She kept it just in case.

"It's common for kids to run away to the other parent, but in this case that seems pretty far-fetched," Deidre Swenson said.

"Unless—could he be here? The UN is headquartered here."

"She doesn't think of him as her father," Alice said defensively.

"Are you sure?" Tom Murray asked. She stared at him. She wasn't sure about anything anymore.

"There's been publicity with the St. John kid's death. Maybe this Oliver contacted your daughter."

*St. John kid.* "No! He'd never just do that." *This Oliver.* What if he'd found out she'd lied? "Besides, she'd tell me."

Deidre Swenson stood up. "We'll get going, then."

It was so sudden. But she wanted them to. "How will I know what's happening?"

"We'll be in touch with Makena's foster mother," Tom Murray said. He looked at his paper. "Patrice Washington."

"But I'm her mother!"

He put up his hand. "Ms. Wangera, your daughter is a ward of the State of New York."

"But—*I* decided—Kena being with Patrice—*I* decided."

"Well, the state decides things now." He scooped up a photograph and left.

The horrors she'd been keeping at bay seized Alice. How quickly Kena could be taken. She was so small. She *trusted* people. Alice grabbed Deidre Swenson's arm. "But will you do an Amber Alert?"

"There's another level called Kid-Find, that's used when it's not an abduction."

Not an abduction? How do they know it hasn't turned into one!

*Don't.* Alice fumbled to collect her photographs. Tom Murray had taken the cotton candy one that Adam took at the circus. Cloud on a stick.

Deidre Swenson turned at the door. "How do you do it? I mean, the HIV—the possibility—" She trailed off. "Never mind, it's none of my business."

Alice spoke to the table. "I'm pretty much terrified all of the time."

"Ms. Wangera—Alice—Tom Murray is—" Deidre Swenson lowered her voice. "He's seen a lot of bad stuff with kids and parents. He's not tactful. But he'll work around the clock for your daughter."

Alice stood up and held out her hand. "Thank you."

Carla Santiago was at the door. "I'll escort you back."

The three women hesitated for a moment. Mothers all, though they would never know it.

# Chapter 18

## Gideon

Gideon had mixed feelings about being back at The Lake House. His first visit had been on a kindergarten field trip. They were served fruit cocktail from a can big enough for a giant and watched a ham get sliced with a huge blade that showed up in a nightmare that night.

Until the divorce, he'd had countless dinners with his family on the back porch. His bar mitzvah party had been there, including a DJ, although only the girls and Adam danced. There'd been a creepy magician who stuck a long needle through a balloon.

He liked studying the sepia-colored photographs of dour Samuel Farley and his five sons standing next to old farm machinery, and Berit Farley and her four daughters holding up bumpy vegetables. There wasn't one smile in the bunch.

The high-ceiling rooms were painted a soft yellow, and green rugs lay like islands on the honey-colored floors. The squishy sofas and overstuffed chairs had been joined by the dining room's straight-backed chairs, like relatives from out of town; the tables in the dining room had been lined up for a buffet. He'd set up the slideshow in the side room that had one door to the dining room and another to the living room, and two little boys were running the loop with greater and greater speed, tagging the Christmas tree each time they went by. They reminded him of himself and Adam.

Gideon felt painfully isolated and lonely. Nobody else seemed to have a problem talking to other people, gabbing away as they filled their plates. Maybe he was hungry instead of tense. He'd had trouble telling them apart since the accident. He grabbed a plate and scooped up rice pudding and macaroni and cheese. A roll. It was impossible not to eavesdrop.

"Charlie's famous rice pudding!"

"Robbie, leave some for other people. And only one muffin. Do you want apple butter? It's from Ruth Bayer's orchard. You sure? You don't know what you're missing!"

"Wasn't the concert last night wonderful? The kindergarteners! So cute!"

"That little boy who waved to his parents the whole time!"

"Benji Lamb. His mom is our vet. Do you think Lily will go back now? All these months waiting, can you imagine?"

"Well, you know—it's probably for the best. How is Sally doing at school? Freshman year can be hard."

"She loves it, thank God! What have you been up to lately?"

"Well, we actually got a sitter and went to a movie! With popcorn and candy, the whole works."

He needed to get out of there. Then he saw his father across the table.

"Dad," he said softly, and his dad looked up. Gideon pointed at the door to the porch. Abe nodded and, grabbing two sets of napkin-wrapped silverware, followed Gideon.

There was a space heater to take the chill off, but mercifully no one else was there. A few votive candles were on each table, and their tiny flames reflected on the windows, looking like a coven of fairies. No, that was witches. The last time his family had been there, David ran around on the beach until their food came, but Gideon had stayed at the table to keep his parents from fighting. At least that was over.

Abe rolled out the silverware. "Is your mother back?"

Gideon shook out his napkin. He stuck his spoon into the rice pudding that Charlie was "famous for." He hadn't checked his cellphone all afternoon, he realized with a stab of guilt. "I don't know. I came over early to set up."

"Set up what?"

Gideon was used to his dad forgetting, or half listening, to the details of his and David's lives, as if he always had something running in his head that competed. When they'd still been all together it was supposed to be funny, since their mom had everyone's schedules embedded in *her* head. But after his parents split, it felt like absence, not absent-mindedness. Gideon didn't include his dad a lot of the time and knew it was the same for David; it was how he got away with skipping school when he was at their dad's.

"How's David?" he asked now, a dig at his dad for forgetting the slideshow.

"David? He didn't want to come, and I thought Lily and Enoch would understand. It's tough for a kid his age to hang around at this kind of thing. Hell, it's tough, period. He loved Adam like another brother."

Gideon put down his spoon. He felt like a jerk. He rubbed his hands on his thighs and brought them up to shove his plate away. He hadn't really given David a thought. And how did Lily and Enoch stand it, other people's kids? Especially him.

His dad leaned across the table and covered Gideon's hands with his own. Gideon saw that they'd become smaller than his. Oh, right, it went the other way, didn't it? The kids got bigger.

"It will get easier."

Exactly what he'd said when he moved out, Gideon thought, and had an urge to flip his hands over and pin his father's down against the table. He disengaged and stood up. "I'm gonna get a Coke. Want anything?"

"Sure, if they have any beer going."

Gideon left his dad looking out the window. Communing with the fairies. Or more likely, chewing on a problem with a patient.

He didn't care, either way.

A girl was in the dining room tidying up the table. She looked up and smiled, and an olive rolled off her tray onto the floor. He picked it up and held it out, then, flustered, stuck it in his pocket. Charlie and Clare's kid. Mari. When did she grow up? She's pretty, he thought, and felt his face get hot as if he'd said it out loud.

The two boys ran out of the side room, heading for the living room.

"Stop right there," Mari said. "Red light!" To his amazement, they stopped.

"You two go to the TV room, and I'll put a DVD in, okay?"

"Can we watch *Star Wars?*"

The littlest boy crossed his arms. "No!" He appealed to Gideon for some reason. "I wanna watch *Frozen 2.*"

"You've seen it six times!"

"You watched *Star Wars* 10 times! 12! 12-*teen!*"

Mari looked at Gideon and smiled. "Scoot!" Mari said. "*I'll* choose."

The boys pivoted but when they got to the doorway, the biggest stuck his arm across. "Red light!"

The boy ducked under. "Green light!" They disappeared around the corner.

"Hi, Gideon." Mari was laughing. "What have you been up to

lately?" She began walking around the big table, picking up crumbs, and stopped. "I can't believe I said that! I'm so stupid!"

"What? Oh." He searched for something to make her feel better. "How was China?" God, he was doing it himself. And what movies have you seen lately, and what year are you, again?

"China? Oh, it was—I read your blog. Every week. I'm so sorry. I mean—" She shook her head. "Listen, I better get a DVD in. Can I get you anything?"

"I'm just getting a Coke." He motioned to the cooler in the corner. "But my dad, he wondered about a beer?"

"Sure, there'll be something in the kitchen. My dad decided not to put liquor out. I mean, after—"

"After what?"

"Never mind, forget I said it. I'll just—" She left through the door to the hallway.

After—oh. The crash. He felt like a dope. He grabbed a Coke and drank half of it, suddenly very thirsty. There was laughter from the side room. He walked over and stood to the left of the doorway, out of sight.

"I didn't know they had a Fresh Air kid," a woman said.

"Oh, Kitty, just because she's a little Black girl doesn't mean she has to be a Fresh Air child. And besides, look at the decorations. It's not summer, it's Valentine's."

Adam and the hula hoop. The little girl twirling. He realized, with a jolt, that it was Kena. It had to be her, who else could it be? He was so stupid!

"Is that Wangera's kid?" someone asked. He recognized the voice of Adam's old roommate. God, they were staying at his house!

"Gideon!" His mom came through the door.

"It's a wonderful tribute. To Adam, and to your friendship." She took a deep breath and let it out in a sad whoosh. "Such an inadequate word for you two." She wrapped her arms around him and squeezed. "Oh, honey."

He stepped away before he cried like a little boy.

She touched his cheek. "I know it's been—excruciating—and now that he's really gone—"

Gideon blurted out, his voice tight and high from the tears in his throat.

"It's too fast! That sounds so stupid! I mean…after the accident and all the emergency stuff, and moving him, but then, just waiting, and waiting. Like Adam was on pause." He cleared his throat and looked away. "And then God, or someone, came back from getting a…a fucking snack and pushed the stop button instead of start."

"Oh, sweetheart."

Suddenly Mari was there holding a bottle and a DVD, and he thought, oh shit, did she hear me say fuck? and blushed.

"Marisol! It's good to see you. I'll bet your parents are glad you're back."

"Hi, Ms. Wainwright. I guess they are." She handed the bottle to Gideon. "I better get this on." She held up the DVD. Muppets. She smiled over her shoulder at Gideon as she left. His mom lifted her eyebrows.

"Dad's on the porch." He motioned with the beer.

"I'm glad that's not for you. I think I'll find David. Maybe he'll want to come home with us tonight."

"He's not here. He didn't want to come."

"So, your dad just—" Rachel swept her hand up and back down, then up again. She tucked Gideon's hair behind his ear. "David should have come."

"Mom, it's okay. He'll come tomorrow. It's fine." Gideon was used to being in an advisory role when it came to David. The go-between guy. The go-to guy. The go-from guy.

"Did you talk to him today?"

"No." He wasn't going to admit that he hadn't checked messages.

"Well, he'll be coming home tomorrow after the service. Meeting for Thanksgiving, what is that? Do you know what happens?"

"When I went to their regular Quaker meeting, people sat in silence the whole time and talked if they felt like it. It's not planned, it just comes from the people there, whatever comes up."

"It sounds ghastly."

"It was peaceful, after I quit making up stuff in my head to say." He dreaded it.

"You could prepare something, no one would know."

"I wondered if they'd want me to play something, but I guess not."

"Do you want to?"

"I don't know. I guess not." He held up the beer. "I better get this to Dad."

"I think I'll go find Lily. Have you talked to her?"

Gideon realized that he hadn't seen her. "No. Enoch's parents are here, though, and they're staying with her."

"Bernie and Louise?"

"Lois."

"Lois. Okay, I'll go say hello." She reached up and kissed him on the cheek, waved at a couple filling their plates, and went into the living room.

Gideon handed the beer to his father but didn't sit down. He walked to the windows and looked out at the lake. He rested his forehead on the glass. Were he and Adam out there in another dimension, swimming or digging channels for the water to run into? Or skating. He heard Adam's voice, singing.

*Here, the night is skating in across the sky. Winter's cold, and when the wind blows so am I.*

He heard the sound of a match being lit and smelled his dad's cigarette. He thought of pointing out that there was no smoking and felt mean.

Would there be snow for Yule? They'd loved it, running wild in the dark and throwing sticks into the fire. One time there was black ice, and they'd skated way way out, shouting at first but getting quieter and quieter until it was just the sounds of their blades and their breathing, and then, in silent agreement, they stopped to lie on the ice. He'd never seen so many stars, and decided he'd put the scene in a movie someday.

*Hey Gid, put the camera down. Just be here.*

The town's other bonfire was on Halloween. Adam had been a mad scientist one year. He'd leaped around looking like a hyperactive ghost in a white lab coat Gideon's dad had given him. Afterwards they'd slept in the playhouse, burrowing into their sleeping bags, a little sick from all the candy and hot chocolate. They would sort in the morning. Gideon hated nuts and Adam hated raisins.

There were raisins in the famous rice pudding.

Adam had worn the lab coat the following summer for their soda stand.

Somehow, enclosed in the candle-lit intimacy of the porch, Gideon wasn't surprised with what his dad said next.

"Remember when you and Adam had that Kool-Aid stand? Fizzy Kool-Aid. What a mess!"

Gideon could smell the sticky cherry syrup. It had been a fantastic setup. Four flavors. "We had those bendy straws." His dad was searching for a place to put out his cigarette. "You brought home a box of them from the hospital, a gross. They were rejects for some reason. I didn't know there was another meaning for gross until then." His dad was still searching. "You remember, they were the reason we went into the business in the first place! Adam still had your old white coat, and you got another one for me. You helped us figure the formula. You gotta remember," Gideon begged.

He moved until he was standing over his father, as if everything depended on his remembering. Abe put the cigarette out on his plate and stood up. He put his hand on Gideon's shoulder.

"Of course I remember, Gideon. I remember more than you think."

They stood there not looking at each other.

Gideon saw Lily opening the door to the beach, holding her coat closed under her chin.

"Too cold!"

She walked over and pulled out the other chair at the table. They sat down on either side of her. She grabbed the neck of the beer bottle. "May I?"

They nodded mutely. She tipped it back and drank as if it were water. Then she pulled a wadded Kleenex from under her cuff and patted her lips carefully.

"I wore lipstick." She examined the Kleenex and stuck it back up her sleeve. "I'm glad it's you out here and not somebody else. I've been sitting in the car watching people come." She held the bottle against her cheek.

"Beer gives me an instant hot flash." She looked at Abe's plate. "God, I want a cigarette. Why did I quit?" She opened and closed her coat, fanning herself. "Don't look so worried! I just—the more people I saw, it began to feel like Making an Entrance, you know? So I thought I'd just sneak in." She pointed. "You going to finish the pudding?"

Gideon pushed it toward her. She wolfed it down as if she were starving. Then she polished off the macaroni and cheese.

"God that's good. Abe, I need to talk to Gideon. Is that all right?"

"What? Oh! Oh. Of course!" He put his hand on Gideon's head for a second before he left.

Lily ran her finger over the plate and licked it. She turned the bottle upside down until a little beer dripped out and licked that too. Then she faced Gideon.

*My God.* He whispered, even though no one else was there. "Lily, are you *stoned*?"

"Oh, Gideon! I was never really mad—well, I was, but not at *you*, it wasn't *your* fault, I haven't even asked how *you* felt. I just need to say before tomorrow that I'm *glad*—I mean, if it wasn't me, that it was you. I just wanted to say that. I just—I *wonder*, you know? Did he *know*?"

She suddenly heard what he'd said.

"Oh no! Do I smell? It was just a couple of puffs, or drags, is that what you call it still? And I went out on the porch! And I brushed my teeth!"

"No one will be able to tell." They'll think her red eyes are from crying.

"*You* could tell."

"Where'd you *get* it?"

"Adam's jacket pocket." They looked at each other bleakly.

"I guess I better go do this." Lily sighed and pushed the chair back.

"Want me to come with?" Please, please say no.

"No, I'm good to go. As good as I'll ever be."

Gideon walked her to the door. As she reached for the knob, he said, "I wonder too, did he know. I'd looked away. I'm sorry!"

"Oh, sweetie."

"He just—left." His throat closed up.

She took a deep breath. "I can't hug you. I *do*, I *do* hug you, in my head, but—but if I hug you we'll both fall to pieces." She opened the door and went in. Lily in the lion's den. There was a bombardment of voices.

"Lily, how *are* you?"

"Lily, I'm so, so, *so* sorry."

She should have smoked the whole joint, Gideon thought.

He pulled out his phone. Two voicemails from David.

"Gideon, are you there? Dad said you'd be. I *really* gotta talk to you. There's this little girl on the train; it gets there in 15 minutes, I should've stayed on, but I got scared Dad would find out I skipped. She's meeting her grandfather, but what if he's late or something? Call me!"

David had promised he wouldn't skip again. Gideon knew he couldn't put off telling their parents any longer, at least their mom, but he had to at least warn David, give him a chance to tell on himself. He listened to David's second message, his voice tired and subdued.

"Hey, it's me. Never mind about that girl and all that. I called Jimmy to bike down and she wasn't waiting, so that's cool. I'm gonna watch TV. I guess I'll see you tomorrow—I hope it's not too bad." Another pause.

"I'm sorry, Gideon. About Adam." More airtime. Then, "Okay." Then, "Bye."

The song came through the wall too faintly for the words to be clear, but Gideon had heard Adam sing them a hundred times.

*Now icicles come melting from the warmth of knowing each step leads back home, home is finding where your heart is known, right at home.*

The slideshow would be pausing at the one of Adam and him.

Gideon opened the outside door. He could see his breath. He pulled the Altoid tin from his pocket and an olive came with it. He grinned. He opened the tin and took out a joint. "Puffs!" He laughed out loud.

# Chapter 19

## Kena & Alice

Kena woke up to her watch alarm. It was dark, and she turned Dora on. Polka-dotted shadows flickered up on the ceiling from the snowflakes hanging beneath it. Ceiling snowflakes were better than snowflake sheets, like Keisha had. Keisha had everything, all the things that Kena used to have, but she didn't have this. She swept Dora around the room but didn't see the cat. She picked up the teddy bear.

"*You're* still here!" She wiggled out of her sleeping bag and zipped open the side pocket of her backpack and took out her water bottle, her pills, and two protein bars. She split the big pill in half. Water, pill, water, one down. Water, half, and again. The nurse said she was ready to Go Solo, but she'd never taken them without Patrice watching.

She wished Toby could see.

She sat the teddy bear back on his chair. He slid down, and she sat him back up and took the chair next to him to eat the protein bars. Crumbs fell on the table, and she pinched them between her fingers to feed him.

"There you go!"

And there was the cat, winding around her legs and purring. She patted her lap, but he rolled over, so she went to the floor to stroke his stomach. And then she saw. He wasn't a boy like Sully.

"What's your name?" She rubbed. The cat stretched to lick her hand and touched the cut. Ow! She switched hands. "I know a good name, but first you need to know the story." The cat was looking right at her, ready to listen.

"Long ago, in Kikuyu land—that's in Kenya—there was a famine because no rain. Everybody was hungry. Some children even *died*. Goats too. The people decided someone should go see Ngai—that's like God—and ask for rain. Nobody volunteered until finally a girl said she would go. Everyone went to the river. The girl sang: 'Rain fall and make this ridge green, make this ridge green.' She walked into the river up to her knees. She sang, 'My father said I should be lost, I should be lost.' She went up to her waist. She sang, 'My mother said I should be lost.' She went in up to her neck. She ducked down. And the river took her."

Kena's hand became still as she gazed at the empty river.

"And rain came! Green grass grew, and food. Everybody got fat! The girl, up in the sky world, found her relatives who had died. They asked what she would like. Because she'd been brave. She said goats. They told her to go to sleep."

Kena shivered in anticipation. She loved the next part.

"When she woke up she was by the river, *her* river back home, and there were goats *everywhere*! And her mother and her father were there, and all the people. And they rejoiced." Kena saw them jumping around with their arms in the air. Goats too. They were great jumpers.

"The girl's name was Wanjiru, after one of Ngai's daughters. And that can be *your* name, and Juri for short."

She sighed. It was time to go, and she was scared. What if Adam's mother was mad she came? But she had to. *Had* to. She fastened her star belt around her Big Apple T-shirt and pulled her boots on. She should pee. And do one other thing, like her mother used to do, and now she did for herself. She spread her nightie out on her sleeping bag and tucked Lemmy and the teddy bear inside peeking out. There you go. Then she remembered.

Adam's book.

She hesitated. She could read her favorite part tonight, one last time.

But sitting on the toilet with her pink leggings around her ankles, everything was all wrong. Blue and pink were baby colors. Her heels hurt. And the worst of all, her mother didn't know where she was.

Her bare legs broke out in goosebumps. The ceiling was so high anything could be up there. The mirror above the sink gleamed dimly. Something moved in it. She gasped and began to pee, then saw it was just Wanjiru, licking at the faucet.

She started to cry. Her mother had agreed that Wanjiru probably cried when she went into the lake. Her back was to everybody so they didn't see, but her ancestors could see her tears. Was Adam seeing *her* tears now? He wasn't a real ancestor like Maitu, but he was her Big Brother. She rolled out a fistful of toilet paper and blew her nose.

She'd change to her black leggings.

Kena left her flashlight just inside the door. She stuck her head out to see if anyone was passing and crept outside. She stopped by the stick figure family, making a fourth. The Lake House was lit up from bottom to top and she could see people moving behind the windows. One of them was Adam's mother, who wrote in his book "For Adam, on his 10th birthday! It's about owls! love, Mom."

She put her hands in her jacket pockets and felt something. Her dirty socks! She shook them out and pulled them over the ends of the littlest stick figure's arms.

"There you go."

She edged up the steps and looked in. The girl from the train! Kena ran down the steps and around to the side. There was a square of light on the house next door. It changed color. She looked at The Lake House and back to the square and back to The Lake House. The square came from a TV, hanging up high like at the hospital. She crouched under the window.

She saw a baby with frosting on his face. Then a lady holding the baby, its face cleaned up. A puppy. The picture changed to two boys. Adam and Gideon? Holding swords. Was that the chicken playhouse? Kena watched as the pictures came one after another, with Adam, she now was sure, in all of them. With his family. With his friend. She gasped.

It was *her*! She'd had to show him how to hula hoop, but he caught on right off. He'd licked the frosting off his heart cookie before taking a bite. The popping balloon game. She couldn't, but Adam sat right down on it and POP. The picture changed again, but now everything was changed.

Because she was included. She was his Little Sister—it showed right there for everyone to see.

◊

"Move your ass!"

Alice focused harder on her book. Friday evenings were the worst, when everything that was impossible, everything that was lost and couldn't be mourned for, everything that hurt the most, broke out of the festering wound that was jail.

"Fuck you!"

"Let it go, V."

On the Outside, Friday evenings were free time, recess for grownups. But Inside was a rancid fishbowl, not a speck of privacy.

*Babaamise, banajaanh.* She closed her eyes to see her mother—*fly, baby bird.* She'd been so little when they died that a part of her had never stopped searching for them. Breathe in. But breathing in, in jail, felt like she was poisoning her secret self.

Someone was crying softly.

She pulled her pillow around her head like earmuffs, but she couldn't shut off pictures of Kena crying for her. And worse. When Alice was little, a boy at school said a man was kidnapping Native kids and putting them in bags. She'd been glad she didn't look like her mother and felt ashamed.

"Your time is up!"

On Friday nights, the space in front of the TV was a war zone, and the line for the phone pushed and held secret bruising pinches; taking an extra minute was an insult, not an irritation.

Alice's legs itched to walk. But if she left her cell to walk, she'd be watched, and someone would decide to pick a fight. It wouldn't matter if she didn't react, being a target was enough. The COs wouldn't ask who started it and couldn't dare finding out. She remembered the dirty, white polar bear at the zoo, pacing back and forth while she watched. It had felt wrong, but she hadn't stopped.

Even after all these months, she was still astonished that people would be so messed up in such a public way, or be kind and in the next second, turn around and be just plain vicious. It wasn't that everyone alive didn't carry such contrariness around inside; she knew she did, like the story about two wolves inside, fighting. Which one won? The one you fed, and there wasn't any honey in jail. Jail poked and poked and poked until feelings exploded out like shrapnel.

Sylvie was an alcoholic. She had an AA acronym tattooed on her forearm in fancy script: HALT. Hungry, Angry, Lonely, Tired. Four roads to the dark side, Sylvie said.

Alice kept having to ask again what the letters meant after Hungry, which Sylvie said was "telling" since words were Alice's Thing. Alice made up lists: H: Help, hallowed, heart. A: Africa, Adam. Amends. L: Love. Lost.

Lemmy.

She saw Lemmy at the edge of a road, tossed there, his legs and tail every which way, his face in the dirt.

T. Terror.

She curled up facing the wall and pulled her blanket over her head.

The debate between the merits of *Shark Tank* and *CSI* escalated. The shrillest was Victoria, V, who suffered from a mental illness but state law meant they couldn't force her to take her pills. Fuck was her favorite word. Alice imagined spinning out of her cell like a dervish and hovering in front of the television, pointing down at their gaping face. HALT!

Instant silence, like freeze tag.

Then music would be heard from far away, a lullaby, and everyone would sink down right where they were, sink down to the floor, even the COs, and bow their heads. And weep. It would start in their unit and spread through the jail like fog, right through the steel and concrete, to all the other units and to the warden and janitors and cooks and dishwashers. They would put down whatever they had, the telephone, the computer mouse, the mop, the sponge, the pot, the potato, the toilet brush, the pictures of their baby's first birthday, and they would put their hands over their faces. And weep.

And it would spread. Because weeping from a jail would be so desolate—so *true*—it would be heard outside its walls. Pilots flying over would have to land because they would be crying too hard to see, and all the passengers would spill out on the tarmac and wail, looking at the sky, and fall on their backs and rock back and forth with the pain of their sorrows. People in nearby towns would open their windows and join in the crying. People in the aisles of grocery stores and on the sidewalks would fling their arms around strangers, their tears soaking into each other's collars. It would cross the ocean. It would be heard in Kenya.

And everyone would cry. For themselves, for each other, for each other's children. For Adam's mother and father, for his grandparents, for everyone who loved him and raised him up. For everyone he loved. For Kena.

And to anyone who might hurt her.

God, if you exist—

Ancestors, if you can hear—

Angels—

"Hey, girlfriend, how you doin'?"

Sylvie was teased about being so tiny, but her voice was deep and raspy. "Alice, I know you cryin'."

Alice waved a hand out from the blanket. She rolled over, keeping her face down, and pulled her night T-shirt from under her mattress. She swung around and sat up with it covering her face. She blew her nose. Folding it, she blew again. She looked over it at Sylvie standing outside her cell.

"You look like shit. All alone thinking about bad stuff doesn't seem too smart to me." Sylvie raised her eyebrow. "Seems like all that ej-yu-ca-shun would teach you. My Gramma used to say to keep your brain from eating crap, you gotta bribe it with sugar."

"I tried that," Alice said. She held the book up.

"*When Things Fall Apart*? You call that sugar?"

"It's about peace. Meditating."

Sylvie snorted.

"I need to wash my face."

"You're right about that."

When Alice got to the table, the cards were already dealt. They'd been playing hearts lately, a game Alice taught them, that she'd played at Our Mother of the Blessed Baby Bible Camp every summer for seven years.

She saw that she had the queen.

Cricket put her hand on Alice's arm. "I been prayin' up a storm."

Cricket's prayers gave Alice hope despite herself. All that earnestness must count for something.

"I try to hold her safe, but I'm so scared I can't think," Alice whispered.

"Well, who wouldn't be?" Keresha said.

"Oh, that's a big help, Keresha." Cricket rolled her eyes. "Look, how about we all do it—what Alice said. We all be holding Kena safe, so Alice doesn't have to all by herself. We'll do a caring circle like at church." She stuck her hands out to both sides. "Come on."

Only Cricket could offer such a thing and not be hooted down, Alice thought. Sylvie put her hand out to Alice. Alice put her cards down and reached out, embarrassed. But she wanted it. She'd light a million prayer candles if she could.

Cricket took Alice's hand and kept her other one outstretched to Keresha, who folded her arms. People didn't do this kind of thing. Not her. And for sure not here.

"Keresha," Sylvie said, and she yanked Keresha's hand under the table.

"Okay, okay. But no praying."

"Kena," Cricket said, and she squeezed.

"Kena," Alice and Sylvie said together and they squeezed. They looked at Keresha.

"Kena."

Then they all picked up their cards and examined them blindly.

Alice remembered the L in HALT. Lonely. Growing up, she'd felt like a changling. Except for Kena, and Oliver and his family for that little while, she'd been lonely most of her life. But here she was in jail, and she wasn't lonely.

She tried to take a deep breath, and could.

"You guys remind me of Kenya. I was the only white person most of the time, and I didn't understand what they were saying half the time, but I felt like I belonged." Alice held her cards in front of her face. "I feel like that with you."

"You do," Sylvie said. "Belong."

"Too bad for you!" Keresha said.

They burst out laughing, and Alice did too.

# Chapter 20

## Lily

She hadn't fallen to pieces, but it was still pretty awful. Like when little Andrea Fuller came up and said, "Ms. J, did you see me be a snowflake? Look! My fingernails are silver!" And she had to look, of course, both little hands held up like an offering.

Or when the head of Warm World said, "Remember when Adam's 'most unusual pet' got loose? I *still* make loud noises every time I open up in the morning. As if a mole could live 18 years! But what if it was pregnant?"

At least Evan Fuller, who must have grown 3 inches, said what everyone else couldn't. "Ms. J, it sucks that your son died."

Standing by the Christmas tree, Lily felt rudderless, as if she were listing from one side to the other. But how brave people were to speak to her at all. In their shoes, she'd be scared she'd say the absolutely wrong thing. Because what was there to say? Adam dying was too big for words.

Clare finally ordered her to sit down. And when someone came to say how sorry they were or share a memory, or both, she breathed in the tree's fragrance like smelling salts, looked right at them, and didn't hear a word. She was off walking the dogs.

The week before Adam left for Belize, they'd watched a show on PBS in which elderly men and women—"pensioners," the voice-over said—dressed to the nines, walked down a red carpet to bow or curtsy to Queen Elizabeth, who said, "How nice to see you. And where are you from? Ah, yes, so pleasant there." Over and over and over, for six hours.

"God! What's in her mind, while they prattle on?" Lily had wondered.

"She's off walking the dogs," Adam had said.

Rachel plopped down next to her, setting a bowl of grapes on the coffee table.

"Where'd you come from?" Lily asked. "I didn't mean—weren't you at a conference?"

"Oh, Lily, I wish I could have come back right away!"

"Have you talked much to Gideon since…" And she was stuck. "Passed," people kept saying, as if he'd taken an exam. They studied each other's faces. They hadn't spoken since late October, when Rachel came to the hospital with candy corn-printed socks and a CD Lily played only once because it broke her heart to hear.

"We gave your CD to pediatrics."

"Wynken, Blynken and Nod," Rachel recalled. "And that shepherd one from *Peter Pan*. I never told you how pissed off I was when Gideon came home singing about Jesus. Shit! *Why* did I *say* that? Nevermind, rewind. *So,* are you ready to go home?" she finished, motioning with her wine glass. It splashed out on her hand. "Whoops." She dabbed at her pants. "It's just seltzer."

Rachel was a child psychologist and sometimes came to the school for a consultation. But when the boys were growing up, with pickups and drop-offs and overnights, Lily saw her almost every day. Now they'd run into each other at the library or the co-op or on the sidewalk and have quick, intimate catch-ups. But they didn't move from the sidewalk to Three Cups down the street; maybe they would now. She'd have time. Oh, *God*!

"I keep wondering where he *is*. And all of these *people*. It's just I've been running into them for months and *now* what do I say? And with the service tomorrow, it's kind of like—" Lily stopped, appalled. Like a rehearsal dinner.

There was a burst of laughter from the side room. Then a soft chorus…aw…the kind of sound people make when they see a baby.

"I had a pissy fit today," Lily said. "Well, I tried to."

"You mean hissy?"

Rachel looked above Lily's head.

Lily twisted around. It was Enoch.

"I don't want to interrupt."

Rachel stood up and hugged him. "I need to call David anyway."

Lily felt terrible. "Is he okay?"

"He's fine, he'll see you both tomorrow." Rachel leaned down and kissed Lily on the cheek. She hesitated for a second, and then kissed Enoch's cheek too. "Is there anything I can help with?"

Enoch shook his head. "We're all set. Besides, aren't you hosting the college crowd?"

"I am?" Rachel asked.

"They're setting up the meeting house tomorrow morning. With Abe and Gideon," Lily said and abruptly grabbed Rachel's hand.

"Oh, honey."

Lily let go. "Go call David." Because you can. *God*, was that the kind of person she was going to be now, maudlin and self-pitying? But Rachel went.

Enoch sank down with a sigh. He plucked a grape from the bowl and rolled it between his fingers like a marble. It suddenly spun into the air and into the Christmas tree.

"How are *you* holding up?" he asked. "I'm exhausted."

"You should go."

"It's Khai too. We came in one car."

"People are starting to leave, anyway. And if you leave, more people will. And if everybody leaves, I can."

"What about Mom and Dad?"

"We'll be fine. How was it picking them up?"

"It wasn't bad. Khai knows more about the birds than baseball, but he actually got Dad to talk about the World Series, of all things. Now they're in there, watching—" His gaze slid toward the side room and back. "I couldn't. I mean, I'm glad Gideon made it, but I just couldn't."

"No. Me either." They sighed.

Lois came out of the side room and walked over. She put her hand on Enoch's shoulder. "You look exhausted. You should go home."

Enoch stood up. "I think I will. I just need to find Khai."

"He was deep in conversation with Gideon's father back by the kitchen. Jacob?"

"Abe. Here, Mom, sit."

But Lois still stood. "He's a fine man. So kind."

Enoch was confused. "Abe?"

"Khai. He's a very understanding person, isn't he?" Lois stood there working her fingers. Lily stole a look at Enoch. He'd been waiting to hear those words, or something like them, for 12 years. He met her eyes, and for a second he was the boy she'd fallen in love with.

"Yes. He is." He wrapped his arms around Lois and hugged her.

Lois stiffened and patted him on the back.

Lily started to rise to hug Enoch goodbye but sat back down. It felt like showing up Lois. See, this is how a hug is done. The last thing she'd want to do. Lois surprised them again.

"You've been good parents, the three of you. Good, good parents to Adam." Enoch stood there, frozen.

"Oh, Lois. Thank you, that means a lot." Lily stood up and hugged Enoch after all.

He cleared his throat. "See you tomorrow, then."

"Don't forget the tree."

"Khai's got it covered." Enoch gave a slight wave and turned toward the back of the house.

Lois sat down, so Lily did too. Lois was silent. Lily searched for something to say.

A burst of laughter came from a circle of chairs at the end of the room.

"The Brandt kids," Lily said. "They're so…so *living*." She motioned helplessly. "It's not that they don't care. I could tell how much they needed a hug, and one boy cried."

Lois frowned.

"No, it was okay. I had something I could *do* at least. But later—they get to have their *lives*—" Life begets life. But not Adam's. She wrapped her arms around her belly protectively.

"I know. He'll just be a boy who died, who they knew for a short time, and they'll be—"

Lily saw that Lois's eyes were shining with tears. "I can't imagine ever laughing like that again," she said softly.

Lois opened her mouth in protest. Then she closed it firmly.

"Adam would want me to," Lily whispered. "One day." Her eyes met Lois's in appeal.

"One day you will. You'll be surprised; then after that first time it will get easier. But you'll always have grief."

As if grief were a friend, Lily thought.

"The awful grace of God," she whispered.

"I'm sorry, dear, I don't think I heard you right. Bernie says I'm getting hard of hearing."

Lily wished she hadn't said it. She felt like she had a seed inside that wasn't ready to grow above ground. "It doesn't matter; it's just something I was talking about with Clare."

"My ears are burning," Clare said from a few feet away, holding a plate piled with food. She put it down next to the grapes. "I'll bet you haven't eaten, am I right?"

Lily wanted to tell Clare about being stoned, but Lois was there. And suddenly she had to put her napkin up to her face not to break into hysterical laughter. She didn't think that was the kind of laughing Lois was talking about. And if she started laughing, it wouldn't be long before she'd be crying like a baby.

Clare flopped down across from them. "Lois, how about you?"

"Thank you, dear. But I'm fine."

Lily saw that Lois was stifling a yawn.

"I've been so self-centered! You've been up since dawn, taken two planes, and then this!" And more—*worse*—tomorrow. Lily offered her hand to Lois. "Let's get Bernie and go home. Clare, is it okay?"

"Don't be silly. Mari's here, and Charlie. And Gideon said he'd stay to help."

"Thank you again, Clare, for fetching us from the airport. For everything," Lois said. "I hate to tear him away from the pictures, but Bernie needs a good night's sleep."

"Would you like Gideon to make you a copy of them?" Clare asked.

"Oh. Can he do that?"

"Sure, a DVD. Do you have a DVD player?" Lily asked.

"Well of course we do! You and Adam gave it to us years ago!" Lois put her hand up to her mouth. "I'm so sorry. I didn't mean to snap like that."

"Well, if that's snapping," Lily said, "snap away."

Just then Kitty Bell came up. She grabbed Lois's hand and shook it. "I'm Katherine Bell. I own Snips and Snaps. The sewing store? I know who you are." She turned to Lily. "We have to be leaving, but I wanted to say how lovely the evening's been. And sad. But of course, it's a blessing." She grabbed Lily's hand and patted it. "You can get on with your life, and Adam's certainly better off."

Lily was struck speechless. She was always confused in the face of rudeness if the perpetrator was older than 10, as if maybe they were right and she was wrong.

Lois put her arm through Kitty Bell's, leading her away. "Let me help you find your coat. Or you can help me find mine. Tell me about Snaps and Snips."

Lily and Clare stared at each other.

"It's like those people who say God has a Plan," Clare growled in a whisper.

But Lily was thinking, it's not like I haven't thought it myself.

She had to get her coat from the back porch. She had to drive her in-laws—ex-in-laws? ex-laws?—home and let Homer out and back in, and then she could escape into the few hours Ambien would give her and not think about tomorrow.

◊

Clare popped grapes into her mouth like candy, staring vacantly out the window. She watched Lily cross the porch ahead of Lois and Bernie. Then, like an apparition, small multi-colored beads bobbed along the porch rail and turned to the steps. They were on the head of a child, a tiny Black girl in a pink jacket. Passing Lois and Bernie, she gave a little wave. Clare looked toward the front door. The little girl entered and hesitated, standing on her tiptoes as if poised for flight.

"You're the hula hoop girl!" someone called out.

The little girl smiled and landed and made for the coat hooks. She jumped to hang up her jacket, but the hooks were too high and too full. A coat fell to the floor. She pressed her body against the others but it was no good and more fell around her. She looked around quickly to see if anyone had noticed. Her T-shirt had a clown on it. She was wearing a belt with a silver star. Her pink boots did too.

Clare was enchanted.

# Chapter 21

## Kena

"Hello!"

Kena called up her courage and walked over.

"I saw you outside." The lady pointed toward the window and smiled. "Actually, I saw your beautiful beads first."

"Are you Adam's mother?"

"Oh dear! She just left."

Kena's heart sank.

"I'm so sorry you missed her."

She was nice, Kena thought. Maybe she should tell *her*.

"That's a beautiful belt. And your boots match!"

"I know."

"Are you hungry? I fixed this plate for Adam's mother, Lily, just a few minutes ago, but she didn't touch it."

Macaroni and cheese, a muffin, and green beans.

"What am I thinking? You should pick out whatever you want." Clare pointed. "Want me to go with you?"

But Kena liked that she could eat from Adam's mother's plate. She perched on the edge of the couch, balancing the plate on her knees.

"Just sit on the rug," the lady said.

So Kena put the plate on the coffee table and slipped down. She unrolled the cloth napkin. A fork, a knife, and a spoon fell to the floor.

"Five second rule," the lady said.

But Kena had to be careful with germs. She wiped the fork thoroughly with the napkin. The lady was staring at her. She made herself keep from covering her scar.

"My name is Clare Lewis. Clare."

She'd forgotten her manners. Kena put the fork on the plate and wiped her hand on the napkin before extending it. Her mother said to look right at the person.

"I'm Makena Wangera."

Kena didn't mean to say her last name; it just came out. We'll just tell Adam's parents, Toby had said. No one else. But here was welcome, and kindness.

"Oh! Oh. Well, I'm glad to meet you, Makena."

Clare finally let go, and Kena picked up her fork. She ate all of the macaroni and cheese and examined the muffin. There were dark chunks.

"They're blueberries. The inn is famous for them."

Famous for blueberries? Kena took a bite. It tasted regular to her.

"Would you like a soda?"

"Oh," Kena said, tempted. "I'm not allowed," she confessed.

"How about a glass of milk? There's chocolate." As if she could make things better with soda or chocolate, Clare thought.

"I'd like milk, thank you. But not chocolate."

"Be right back."

Kena stabbed a bean with her fork. It broke on the way to her mouth. She decided she could skip her vegetable on account of the blueberries. She hitched herself up to the couch to finish the muffin. An older lady came out from the room where Kena thought the pictures were, wiping her eyes with a lacy white handkerchief. She smiled, but the lady didn't smile back. Kena put the muffin down and centered her star belt.

Clare came through the other door holding a glass and stopped. "Oh, Louise!"

"Who's that child?" Head down, Kena could hear every word.

"I'll introduce you," Clare answered.

"Well, don't mind if I do." Kena scooted to the very edge of the couch, ready.

"Louise, this is Makena." Kena stood up, glad that the Clare lady hadn't said her last name.

"Makena, this is Mrs. Berdick. She's the principal of Falls Academy, where Adam used to go."

David's school! Where he skipped! The secret gave her confidence. "Hello." She suddenly realized: Adam and David went to the same school!

"Hello, young lady," Mrs. Berdick answered, and sat on the chair across the table like she was staying. Clare handed the milk to Kena. Afraid of spilling, she drank half before sitting down.

"Where are you from, Makena?"

Kena placed the glass down carefully. She patted her mouth with the napkin. "New York City." Queens was temporary.

"Are your parents here?"

Toby said sometimes you just have to tell a Big Lie for the Greater Good. "My grandfather dropped me off." Toby said not to "embellish," but she thought she'd better. "I'll call him to pick me up."

So there's a grandfather, Clare thought. Thank God.

"And you knew Adam?" Louise Berdick continued.

"Yes, ma'am." Louise Berdick waited.

"Adam is..." Kena swallowed. "Was my Big Brother. They thought I was a boy when I signed up. Maybe because of my name.

But after we met we decided not to tell." At least that part was true.

"Was this at Brandt University?"

"Yes, ma'am."

"And what do a Big Brother and Little Sister do?"

Kena stretched her T-shirt out to show the clown. "We went to the Big Apple Circus for his birthday." Mrs. Berdick nodded.

"The clown took money out of Adam's ears! Everyone was laughing."

Mrs. Berdick didn't seem to think it was funny.

"I taught him to hula hoop. And we walk dogs." Mrs. Berdick raised her eyebrows. "From the Humane Society. They had a puppet show. The puppets were as big as real dogs and cats. When the string wasn't pulled they went like this." Kena dropped her head sideways. "To show being sad—to make people adopt a pet." Mrs. Berdick almost smiled.

"We went to the museum." Kena tugged on her hair. She was using up the best stuff she had on this lady instead of Adam's mother.

"Don't pull your hair like that. You'll make a bald spot." Mrs. Berdick reached over and took Kena's hand. "When Adam was in seventh grade we read a book about two children who ran away and slept in a museum. He wrote to the author, and she replied."

"He told me! *The Mixed-up Files of Mrs. Basil D. Frankweiler!*"

Mrs. Berdick squeezed Kena's fingers gently and let go. "You're fortunate to have had Adam St. John for a big brother." She smiled, but her eyes were swimmy with tears. "Such a loss."

"Adam's not lost!" Mrs. Berdick looked surprised. "He's with his ancestors."

"His ancestors?"

"Yes. My fath—a friend told me, and it's true. He's from Kenya. I was born there."

"Well, that's a comfort. I'll remember that, about ancestors."

"You can call me Kena."

Mrs. Berdick stood up. "It's been a real pleasure meeting you, Kena." And abruptly, she turned and left.

"Well! Louise Berdick! Who would have thought!" Clare said. "You just never know. Kena, would you like dessert?"

Dessert. She needed food for breakfast too. And Wanjiru. "May I get something for my grandfather?" She heard a phone ringing. Hers? What if Toby was calling?

"I should check my phone."

"Come to the dining room after and you can pick out what you want."

Toby hadn't called, but Kena held the phone as she picked out food for the morning. She put the phone down each time she took something, until she had the idea to put it on her plate. Protein. Ham and cheese—cats liked those. Fruit. Grapes. The rice pudding probably had sugar. Anyway, there were raisins. Adam didn't like them either.

The phone chimed, and Kena jerked and tipped her plate. Everything except the cheese rolled off, and the grapes had gone everywhere. She got to her knees.

"I've got this. You get your phone call."

It was a girl, on her hands and knees on the other side of the table, chasing grapes. "Don't worry, go ahead!"

Kena picked up the phone. "Kena! It's me! Toby!"

He was practically shouting. Kena wiggled backwards and stood up and looked around. She darted through a doorway and saw that she was at the end of the hallway with the coats. She could hear voices and running water coming from behind a door. There was another door with a cardboard Santa Claus holding a sign: Good Boys and Girls.

Toby kept talking. "The cops stopped us and asked if I knew

where you are! They did the siren. My mom freaked. Did you go without me?"

When she closed the bathroom door, it was pitch dark. She slid her hand along the wall, feeling for the light switch until she found it. Ow! Stupid cut. "Did you tell?"

"They asked what we did together."

She put the toilet seat lid down using her foot. "Toby! Did you tell?"

"I didn't squeal! Good thing you left the paper for the phone, though, to call you. Where *are* you?"

"In the bathroom."

"In what bathroom? Are you—"

"At the inn!" Kena interrupted. "I'm at that inn! But Adam's mother and father left. I have to wait until tomorrow!"

"But Kena! Where will you sleep?"

"In your sleeping bag at the library," she bragged.

"The library?"

"There's a cat."

"Is there a librarian?"

"There were kids who lived for a *whole week* in a museum. I can take care of myself!"

"You're crazy! You have to be with a grownup! You're too little, Kena."

"I'm not little!"

"You have to tell a grownup! *Now.* I'll wait." His voice changed. "Or I'll tell my mom."

"No! Toby, if you tell, they won't let me go to Adam's funeral!" Kena wailed. "Toby, please! The library's right next door. And it's a *house.*"

He didn't say anything.

"Toby! It's just a little town. It's not like the city with people all over."

"Okay, okay! I'll call you in the morning before we go."

"Go where?"

"To see my dad. It takes an hour and a half to get there, and we have to sign in."

To the prison. She was glad for him, but it felt like he was leaving her all over again. "You can call me in the afternoon. I'll be busy!"

"Kena, you should tell somebody."

"No."

"Oh, Kena."

"It's just sleeping. The librarian will come back in the morning."

"I'll call you before we leave. At eight. And I'll bring the phone into my room tonight so you can call me if you need to."

"I won't." But she felt relieved.

"Did you see Gideon?"

"No."

There was a knock on the door. The door opened.

"Oops!" The door closed.

"Toby, I have to go," she whispered.

"Okay. But Kena, if you don't answer in the morning I'm gonna tell."

"I took your Snickers bar. Bye." She opened the door, holding her other hand high. A tall man stood there holding two toilet paper rolls.

"Sorry to barge in like that," he said. "I'm Charlie." He looked at her hand. "Are you all right?"

"Yes, thank you," Kena replied, stepping into the hall. He ducked into the bathroom.

But she wasn't all right. Toby was with his mom, and hers didn't even know where she was.

"There you are!" It was the girl who'd picked up the grapes, holding a box like the one they got General Toe's chicken in. "Mom said you were fixing that plate for your grandfather."

"That was him. On the phone. He's waiting outside." She looked away.

"I packed what you'd picked out. And rice pudding. I didn't do salad. Want me to get some?"

"He doesn't like it." She thought of Oliver's mother. "His teeth, that's why."

There weren't many coats left, and someone had hung them all up, including her own.

The girl reached up. "This pink one?" She opened the jacket and pulled it up over Kena's arms. "You're bleeding!"

Kena stuck her hand in her pocket.

"Do you want a Band-Aid? We should put something on that."

Kena shook her head. "I'm fine."

"Want me to zip your jacket?" She handed Kena the food. "My name is Mari." She zipped. "Mom said you were close to Adam."

Was Clare her mom? They didn't look alike. This girl looked like Ms. Chau, her teacher.

"Our moms are best friends—I mean, Adam's and mine—but I've been gone. I didn't realize. I should've known from Gideon's blog. My mom didn't let on how bad it was."

She knew Adam, this girl. And Gideon?

"I feel so sorry for everyone. And Adam! But I think you're lucky to have had him as a friend."

Kena stood there holding the box, her hand throbbing. People kept saying she was lucky, but it wasn't lucky that Adam died. It wasn't lucky that her mother was in jail. She wasn't lucky *at all*. And it would get worse if she didn't talk to Adam's mother.

"Anyway." This girl looked so sad.

"I'm Kena," she offered.

"Kena, can I give you a hug?"

Kena tipped forward, and Mari bent over, laying her cheek against

Kena's hair and hugging her, food and all. Then she opened the door and Kena stepped onto the porch. She felt her hood being pulled up. She saw a car with its lights on down the street and pointed. "There he is!"

◊

Locking the library door behind her, she called. "Here, Juri!" But there was no cat thump, no meow. There were lots of places to tuck yourself into in a library if you were a cat. She felt in the box for the slice of ham. She held it up in case Juri was watching. She put it on the floor. "There you go."

She turned the flashlight on. "I'll be right back, I need to wash my hand." But when she swung the door to the bathroom open, she felt cold air; the bottom of the curtain was moving.

Oh, no!

"Wanjiru, Juri!" She whispered, as if someone besides the cat might hear through the open window. "Please, Juri!" She made a kissing sound. She wrapped her hand in toilet paper and searched the library, sweeping the light under tables and chairs and across windowsills and bookshelves. Stuffed animal eyes gleamed back, but not Wanjiru's. And the ham hadn't been touched. Kena picked it up and went to the front door. She popped the lock and went outside. She ran around to the back and crouched under the bathroom window facing the lake.

"Wanjiru!" she called softly. "Supper!" Was Juri hiding, scared? Or was she having the Time of Her Life, like Patrice said when Sully got out. She waved the ham. She huddled against the building, shivering, suddenly scared of the dark and the night coming up. "Juri?" she whispered.

When you're scared, do something brave.

She stepped out from the safety of the wall. The ice on the lake sparkled. Everything was still and frozen. She stepped into the moonlight. Raising her arms, her shadow moved with her. Even the ham had a shadow. A moon shadow, like a song her mother sang. She spun. She waved her arms above her head. She spun again and again. *I'm being followed by a moon shadow.* She went up on her toes. She was a sugar plum fairy.

Her shadow disappeared. It was a cloud. And there were more clouds skittering across the sky. Someone off stage had shoved them out there. And there was the cat, weaving around her legs. Kena stooped down and the cat grabbed for the ham, and when Kena picked her up, she began to purr, kneading into her jacket. Kena held on tightly, went to the window, and pushed it up further. The cat grabbed the windowsill and Kena pushed, and when the cat dug in, Kena shoved. Meowr! Thump.

Kena slammed the window firmly.

There you go! She ran. There were voices coming from the street, and she peeked around the corner.

"Look at the moon! It's moving!"

"It's the clouds moving."

"It's supposed to snow overnight."

"Does anyone know where we're going?"

"Gideon told me. It's just a few blocks."

"Imagine growing up here. It's like *It's a Wonderful Life*."

"Did you talk to Adam's parents?"

"His mom."

"I chickened out."

"No. I mean, it was good."

"Why didn't Gideon come with us? I mean, it's kind of weird, don't you think, just showing up without him?"

The voices became soft, as if somebody had turned them down. And then she was alone. The inn's porch light went out. The

Christmas tree lights shone through the side of the bay window, and another window flickered blue. Was Gideon there? She shivered. She wasn't supposed to get shivery.

"Adam, are you there?"

The words made clouds in the air. Voice shadows.

She shivered. Can a person get sick from loneliness?

◊

She brushed her teeth without water. She put on her nightie. She set her watch for Toby's call. She snuggled into his sleeping bag with Lemmy and the teddy bear, the phone in reach.

"Bless Mama and me and Oliver." It was daytime in Kenya. "Bless Karimi and Nia and Homer and Too and Juri and Sully. And Daisy. Bless Toby and Patrice and Jackie and Peter." She paused. "And Keisha."

Bless Adam. "Goodnight, Mama." She aimed Dora on Adam's book to where Billy put the doll clothes on the owl for the pet parade.

She listened to Adam's voice as she drifted into sleep, her tears drying on her cheeks.

# Chapter 22

## Gideon

Gideon sat in the dark watching Kermit sing "The Rainbow Connection." A voice joined Kermit from behind him. Gideon pressed STOP, mortified. He quickly wiped his tears with his sleeve before twisting around. Mari was in the doorway, the bright colors from the TV flickering over her face. She'd fastened her hair on top of her head with a pencil.

"I didn't know anyone else was still here."

"It's just me, everybody else is gone," she said. She pulled out the pencil, her dark hair tumbling down. "I get hot, loading the dish machine." She walked in and fell back on the couch next to him and sighed.

"I love that song." She sang the ending again, her voice off key.

Gideon thought she was perfect.

She brought her knees up under her chin and hugged her legs. "I was just finishing the lights and saw you were still here."

"I should go." He jumped up.

She followed him into the living room and disappeared around the backside of the Christmas tree. The tree's lights went out, making it loom larger. Its pine smell grew too, as if being in the dark brought it out. Did the tree have feelings about being chopped down? About being chosen? He and Adam had discussed the question seriously more than once.

"You live by the woods, don't you?" she asked, crawling out and standing up, brushing needles off her sweater. "The house with the turret, right? Is that a room?" Seeing his expression, she asked, "Is it yours?"

He nodded.

"Did you ever read *The Sword in the Stone*? Remember Merlin's turret?"

Gideon remembered. And Merlin's owl, Archimedes.

"Time went backwards for him." She walked backwards toward the hallway. "Would you want to? I mean, to go back in time? Oh! Of course you would, you could stop—"

It wasn't *back* in time, it was back*wards* in time, Gideon thought. So Merlin got younger while everyone else got older, and it made him sad.

"Did you play knights growing up?" Mari asked.

"We had homemade swords."

"You and David?"

"Me and Adam."

His parka, slumped on the floor, looked like it had fallen asleep waiting.

"I don't want to go home," he said, surprising himself.

"Why not?"

"It's just…there are a bunch of people from Brandt staying, and I don't want to talk with anyone right now." But he was, to her. "I mean, I don't want to hang out or talk about Adam." But he was, to her. His phone vibrated. He pulled it out. David. "Hey. I was going to call back after—"

"Gideon, that girl! She's on TV! It's one of those alert things! I just saw it!"

"What are you talking about? What girl?"

"The train! From the train! Turn on the TV!"

"I'm not home."

But Mari heard the last part and crossed back to the TV room, picked up the remote, pushed a series of buttons.

"Oh my god!" Mari said. She turned up the volume. "She was *here*!"

"—website below or local or state police. Again, 1-800-KIDFIND. Now back to our regular program."

Mari pressed mute as *Shark Tank* appeared on the screen, the 800 number scrolling across the bottom. She took her phone out of her pocket.

"Did you see? Did you see it?" David was asking.

"Are you saying that's the kid from the train?"

"Yes! It's her!"

"Is Dad back?"

"He went to bed."

"Well, wake him up and tell him."

"But why was I *on* the train? What'll I tell him?"

Gideon had forgotten about David skipping school. Fuck.

"It doesn't matter. You'll just have to tell the truth. The important thing is the kid."

Mari clicked 1-800-KIDFIND into her phone.

"A recording," she whispered.

"My name is Mari Lewis. I'm calling about the missing little girl. On TV? She was here at our inn—in Farleys' Dock, New York. She left with her grandfather a couple of hours ago. You can reach me at this number."

"Wait, she was here tonight?" Gideon asked.

Mari nodded. "But she was fine. She got picked up. She's really sweet."

"David, she was here," Gideon said. "I mean, at the inn."

"The inn?"

"Yeah. It's gotta be some misunderstanding."

"So I won't wake Dad." Gideon heard the relief in his brother's voice and felt complicit. How many times had he rescued David? How many times did they Not Wake Dad?

"No. Wake him anyway. Because I'm not gonna lie if the police come here. And it's better if he hears all this from you." There was a heavy silence from David's end.

"Why would they come if she's okay?"

"They probably won't. But Mari called them. The KIDFIND number."

Another silence.

"Mari?"

"Yeah, you know the inn people, Charlie and Clare? Their daughter."

"She's there?"

"Yeah." He looked at Mari, watching him.

"Jimmy said she's hot."

Mari looked away, laughing. Gideon blushed.

"I guess I better get Dad."

"I guess you better."

"Okay." Resigned, David hung up. Mari was scrolling on her phone.

She held it up. A photograph.

"That's *her*?" Gideon asked. It all fell together. "But that's—"

He took the phone.

"Gideon, what's wrong?"

"She's Alice Wangera's daughter. Kena."

"Right, Kena, that's her name. Who's Alice Wangera?"

Mari had been in China.

"The person who killed Adam."

Mari put a hand over her mouth. "I thought it was an accident!"

"She was drunk driving, and *she* was there too. Kena. She got hurt too. She was in the hospital in White Plains with Adam before they moved him to the city."

"Where's her mother, then? Kena was with her grandfather."

"Mari, she's in *jail*. Her mom's in *jail*. They were friends. Adam and Kena and her mother."

"Jail?" She looked toward the front door. "That little girl!"

Gideon stared at the picture. Adam's "little sister." Adam loved her.

He was so stupid to have missed it—the pink dress and the decorations in the photograph. He'd been invited to go along. *C'mon, what else are you gonna do? It's Valentine's Day!*

"Her hair smelled like coconut," Mari said softly.

◊

Aren't we cozy, Gideon thought. Like those old Miss Marple movies, cloistered together, waiting to be grilled. His dad and David had arrived to join Mari and her parents and him, the only light the lamp hanging over the long butcher block table, the rest of the cavernous kitchen in deep shadow.

Gideon had shown them the photo of Kena and Adam with the hula hoops. Then they'd watched the entire slideshow on his laptop to the accompaniment of the whooshing of the big dish machine, their feelings too raw to talk.

The clock chimed 10:00, pulling them back to the present.

Clare told about the dog-walking, the museum, the Big Apple Circus and the clown, and Kena became a real little girl. Gideon felt ashamed not to know everything. He was Adam's best friend!

"Can we keep this from Lily?" Clare asked no one in particular.

When David had walked in, Gideon could tell he'd been crying.

But now David peppered Gideon, as if he should know: Where was Kena now? Would she be at Adam's funeral? Do Adam's mom and dad know her? Dad said her mom was in jail! Why hadn't Gideon *told* him?

And finally, "I never should've gotten off! But Jimmy went to look, and she was gone!" Like he was begging for a do-over.

Gideon watched their dad do the dad things, putting his hand on David's head and pulling him over to his shoulder. He watched Charlie put a cup of hot chocolate in front of David. He watched his dad hand him a paper napkin. It's what he'd said to himself—and to Adam, too many times to count—that his dad needed to step up. So why was he feeling more and more angry?

Charlie put down a pot of tea and set out a plate of Christmas cookies, fussing with cups and milk and sugar until Gideon wanted to scream.

*Gideon, you gotta meet her. She's great.*

*Gid, we're going to Ben and Jerry's. Want to meet us for a cone?*

But he'd been "busy" feeding his misery.

They all looked to the door when Rachel rushed in, thinking she was the state police.

"What's this about the train?" she demanded.

Gideon watched David slink down in his chair, wiping his mouth. He watched his mom check herself from going straight to David's side. Instead, she slid in next to Gideon.

"What's this about the train?" she repeated, looking at Abe, who opened his hands to show his innocence. "What's happening?"

Clare responded. "Waiting. They want to interview anyone who saw her. I feel like an idiot."

"*Mom*! Why would you have thought anything?" Mari asked.

"A child that young by herself? I think when I realized she was the daughter of—" Clare pursed her lips together. "My common sense flew out the window."

"But her grandfather picked her up," Mari said.

"I don't get it. If she's with her grandfather, what's the problem?" Rachel asked. They stared at her, faces blank.

"What about the train, David?" Rachel asked.

"She didn't say she was coming for Adam's funeral! Maybe it was *all* lies! Africa! And the elephant!"

"Elephant?" Rachel asked.

"She got cut by a tusk. She *said*. She said *gored*. She has a scar." David touched his forehead.

Could it be true? They fell into silence. The dishwasher whooshed. The clock ticked. Rachel spoke softly to Gideon.

"When do you go back to school?"

"I don't know."

"What does that mean, 'I don't know'? Gideon, I'm just asking." She sighed. "Maybe a semester off would do you good. You liked making videos with those kids at that middle school. Berdick would snap you up in a second if you were around to work with the Academy kids. And David—"

There was a chime from the front of the house. Charlie got up and left the room. David looked stricken.

There were two of them, a burly guy with a buzz cut and a tall blonde woman. They looked too big for the kitchen in their bulky uniforms and alien plastic things hanging off them. They said their names: Officers Murray and Swenson.

"Can I get you anything?" Clare asked.

"Would you like a cup of tea?" Charlie asked.

"May I take your coats?" Clare asked.

May I take your guns? Gideon thought.

The officers sat down with a great deal of creaking and rattling and shuffling. The woman accepted a cup of tea and added milk from a pitcher shaped like a cow. The milk came out of the cow's mouth, and some spilled on the table. She wiped at it with her finger and met Gideon's stare. She smiled slightly. He looked down, flustered.

"My Grammy used to make these," Tom Murray said. "Mexican teacakes." Grammy? Not such a tough guy now, Gideon thought.

"No, they're snowballs, Tom," the woman said.

"We called them teacakes."

"Snowballs to me," she repeated.

"Oh, to *you*," Tom said, as if they had a routine. It was the Madhatter's Tea Party, Gideon thought. Tea-cake Tom held a hand under his chin to catch the powdered sugar when he took a bite. One more and it was gone. He reached for another. "You know, a cup of tea sounds good."

Surreal.

Gideon wished—*ached*—to get up and walk out. And walk and walk and walk. Walk away from them all.

"All right, then," Officer Swenson said, wiping her hands on a napkin. Getting down to business. She placed a photograph on the table. "Just to be sure we're talking about the same child. This is Makena. Oh, and does anyone live south of here?"

Abe put his hand up like they were in school. "I do, why?"

"Snow's started, and they're saying it could be a couple of feet."

They looked up at the windows.

"Stay with us," Rachel said.

"That's probably a good idea," Abe nodded. "Though what I'll wear tomorrow—"

"It's *Quakers*," Gideon mumbled. "Wear pajamas if you want, no one cares." He cut his eyes to Mari. She was looking at the picture of Kena.

Officer Murray turned to David. "Tell us about the train."

David darted his eyes from his mother to his father and back, and gulped. "Okay. She was at the ticket booth in Grand Central, and she said here—Farleys' Dock. And she tried to use money from some other country, but he wouldn't take it. So I bought her ticket."

"You bought her ticket?" Rachel interrupted. "What were you *thinking*?" Abe shook his head to stop her.

"Don't you shake your head at me! I think we'll find he never skipped school on my watch!"

"Mom! Mom. It's my fault. I knew he was skipping and didn't tell Dad," Gideon said.

"You *knew*? And you didn't tell *Dad*? What about telling me? *Mom*?"

"Stop! It's not Gideon's fault!" David turned to Rachel. "*Please*, Mom, can't we talk about this later?"

Rachel was embarrassed. "Of course." She looked at Abe apologetically and turned to Tom Murray. "And I'm the therapist in the family."

"Okay, David, go on," Deidre Swenson said gently.

"We got on the train. She talked about Africa. About an elephant place where—it's not important. She told a story, and she sang. The story had a song, and she sang out loud right on the train."

Gideon heard awe in David's voice.

"Did she say anything about a grandfather?"

"He was meeting her. But I gave her my cell number if she needed to call," David said defensively.

"She had a cellphone?"

Mari spoke up. "Her grandfather called her here."

"When did she arrive?" Tom Murray surveyed them.

"8:00? It was right after Lily—Adam St. John's mother—left." Clare looked around. "I guess we have to tell Lily, but I hate to."

They all began talking at once:

Lily needed to know. She'd want to know.

She should be warned.

Did Lily ever meet Kena?

Is there a dad?

What if they show up at the service?

Someone should stop them; it's not right.

What are you talking about? She didn't cause the accident; she was a victim too. And her grandfather wasn't even there!

"She was there? In the car?" David interrupted.

"Her mother's in jail for it," his mother said.

"She was *there*?" David asked again. He put down a gingerbread boy, its legs gone.

Amputated, Gideon thought.

"David, what was she wearing?" Officer Swenson asked.

"I don't know. Pink stuff. Like they said on TV." He looked at Gideon. "She had on a Brandt sweatshirt like yours from Adam."

Gideon's head snapped back like he'd been slapped.

"She was wearing a T-shirt with a clown at the inn," Mari said. "And a belt with a star."

"From the Big Apple Circus," Clare said. "And pink cowgirl boots with stars on them."

Gideon wanted to throw the snowballs, "no, tea cakes," at them all.

Who fucking cared about pink stars? Teacake Tom left the kitchen. He wanted to get up and follow. He'd keep going, out into the snow, into the street. He could see it. He knew every step of the way, the long walk to Adam's house, the tree branches turning white like a negative. His would be the only footsteps, and they'd disappear behind him as if he were a ghost.

The snow, drifting down in slow motion, would be backlit by the porch light that Lily always turned on when they were going to come home late. He'd open the door, and Homer would come, happy to see him even if he was second best. He could've gone to that circus. He wanted to cover his ears. Couldn't they *see*?

His heart was breaking.

# Chapter 23

## Alice

Tom Murray pulled out his cellphone, walked to the front door of the inn, and looked out. The snow had covered the sidewalk and road and didn't look like it was going to let up. He wouldn't be home to see Sophie's face in the morning. Her first snow. Those stick people needed snowsuits. He pulled out his notebook and punched the number in.

"Hello?"

She sounded breathless, as if she'd been running. "Ms. Washington, this is Tom Murray with the state police. You talked with my partner earlier."

She went right to the point. "Did you find her?"

"Several people saw her. They say she received a call on a cellphone here at the inn in Farleys' Dock. From her grandfather."

"She doesn't have any cellphone *or* grandfather. And as far as *I* know, her only relative in this country lives in Wisconsin and suffers from nastiness. Her mother didn't want Kena anywhere near her."

"Well, Kena was picked up a couple of hours ago by someone who apparently called her on this cellphone that she apparently doesn't have. If we knew whose phone it is, we could trace it. That's what's frustrating me."

"That makes two of us! I've been 'rackin my brain tryin' to figure this thing out. She got wind of that boy's funeral and got it into her head to go. So she snuck off to do it without a by-your-leave."

"Why wouldn't she ask you to bring her?"

"Because she knew I'd say no. And I'm a fool. A *fool*. She loved that boy like a brother, but all I could imagine was his family all upset to see her walk in. Not that poor child!" Walking in with *her*, in that lily white town.

"Well, that 'poor child' is certainly resourceful."

"Has anybody told her mother about Kena bein' at that inn? Poor Alice must be out of her mind. I told that police lady to call her. What's this grandfather look like, anyway?"

"No one saw him; that's the problem."

"What does that mean, no one saw? She's eight years old!"

"I'm very aware of that. We've checked the one motel by the freeway, as well as those in the towns north and south. We're parked at the exits from town now, and anyone exiting will be checked. We'll continue to circle around. If she doesn't appear at the funeral tomorrow, we'll start door to door."

"Why aren't you doin' that 'door to door' now? I ask you!"

"She was clearly fine just two hours ago. This doesn't look like a missing child, more like a misunderstanding, but we'll keep KIDFIND active." He rubbed his face. He'd need to track down a razor somewhere. Maybe here at the inn—didn't inns have toothbrushes and things? "And I'll call and make sure her mother is brought up to date."

Patrice heard him sigh before he hung up. She put the phone back and sighed herself. "Fools!" Sully looked at her from the top of the radiator. "Oh, Sully, what are we gonna do?"

The words came up through the floor from the apartment below.

"—missing since—"

She put her hand on the banister and went slowly up the stairs. She peeked into the boys' room. She shook her head. Jackie was sleeping in the top bunk with Peter. Peter would be sorry if Jackie wet the bed. She tiptoed to the girls' room. She sat on Kena's bed, swung her legs up, and put her head on the pillow. She folded her hands and closed her eyes. She prayed.

She waited. And waited some more.

Then she swung her feet to the floor and walked out of the room, purpose in her step. She stepped into her shoes at the back door, pushing Sully away, opened it, and went down the steps and under the porch. She knocked, then knocked again. The TV volume went down. She wrapped her arms around herself. And the door opened.

"Mr. Steckle, I'm glad you're home tonight. I have a family emergency, and I'm hoping I can borrow your truck."

He frowned. He pursed his lips. He nodded. "I saw on the TV. You'll have to gas it up." He scratched his chin. "The tires are just all-season and the back ones are working on being bald. They're saying a foot overnight."

"I'll take it slow. I'll be leaving when my sister comes in the morning, and maybe the plows will have been out."

"I'll get the keys."

When she walked out from under the tiny porch, something struck her cheek. She lifted her face. Snow. Just in time for vacation. The kids would go crazy in the morning.

◊

"Wangera! It's your kid!"

The babble of excited voices drowned out the announcer until Alice got close, when everyone became silent. All eyes went to her, then swiveled back to the screen, which was filled with Kena's old school picture.

"…wearing a pink jacket, carrying a pink backpack."

"She sure likes pink!"

"Shut *up*, V!"

"…scar above her right eye."

The screen switched to a man behind a desk.

"Again, eight-year-old Makena Wangera is missing from her home in Queens, New York. The number to call is 1-800-KIDFIND, or your local police." Kena's photograph popped up in the corner with the number. "Now back to our regular programming."

Not one person complained while Alice held the remote and made the rounds of the channels over and over, trying to shut out the vision of Kena in dark alleys and dark abandoned buildings. The trunks of cars. All of the New York stations were showing Kena's picture, and the entire unit sat riveted to the television in solidarity, even V. No one told anyone to get her ass out of the way. If the chairs weren't fastened down, they would've huddled around Alice. As it was, everyone tilted her way whenever Kena appeared.

Kena's face began to be followed by storm warnings. Up to a foot or more of snow, and more tomorrow afternoon. Alice's fear coated the roads in ice.

"Wangera!"

The CO pointed to the door.

Hands patted Alice as she got up on shaky legs, like a player being given strength by her teammates. Lieutenant Tomas was on the other side of the door. Her stomach roiled. Then she looked at his face, really looked. Whatever he had, it wasn't worse.

"Kena was seen in a town called Farleys' Dock. And she was fine."

Alice sagged, and he grabbed her arm. Of course! Stupid, stupid! So stupid! Adam's town. What was *wrong* with her?

"She was at an inn where Adam St. John's family and friends were gathered. The funeral's tomorrow."

Oh, baby.

"She went there on the train with a boy, and her grandfather picked her up."

Toby?

"The boy's name is…" He checked a piece of paper. "David Wainwright?" Bewildered, Alice shook her head.

"And her grandfather? They need his name and address and phone number. Tom Murray is fairly ticked off that you withheld the information. From her foster mother as well, it appears." He tapped his pen on his hand like a ruler about to come down on her head.

"But I didn't! She doesn't *have* a grandfather! Who's this boy? How old is he?"

"They're talking to him now. He's a teenager, I think. But he's not with her anymore. It was *his* father who called the state police. Oh, another thing, they say she has a cellphone. Do you have that number?"

A cellphone? Her heart sank. The more he said, the more it sounded like some other little girl. Except for Farleys' Dock.

Tomas's phone buzzed. Carla looked up from the magazine she wasn't reading, and her eyes met Alice's.

"Lieutenant Tomas here." Alice thought she heard Patrice's voice.

"Yes, I got your messages. No, no word yet. I just told her, she's right here. You can talk to her yourself." He handed the phone to Alice.

"Patrice? They saw her!"

"I heard too," Patrice responded. "Alice, I've decided. I'm goin' up there. Rosie's comin' in the morning, and I'll head up there first thing. If they don't find her before, I'm betting she'll be at that funeral, and I aim to bring her home myself so she doesn't have to ride in any po-lice car."

"But where *is* she?! They said she has a grandfather! Maybe it's not her."

"Alice, the description fits her exactly, except for some boots, and don't I know where they came from: two dollars at the Goodwill! They saw her picture, these people."

These people. Adam's people. Were they kind to her? Oh, Kena.

"Is it snowing?"

"It's started. But I'll get there. My neighbor, it's his truck, a big old heavy thing. I'll be fine."

What else, what else? Alice clutched the phone, loathe to give it back.

"Patrice, should she get to *go* to the funeral? I mean, she loved Adam, and he loved her, but Adam's parents wouldn't like—oh, what's *right*? When you get there, if she's at the funeral…"

Lieutenant Tomas took the phone.

"Ms. Washington, do I understand that you plan to go to Farleys' Dock?"

"Yes, first thing in the morning."

"You understand that you can't take Makena without clearance from the state police, right?" Even Carla at the desk could hear Patrice's response.

"Whose child do you think she is! I'll do what's right for *her*, not any PO-lice!"

"Just don't head back to Queens without permission."

"What about the other way around? Are they allowed to bring her back without *my* permission? My *clearance*?"

He sighed. "Do you need another minute with Ms. Wangera?"

"That would be a kindness, thank you."

"Patrice?"

"About the funeral, I guess we can sit in the back and just slip out after, if she's that determined. Alice, it's a tiny little place, just a dot. I looked it up. And I talked to that state policeman, and he's there with a whole bunch of folks who know every inch of it. So don't you worry."

Of course, they'd both be awake all night worrying.

"Oh, God! Okay. Okay. What would we do without you?"

"God's gift, that's me. I blame myself. But that's water over the bridge. Of course later, we'll have to come up with something, but offhand I can't think of any 'logical consequence.' I'm just tryin' to figure how to act when I get there, I guess. The two of us are gonna stand out, I expect; I don't suppose there's many Black people there. You have anybody to hang out with tonight, honey?"

Alice turned her back on Tomas. "I'll be okay." She wiped her cheeks.

Patrice could barely hear her. "You raised a strong little girl. I'll bring her back tomorrow, and we'll come see you Sunday, like always."

Alice handed the phone back to Tomas. He put his hand on her shoulder for a second, and she let out a cry. Then she straightened up and went to the door.

She was back just in time for lockdown.

◊

*Kena pressed into the damp red earth between the prickly rows of tea and Nia squished in next to her. The leaves stopped rustling and the birds grew silent. They heard footsteps running, smack, smack, and Kena pulled Nia close. She put her fingers to her lips, shhh. The footfalls stopped. Then started, slow and sneaky. Kena could hear Wanoi's breathing, as distinctive as her voice. She put her hand over her mouth not to giggle. Nia, just five, giggled anyway, and Wanoi called out, "I hear you, Nia!"*

*Kena squeezed Nia's fingers. Sasa! Now! They leapt up and took off in opposite directions. Kena's rubber boots slapped, slapped, slapped as she ran. Shoots scratched her knees. She slipped and fell, holding Lemmy high, away from the mud, laughing. Wanoi called out, "Nia's It!" The field was suddenly shadowed. Kena looked up at glowing yellow eyes. The shadow swooped and bit her hand and snatched Lemmy. Mama!*

*She was lying in Mugumo's cool shade with her bare feet sticking out into the hot sun. Mugumo rustled, and she made herself be still. It might be a grouchy spirit woken from his nap.*

*"Kena!" It was Adam's voice, happy.*

*She looked up. He was straddling a branch, holding a cat against his Big Apple T-shirt. Was it Too? There was a chameleon on the clown's face. Adam plucked it off and put it on a leaf. The chameleon turned green. The ground trembled.*

*The trembling traveled up the trunk, and Mugumo began to shake. Run! Run! She ran out into moonlight. The shadow loomed over her. Lemmy's long tail swung across the ground, and she jumped and grabbed him. She held him tight against her chest. She looked back to the tree but it was gone, leaving behind a deep and dark hole. It was so wide she couldn't see the other side. Where was Adam? Lemmy struggled against her. He would fall into the hole!*

*Deep inside of it, somebody was crying, A red light swept across the hole, blinking—off, on, off, on—*

Kena woke up, gasping, squeezing Wanjiru.

"Meowr!" The cat leapt away. A red light pulsed behind the shaded window. Then it was gone. Her cheeks were wet.

Wanjiru's eyes glowed from under the table. She pressed her hand to her mouth and tasted blood.

*Kena.*

It was Maitu, her birth mother, who spoke.

*I'm here, Kena. Go to sleep now.*

So she did.

# Chapter 24

## Lily

Lily was in Adam's bed, spinning everything she had to do like socks in a dryer. No wonder so many went missing; they were escapees from the relentless cycle. But she couldn't escape.

It was like the night before Adam went to college, when she'd spent the night folding his brand-new laundered towels and sheets over and over and over in her head, trying to fit them into his brand-new laundry bag with the comforter her mother had made for him. She'd finally crept out at dawn and saw that Adam had packed everything himself.

She dropped into a restless sleep; her spinning became a dance of napkins: the picnic checks and Christmas trees and sunflowers. A prickly pear and Christmas cactus entered in, then brownies marching on cartoon feet like at the drive-in movie, blondies right behind. Where was her Tender Shepherd vase? *Where?*

No Time! On to the meeting house, sweeping and sweeping and sweeping like the sorcerer's apprentice. Chairs! Chairs in a circle that didn't end, a mobius strip of chairs and more chairs and more. Dining room chairs, a rocker, a highchair followed by a red Adirondack chair. And the tree! Clothespin angels danced around it like the second line at a funeral in New Orleans. Stars hovered in the air, shimmying. Words! She needed words!

*Now I lay me down to sleep, amazing grace how sweet the sound, love of my life I am crying, I am not dying, I am dancing, sometime at evening when the tide is low…*

She spun around and around, faster and faster. Sticky notes flew off her body. Christmas lists, birthday lists, grocery lists. To-do lists. Yesterdays and tomorrows, maybes and forevers, and never-agains.

Was this what happened to Adam, spinning, spinning around and around, trapped in his mind?

Her mind skittered away from the horror and began to paw through the kitchen junk drawer for his postcard from Belize. Too late, too late, too late! She fell into a new dream.

*She was going through the house looking for Adam, playing hide and seek—pretending, knowing he was under the skirt of the big red chair.*

*Where is Adam? Where is that boy? Is he behind the door? Is he behind the couch? Is he under the table?*

*Adam laughing so he'd be found.*

*Where is that boy? Is he under the chair?*

She shot out of the dream before she could lift him up. Before she could hold him. Waves of pain raked her skin like nails of fire. She lay in Adam's bed, her nightshirt soaked with sweat, remembering. The time Adam swallowed his tooth and examined his poop—"scat"— every day until it emerged. The time he'd kept a garden snake in his drawer and fed it for days before she discovered it while putting the laundry away. The time he fell off Gideon's bike on his head and "saw stars, Mom! For real!"

The time he begged her, *begged* her, for them not to get the divorce.

The time, maybe the first time, when he hugged Khai, both of them in puffy jackets and fat gloves, the sound of their padded hands thumping. Thump, thump. Thump. Then parting and not looking, as if it were no big deal.

Reading the poem at her mother's funeral, and his voice cracked, and she longed for her mom to see him in his first ever suit.

"I shall have peacefully furled my sail

In moorings sheltered from storm and gale

And greet family and friends who have gone before

Oe'r the unknown sea, to the unknown shore."

She tried to picture her mother holding her arms out to Adam on the "unknown shore," but all she saw was Max sailing to the land where the wild things are.

Where is he? Does he feel? Is he wanting to come home?

I wasn't there! *Adam! I'm sorry!*

Oh, *why* did I say yes to a Quaker service?

If I move my body, my head will have to go along.

She rolled over and opened her eyes. The light was funny. She pulled her shucked-off socks out from under the covers, put them on, and went to the window. She pushed back the curtain. The sun must be rising somewhere, but here the world was swirling snow.

"Shit." She shuffled into the hall. She smelled coffee. It had to be either Clare letting herself in or Lois. Bernie would never.

She closed the bathroom door as quietly as she could. The hair on her chin was back. Her witch's whisker. She squinted, then tugged. How could one little hair hurt so much? She took her sweatpants off the hook and pulled them on. The phrase "girding her loins" popped into her mind. Not very Quaker-like.

Homer greeted her at the bottom of the stairs.

"Did you make coffee?" she whispered. His head was damp. Had he been drinking from the toilet again? He'd hate this day. She'd have to shut him in upstairs or he'd exhaust himself going to the front door for each arrival, just in case it was Adam.

"Oh, sweetie." She went to the front door and looked out.

The snowflakes were fat and slow. It would be a snow day if it was a school day; it would be a beautiful snowfall if Adam were alive to share it. She wiped her cheeks with the back of her hand. She had to do better than this.

Coffee. Cinnamon?

Homer pushed around her, his tail whacking the doorframe.

"Enoch?"

He stood up, sliding the chair back from the table. "It's me. I'm sorry, I just—"

"No. No!" She leaned over the table to kiss his cheek. It was cold. His hair was wet.

"I stopped and got those Cinnabons we used to get. I followed a couple of plows. The hardest part was right here. I'm parked on the road, but it's one lane, so I need to get the car into our driveway."

*Our* driveway.

"We'll need a place for cars later too. I'll call Hank. Oh, and I made Homer go out."

"I use McCauley's now. Hank retired. His heart."

"He'd hate that." Their eyes met. There were worse things.

She took her mug out of the dish rack. Snow was mounded on the neglected bird feeder outside the window. "What if people can't make it?"

"Well, there's not a thing we can do about it. They will or they won't."

She felt a stab of irritation. But he was right, unless they postponed. She'd never heard of a postponed funeral, but it must happen sometimes. She poured herself coffee and sat down across from him. She tore off a piece of his cinnamon bun, but the second she tasted it her throat closed against its sweetness. She got up and surreptitiously dropped it in the sink. She handed Enoch a dish towel.

"Here." He looked at it as if he'd never seen one before.

"For your hair."

"Oh." He took it, ducked his head into it, and rubbed with both hands. *Like Adam.* And if it were Adam rubbing his head, she'd be thinking, *like his dad.*

"I slept some," Enoch said, "but then I just lay there thinking. It was torture. Then I wondered how you were doing, were you doing the same thing?" He bunched the towel on the table and she picked it up and hung it over the back of the other chair. "And I just ended up here. I just needed to…I don't know, sit here in the kitchen. See you sitting in the kitchen."

They were sitting in the same places they'd always sat, she thought. This room was always cozy in a snowstorm. Listening to the school closings on the radio, waiting for hers, then waiting for Adam to wake up and discover it was a snow day. She fumbled away from the memory.

"Would it be okay if I looked through the Christmas stuff for an ornament?"

Christmas. There would be Christmas.

He took a bite of the Cinnabon. How could he be *eating*? He took the towel and wiped his mouth.

"I can't believe you can eat that!"

"What?" He draped the towel back on the chair.

It was lopsided. She moved to straighten it out. "You never *look!*"

"Lily," Enoch said softly. "Stop." She stopped.

There would be Yule, and then Christmas. *Who said remembering the future that wouldn't happen is the greatest suffering?*

"Lily, can you pre-forgive me, just for today? I think I'll need extra latitude."

She tossed the towel to the floor as a peace offering. "Should we put the star on top of the tree?" she asked.

"It'll bend over like Charlie Brown's tree. Seems about right."

She left the room and came back in a minute with the box of Christmas ornaments and set it on the table. He stood up.

"Enoch, your pants are soaked!"

"Yeah, the snow's pretty deep."

"You should go change."

"Into what?"

She looked up at the ceiling.

"I can't."

"Well, go put on my robe—it's in the bathroom—and I'll stick your pants in the dryer." As Enoch sidled around the table, he bumped the corner of the box. He tried to catch it as it fell to the floor. They watched as a few ornaments spilled out. Homer got up and shuffled through the door to the dining room. They knelt on the floor.

Enoch reached for the square gold box. Yellowed scotch tape curled away from the lid. He pried it off and folded back the tissue paper. A point of the star broke away as he lifted it out. He placed the star back in its nest, tucked the tissue paper around it, stood up, and walked to the window.

"I know…I know a lot of the time it was like we were just sitting by his bed waiting, waiting for someone…waiting until—A blessing. That's what they're saying. A blessing. Oh, God, Lily, I thought it myself. But now…now…" He put his hands on the edge of the sink and began to sob. "At least then I could touch him."

She put her arms around him from behind. He turned and put his arms around her, the wounded star at their feet.

# Chapter 25

## Gideon

By the time Gideon got to the highway, the cold radiating from his glasses had taken over like a horrible toothache until, finally, he grabbed them and stuffed them into his pocket. The snow was so thick that he couldn't see more than a few feet ahead anyway. A car suddenly loomed, passing him, a red light glowing on its roof. He jumped away, into deep snow. State police? Still searching?

The shortcut he and Adam took through the woods from town was a short way across the field. He rejected it a second after he thought of it. Snow began to coat his cheeks and eyelashes. Like the shot in *Dr. Zhivago*, that sudden close-up of someone, eyes seemingly frozen shut, appearing out of the storm like a snow zombie. He pictured the shot of himself from overhead, his dark figure moving through a blurry scene, the hissing snow the soundtrack.

The meeting house emerged like a developing photograph. It might have looked the same 100 years ago, the old one-room schoolhouse framed by snow-bent trees, sitting back from the road narrowed to one lane by snowbanks. The tallest one, near the door, was perfect for king-of-the-hill. Adam had ruled the big snowbank in front of the co-op when they were growing up.

Someone had shoveled a path to the door to the schoolhouse, and when Gideon entered he saw that the chairs were already arranged in circles. A potbelly stove sat in the outermost circle like a fat little man, steam rising from a kettle like he was smoking a pipe. The only other furniture was a small table covered with a motley assortment of cups and an old upright piano. The back door opened with a kick. His dad and David came in stamping their feet, their outstretched arms piled with wood. David's good pants were sprinkled with woodchips.

"Gideon! Good morning! God, look at you! Did you *walk*?"

It was his mom's voice. She was coming out of the bathroom waving her hands in the air. He didn't bother to remind her that they'd taken both cars. Where *were* the cars?

He jumped at the sound of the wood rattling into the box. He pushed his hood back and took his glasses out of his pocket, stuffing his gloves into it.

"That should be enough," Abe said. "I hope so, because the rest is still buried."

"At least it was already warm when we got here," his mother said, and put her hand on Abe's arm. Gideon looked away. As if a Service of blah blah blah Whatever wasn't enough, his parents were making nice. He walked over to the stove. He stretched his hands out over it.

"I'll try to get it pumped up." Abe rubbed his hands together.

"You don't know a thing about woodstoves," Rachel said.

"It's chemistry. And mechanics. People have been combusting wood forever. I should be able to figure it out," Abe said, and leaned over to investigate.

Rachel raised an eyebrow. "We need to call and ask Charlie or Clare to bring guest soap and hand towels," she said. "Maybe a space heater."

Gideon unzipped his parka but left it on. He pulled out a shirt-tail and wiped his glasses. "You must have been here at the crack of dawn. Where are the cars?"

"Your dad was. The chairs went fast. The Brandt kids took the cars and went for coffee at the co-op. I guess you didn't come across them stuck on the way."

"Who'd you let drive in this?"

"I gave my keys to that boy from Vermont. I don't know who drove your father's."

"All I saw was a state police car."

"I don't think they found her yet." There was something hopeful in the way David said it.

"Well, I hope they do soon. Think of Lily! Oh, Enoch called. He's there. At Lily's. Khai's bringing the tree," Rachel said. "I wouldn't mind some coffee myself, although that might make it seem even more like an AA meeting. When I walked in and saw the chairs in a circle, I almost sat down and said the Serenity Prayer. I hope I don't say Hi so and so,' if someone stands up and says their name."

David gave Gideon a pleading look. He hated it when their mom brought up her alcoholism.

"Should I turn the piano so people can see if someone plays?" Gideon asked.

"Is music allowed?" Rachel asked. Gideon pressed middle C.

"Anything's allowed, even 'The Serenity Prayer.'"

"Ha ha. Sure, turn it. We could take some of the pine from the windowsills for on top. I mean…do you think the Quakers would mind? Are the lights around the windows for Christmas, do you know? Do they *do* Christmas?"

"Fuck!" Abe said. They turned to see him grimacing with a hand tucked between his legs. He waved them away with his other hand. "It's nothing!"

The St. Johns did do Christmas, Gideon thought. First Yule, then Christmas. How would Lily bear it this year? He pushed against the piano. "David, give me a hand." They leaned hard and swiveled the piano around. Gideon scraped a chair over and sat down. He played a couple of scales.

"Clare gave me some of those tiny candles…what-cha-ma-call-its…" Rachel dug in her big canvas bag and pulled out two big Ziploc bags. She handed one to David. David opened it and sniffed.

"Strawberry. Notives."

"Votives!" Abe called out.

"David, what did you *do* when you skipped school?" Rachel asked.

It was her I-don't-need-to-know-I'm-just-wondering voice that meant the opposite. David dumped the votives and small glass cups onto a chair. A cup slid into the candles, bowling several to the floor. He got down and scrabbled for them.

"Oh, David, your pants!"

"It's okay, Mom."

Rachel rolled her eyes over his head to Abe. Abe looked at his own pants. He shifted from kneeling to squatting. The notes of "Sweet Baby James" rose from the piano.

"What about these?" Rachel cradled the other bag as if its contents were fragile. "I don't know what Lily wants us to do with them."

"Call and ask," Abe said.

"I can't."

"I have my cellphone."

"No, it's not that." Rachel hesitated. "I'd feel like I was lying."

"About what?" Abe asked.

"That little girl. I don't want Lily to know and worry."

"But if Kena comes," David said, hope in his voice, "won't she see her?"

"Well, let's hope she doesn't," Rachel said. "Come."

Gideon hunched his shoulders. He moved into "Hey Jude." David brought four candles to the piano and spaced them along the top.

"But David, I just wonder *why*. Did you have a reason to skip?" Rachel persisted. "Is there anything going on at school?"

Gideon interrupted, pointing to the Ziploc bag she was holding against her dress. "What're those?"

Rachel sighed and pulled a card out of the bag. "I don't know where to put them." She pointed. "David, could you move those cups somewhere?"

Abe spun a knob. "I think I've licked it! See? There are two means for controlling the burn. This, and the damper."

Gideon walked over and took the card. It was 5 x 8, black and white. *Meeting for Worship in Thanksgiving for the Grace of God as Shown in the Life of Adam St. John.*

Two verses of "For the Beauty of the Earth."

Gideon felt stomach punched. They'd decided to have a song after all. And they hadn't asked him to play, or what Adam might like. Or anything.

He slapped down the hurt. Fuck them.

He turned the card over. It was the picture of Adam and Homer where Adam was missing a tooth. It was a picture of joy. Like the hula hoop one.

He felt like he was tripping, spinning. Like a tornado had been brewing and now it was here and he was in its funnel—he *was* the funnel. He didn't have anything to hang onto. He turned away toward the wall.

*God!*

He'd thought *fuck* them. Lily. And Enoch and Khai. *Lily*. What was *wrong* with him? He heard his mom say, "How could I not *know*? I mean, what about the *school*?"

He heard his little brother say, "It was only at Dad's that I skipped."

He turned toward the door.

He turned toward the wall.

He turned toward the door. He turned in a circle like Homer, except he didn't have a duck or anything else to hold on to.

"I guess Clare can bring a basket for the cards along with the soap and towels," Rachel said. "Where should the tree go?"

"How about here?" David said. He stood in the center of the chair circle with his arms out, cups dangling from his fingers.

"'O Tannenbaum!'" Abe sang out.

"How tall is it?" David asked.

"Maybe four feet?" Rachel held her hand out. David got down on his knees.

"David, your pants!"

David scrambled to his feet. A cup fell to the floor, and the handle broke off.

"David!"

Gideon spun around. "Mom, give it a *rest*! *Fuck*!"

He fled to the piano. He slammed his hands down on the keyboard, freezing his family in place. Oh God, oh God, oh *God*! Monsters burned down his arms to the tips of his fingers and flew over the keys. Their screaming voices leapt up to the roof. Sorrows and joys that had been felt and shared for 200 years gathered them in.

*Oh God, oh God. Oh God!*

He'd known some of the monsters a long, long time. There was the huge jagged one that was his human father. There was the one who cowered behind anger that was fear. And there was the worst one, the one that he'd been feeding until it had grown tentacles and was starting on claws. The monster that was Alice Wangera. Who was Kena's mother. Her *mother*.

Mommy. Mama.

And Adam's friend. Alice. A real person.

The door burst open with a blast of cold.

"Here's the tree! Where do you want it?"

Khai knew right away, though, that he'd walked in on something, a strange tableau: David holding a cup and Rachel hugging a bag, both looking at Abe standing by the piano, cradling Gideon's head against his chest.

# Chapter 26

## Kena

Molly Mulligan walked gingerly down the center of the white street, attentive to her slippery boots. Which were all show. Her serviceable old Mucks were cozy at the library, doing her no good at all. But still, it was wonderful, like Jack Frost had painted the town overnight. When she got to the library, she'd put out snow books: *Snowflake Bentley. The Snowy Day* and *Snow Lion,* and her favorite, *The Snowman,* by Raymond Briggs.

The county had been around to plow and would be again, but she worried about the road to the meeting house. She'd seen a state police car, though, so they must be aware of the need for people to get to the service.

Approaching the library, she studied her own need: how to get to the door. Finally, she used her bookbag to sweep away the top foot or so. Then again, and she minced along like a tightrope walker. She dug the key out from its hiding place, opened the door, and swung the canvas bag inside.

"Eowr!" Something streaked past her. She yelped and flailed and grabbed the doorframe, one foot in and one foot out, her long skirt keeping her from doing the splits. She must be quite a sight. If anyone was looking. Which no one was. Get a grip, Molly. Realizing she *had* gotten a grip, she laughed out loud.

Her fancy boots went on the mat next to the Mucks.

"Now, you all get along."

She shook out her coat and hung it up. She hitched up her skirt and pulled up her tights. Her slippers and mended books had spilled out on the floor. It was an effort to kneel down. She began to put them in order. What had that *been?* "It screeched like a banshee" popped into her head. A banshee was something from folklore that warned of a death.

But the death had already happened.

"Hi."

Startled, Molly jerked, and the books slid every which way again. The little girl from the day before was in the doorway, covered in snow as if she'd rolled in it, a pink backpack at her feet. She held a cat, its hind feet pumping. It pushed off and ran into the children's room and under the table.

Not a banshee, then.

"Good morning," Molly finally replied. She began to rise, and the child rushed over and held out her hand. What was her name? Gladness, Gladys, happy one. MacKenzie? Makena!

"I know I'm too early. I mean, you're not really open."

"No, no. It's fine."

Makena didn't waste any time. She put her boots next to Molly's and hung her jacket up. Snow plopped into one of Molly's Mucks.

"Was that cat in here?" Molly wondered.

"Isn't she your cat?"

"My cat? My cat's at home. His name is Jelly. From *The Song of the Jellicles* by T.S. Eliot. Jellicle cats. They *caterwaul.*"

Kena was captivated by the words, and by Molly. Who was wearing a *red* skirt. And a blue sweater with snowflakes. No black anywhere.

"What's cater—"

"Caterwauling. Howling."

Kena nodded. She knew that sound from the back fence at Patrice's.

"That's a beautiful dress," Molly said. "Look at those flower buttons! Someone went to a lot of trouble to make it special." It was an invitation, but Kena didn't know who went to a lot of trouble.

"Maybe I can help you until…" She couldn't remember the words for Adam's funeral. "I spend a lot of time at libraries."

"I'd welcome your help." Molly pointed to a box with wheels. "You could put those in the proper bins. The letters on the front are—"

"Author letters! I know all about them!"

Molly turned on the light, and the kids' room sprang into color, the snow outside making it cozy. Kena went to work. L. Lobel. It was the *Frog and Toad* book where Frog reads poems to his seeds.

"There you go," she said, tucking it into the L bin with her good hand. She'd forgotten to put the salve on her hand until that morning. She'd put on four Band-Aids, criss-crossed, but they were already peeling at the ends.

She picked up the next book: *Cannonball Simp*.

It was like finding old friends.

"I found a clue!" Molly called out. "Come see!" She pointed to a paw print on her desk. "The Mystery of the Cat's Paw Print," she said dramatically.

Kena returned to her work and peered around. Juri was no longer under the table. When she pushed the emptied box back into the hall, Molly pointed to a book on her desk.

"T.S. Eliot. Jellicle is in there," Molly said. There were cats wearing hats on the cover. Kena opened the book. It was poems.

"I should find the cat."

"He'll come out eventually."

*She*, Kena wanted to say. But she went back to the children's room and sank down on a pillow. "The Song of the Jellicles" was on page 25. There were words she'd never heard of. There was *roly-poly*. There was *terpsichorean*. One time a reviewer had said her mother shouldn't have made up a word, and her mother said, "Where does he think words came from, God?" Even though Calliope was the Greek goddess of poetry.

A card fell out from the back of the book. It had names in a row with numbers next to them. One of them was *St. John*. She walked out to the desk.

"Did you find the cat?" Molly asked. Kena held the card out.

"Oh! I like to keep the pocket cards in the really old books, kind of like a memento," Molly said.

Kena tugged on her hair. "It's Adam's name."

Molly looked. "Oh! That's Adam's mother, Lily. She took out poetry to read to him, especially about animals. Let's see the date. Adam must have been about six or seven. Oh, my." She put her hand over her heart.

Kena returned to the children's room, picked up the book, and slipped the card into the pocket, then out, then in. Did Adam sit on her lap? Lily.

She'd have to give Adam's book back today. And she needed an ornament. When Toby called that morning, he'd said she should Lay Low because she was a Missing Child on TV. "If the cops see you, you'll never get to that funeral."

A missing child. The whole time getting dressed and taking her pills and hiding around the corner in the cold and slipping and falling into the snow, she hadn't cried. Toby had been excited, like being missing was fun. But he wasn't missing. She went to the farthest corner with her back to the door to get herself under control.

"Makena?"

The librarian came up behind her, smoothed her hand across Kena's hair, and rested it on her forehead the way her mother did. Kena stiffened. Then she turned and pressed the top of her head into Molly's stomach, holding the book against her chest. They both felt it, the cat's warm body winding around their legs.

Molly held out a handkerchief, white with blue flowers. "Blow. That's what it's for." It was soggy when she finished, but Molly held out her hand for it anyway.

"No, it has germs. You should put it in a baggie."

"Don't be silly."

Kena hesitated. They were just starting to be friends. "You need to put it in a baggie. Please."

The librarian left the room and returned with a baggie over her hand. She scooped up the handkerchief and turned the baggie around it, the way Adam picked up dog poop when they walked the dogs at the humane society.

Kena gave her the Jellicle book too and scooped Wanjiru up. "We could call her Wanjiru. Juri could be her nickname. Like Jelly."

"Wanjiru? There's a Mungojerrie—"

"It's from Kenya."

"It can be her library name until I find the owner," Molly said. "It's a girl?"

Kena tried to show her, but the cat jumped down. "I don't have an ornament." She pulled on her hair. She stopped when she saw Molly watching. Or was she looking at her scar?

"An ornament?"

"For the tree," Kena said.

"What tree?"

"I'll show you."

Kena returned with the paper Toby had printed out and read it out loud. "Those attending the service are invited to bring an ornament to hang on a live pine tree that will be planted at the library in the spring."

At *her* library? Molly took the paper. "See? Do you know where I can get one?" Kena was asking.

Why hadn't they asked her, Molly wondered. Oh, what did it *matter*? It was a good idea. But was it some other library? At Brandt? She felt jealous of that other library, wherever it was, as if hers were just a country cousin.

Oh, get a grip!

But Adam loved it here. It should be *here*.

"What are *you* going to do?" Kena asked. "For the ornament."

Molly handed the paper back. She knew *just* what to do. Returning with a cardboard box, she said, "Handmade ornaments are the best, in my opinion."

Kena ducked her head into the box. It was a treasure trove. There were small containers of sequins and buttons and beads. There were popsicle sticks, clothespins, and balls of yarn. There were pipe cleaners and every kind of paper scrap. There was tissue paper. There was glitter glue. She could make a clothespin angel. Or a glitter star. Then she knew.

Kena found two green pipe cleaners and sorted through the tissue paper. She began to fold. Molly took a piece of shiny gold paper, and her hands got busy too.

"What happened to your hand? I have gauze if you want me to wrap it." She held up a golden bird. "It's a phoenix."

Kena picked up the scissors. "Feenicks?"

"Do you know about myths?"

"*Lots* of them. *Wanjiru* is in a myth." Kena put down her scissors, defeated; her circles were ragged looking, like someone had chewed on them.

A humming filled the room, making the windows shake. Kena

grabbed Molly's sleeve.

"It's Charlie, from the inn. He does our walk."

"Is he Mari's father?" Kena remembered the man with the toilet paper.

"You met Mari? She must be home from China. Yes, Charlie and Clare are her parents. She used to come here almost every week to help with Saturday storytime."

"Is there storytime today?"

"No."

"Because of Adam?"

Molly nodded.

"Do you know everybody?"

"Now I know you too. Anyway, the myth is that the phoenix lives for a very long time, even up to a thousand years. Then it bursts into flames and burns itself into ashes. And a young phoenix rises out of those ashes."

"But its mother burned! Who takes care of it?"

"I never thought about that." Molly picked up Kena's scissors, picked up Kena's circles, and trimmed them, little pieces falling like confetti.

"Does it cry for its mother?"

Molly frowned. Then her face cleared. "It's said that the phoenix's cry is a beautiful song, so it must be okay."

"Other birds come when they hear the baby," Kena declared. "The Sparrow Lark and the Golden Weaver and," she watched Molly's face, "the Scaly Babbler."

"Scaly Babbler! I'd love to meet that one!" Molly laughed.

Kena began to thread her circles onto a green pipe cleaner, alternating the pink and orange ones. She bent the pipe cleaner at the end to keep them in place. "Did you go to a funeral before? I guess you did a lot because you're old."

"I suppose I have."

"I went to a funeral. I didn't remember the person, but they said she helped me get born. She was in a long skinny box and people carried it behind a house and there was a big hole in the ground. My mother got worried I'd fall in." Kena rolled her eyes. "Lots of people talked, telling her whole life. She helped lots of babies get born, not just me. Then everyone helped put the dirt in, even me. There was a bucket of flowers and we made a garden on top. It was really pretty."

"You planted a garden on top of her?"

"We just stuck them in."

"That's very moving, picked flowers standing up on a grave instead of lying on their sides. Ephemeral," Molly said.

"What's effemeril?"

"Fleeting…short-lived."

"The lady wasn't short-lived. She was really old. I know a myth too, if you want." Molly nodded.

"One-day Ngai…that's like God…Ngai decided he wanted a lot more people on the land." She fluffed her flower. "Ngai said," Kena made her voice low, "'Chameleon! Go and tell everybody to have more babies and their children will never die!' Chameleon waited to see if there was more to Ngai's message. She was a slow animal and didn't like to have to come back. Ngai shouted, 'SASA!' That means now. After changing color from fright and changing back again, Chameleon set off."

Kena twirled her flower. "I saw chameleons, they're hard to see, but we caught one, me and Nia, a pygmy one. Do you know what that means? Not a pig."

"A smaller version?"

"Yes. But Wanoi made us let him go." Kena put the flower down. "Chameleon walked *very* slowly. It took her such a long time that a *lot* of babies got born like Ngai wanted. When Chameleon finally got to the people and was beginning to say her message," Kena made her voice squeaky, "I wa-was-to-told-to-to-tell-tell," She checked to see if Molly was smiling. "An owl came flying down and copied Chameleon, making fun of her, or maybe just being itself. Whatever the reason, the damage was done. Chameleon got so embarrassed, she changed colors many times and slunk away. She never said the whole message, so people died like always and didn't get to live forever. But Ngai said they could come back and visit," Kena concluded. "And sometimes they're an animal."

"You mean, reincarnated?"

"I don't know that word."

"It means…it's someone returning to have another life. Except I don't think they remember the last one."

"But if you don't remember—" Kena frowned. "It's not that anyway, because they *do* remember, they just *pretend* to be something else. And they can visit their alive relatives."

"Who would you like to visit you?"

"My birth mother, and Adam." Kena studied Molly's face. "Do you think he will? He will," Kena said. But her eyes held Molly's like a question.

Molly understood why people told children there was a heaven, but she'd never been tempted herself. Until now.

"Do you think it hurts to die?" Kena added.

Oh, dear. "I…I like to think that it feels wonderful. And perfectly right, like being born into another brand new world. Or going back to where we came from, like going home. And why not think that? Since we don't know one way or the other." Molly flew her phoenix to Kena's flower. "Do you want to make an ornament for your grandfather to bring?"

Kena turned and began to pack up the box. "Actually…*actually*, he's not feeling good, so I'm going by myself." She began to scoop up the tissue scraps and peeked at Molly. "Maybe I can go with *you*." Molly sat back on her heels, confused. What kind of person would let a little girl go to the funeral of her friend alone!

"I wouldn't be any trouble," Kena continued. "My friend Toby told me all about funerals when his grandmother died. I know how to be quiet and follow rules."

"I'd better go next door and talk to him. He'll want to meet me."

"No!" Kena was around the corner and pulling on her jacket. She shoved her feet into her boots. "I'll tell him!" And she was out the door.

Molly watched from the doorway. The snow was so high on the sides of Charlie's path that all she could see of Kena was her beads, bobbing up and down as she ran toward the inn. The beads were passing Kathleen Hollins coming toward the library. Molly waved. The red pompom bobbing in front of Kathleen would be her son Peter's. She went in to find *The Snowy Day*.

# Chapter 27

## Oliver

Oliver didn't think he could feel more lonesome. His eyes were parched for something green. The cars in the parking lot below were buried under the snow, no distinguishing features visible. Poor Nigel. He leaned his forehead against the cold glass and punched in the string of numbers. Please, please, please. It was almost suppertime; surely someone would answer the phone!

"Ii? Bakari, you're supposed to be setting tables, not playing tag!"

"Wanja, it's me."

His heart filled with the sounds of kids' voices and clattering dishes.

"Oliver! When I told the kids about the books—and Jaafar! He hasn't stopped pestering. Today! He must learn to read today! He must get ready!'"

"Books?"

"There's an e-mail, didn't you see it? A church there in Washington? And they're doing a clothing collection and want to know sizes! Even shoes! The books are already on their way!"

*For the kiddies.* He sank down on the bed.

"But, Oliver, did you get to see Alice?"

"Not yet. I needed to get a special pass, since I'm not a U.S.

citizen, but today I should be able to."

"Do you know anything more?"

"It seems Kena's in a foster home."

"Oh, Oliver!"

"Why didn't she *tell* me? Why didn't she ask *me* to take her? I could take time off or maybe gotten work at the UN here. I don't understand."

"I don't either, I confess."

A slap of wind hit the window. Oliver shivered.

"It's been snowing here all night, and there's more to come."

He'd spent Thursday in the motel, mining the internet for information. Then he'd spent Friday at the jail waiting for his clearance and reading a local paper front to back and back to front. Imagining Alice someplace in the same building. Could he bring her socks? Her feet were always cold in the winter here. The newspaper had an advertisement for a kids' movie at a shopping center. He imagined taking Kena and visiting Father Christmas afterwards. Did she still believe in Father Christmas?

There was a photo of people skating, and he remembered the time at Rockefeller Center, watching, with Kena strapped to his chest. Watching Alice…spinning, going backwards, going fast with her arms out, her hair flowing behind under her bright blue hat. So happy. Kena had been mesmerized by the huge tree with its hundreds and hundreds of lights.

Wanja broke into the memory. "Don't forget to tell Alice I'm minding about her and ask if I can write. Don't forget! Will the snow be a problem driving?"

"I'll be slow. No worries." His stomach tightened its knot.

"Tata Wanja, who you talking to!"

"Anka. Oliver."

"In America? It's Uncle! Come on, it's Anka in America!"

He heard a polyglot chorus of high voices. "Hello, hello! Habari! Hujambo? Are you fine? Ni Wega! When are you coming back? We're getting books!" With each voice, he felt warmer.

"Remind them I'll be there for New Year's," he said, renewing the promise against his lonesomeness.

"I love you!" Wanja had to raise her voice to be heard.

Then a piping voice, "She loves him! She loves him!"

"She's his sister, stupid."

"You're not supposed to say stupid!"

"We'll see you soon!"

"I'll see you when you see me," he said softly, but they'd hung up.

◊

"You're gonna have to shuck those shoes."

Oliver looked down. They weren't *that* wet.

"This your first time, honey?"

The woman was stuffing a coat and purse into one of the other lockers.

"Me?" But of course she was talking to him. There were two walls of lockers and five rows of plastic chairs fastened to the gleaming linoleum, but it was only the two of them who'd braved the snow that early in the day. "Aii. Yes. First time."

"Your watch too. Anything metal, like your belt buckle."

And like the miniature Christmas tree that took batteries that he'd bought at the store attached to the petrol station. He put the bag into the locker and slipped off his watch. He zipped it into the pocket of his anorak before rolling it tightly into the locker. He began on his belt. "My shoes aren't too wet."

"My husband has shoes like yours that have metal arches for some fool reason. You don't want to find that out in the metal detector when it's too late." She pulled her purse and coat out and shoved them at Oliver to hold. Her hand went back into the locker and emerged with a pair of canvas slip-ons. "I got these for him over at the Dollar Store. Somebody might as well use them. He claims his sciatica is too bad to visit, but truth tell he's just too sad."

The shoes were too small.

"I have something in the car," he said.

"Well, it's just you and me, so you wouldn't think a couple minutes would matter, but they put a lot of stock in their rules. You'd best hurry!"

When he got back, she was waiting with a plastic bag. When she saw the flipflops he was carrying, she laughed and shoved the bag at him. "Your shoes will melt all over the locker. And tuck your socks down in the toes."

He felt like he was about 12, but it felt fine.

"We missed the time, though."

"You didn't go?" Well, of course not, she was standing right there.

"Thought I'd wait for you so you wouldn't be lonesome. We'll talk. Where you from?"

"I'm from Kenya."

"Long way from home." She patted him on the arm. "You'll be fine now."

So Oliver heard all about her daughter, Christina, who was called Cricket because she never stopped talking and was in for drug possession for a year, and Thank the Lord she hadn't had to go Upstate, it being a second offense and not a third, three strikes you're out, and *then* what about baby Tanya, who was cutting a molar? And she knew all about Alice and Kena and Patrice, Kena's foster mother, and prayed for them every Sunday and Wednesday in the All Souls' Baptist Church Ladies' Caring Circle.

"Line up!" a voice called out.

She grinned at him, at the silliness of the two of them lining up.

She stepped through the metal detector, and then it was his turn. He'd forgotten to put his locker key in the bin, and the correctional officer didn't hide her annoyance. Finally the door opened with a buzz and clang, and they entered a room like an elevator with a door on the other side. After the first one closed, the second one buzzed and clanged open, and there they were.

"Take a seat," the officer said.

Oliver adjusted his beltless trousers and ran his hand over his hair and his shirt front, still damp from his run through the snow.

"Don't you worry, you lookin' good," Cricket's mother whispered, before she walked to the front of the room and sat down to wait.

He picked a spot in the back, his legs barely squeezing under the table.

Then he saw her, coming around a corner, rushing as if she couldn't wait. He stood up, banging his knee. But when she saw him, her face froze.

She looked around the room, as if to give it another chance. Finally, she walked toward him and stopped a few feet away.

"Alice," he said. Her eyes kept him from touching her. He put his hand out, open, but he didn't have anything to give except himself. No Christmas tree. No socks. The petrol station hadn't had any, of course.

She put her hand up. Stop. She looked away, stiff-faced. She was wearing an orange coverall, a color he knew she hated because of her hair. There were deep circles under her eyes. She was too skinny. Her freckles stood out against her pale cheeks. Her hair was cut off like a boy's.

She took his breath away.

"I came as fast as I could when I found out."

"You shouldn't have." As if her voice had crossed its arms against him. "We have to sit down."

He squeezed back onto his stool, and she sat on the other side of the barrier, her hands tucked into her armpits, her shoulders hunched, stretching her eyes not to cry, he could tell.

"Why didn't you *tell* me?" he blurted out. "I would have *come*."

She folded over and began to cry without a sound, and then with little high squeaks. He stood up.

A CO called out. "Wangera, you gotta keep it together." Oliver froze. He had to keep it together? "And you, you have to sit down." Oliver sat.

Alice's squeaks turned into hiccups. Hic. Hic. The CO was there, holding out a striped paper bag. "Breathe into this." Hic. "It only had plain popcorn," the CO said, and walked away.

Alice squashed the bag over her nose. Hic.

The bag went in and out. Hic.

"Wanja says hello. She'd like to write. Our mother sends her love." He knew she would if she knew.

The bag went still, then started up again. Hic, hic, in and out. Alice looked like a clown with her fuzzy red head and her eyes staring at him over a bulbous red and white nose. If she could see herself, she wouldn't be able to keep from laughing.

"Remember Nia's chicken-aunt? Still on duty."

Then, not much of one, but a promise of a smile peeked over the bag. Or maybe it was just his hope inventing one.

"I'm here in the U.S. getting help for their new clinic. And then I saw…I read what happened. Was it a lie, then? Not wanting to see me anymore?"

Alice put down the bag. "I was scared you'd take Kena! And you would have. Don't pretend you wouldn't have."

"She's in a foster home! What were you thinking?"

She glared at him. Like old times.

"You wish I hadn't come."

She shook her head. "I thought—I hoped—you were Kena with Patrice. Oliver, listen! Listen! She ran away. To go to Adam's funeral! Adam St. John, the boy—"

"I know who he is."

"I thought she'd been kidnapped!"

"What?"

"She took the train from the city to Adam's town. By herself! Patrice, that's her—"

"I know who she is."

"Patrice went to get Kena there. But all night I didn't know where she was!" She smiled then, her tears spilling over and running down her cheeks. "But they told me this morning. She's there, at Adam's service! Oh, Oliver! She's safe!"

Oliver didn't look out for the CO. He just went around to the other side, slid onto the stool next to Alice, and put his arms around her.

"I was so scared," she whispered into his neck.

"Wangera!" The CO was heading their way.

"Come on! Leave them be! It's just us in here—they're not hurtin' anybody!" It was the voice of his shoe mentor. "You've seen that little girl in here! Where's your heart?"

Alice stood up. "Cricket! She's safe!"

"Praise the Lord!"

"I'll go there." Oliver started to rise.

"You can't leave. One time Kena *threw up*, and she still had to stay to the end." Alice pushed Oliver away. "You have to sit across from me."

He went back to his own side. "The newspaper said she had a concussion. What happened?" He reached his hands out for her while she twisted hers in her lap. If he could take them into his, the past would be over, he was sure.

"What happened." Her voice went flat, as if she were giving dictation. She shook her head.

"Tell me."

She looked down and told the table. "They came back from walking dogs at the animal shelter and having supper at a waffle place near there. They did that most weeks after Adam got out of school. He was taking the Metro back to Farleys' Dock. He'd come down for the day. But Kena had cooked up a plan: If I drove, we could stay over and meet his mom and maybe his dads." She half-smiled. "I think she thought they would look like twins." She looked up and began to rock back and forth. "Kena was so excited that I gave in, even though—" She rubbed her hand across the table.

"I knew I shouldn't have said yes. And then it started raining halfway there." She was looking at him but was seeing back then. "The freeway kept switching…from three to two lanes to one lane to two to three…and it began to rain hard. It was one of those long June evenings, but it got dark and everybody's headlights came on. There were cones and cement barriers and cars kept passing on one side or the other and honking like they were mad because I was too slow. Kena and Adam were singing to Kena's CD. It was the soundtrack from *O Brother Where Art Thou*." She stopped rocking.

"Then the exit was there." She blinked and shook her head. "It was so *sudden*—I tried to get across, to cross—" Her eyes were pleading. "There was a wall, they were singing—"

*Mama!* Alice covered her ears. "They said the car…someone said the car *bounced*."

*Mama! Mama!*

I'm here! I'm here!

Like *Horton Hears a Who*. I'm here.

"Kena was in her car seat. They said it saved her. I couldn't *see* her!" Alice lifted her face. Oliver's face showed only compassion. No judgment. She looked for it: maybe it was waiting. "There was glass, and a piece—" She looked down at the table. There was a spatter mark where the finish had bleached away. She rubbed at it with her finger.

The windshield was bleeding.

NO. Look at Oliver.

"She stopped calling for me! I thought—"

Alice put a hand over her eyes. "I couldn't get out! I pulled and pulled and pulled but I couldn't get out!" It was the hopeless wail of a child, as if everything would be different if she only could go back and get out.

"I don't remember putting my arm across Adam, but for days after I could barely move it, and they made me see a nurse and she figured it out. But I don't remember Adam at all!"

"It was an accident."

"*Not* an accident. *Not.* Oh, God! How can everything change in a second!" She stopped abruptly. She whispered. "I killed him."

He shook his head.

"No! Remember my parents, how they died?"

"Of course I do."

"Oliver, I was *drunk.* Drunk! Just like that woman who ran into them. I was drunk. 'Class E felony, DWI, a child in the car.' Manslaughter! Homicide. It will be years and years. Years. And I *deserve* it." She hung on his eyes. "But Kena doesn't."

She swallowed. "I was embarrassed. I was *embarrassed* to say I couldn't drive. How could I say I'd been *drinking?* I'd been drinking most of the day! And I was jealous—*jealous*—of Adam. Because he had everything, a mother and father—*two* fathers—and growing up in a town like…I was like—what about me?" She shook her head. "But Kena was so excited! She was going to meet his dog. She was so happy."

"Five minutes!" the CO called out, and like a shade going down, Alice went silent. Oliver thought that in the outside world, such feelings, such life-altering earthquakes of feelings, would have room and time to do what they needed to do. But in jail there wasn't room, not even for tremors. Feelings had to be locked down and hidden, sometimes even from those holding them. It must be crazy-making.

"If I'd stayed, none of this would have happened," he said, as if together they could beg the past and choose all over again, make everything different.

Alice looked at him, flat-eyed. "Don't. It's bad enough without ifs, like whiny ghosts." She bent forward as if she had a secret. "Remember that head at the museum with two faces that couldn't see each other?" She crossed her arms and tucked her hands into her armpits.

"One face is fine. Just *fine*. I have to get out of here for Kena, so I'll be *fine*." She crossed her arms the other way. "The other face is not fine. It's cracking into pieces." She held his eyes as if her life depended on his not looking away.

"It didn't even take a minute for me to break everything," she whispered. "It's *forever*. His parents, how do they live now? How do they *live*? Lily and Enoch. Their names are Lily and Enoch. Lily will look for Adam for the rest of her life, even when she thinks she's used to it; she'll follow a stranger whose back looks like Adam's down a street, hungry for her boy."

She closed her eyes. "He was right next to me, hanging upside down. But I don't even remember! I didn't take care of him! I didn't talk to him! I never even looked at his face! I didn't do *anything*! All the time, all the time, the cracks—it was Adam's blood on the windshield! Oh, oh!" A tear trickled out from under her eye. She swiped it away and looked at Oliver.

"Alice," he began. She put her hand up to stop him.

"It was his head! And I didn't do anything!"

Oliver flailed for something to say. "Would Adam want this for you? What if it was me who had done this? People make mistakes, but that doesn't mean you're…we're…bad. It means we're human."

"Time's up!"

Alice wiped her cheeks. "Oliver, I'm sorry I didn't tell you."

He walked around the table. "I'll go find Kena."

They looked at each other helplessly. Alice got just a second to feel his arms around her.

"Alice, you're gonna get points!" Cricket called out from the front of the room.

Alice stepped away and touched her forehead. "Oliver, when you see her—she has a scar."

# Chapter 28

## Kena

Adam's funeral started with a parade. A snowplow led the way, followed by a string of cars, people squeezing together inside them, Tupperware and children perched on their laps. The school bus came next, and taking up the rear were two state police cars.

Molly had dug a hat and mittens out of the lost and found for Kena. The hat was bright red, had a fat green pompom on top, and didn't go with her jacket and boots at all. Molly said she'd be glad to have it for the long walk to the meeting house and told her to wear her leggings over her tights. Ug-*ly!*

Would David be there?

But when they turned the corner by the school, they stopped in their tracks.

Kena had never seen anything like it. Cars were parked every which way with their doors open, and puffs of steam were rising from a school bus like it was breathing. A school bus! People were laughing like it was a party, not a funeral at all. Most of them were carrying dishes of food.

"A bus! What a good idea!" Molly said, taking Kena's hand and leading her over to it. She pulled herself aboard. "Iva! Back in the saddle!"

"I'm glad I can do something for Lily. I can still picture Adam on his first day with that Star Wars lunchbox."

"This is Makena, Adam's friend."

Iva's face wrinkled up like a walnut. "Pleased to meet you, Makena." Kena felt shy. People were staring.

"Kena!"

It was Mari, and Clare was sitting next to her. Kena hurried to sit in front of them, and Molly followed. Then Clare stood up suddenly and walked up the aisle and out.

"Is your grandfather here?" Mari asked, looking toward the front of the bus.

"Is he feeling better, then?" Molly asked Mari.

Caught between competing lies, Kena didn't know what to say. She looked out the window. Mari's mother was talking to a policewoman! She slid down in her seat. As soon as Clare returned, Iva closed the door, and Kena took a big breath before worrying about the next thing: she hadn't brought any food.

Back in caboose position, Officer Deidre Swenson called in the information that Makena Wangera was on a school bus with the town librarian, improbable as that sounded. Would someone inform Alice Wangera?

◊

Lily, Lois and Bernie next to her, had welcomed the few people who'd arrived. She was increasingly sure that the snow was either keeping others home or delaying them so much she'd have to make small talk forever in the sprightly voice she seemed unable to modulate. Enoch was examining a space heater with Abe and Charlie as if together they might know something, which she doubted. Gideon was hunched over the piano, playing snatches of Beatles songs. Rachel was lighting candles, and David was at the little tree, a small paper snowflake dangling from his hand.

But Khai, thank God, was shepherding people to hang their coats, to hang their ornaments on the tree, to sit. To anywhere but her. She heard a familiar swoosh of air brakes. The school bus? Suddenly the whole town seemed to be pouring in, stamping their feet and talking. She recognized Susie Patterson's voice: "Mark, you come down from there right now!" And others. Voices she could close her eyes and know.

"It took us over two hours!"

"They'll never have a Christmas without this being part of it."

"Did you see Hank Whittaker with the plow?"

"And old Iva Winston is driving the bus!"

Enoch sat down, and Lily grabbed his hand.

The coat pegs were quickly overwhelmed, so people draped their coats on their chairs and set their potluck dishes underneath. They hadn't followed directions and had brought casseroles as well as bars and cookies. Soon there weren't enough chairs, and people sat on their coats around the little tree. Lines converged like a roundabout as people made way for each other, holding up ornaments.

"I found it at Nearly New up in Brewster. Adam loved any animal. Isn't it cute?"

"We hung all the breakables at the top this year. Maddie grabs everything she can reach. She put a silver ball in Harriet's water bowl this morning. The thing is, that darn cat didn't come home last night. She's done it before, but still...all this snow! I hope she found a place to shelter."

"Sam said Ms. J likes glitter."

It was nothing like Lily imagined. How Adam would love it!

The snow, the bus, old Iva Winston coming through the door. And the colors! How did they know not to wear black? Some touched a hand down on her shoulder as they went to sit, like a blessing. When the tree got too full, people put their ornaments underneath, like presents, and on the piano.

Gideon arranged them, pairing a bobble-headed turtle with a penguin.

"It's okay. Kids don't need to bring food." It was Mari's voice, and Gideon looked over. Makena Wangera was sitting on the floor between Mari and his brother. So she came. She was tiny in real life. Her face was solemn, and a big pink scar cut her eyebrow in two. Where were those state police?

David saw Gideon and waved, and Kena looked over. David said something to her. And suddenly Gideon was struck by the force of Kena's smile, as if she already knew him, as if they were friends. He reared back. Her smile faltered, and she looked down. He turned away and fumbled with another ornament. Had *she* brought one? He hadn't; he'd forgotten.

Clare cracked the door and stuck her head out. The road had become a parking lot. Exhaust from two state police cars hung in the air. They'd told her someone was coming from the city to get Kena. In this snow!

Mark Patterson slipped in. "Hi, Ms. Lewis."

The Last Kid Standing, as usual.

She closed the door and turned half of the lights off, and the fairy lights around the windows seemed to double in size. People quieted, gazing at the tree and its peculiar glory, its star bent and bowing to a pink and orange tissue flower. A man wearing a red bowtie rang a bell no bigger than his thumb, waited for the room to quiet down, and rang it again.

"Hello. I'm Roger Caldwell and I'm an elder here at Falls Meeting. Welcome to this Meeting for Worship in Thanksgiving, for the Grace of God, as shown in the life of Adam St. John."

The fancy words took on new meaning for Lily. Grace. Something lurking in a fold of her heart peeked out. Maybe Meeting for Worship in Thanksgiving could be more than something she had to endure.

Roger continued. "Many of you aren't familiar with our service, so I'll take a moment to explain. We don't usually sing, but because this Meeting for Worship is held to honor Adam's life, we'll begin and end with a song requested by his family."

"Oh, no! The cards!" Rachel interrupted. "I'm *so sorry*. So many came at the same time…we have cards with the words. We have cards." She glanced at Lily and made a rueful face. Lily looked down so she wouldn't laugh. Laughing was awfully close to crying.

Abe was already at the table, where a child-sized blue fleece was draped over the basket of cards, hiding it from view. He held up the fleece.

"That's mine!" a child's voice said indignantly, and everyone laughed, and it was all right.

"I don't think there are enough cards, so you'll need to share," Rachel apologized. It was the opposite of an offering, the basket emptying as it was passed hand to hand. By the time it got to the people on the floor, there were just a handful left. Mari took one and gave it to Kena.

"Is that Homer?" Kena asked David.

"He's really old now," David said. "My brother takes him for walks."

It sounded like bragging, Kena thought. Like she'd done about the elephants, except she'd lied. Longing for her mother struck her and she leaned over to hide her face. She grabbed her hair and quickly let go. Her hand throbbed.

The bell rang.

"Okay—take two," Roger said. People laughed again. "After singing the first verse, we'll move into Open Worship, during which anyone may stand and offer words…or music. All are welcome to, regardless of age or faith, or no faith, for that matter. Please sit in silence between folks for a few moments, for reflection, and to feel the spirit. Thank you." He sat down.

Khai stood up. "Please join me in singing the first verse of 'For the Beauty of the Earth.' The words are on your cards." He hummed a starting note.

"That's Adam's stepdad," David whispered.

Khai, Kena thought.

> "For the beauty of the earth
> for the glory of the skies…"

Kena held her card up for Mari and David and blinked and blinked against the stinging in her eyes, determined to sing for Adam.

> "For the love which from our birth
> Over and around us lies
> Source of all, to thee we raise
> This, our hymn of grateful praise."

Khai waited for everyone to settle again. "Let us open to a place of quiet and the gentle spirit of love."

A few knew the fragrance from the woodstove was apple wood; it mingled with the smells of cinnamon and sweet strawberry candles like dessert. The words of the song lingered in their hearts. The lights around the windowpanes glowed. Small creatures watched from the little tree and the piano. A light beamed off the golden wings of a bird.

Hush.

Shhh.

Adam's Meeting sighed.

# PART TWO

*The wolf shall dwell with the lamb,*

*and the leopard shall lie down with the kid,*

*and the calf and the lion and the fatling together,*

*and a little child shall lead them*

*Isaiah 11:6*

# Chapter 29

## Lily

Murmurs. Sniffles. Snow whispering on the windowpanes. A woman in a red pantsuit stood up.

Lily didn't recognize her for a second, and then almost stood up too, ready to take comfort from the warm embrace she'd received so many times. And that she'd *come*, with all the snow. And red! She'd never seen her out of her pastel nurse's scrubs.

"My name is Ellie. I'm a little nervous, but if I speak first off, I'll be able to listen to you all. And besides, I don't want Lily sitting there worrying no one's going to talk." She held up the card.

"I was privileged to know Adam and his family at the hospital. That might sound funny—I mean about *knowing* Adam. I never heard his voice, or saw him smile, or met his eyes. But I took care of him almost every day, and that's a special kind of knowing. And I got to know Lily and Enoch and Khai." She looked over to the piano. "And Gideon."

"I liked to go in after my shift to sit with Adam. Sometimes I'd sing to him or tell him little things I thought he'd like to hear. I'd tell him about the sky outside his window and about my dog, Gladys. And other things." She looked around. "Holding Adam's hand, looking at the funny things hanging around his bed—all a little odd, like the tree here. You know how it is to hold a sleeping child, that tenderness and kind of…holy feeling?"

She looked at Lily and Enoch. "I feel blessed to have known him. Your beautiful boy." She sat down. A woman next to her, a perfect stranger, took her hand and squeezed it.

Lily took Enoch's hand and hung on hard. Khai let go of Enoch on his other side and stood up.

"I'm Khai, Adam's stepdad. I felt a little shy with Adam when Enoch wasn't there. I wasn't around during the lap-sitting years, so I was careful to wait for Adam to make those first moves. Maybe too careful. I mean, like when he came for the weekend, if Enoch wasn't home yet, we'd hide in our books. Then one time I noticed he was reading *White Fang,* a favorite of mine. We started sharing authors, and last winter we both read Wendell Berry's *Jayber Crow* and got into exchanging Berry quotes. One's up in my office—the one about how it's the rocks in the way that make rivers talk. I think the metaphor is one Adam wanted to live by, being curious about where obstacles and detours might take him. And it's not hyperbole to say that he had a lot in common with the animals he felt so at home with…to take things as they came and live the day he was in fully. He was a gentle and accepting boy and man."

Khai smiled. "Sometimes he sent me things from the classifieds. 'Lost: tortoise-shell female cat named Screamer; use gloves.'" Everyone laughed.

"Like Ellie said, I'm blessed to get to love Adam and, I think, be loved back." As Khai sat down, people looked at their laps, or up at the rafters, or anywhere—just not at Lily and Enoch.

A big bear of a man stood up in the back row.

"Adam worked for me summers and vacations, helping with check-ups, shots, and whatever he was up for, which was most anything.

Oh, I'm a vet, I shoulda said. A veterinarian, that is, though I'm a Vet too, but that's a whole 'nother story. Anyways, what I was saying… here's a story that's pure Adam."

He paused like a seasoned storyteller, sticking his thumbs behind his red suspenders. "We get a wild animal occasionally, hit by a car, birds flying into windows, stuff like that. Once we had a raccoon that mixed it up with a cat, and it was the raccoon that needed stitches." His beard bobbed as he shook his head.

"Anyways. Last April, this guy from Weebotok Camp, he brought in a half-grown barred owl that had been attacked by something, maybe a fisher; they'd found it crouching in a corner of one of the lean-tos. Well, I sewed the little guy up. He was mad as heck, but we didn't want to sedate him, and Adam helped me splint the wing."

He held his hands up to show the size, like he was telling a fish story.

"We stuck him in a cage in the office for extra looking after. We knew he'd never go back to the wild. One eye, especially, would never be right. Adam stayed around the clock the first couple days, feeding him chopped up mice like a mother. He put the bits down the owl's throat with tweezers—owls don't have any gag reflex—but after a few days the owl ate on his own. Adam got on the internet and learned the juvenile's sounds, and he'd make these noises, these clicky-throat sounds."

He grinned. "The owl whisperer. And wouldn't you know it? Pretty soon, when he heard Adam's voice, the little guy called to him. Adam would close the baby gate at the door and open the cage. And that owl would come out and walk around, looking kind of drunk because of the injured wing and eye, the two of them bobbing and weaving and clicking down on the floor, telling about their day or maybe secrets." He rocked back on his heels and stroked his beard.

"It was something. Course we couldn't keep him, so Adam took him up north to a raptor sanctuary. I expect he cried some. I know

I teared up, seeing them drive away. He never named that owl, said teaching a wild thing a name took away its wildness. But love does that too, and Adam truly loved that little owl."

He looked over at Khai. "Like you said, Adam had…*has*, who *knows*, I surely don't…a gentle soul. I hope I never lose the picture in my head of that owl turning his head prid' near all the way around and looking at Adam looking at him. Like they both were seeing God."

Lily didn't think she could stand it, her brimming tears turning the candlelight on the piano into stars. A young woman got up from the floor, using the hand of a woman in the chair behind her as a brace. She had an envelope in her hand.

"Hi! I'm a friend of Adam's from school. From Brandt. I didn't think I'd speak today. Gideon told me kind of how it worked, but after hearing—well—Adam gave me this." She pulled a card out of the envelope and a piece of paper from inside the card. She unfolded it.

"*Dear Madison.*" She stopped and swallowed. "That's me. It's from Adam to me. *I heard about Taylor, and I'm really sorry. I didn't know him, but I know you were really tight. I spent a long time trying to find a card and even called my mom, and she said pick a card you like; it doesn't have to be a sympathy card. She said just go from your heart.*"

Madison held the card up to show a monarch butterfly, its wings half open. She went back to reading.

"*When I was in kindergarten my mom was my teacher. She sent away for butterfly larvae, and we made leaf and stick houses for them to make their chrysalis inside of. My mom is good at finding lessons in things, so besides learning about the life cycle of a monarch, which was very cool, she showed us that a life can have different forms. When my butterfly emerged, he stretched his wings for a whole afternoon, and then I carried him outside and held my hand up and waited. And he flew away. I cried. But not for him, for me. He got to be a butterfly. Maybe somebody's body dying isn't the end of someone. Maybe our bodies are kind of like a chrysalis. Not exactly like a butterfly—the pupa stage is*

*pretty gooey—but some human stage, and not finished. I hope it's okay to write*
*all this. Adam."*

"Adam was…I just…it was a comfort to me." Her face crumpled. She folded the paper, tucked it into the card, and tucked the card into the envelope. She stepped toward Lily. "I'd like to give it to you."

No, Lily thought, I can't. But she took the card, along with a hug. Then people passed Madison from hand to hand until she got back to her place and sank back to the floor. And it was as if everyone sank down with her, and the room's heartbeat slowed.

A few soft notes came from the piano.

"Hey. Well, that picture you all have there is Adam, of course, and that's Homer. We grew up together, us three. I'm Gideon. We grew up together and had a lot of adventures. Homer's not one for leaving home. Maybe you'll meet him later. But lucky for him, his place has woods and a river, and if you wandered around you'd find things that remind you of Eeyore's house, and they would be what's left of our forts."

Gideon shook his hair out of his eyes.

"Homer put up with a lot: He's been a pirate, and a horse on the Pony Express, and a rescue dog with Koolaid hanging off his neck, and a messenger behind enemy lines with secret papers in code strapped to him. Adam tried to put him in the Halloween parade once but it didn't work out. Homer disapproves of firecrackers."

Gideon pushed his glasses up. "There was this one time he left home on his own, though, and we never figured out why. It was the last week of school, and it was way hot. We were s'posed to be reading, but mostly we were looking out the window or at the clock. Then, all of a sudden, this girl Elaine screamed, "Adam, isn't that your *dog*?!" Gideon pitched his voice high.

"Homer was at the door with his tongue hanging out like he'd just run a mile. Which maybe he had. As soon as Adam said his name, he took off down the aisle and tried to get in his lap. The teacher let him stay until it was time to go home." Gideon looked at his feet.

"I'd say Homer knows all the right things about being a friend, and Adam does too, wherever he's gone off to." Gideon turned, his back to everyone, and set his hands on the piano keys.

> "I had a dog
> and his name was Blue
> And I betcha five dollars
> he's a good dog too.
> Come on,
> Blue
> You good dog,
> you
> I—"

He stopped. He stuck his arm up and made a victory fist. People held their breath, as if there might be more. But there wasn't.

Then, without any pause at all, Bernie started talking.

"I'm Adam's grandpa. I hope you'll excuse me if I don't stand."

It took a few beats for people to find him.

"Gideon saying that about pirates, this poem popped into my head. When he was a little guy and we visited, I got to read to Adam at bedtime, and there was a book of poems—what? What's the matter, I can't talk?"

"You need to speak up, Dad."

"Oh." He stretched his neck. "Can you hear me, back there in the cheap seats?"

"We can hear you fine, Mr. St. John," the vet called out.

"They can hear me fine," Bernie said. "Don't worry." He leaned across Lily and patted Enoch on the knee.

"The poem's called 'Pirate Story.' They played pirates, like

Gideon said. I helped them make wooden cutlasses, and they ran around whacking each other. But the poem…" He looked up toward the ceiling.

> "Where shall we adventure, today that we're afloat,
> Wary of the weather and steering by a star?
> Shall it be to Africa, a-steering of the boat,
> To Providence, Or Babylon, or off to Malabar?"

Bernie smiled at the memory. "Then one day I heard Adam singing: 'Where shall we adventure, today that we're afloat, weary of the weather and steering by a star? Shall it be to Africa, a-steering of the boat, Probably to Babyland to get a Mallomar.'"

Bernie slapped his knee. He said it again, softly. "'Probably to Babyland to get a Mallomar.' That's what I got to say." Lois looked at him in astonishment.

Kena knitted her forehead. What was a Mallomar?

Enoch reached under his chair and stood up, holding his flute.

"Adam and I hiked a lot of trails, often with Gideon. But I want to tell you about a time when it was just the two of us. We'd made camp on a cliff above this long, narrow lake and went right to bed to get away from the no-see-ums. The next morning when I crawled out of the tent, there was just the slightest hint of the day to come and the air was chilly and damp. I walked the few feet to the overlook. The lake was gone." He looked over their heads as if he was seeing it.

"I was looking down at a cloud, roiling like a giant's cauldron. I woke Adam up. I remember I whispered, as if talking out loud would break some spell. We dragged our sleeping bags out, wiggled into them, and sat watching. I don't think we said a word. At some point, we could make out the tops of the pines across the lake…it was as if they were rising out of the cloud, like Shangri-La. And then we heard a loon calling."

Enoch closed his eyes to hear it better.

"That call—if you've ever heard it you never forget—sounds like all the world's sorrow." He opened his eyes.

"And then, when there wasn't a wisp of it left, there was an answer from the other end of the lake. And then the first one, and back and forth, and then changing to that crazy, wonderful laughing call. And as the sun rose, the cloud lifted off the lake like a flying saucer, bright pink and orange, and dissolved into the sky. The loons had laughed in a new day."

Enoch looked up at the peak of the meeting house.

"I can't think that there's a heaven. But I can imagine that our atoms, our molecules, our quarks, or whatever the latest particles are, join all the others in the universe, making and remaking this beautiful world. And so I imagine that Adam can be a part of loons and lakes and clouds and the sun and owls…and no-see-ums. Part of the beauty of this earth, and maybe another earth we haven't met yet, but maybe Adam has."

Enoch raised his flute. He hadn't known if he would play. But now he just played the way he did at home sometimes, the notes flowing through him from a mysterious place. Touching tenderness. Touching sorrow. Touching joy and hanging in the air.

Rachel wiped her cheeks. She should have brought boxes of Kleenex!

Molly put her hand on Kena's head.

Mari ached for Gideon, alone by the piano.

David took Kena's hand, so she would be holding his.

Kena removed her spirit from Molly's hand on her head, and her fingers from David's. If she stayed very still, she'd be okay. She heard her name, whispered.

"Kena," Mari whispered again.

No, Kena thought. When Mari's arm went around her, she drew away. No. She shook her head so slightly it could barely be seen. No.

Mari took her arm back and looked at Molly in appeal.

David watched a splotch drop on Kena's pink dress. He leaned down to see her face. Another tear dropped.

Suddenly the meeting house was flooded with light. The sun had come out. Kena wiped her cheeks and blinked directly into the bright square that a window had become. Adam!

A humming started from somewhere. Someone joined in and then another. Lily recognized the song: "Morning Has Broken." How can so much pain be so close to joy? Like vines wrapping around each other for support.

Kena got on her knees. She cupped her hands around Mari's ear and whispered. To Mari it felt like how butterfly wings might feel. She couldn't understand a word, just the intonation, the lifting at the end, a question. She lifted her hair away to hear better. Little puffs and a word…

"Puff, puff, puff, puff, puff, puff, okay?"

Mari nodded. Kena stood up in her stocking feet. People watched the little girl run her hands down her pink dress. They watched her hand go to her hair and freeze. Some noticed that her buttons were daisies. Some noticed a butterfly in her hair. Some noticed *Toy Story* Band-aids on her palm.

The little girl spoke to Lily. "Adam told me he saw a island floating down a river, and there was a tree in the middle of it. He told me it waved at him. Adam would say Today is an Ordinary Day or Today is a Special Day. Ordinary was the library. Special was the circus. When a island floats by, it makes a ordinary day a special day, just like that, he said. A ordinary miracle, he said. Like that song."

Lily pressed her lips together to not cry out. Kena rocked from her toes to her heels to her toes.

"I was minded of a song. In Kenya it's a game, but I made it a song for Adam, and he copied me." She put her palms together, lifted them over her head, and followed with her eyes. "*Muti muhande rui-ine,* a tree planted on the river."

Lily couldn't take her eyes off the scar.

"One i mathangu maguo, look at its leaves," Kena sang, her voice high and thin. She looked at Lily again, as if to say, "Watch!"

And suddenly she was a different child, a child from another place. She swayed, her fingers dancing, and her hair too, until every inch of her was dancing. She spun.

"Magithaka na ruhuho, playing with the wind." She dipped her arms down and back up, down and back up, her hands and every finger moving faster and faster. "*Na ithui nituthake na ruhuho,* even us let's play with the wind." She swayed and dipped to the rhythm of the wind, and her voice sang in the cadence of Africa.

> "Na ithui nituthake na ruhuho
> Even us let's play in the wind
> Na ithui nituthake na ruhuho."

Kena flung her arms wide. "Na ithui nituthake na ruhuho!"

Lily had realized who she was with, "Today we will have a special day!" And then, "Ordinary Miracle." And watching, Lily was spun around and set down facing in a new direction. Even as a storm of contrary feelings pummeled her, she was riveted, imagining Adam's arms going up, Adam's hands waving, Adam copying Kena's every move. He'd be grinning from ear to ear. He'd be enchanted.

Kena Wangera. The scar cut her eyebrow in two.

Adam had wanted Kena and her mother to come up and meet her and see the town, and she'd put him off time after time. Then, that day, she gave in and said yes.

Lily closed her eyes.

She hadn't even told Clare about the night in the White Plains hospital when she'd asked a nurse about "the child." She'd been led to a darkened room in the pediatric ward. There was a red sign on the door: "STOP. MASKS AND GLOVES REQUIRED." The nurse slipped on a surgical mask and gloves and motioned for Lily to do the same.

There was an IV drip. Kena's tiny face was swollen, and dark bruises were beginning to have a yellowish cast. A bandage was wrapped around her head and forehead like a turban. She was barely a blip under the sheet, except for the bulky cast bound against her small chest. The nurse bent and whispered.

"Makena, there's someone here to see you." But Lily was shaking her head no.

"I'll leave you alone," the nurse whispered. Kena opened her eyes. Then she closed them and was back asleep. Lily remembered Adam doing that, waking but not waking.

They'd missed a spot of blood on her ear. Lily took a wipe from a box on the table and gently patted it away. It had crusted, and it took a long time. The gloves made her clumsy.

How could she *not* keep vigil? How could she not take Kena's hand to hold between hers, wishing she could take off the gloves? She sat there until daylight began to creep in around the blinds. Then Kena stirred, and she fled.

That was the day they moved Adam into the city, and she'd shoved thoughts of Kena away. How could she not?

Alice Wangera. What was she *thinking*, to allow Kena to come here?

How easy it could be to hate, like she had a place ready, just the right shape, waiting for it. Lily wrapped her arms tightly around herself. She looked for Clare, and there she was, rising, as if she knew Lily needed her.

But instead, she was holding up an open book. Oh, God. At the last minute, she'd asked Clare to read that thing from *The Prophet*.

Lily shook her head vehemently. No.

Clare held the book up. No?

No!

Clare put the book on her chair. "Thank you all, so much, for coming today, and through all the snow. The buses will take you to the St. John house, and everyone is welcome. Or you can walk, it's just half a mile. And the sun's out! But first…please stand to sing the last verse of 'For the Beauty of the Earth.' Enoch will play accompaniment."

Enoch walked over and took Gideon's place.

"Oh, I almost forgot," Clare said. "After the song, it is the custom to shake hands with your neighbors."

> "For the joy of human care
> sister, brother, parent, child
> for the kinship we all share
> for all gentle thoughts and mild
> Source of all, to thee we raise
> this our hymn of grateful praise."

But they didn't shake hands.

Enoch hugged Gideon. And Gideon held on. And Khai hugged Lily, who hugged Lois, who hugged Bernie.

And pretty soon everyone was hugging everyone. It was Pass the Hug.

Oh, how Adam would love it! It was like the story in *Somebody Else's Nut Tree,* Lily thought…the boy hugging the sky things, floating down to Earth, to a tree and his train, to his mother. To his mother.

Her beautiful boy.

# Chapter 30

## Kena

Kena left the tiny bathroom, her leggings tucked deep inside her backpack. When she stepped outside, the sun burst through a cloud and made glory-rays. Adam!

She saw David on top of a snowbank with another boy.

"David Wainwright, get down from there and go inside and help your father!" someone said sharply. He slid down and landed in front of Kena, spraying her pink tights. "Mothers," he said. He grinned, but then turned bright red, like he'd done something wrong, and hurried inside.

Kena saw Clare talking to someone through the window of a police car and ducked behind the snowbank.

Mari came out the door, pulling on a red stocking cap, Molly behind her.

"Kena, what are you doing back there?" Molly asked.

"Want to walk with me? It's not far," Mari said.

Kena wanted to, but did Molly? Then she remembered: Molly didn't like "chitchat." "If you don't want to come, I can go with Mari."

"Oh! Well," Molly said. "Your grandfather…when is he expecting you back?"

Kena felt worried for a second, as if he were real, and she'd abandoned him. "Not 'til later. He's probably taking a nap."

"I can bring her back," Mari said.

"Well, I wouldn't mind. I'll check on Wanjiru. I might know who she belongs to." Molly smiled at Kena. "Would you like to correspond?"

Kena was thrilled. "Yes! But I need your address!"

"Just write Molly, Farleys' Dock Library, New York. Ask any librarian for the zip code." Kena hugged Molly and her puffy coat. "Tell Juri goodbye," she whispered.

As they walked, Mari told Kena about the solstice celebration called Yule. Adam had told her too, and she'd expected to go one day. But that day was never going to happen now.

Adam's driveway was long and filled with cars. The snow on his house looked like frosting. And there was the playhouse, glittering like a cupcake.

And the barn. And the swing. She stopped.

Mari took her hand. "Feeling shy?"

Kena shook her head. Adam was missing.

Inside was crowded with strangers. Some of them smiled at her, and it was horrible because she should smile back, and she couldn't, she just couldn't. She didn't see Gideon. Or Homer. Mari pointed to where David was sitting with another boy. Kena slid her backpack under a table and went up to them.

She put her hand out. "I'm Kena."

"This is Jimmy," David mumbled.

"Hi." He didn't take her hand.

"David, I need to talk to you," she said. "Private."

David looked at Jimmy and shrugged. "Kids." He got up and walked into the hallway, and Kena followed.

"Okay, what's private?"

"That was rude! And don't say kids!"

"You *are* a kid." She narrowed her eyes.

"Okay, I'm sorry," David said. "What's private?"

"Will you go with me to the train?"

"What are you talking about?"

"The train, I have to be there at three! Will you go with me?"

"You can't do that! And besides, you lied to me. I know every-thing! I know how you really got hurt, and I'll bet you never even saw any elephants! I know all about you."

She looked over his shoulder. Jimmy was staring at her forehead.

"And the police are looking for you, anyway. You can stick by me until they come get you."

"Don't you *dare* tell about the train, David!"

"Kena, you can't take the train."

"The police don't matter because I'm gonna talk to Adam's mother!" Chin up, she walked away.

David went back to the living room.

"Isn't that the missing kid?" Jimmy asked. David hesitated. Then he shook his head.

Kena found Adam's mother sitting by a big piano. She went back to the hall, pulled her backpack out, and took out Adam's book. She hugged it as she wove through the crowd. There was a postcard on the piano leaning against a statue of Jesus. Except Jesus was white-skinned, not brown like the picture above Patrice's bed.

Adam had sent her a postcard almost exactly like it, maybe the same leopard even, but it wasn't one of the things Tam knew to bring from their apartment. She reached, then took her hand back. Letters were private even when they were a postcard, her mother said.

Kena wanted it, wanted the postcard with all her being, jealous of Adam's mother who got to have it, and the book too, and this house and the playhouse and barn, and Homer. A mean feeling was growing inside of her. She thought of the room she had to share with Keisha. She thought of her old apartment and some other girl in her bed. She thought of her Big Apple T-shirt and her Brandt sweat-shirt in her backpack and rejected them like clothes for the ragbag, rejected them out of her bad feeling even though they were her most treasured things, along with Lemmy and her picture of Oliver.

She thrust the book at Adam's mother.

"Here. We were reading it. Me and Adam."

"Oh! *Owls in the Family.*"

Kena pulled out her charm and held onto it, trying to wish away her mean feelings.

"What is that?"

Kena covered it with her hand.

"You have to help my mother!" she blurted out. "My mother isn't mean EVER. Adam would say too." She perched on the edge of the piano bench so they were face to face. "She didn't mean to do it! You need to tell them! She loves Adam too!" All the fight had gone out of her, and she was pleading. "You need to *tell* them. Please won't you tell them so Mama and me can go home for Christmas?"

But Adam's mother just looked at her, and it was no good, Kena could tell. She blurted out her last and biggest wish, her worst fear. "You need to tell them not to make my mother be in a prison! Toby said they listen to the family, what Adam's family says, and you're his mother, so you need to tell them!"

Adam's mother slid away to the end of the bench. "I can't *believe* your mother let you come here! You're just a child! How *could* she!" She stood up. "And anyway, there's nothing I can do. It's not up to me! And if it were…oh, my dear…" She touched Kena's cheek, and Kena flinched and stood up too.

"It's okay," she managed. She held her face still with sheer willpower, not to embarrass herself more. "Excuse me."

She turned and walked stiffly through the crowd to the hall and the bottom of the stairs. She kept her back straight as she went up and pressed her injured palm down on the banister to keep from crying. When she got to the top, she saw a bathroom straight ahead and she ran for it, shutting the door and sinking to the floor with her back against it.

And she let her tears come, all those tears she'd stuffed down while she held up her hope like a flag.

And fresh tears of humiliation for spilling out that hope. And more, the worst, because Adam was dead. *Dead.* And she didn't even get to see him before he died. He was supposed to be here to show her the river and Homer and Too—and *everything.*

And then even more tears because she still had to get to the train, and without David, who she thought was her friend.

And then a whole new wave, the *worst* worst that she couldn't bear to think about most times, but now she'd lost her strength not to: no back home and her room and Mama—no happy ending. It was supposed to be like *A Little Princess* when Sara was reunited with her father and all of her beautiful things. Adam's mother was supposed to take her on her lap and make everything all right.

But Frances Hodgson Burnett wasn't writing her story. She dropped her head to her knees, stretching her dress over them. Ugly dress, ugly boots. How she'd loved them! She'd never-ever wear them to a *prison.* She'd throw them in the *garbage* before she ever did that!

She sat for a long time.

Then she pulled off a wad of toilet paper and blew her nose. She wet a corner of a towel and wiped the snot off her face. She gingerly washed her hands, wincing at the sting of the soap. Her Band-aids got soaked and fell off. Her palm was swollen and red. She stretched to see in the mirror—blotchy face and red eyes. She peed and threw the Band-aids into the wastebasket. There wasn't any laundry basket for the towel. She cracked open the door and peeked out.

There were three doors, and one of them was Adam's. She wished she could go in and take a little rest. Like Goldilocks. She heard scratching and a whine. Which door? And more scratching. Homer! She turned the knob. She slipped inside.

He launched himself at her, licking her face, stopped to make a circle, then licked her face again, his tail wagging furiously. Kena flung her arms around his neck, and they rolled onto the rug. Kena lay there and Homer stood over her, panting and drooling in happiness.

"Did they make you stay up here?" Kena knelt and rubbed behind Homer's ears. "Did they?" She ran her hands over his head and back, and he sat, tail thumping, basking in the attention. "Well, you're not missing a thing! You wouldn't like it a bit!"

He put out his right foot.

"Oh, how do you do?" She shook his paw. "I'm Kena. Oh, Homer, I'm so glad to meet you! Adam was going to bring me at the Fourth of July. He said you'd hide from the fireworks, like Gideon said. But I'd stay with you, I would!" She snuffled her face into his neck. "Oh, Homer, we miss him!"

She looked around. The bed was big, and the dresser had a lacy cloth on top. It didn't look like Adam's room at Brandt at all. There was an open suitcase on a chest under the window. She walked over and looked out. There were the woods. They looked like woods in a fairy story, mysterious under a blanket of snow. The sun was gone, and it was snowing again.

Pretty soon it would start to get dark.

When he'd heard "Adam," Homer had walked to the door, and now Kena was forced to push him away. "Homer, I have to go." She knelt and hugged him. "I wish you could come too."

Homer whined, looking from the door to her.

"No, you have to stay," she said firmly, working not to cry. She opened the door to squeeze through. But Homer pushed around her and made a beeline to the door opposite and stared at the doorknob. Words wouldn't have been clearer. Kena tiptoed across and turned the knob, and peeked in. She saw the end of a bed and legs crossed at the ankles, their stockinged feet bobbing.

Her heart skipped a beat. For a second she thought—she swung the door open, and Homer rushed in.

It was Gideon on the bed. He lurched up. "Homer!"

His eyes were red. Had he been crying? Now that she was up close, she saw that he looked like David, thin and dark, except his hair was long and shaggy. And glasses. He took out earbuds and leaned across the bed to scratch Homer, looking at her.

"Hi, Kena," he said. He said it just right, like they were already friends.

"Hi, Gideon," she said back. Struck with shyness, she looked at her feet.

"Cool boots," he said.

Gideon could tell she'd been crying. He felt dumb and clueless. All the questions he'd imagined asking were ridiculous; she was just a little girl.

"Oh, Too!" Her face lit up. But when Kena went to pet the cat, he jerked away from her hand and skittered out the door.

"Too doesn't like me," she said forlornly.

"Too takes a while to warm up, is all."

But Kena didn't have time for Too to warm up.

Adam's laundry bag was in the corner. Adam's room. There were two framed pictures above a desk. Adam's desk. She walked over to look at them, the one from the service and another one of Adam and Homer grown up.

"I took that," Gideon said.

"You took pictures when you were little?"

"The other one. But we were friends then," he said. "I met Adam in kindergarten." He blushed. He'd said it like a boast: He was *my* friend first.

"That's Adam's T-shirt."

They both looked at Gideon's chest, at the swirling music notes. Gideon crossed his arms.

Adam's watch was on the dresser. He *always* wore his watch.

She backed away and sat on the edge of the bed on her hands to keep them from grabbing it. "I read the computer, what you wrote every week."

It was the furthest thing from what he'd ever thought. He'd kept her and her mother sequestered off to the side all this time, never thinking they might read the blog like everyone else. But of course she'd been worrying about Adam too, all this time, and hadn't even been able to see him. She probably thought about Adam every day. More than every day. And her mother—her mother was in jail.

Everything was on its head.

Homer suddenly got up from the floor near Gideon and walked around to Kena, as if taking sides. He jumped and scrambled up next to her. Kena scooted back, and Homer adjusted himself so he could rest his head on her lap. He sighed.

For Gideon, it wasn't a rebuke. It was more like Homer was showing that he, Gideon, had a choice too. He gazed blindly out the open door. There was a hum of voices from below, and now and again distinct words drifted up the stairs.

"…lovely…"

"…another foot or so…"

Kena began to sing softly, rubbing Homer's ears. "Little bird, our soft and downy bird."

"Have you seen Kena?" Gideon heard Mari ask below.

"Is she here?" It was Clare's voice. "That could be tough for Lily. We need to tell the police."

Gideon jerked and swung his head…had Kena heard?

"Singing in…" Kena stopped singing, listening, meeting Gideon's eyes.

"Have you seen Gideon?" It was his mother's voice.

Gideon got up, closed the door, and leaned against it.

"You came on the train with my brother David."

Kena stiffened.

"Did your mother tell you to?"

"No! She doesn't know!"

Gideon knew he could make a mess of things. He needed help. His mother? No, she'd take over. And not Lily. Definitely not Lily.

Mari.

"Stay here. I'll be right back. Just stay!" Homer sat up. At attention.

After the door closed, Kena gave a deep sigh and put her arm across Homer's back. She wished *she* could "just stay." Was he getting the police?

She had to go. She looked around, longing to curl up under Adam's comforter and sleep and sleep and sleep. "Adam," she whispered.

She rolled off the bed. She went to the dresser and picked up Adam's watch. She stroked her cheek with its cool face. She put it back. She fell to her knees in front of the bookcase. She saw another book by the owl author. A dog wearing goggles. She looked. Nobody had written in it. Then she saw it: *From the Mixed-Up Files of Mrs. B. Frankweiler.* It was stamped inside: *Property of Falls Academy.* He'd stolen it.

Homer was watching. He wouldn't tell on her. She went for one last hug. "I have to go, Homer. You stay. Good dog."

She closed the door behind her. Homer went to the door. He had a lot of practice with this particular knob; it just took time.

Kena waited at the top of the stairs for a couple to leave. Then she scurried down and grabbed her jacket and backpack. She wished she could say goodbye to Mari. She'd never see her again.

She opened the heavy door to a blast of cold, and it shut solidly behind her. She got into her jacket and pulled her hood up before zipping it to the top. She shoved *The Mixed Up Files* into her backpack and dragged the pack to the steps, went down a step, and backed into it. The cars parked along the driveway hadn't included that police car, but she couldn't risk the road.

The snow bit her hands and face. She put her hands into her pockets. Adam had told her about a shortcut he and Gideon took on the old railroad tracks. She wound her way around the highest drifts of snow and passed the playhouse with a pang. She saw the opening in the trees and, head down, aimed for it.

◊

"Hi there! You must be Homer! What is it, boy? Ah. When you gotta go, you gotta go, I guess, no matter what the weather. Well, here you go, then. Glad I'm not a dog."

# Chapter 31

## Lily

Lily went to check on Homer and found a wet towel in his place. But Gideon was missing too, and Mari. Had they taken Homer out? In the snow? But she felt a lift of spirits; Gideon had been so alone.

She was on her way to tell Clare when they burst through the door, snow-sprinkled and so sparklingly alive she had an urge to push them back into the cold. She looked around them. "Where's Homer?"

Gideon and Mari exchanged a look. A not-so-happy one.

"We've been searching for him, and for Kena, too," Gideon said.

Searching for Too? But she'd just seen Too, curled up in Lois's open suitcase.

Ellie walked up to her. She was in a poppy-red coat, looking like an exotic flower. Lily felt like a child in her wish for Ellie to be wearing her familiar scrubs. At least she smelled the same, like the lotion she used at the hospital. But they'd barely talked, and she hadn't said the important things.

"I best be on my way. I expect it will be slow as mud, and I'm on duty tomorrow," Ellie said.

But Lily wouldn't be there; her own being on duty was over. What would she do now?

Ellie opened her arms as she had so many times. When they stepped apart, Lily squelched her impulse to smooth the way with "we'll be in touch" and "let's have lunch sometime." They'd been through too much for that.

"You'll always be right here," Ellie said, patting her heart. "With Adam."

Lily followed her across the porch in her stocking feet. The driveway had inches of new snow. She hugged herself, watching Ellie brush off her car and get in. She heard the wipers grind then break loose. She lifted one foot and then the other. Like a duck. Ellie's headlights went on, lighting up a scene from a Christmas card. If she waited, would a doe and her fawn walk into it?

And what about Homer? Behind her was her house, full of people who loved her, but she'd never felt so lonesome.

"Homer! Ho-mer! Come on, Sweetie!"

She'd have to put on her boots and coat and take the flashlight. He could be in the barn. It was odd that he hadn't come for Gideon. Maybe he really was going deaf.

She went in to tell Clare she was going out. Enoch was in the living room with his parents and Khai, she was glad to see. Somebody had put on a Christmas CD. Most of the crowd had left, including, thank God, Kena Wangera, but where had Gideon gone, and the others?

*Ah! Ah! Beautiful is the mother. Ah! Ah! Beautiful is her child.*

When she pushed open the kitchen door, she got her answer.

"She must've gone with the state police," Rachel was saying.

"No, they're parked on the road," Gideon said. "But Mom, you're not listening! She was in Adam's room with Homer. I just left for two minutes!"

"Do you suppose her foster mother came? She was coming up from the city," Clare said right over him.

"Where's David?" Abe asked. "Could—"

"David went home with Jimmy," Rachel said. Lily tried to make sense of it.

"But what about her grandfather?" Mari asked. She looked from Clare to Rachel.

"There is no grandfather," they said in unison.

"Where is he?" Mari asked.

"He *isn't*. He never was. She apparently made him up," Rachel said.

"She made him *up*? But last night! Was she *alone*?" Mari was horrified.

"Who is 'she'?" Lily finally asked, but she thought she might know and dreaded the answer. They turned and stared at her.

Clare took it on. "The little girl who did the song?" She studied Lily's face. "She's Kena Wangera."

"I know that," Lily said. "Oh! 'Kena too.' *That's* what you said, Gideon. You were looking for her *outside*?" She looked wildly around, as if Kena Wangera might be hiding in a cupboard.

"The state police," Clare asked cautiously. "Do you know that too?"

"Know what too?"

"We didn't want you to have more on your plate, so we didn't tell you. Kena Wangera was missing…there was an Amber Alert," Rachel said.

"KidFind," Mari corrected.

"She came to the inn last night," Clare said. Lily heard something in her voice, something like awe. "She told Mari her grandfather was picking her up."

"She lied to David, too, on the train," Gideon added.

It was like a farce, Lily thought. They had no idea she'd had a part in it, but they were looking at her as if they were waiting for a cue. "She came on the train?"

"She lives in Queens. But it was just a fluke she met David,"

Rachel said.

"You mean last night? She went to the inn with David?" Lily asked. No, he didn't come, she remembered.

"I thought it was odd she was alone, but I was so—" Clare said.

"What? You were so what?" Lily asked.

"Charmed," Clare confessed. "She'd come to see *you*."

"But I was there."

"You'd left."

"Why didn't you call me?"

"Well, you had Lois and Bernie and I just…then Louise Berdick came up, you know how she is, and then she got a phone call…"

"That's no excuse, Louise Berdick getting some phone call," Lily accused.

"No, *Kena* got the phone call from her grandfather."

"But she doesn't have one!" Mari said. "You just *said*, Mom."

"There's an Amber Alert?" Lily asked, frowning.

"David saw the Amb…Kid thing on TV, and Abe called the state police," Rachel looked apologetically at Lily. "Last night."

"We met with them. David too," Clare went on. "And Charlie," she added, spreading the guilt.

"*All* of you? You all knew about this. Enoch and Khai too?"

"No, no, not Enoch or Khai," Rachel defended, "or Lois and Bernie either."

"Am I to understand she was *alone*? And no one knew where she was all night? Did any of you *sleep*?"

"We still thought she had a grandfather, and she was with him," Clare said. "And the police were going to look," she added feebly.

"She has a foster mother?" Lily remembered.

"She's coming from the city to get her," Clare said. They looked at the dark window over the sink.

"And you were going to tell me this *when*?" Lily looked from one guilty face to another. "You weren't! You hoped the problem would disappear. This foster mother from Queens would appear like a fairy godmother and sweep her away. And I'd never be the wiser."

But she was the wiser. She'd told Kena Wangera she couldn't help. She'd said Go Away. Maybe not in those exact words, but that's what she said. And now look.

Lily prided herself on rarely raising her voice, no matter the provocation…a pants-wetting five-year-old, a gallon of spilled tempera paint, her husband keeping the most important thing about himself a secret for seven years.

A drunk, driving her son into a concrete wall.

She'd raised her voice to Kena Wangera. A little child. Who was alone.

Lois and Enoch were at the door.

"What's going on?" Enoch asked.

Lily fled the kitchen, shoving Lois and Enoch aside. She saw Lois's stricken face, but she didn't care. Didn't want to care.

All these months. Adam would never have stood for it. How old was she? Seven, six? She didn't even know *that*. When she got to the hall, she grabbed her coat. She sat on the bottom step and pulled a boot on, shaking. First she'd tell the state police, then—"

"Have Yourself a Merry Little Christmas" from *Meet Me In St. Louis* was playing in the living room, and she remembered Tootie running outside in her nightgown barefoot, crying, and knocking the heads off her snow people because she couldn't take them along when they moved.

Lily wished she had a whole yard of them: bam—bam—BAM.

Adam loved Kena. Loved, *loved* Kena Wangera, and she'd—what was *wrong* with her? Leaving Kena at the hospital all those months ago. For someone else to take care of. Who? *Who?!* Her mother was in jail.

She stamped her other foot into her boot. BAM. She'd been so selfish, so…so unmindful. So *heartless*. Pictures spun through her head: the hospital, the cast, the huge bandage, her face. Her face. *Oh, God!* A foster home…all this time.

Her pink dress. *Today is a special day.* The scar.

*Oh, Adam, forgive me!*

There were sounds on the porch. She rushed over and flung open the door. A couple stood there. A Black couple. She'd never seen them before.

"I'm here to pick up Kena," the woman said.

# Chapter 32

## Oliver

The door opened before Oliver had even knocked. A white woman stood there, dressed to go outside. Her face fell when she saw them.

"I thought you were Kena and Homer."

It was the second time that day that Oliver had been a disappointment because he wasn't Kena, although maybe this woman was disappointed he wasn't Homer.

But if she thought he might be Kena at the door, where was Kena?

Farleys' Dock was supposed to have been "less than an hour, easy." But that less-than-an-hour had ballooned into two hours as the snow mounded up. He'd crept along, gripping the steering wheel, stiff with fear he might drive right off the road. He barely made out the exit sign and slid down the ramp, braking. The car made a full circle at the bottom. Heart still in overdrive, he entered the town. The only lights he saw were at an inn. Maybe someone would give him directions.

When he finally found the driveway the innkeeper had directed him to, he braked, skidded, and smacked into a truck. He turned off the ignition, cutting off the irony of the radio singing "I'm Dreaming of a White Christmas." And then he shook, not just from the cold.

Staring at the windscreen as snow covered it, he imagined blood.

When he stepped outside, it was into deep snow. Poor Nigel looked like he was taking a bite out of the truck's tailgate.

He slipped and slogged toward the big lit-up house. When he saw a woman grab at the railing on the porch steps, he hurried to help and his feet went out from under him, and he fell. She gave him a hand up and they clung to each other as they minced across the porch.

Now inside, on sure footing, his new friend took her hand from his arm. "I'm Patrice Washington, Kena's foster mother." He gaped at her.

"You're Patrice? I'm Oliver Wangera."

"Oliver? From Kenya?"

The white woman reached around them to close the door. "Look at your feet! And your pants! Come in, come in! I'm Lily St. John."

"You thought we were Kena," Patrice didn't budge from the doormat, didn't begin to take off her gloves. "And a boy. That boy from the train?"

"No, no…our dog. Homer. I was just going out to look for them. Did you see a state police car down on the road?"

Patrice raised her chin. "They left. I insisted. They can talk to her back home if they need to. But not today, the day of her friend's funeral, like she did something bad. Kena doesn't need any truck with any po-lice."

The truck! He had to tell someone about the truck. Oliver tried to control his shivering. "Kena's out there with your dog?" He abruptly turned to go back outside. "Bloody hell." Patrice clutched his arm again as a crowd of people entered the hall. They began pulling on coats and hats and sorting through a mess of boots, talking the whole time.

"Someone should go to the river. Homer goes there all the time."

"What about flashlights?"

"Use your phones."

"Gideon, call David—maybe she said something."

"I'll take the road to town."

One by one, they noticed Oliver and Patrice and stopped talking. Patrice pulled her coat close against their scrutiny. They turned to listen to Gideon.

"David, do you know anything about Kena Wangera? She's not here. She's what? Jeez, David, why didn't you—" He looked at his watch. "No, every three hours on the weekend. Okay, I'll wait." He peeked at Patrice and Oliver.

"You're shivering," Lily said to Oliver. "We've got to get you out of those wet things." She sat on the bottom step to take her boots off.

"David says she was going back on the train," Gideon told them. "But Jimmy's dad says they've stopped service because of the storm."

"Of course! She came on the train!" Rachel said. "Oh, dear!"

An Asian man put his hand out to Patrice, and she started to pull off her gloves. So he put his hand out to Oliver. "I'm Khai. My God! You're ice cold!"

Lily pulled herself up by the banister and went up the stairs.

Another man put his arm around Khai. "I'm Khai's husband, Enoch St. John."

"I'm Oliver Wangera." They were all gawping at him as if he were some kind of apparition.

"She was with *you*?" a girl almost shouted. "Oh, I'm so *glad!*"

"You mean Kena?" She nodded. He hesitated. "No. She hasn't seen me for a year and a half, back home. In Kenya. The innkeeper in town told me she might be here." They kept staring, as if there were more to the story. So he added, "He gave me a tin of biscuits. Homemade." As if that made any difference.

"That's my dad! I'm Mari."

"What about the state police?" Khai asked.

Patrice froze, one glove off. Oliver took her elbow.

"They left. Someone should call them," he said.

"I'll do that," Khai said. "Enoch and I are taking the road to town. We'll check the meeting house on our way, but it makes sense that we all work our way to the train station, don't you think?"

"I'll take the river path and the old railroad tracks to town," Gideon said. "Adam and I used to go that way."

"I've got the woods, then," Abe said. "Just in case."

"I'll go with you," Rachel put her arm through his.

"Everyone have each other's numbers?" Khai asked.

"Call here on the landline if you find her," Clare suggested. "Or Homer." She looked at everyone's feet and put her boots down. "I'll tell Lois." Patrice backed into the corner as they paraded past her.

"Gideon, can I come with you?" Mari asked, following him out the door.

Patrice and Oliver were alone. He unzipped his anorak and pulled it off, shook it, and hung it on the doorknob. He reached to take her coat. "Let me help you."

Patrice didn't move. She whispered, "That was Lily St. John, that boy's mother." She pointed up the stairs. "She looks like she's about to fall apart."

"It's got to have been a difficult day."

"And now me, like salt in her wounds." Patrice shook her head, frowning. "What was Kena thinking? Nevermind, I know what she was thinking, I'm just worried to death."

Clare was so quiet in her stocking feet that they hadn't noticed she'd come back. An older woman was at her side, wiping her hands on a dish towel.

"Lois, this is Kena's foster mother...I'm sorry, I don't know your name."

"Patrice. Washington."

"And this is Oliver Wangera, from Kenya. Kena's—what relation are you? You're way too young to be anyone's grandfather! This is Lois St. John, Adam's grandmother."

"I'm so sorry for your loss," Patrice said. "And here I am, causing more trouble. I just meant to pick Kena up. And now this."

Lois ignored Patrice's outstretched hand to give her a hug. "You must be worried sick!"

"I'm going out," Clare said, looking at Oliver. "Tell Lily I'll check the barn and playhouse again, okay?" She stepped into her boots, pulled up her hood, fastened its flaps under her chin, and left.

Oliver had no idea who she was. "I might be blocking the road. And to top that, I'm hooked up on somebody's truck."

It was the last straw for Patrice, and tears started coursing down her cheeks. She turned to go out, clutching her pocketbook to her chest, and her gloves fell to the floor. She reached down. Oliver saw her sway and grabbed her arm.

"You two come with me. We need to get some food into you and get you warm," Lois commanded.

"I have to move my car," Oliver said. "And I'm going to look for Kena."

"Not like that, you aren't. Look in the closet, there should be something." Lois put her arm around Patrice and walked her across the hall and through a doorway. "I'm sure Homer has some blood-hound in him along with everything else, and it sounds like that little girl of yours has gumption to spare."

"Here you go."

Oliver looked up the stairs. Lily St. John had her arms full, and when she got to the bottom, she put the stack of clothing in his arms. She looked at his feet. "You need boots, too. I hope size 10 fits; it's all I have."

Their eyes met, and he was looking into unfathomable sadness. She looked away.

"There's a bathroom down the hall." He didn't move.

"Don't be silly," she said. So he obeyed. As he was stepping out of his trousers in the bathroom, there was a knock. "They want your car keys!"

"In the jacket hanging on the door."

When he returned, the hall was empty except for a parka hanging on the newel post, a pair of boots beneath it, and a hat and gloves on top. He was pretty sure he knew whose they were, and the last thing he wanted to do was put them on.

Don't be a fool. Kena was out there. He reached for Adam St. John's boots.

# Chapter 33

## Alice

"Wangera! Attorney."

Alice groped her way out of sleep. She tried not to sleep during the empty weekend hours because she'd pay later in the empty nighttime hours, but the relief of Kena, and then Oliver—*Oliver!* She'd dropped into a dreamless sleep, and for that little while she'd been free.

She rubbed cold water over her face and grabbed her Abbott papers, trying to keep her racing thoughts in check. Why today? A Saturday. In a snowstorm. And even though he was a public defender and had no choice about defending her, she dearly wanted Brian Abbott to think she was a good person. Not just good…*equal,* a professional…like him. Not just a "felon." As if he'd pull something special out of a special legal hat he kept for his *professional* felons. She thought of Sylvie and Cricket and Keresha and felt ashamed.

Always a gentleman, he stood when she entered, shook her cold hand, and waited for her to sit before sitting himself. He was wearing a flannel shirt and jeans instead of his usual three-piece suit.

"How are you? I imagine it's been a tough few days," he said.

"Well, all's well that ends well," she said ruefully.

He looked startled. And like he was disappointed in her. What had she said?

*God.* He was referring to *Adam.* She blushed.

"I didn't mean Adam. I meant Kena. I meant my daughter."

"It's of no consequence, it just sounded odd…under the circumstances."

"But it *is*, I mean…of consequence. Do you know about Kena?" And Oliver, she should tell him about Oliver. But she didn't want to; she wanted to keep Oliver to herself.

He swung his briefcase onto the table. "I was on the way home from Plattsburgh early and realized it would work to stop on the way." He drummed his fingers on the leather. "Robin Barker sent us the charges. She'll be announcing them Monday at a press release, and I didn't want that to be how you got the information." He unzipped the case and pulled papers out, handing her the top one.

"You'll need time to digest everything, but I'd like to just touch on our likely next steps, and I have a procedure I'd like to move on immediately, if you agree." He folded his arms against his chest, averting his eyes to give her privacy.

She wasn't ready! It was too fast. Couldn't she have one more day of not knowing? One more day of Kena safe? Of Oliver?

Her conscience recoiled. Her *one more day* was the day of Adam's funeral.

She fixed her eyes on the print. After reading the first awful words three times, she began to take it in. The bold face and the italics, the stiff formal language, were the stuff of her middle-of-the-night horrors. She broke into a sweat. It could mean ten years.

"Ms. Barker aims to be the next DA when he retires next year," Brian Abbott said. "And those DWI fatalities up in Clinton County are having an influence. We were lucky in August that nothing occurred just before your plea. She could have put a lot more time on your current sentence, you might recall."

Alice did recall. She could have been sentenced up to 15 years for Kena's and Adam's injuries. There were plenty of missing pieces from the summer and fall, when she'd been too stunned to do much more than drag her body to the table or wherever it was supposed to be, but she never forgot Leandra's Law, named for someone's child who died in a DWI accident. What was it like for those parents, having a law named after their child? Never knowing when everything that happened would be flung up again because of someone like her.

She'd thrown up every day—her body's reaction to what she'd done and how small she really was, as insignificant as the rest of the women who couldn't be raising their babies, some of them practically babies themselves, like Cricket. She was ashamed of how patronizing she'd been to the others in the jail, thinking she and Kena were different. Better.

More deserving.

And then the offer had come…one year, as if they *were*. For a couple of days she'd been almost euphoric: *not* 15, *not* even 5. One. *One*. But now—Adam had died, and it would probably be 10 if they made a plea, and she deserved it.

But Kena didn't. She wiped her hands on the legs of her jumpsuit.

"We'll give Ms. Barker reasons she can use publicly to justify a lesser charge. She's not unsympathetic," Brian said. "This is just the first step in a long dance."

Alice had searched the newspapers for clues. Robin Barker was a graduate of NYU Law; she wore pastel pantsuits and dangly earrings; she was a single parent of two teenage girls. She was Black. Like Kena. Was that good? Was it bad?

"You've proven yourself to be a model inmate. You've been entirely cooperative with Child Protection Services, seeking their help rather than waiting for the court to order a placement. That's important."

He was probably talking about something important, but she was stuck on 10. The math was simple. This year plus 10 equals 11 equals Kena's whole childhood.

"Alice?"

"Yes."

"Let's look at what we might bring to a plea—"

"But I already said I was guilty."

"Of the Aggravated DWI, yes. This is a new charge. Your new plea will be regarding Adam St. John's death."

But she was guilty. She was.

"You have no prior history, no DWI other than the one you're serving for the same accident. Your BAC—blood alcohol concentration—was .10."

Another 10.

".05 is driving under the influence and .08 brings it to driving while intoxicated, as you'll recall."

He liked the word *recall*. She knew the numbers by heart.

"The court has seen countless repeat offenders getting off with fines and suspended licenses. People who have been lucky. Not innocent. *Lucky*. A future accident, a future fatality, walking out the door."

She *would…not…cry*.

"I can return next week after you've had some time to take it in, and we'll go over the rest then. It's a lot to absorb."

"No. Please. Just don't be too nice about it."

"All right." He cleared his throat. "Have you thought about what I talked about? Alcoholism is a disease, and…"

"I borrowed a book about it; the thing is, it was never a problem for me before…" *Before Oliver left*. "I know I won't ever drink again."

But she'd seen herself in Sylvie's AA book, how she'd feel impatient waiting for Kena to go to sleep, how her spirits lifted as it got closer to the time she could pour a glass, how she'd make sure she always had a spare bottle. Sneaking a drink earlier and earlier in the day. Even in the morning.

*That* morning.

"It feels like saying I'm an alcoholic is an excuse, all that 'disease' stuff, like it's not my fault. But it is."

"Not an excuse. A mitigating circumstance. There's an outside AA group that meets here at the jail so inmates can attend. The state can't impose it, which is good, because we can show you're going voluntarily. I don't mean to say you have to attend meetings, but going might help you personally too."

"My friend Sylvie goes." Oh! She covered her mouth. It was supposed to be anonymous.

"As do I," Brian Abbott said. "Twenty-two years come March."

*Him?* In his three-piece suits? *Twenty-two* years?

"We'll offer counseling. And community service; we'll bring up the writing group you've been facilitating. BAC testing. Ignition locks and driver responsibility assessments would be required for probation, but we'll bring them up proactively."

He pulled out a paper.

"But about this coming Monday. I'd like to ask the court to appoint an attorney for Makena, called a guardian ad litem, to represent her needs. They'll make a report, and I haven't a doubt that it will state that a shorter sentence is in her best interests. A guardian ad litem would solicit opinions from her foster mother, her teacher, and others who can testify to your relationship and stability and to Makena's needs. Her unique needs."

Alice started shaking her head.

"Just bear with me. I want Robin Barker to see the kind of public sympathy I could bring to bear—how you rescued Makena as a baby, an orphan. A child with AIDS."

"*No!* I *told* you, no publicity about Kena's HIV! And she's HIV positive; it's not the same as AIDS!"

"I haven't forgotten. It doesn't necessarily mean we'd use it publicly, but the idea of it might sway the sentencing. It could mean less time in prison and more time with your daughter. It should be taken into account. Until this, you've been an excellent mother." He put his hand up. "Not being nice, just a fact. You've shaped your life around a child who needs special care, a child who would have no parent if you hadn't volunteered. A child who might not be *alive* if it weren't for you. You saved a child's life, and the tragedy of Adam St. John's death is at least somewhat balanced."

Alice realized that what was growing inside of her was anger. Intense, red-hot anger on behalf of Lily and Enoch St. John.

"No. No. You have to stop. There can *never* be any balance. Never. Kena's alive. And Adam isn't." She whispered. "Their child isn't."

"All right," he said gently. "Let's stop for today."

"No, let's finish what you came for." A day at a time, Sylvie said, sometimes wasn't enough. Sometimes it was a heartbeat at a time.

"Will I be there, or Patrice, if Kena meets with this guardian person?"

"No. That's why it's so good for you. You have no influence, although you'll be interviewed as part of the process."

"What if it's a bad report? Can you decide not to submit it?"

"It would be a court appointment, and once it's in play I have no control. But do you really think…let me put it this way. *I* know it's not possible you'd receive a negative report. It's a slam dunk."

Alice was taken aback. Slam dunk.

He didn't know, though, about Farleys' Dock. He'd been in Plattsburgh.

Brian Abbott checked his watch. "There's one other thing called a

Victim Impact Statement. A member of the victim's family can make a statement on the victim's behalf, including the impact of the death on their family, before the sentencing."

Alice flinched. Not "victim." Adam. *Say Adam.*

"It's their choice if they do, but I want the report from the guardian ad litem to be available to them prior to making it, to remind them of Adam's friendship with Kena."

It was almost funny.

"I don't think they'll need any reminding about Adam's friendship with Kena. And Kena's already been in the news."

At least now he'd understand why she'd said "All's well that ends well."

# Chapter 34

## Kena

Kena shoved her feet, like two arctic explorers, between the railroad tracks, following Dora's beam of light. She was too tired to lift them up. Now and again she tripped on a tie and fell. Her legs were soaked and beginning to freeze, and she couldn't feel her fingers inside her stockinged hands. Adam had called this a shortcut, but he should have called it a longcut!

The tracks suddenly went downhill, and she fell and slid. There was a tunnel ahead. She tried to see the end of it, but Dora only lit up a few feet ahead of her. And what if a train came! She crawled up the bank. There was a road! Accustomed to the deep snow, she wobbled, one foot hanging in space, then came down hard, as if the pavement had risen up. The road had been ploughed but was covering up again. There weren't any car tracks. But across the road was the railroad station; a light spotlighted a sign over a footbridge that crossed the tracks: New York City. She'd done it! She turned Dora off and tucked her into her backpack.

The ice-covered railing burned her hand, and driving snow peppered her face as she crossed the exposed bridge. By the time she got across, every part of her was shaking, even her lips. She cleared a space on a cement bench with her arm, sat down with her pack on her lap, and tucked her arms behind it and her face into it. She only had one prayer.

*Mama.*

Then, as if in answer, she remembered Adam and his dad in their sleeping bags, listening to the loons. She tugged Toby's bag out and wiggled herself in, boots and all, like a caterpillar in its cocoon. She'd said flutterby when she was little. *Mama.*

Did Adam have wings?

The train would be warm.

She hurt all over, and she knew what it meant; she was sick. She was sick and her hand throbbed. It might be infected.

She heard a bell and jerked her chin up, her heart lifting too, and looked down the track. All she saw was snow. She heard it again.

Toby! The phone was in her pocket. Frantic, she pulled the sock off with her teeth and groped for it.

"Toby?"

"No, it's Santa Claus!" Light and warmth flowed out of the little phone.

"I'm at the train station! It's FREEEE-ZING here!" It could be an adventure, now that Toby was there.

"Kena, it's suppertime! You should be home by now!"

Didn't he know anything? "Toby, there's a blizzard!"

"Well, how was I s'posed to know? There's no blizzard here! But Kena, wait 'til you hear! I'm gonna stay! I mean, I get to stay with my mom, I don't even have to go back for my stuff, social services is gonna get everything."

Kena was stunned. But Toby went on, oblivious.

"You can keep my sleeping bag, though, and my Harry Potter pillowcase."

As if that made everything okay.

"I'll go to the middle school on the bus. And listen to this! They have a climbing wall! And a hiking club! They even hike in winter!"

She pressed her lips shut tight.

"Kena, are you there?" She turned her face away, as if he could see.

"Kena, Kena, where are you?" It was the sing-songy voice that he used for Jackie. Like she was a baby.

"Kena, say something!"

But she couldn't. She flailed at the sleeping bag. Which was covered with Superman and Batman and some other ugly man, all green and muscly. *Toby's* sleeping bag. She hated him, off having his happy time! Climbing wall! He didn't even ask how she was! She stood up, and the sleeping bag sagged to her knees.

She shuffled forward and drew back as far as she could. She took a big breath in and threw the phone with Toby inside it as hard as she could. It went spinning, all the way across the tracks. It was probably the best throw she ever made. She started to cry. She'd never see Toby again. Her only friend in America.

A shadow sprang out of the darkness on the other side. A wolf! She tried to step back and fell over her backpack, hitting the back of her head on the bench. Then she heard a bark. And another. She struggled to her feet. It was Homer on the other side of the tracks, running back and forth. He ran to the edge of the platform as if he might jump.

"No, Homer! No!" What if the train came? She frantically kicked at the sleeping bag to get loose.

"Homer, stay, STAY! I'm coming, STAY!" She kept shouting as she grabbed her backpack and dragged it to the bridge.

"STAY, Homer, STAY!"

Stumbling across, she looked over in horror. Homer was gone. Then she heard him whining, and there he was, trying to scrabble up the icy metal steps.

Kena slid her backpack down and followed on her butt, her head pounding like it was being hit with a hammer. When she got to the bottom, Homer dropped the phone in her lap.

"Homer, you fetched!" She flung her arms around his neck. He licked her face, whining, and pushed his head against her stomach and chest and face and then all over again, as if he were checking her for injuries. He licked her hand, and she jerked it away.

"Oh, Homer."

She'd have to take him back.

She slid the phone into her pack. She'd left one of her socks on the other side. She gingerly switched the remaining sock to her hurt hand and went for her pack. Then she remembered what Gideon had said.

But Homer kept going in a circle, trying to get his teeth on the strap.

"Homer, stay!" And he did, while she pulled one front leg and then the other through the straps, trying to perch the pack on his back with her arm. She finally got the waist strap under him and clicked in. She tightened it.

"Okay, Homer, time to go!"

He didn't budge.

"Homer, we're going home. Home!"

He held up a paw. She leaned over to shake it. A sharp pain shot through the back of her head, and she fell to her knees. He pawed at her arm. She took his foot, feeling dizzy. There was ice between his toes.

"Oh, Homer, I'm sorry!" He stood patiently while she pried the ice away. "There you go!" A wave of sickness swept through her, and she abruptly threw up. She knelt there, shivering, until Homer nudged her. She pulled her hood back and felt the back of her head. She held her hand up. Blood. She wiped her hand against the snow, and Homer tried to lick it. "No, Homer." Can a dog get HIV?

She turned Dora on, and they crossed the road and entered the woods, retracing the way they'd come separately, but now together…a team. The erratic beam of the flashlight bounced off the falling snow, so Kena aimed it straight down and soldiered on, hunched over, her injured hand in her pocket. All she had to do was go back the way she came. And Homer wouldn't let her get lost. But still.

"Maitu," she pleaded. "Mama."

The darkening woods would be filled with animals sleeping in cozy burrows under the snow. She pictured the map of the Hundred Acre Wood with the trees and everybody's house, and Eeyore's down in the corner. Eeyore's Gloomy Place. And the time Pooh and Piglet went to see Eeyore in the snow, and they sang Pooh's song to keep them going. She and Homer were like Pooh and Piglet, making their way. Lemmy was safe in her backpack, but she wished he was inside her jacket next to her.

What was a acre?

*Nobody KNOWS tiddly-pom, how cold my TOES, tiddly-pom, are growing. Adam.*

Her toes hurt with every step. Would they have to cut them off like that man who climbed that mountain? She tried to rub her fingers together. They felt numb and fat. That man's fingers were black like they were burned in a fire. Don't cry! Your face will freeze. That man's nose froze and fell off. The picture Toby showed her haunted her for weeks. She swayed, stopped and watched the snow cover her boots. Homer whined. He pushed her legs.

He had found her and was supposed to bring her home.

Kena jerked her eyes open. She had to take Homer home.

"I had a dog and his name was Blue…" Her lips were stiff; her teeth clacked against each other. "Betcha five dollars he was a good dog too…" Each step felt like a hundred pounds. She fought against waves of sleepiness. She slipped and fell to her knees. She'd rest for a little bit.

Homer barked. The snow kept falling and falling and falling, covering her like a blanket. Homer barked and barked and barked.

# Chapter 35

## Lily

Lily pulled her boots on. Again. She felt mulish and mean. All she wanted was to retreat upstairs into Adam's bed. But instead, she tucked her hair into her hood and tightened the cords. As she reached for the doorknob, it chimed. She jumped back as if she'd been stung, looking down. It was the phone in Oliver Wangera's flimsy jacket that was ringing.

She took another step away. What if it was Her? Alice Wangera?

Oh, stop! It could be about Kena!

"Hello?"

She heard heavy breathing.

"I'd like to speak to Oliver Wangera, please."

So not a Heavy Breather, which would have been the absolutely last and final straw.

"I'm sorry, but he's not here."

"Oh, dear!"

Lily's manners kicked in. "Would you like to leave a message?" She went to the table for something to write on. A book was propped between two balusters. She slid it out, and a jolt went up her spine. There on the cover were Billy and the owls. Meeps. No. Weeps. And

Wol. She looked up the stairs. Her heart speeded up, as if Adam could have just been there. But she knew who'd left it. Kena Wangera.

"Hello?"

Lily cradled the book and took a pen and a sticky note from the drawer. "I'm ready."

"This is Maggie Wells…at the LuluWells Foundation."

Lily wrote *Maggie.*

The dog on the cover of the book was called Mutt.

Homer!

"Listen, I have to go, but I'll tell him. Maggie Wells."

"And tell him it's *not* about the orphanage. I don't want him to get his hopes up."

"I have no idea what you're talking about," Lily said, impatient to be off.

"The clinic. Kirinyaga?"

"Kirin-what?"

"Kirinyaga Children's Home? HIV kids? Kenya?"

Kenya? HIV? It was so unexpected it felt like another language.

Lois waved from the doorway.

"Just a second."

Looking at the phone, Lois whispered, "They found a sleeping bag at the station."

Lily pressed the phone to her stomach. "A sleeping bag?"

"Superheroes. It doesn't sound like a little girl's." Lois returned to the living room.

"Are you Alice?" Maggie Wells asked.

It would be funny if it weren't so *not funny.* Lily took a big breath. Count to five. Let it out. One more time.

"My name is Lily St. John, and I live in Farleys' Dock, New York. Oliver Wangera just arrived here looking for his daughter, Kena. Who seems to have taken my dog out into a snowstorm. So I have to go."

"Is Alice there?"

She didn't know a damn thing, this Maggie Wells.

Lily hugged the book she'd given Adam when he wasn't much older than Kena. Who should *not* have come there. At All. And it was not fair that she had to be talking to this lady who only cared about the Wangera family.

Not hers AT ALL.

On the very night of Adam's funeral.

There was *so not* any grace.

And orphans? Lily did care about orphans, of course she did. And HIV.

But at least *they* still had a chance; they were *alive*. She would've taken Adam any way she could; hadn't she tried to bargain with every-one? Jesus and Buddha and every star in the sky, holding Adam's hand and breathing with him, holding his breath in her heart and breathing him into the next one, and the next, and the next. Imagining him in a wheelchair, imagining him *paralyzed*, allowing the worst she could think of, tossing away all hope for his body in favor of his brain. Or his soul. Just leave me his soul. Just leave me *Adam*.

"*Listen.*" She was so mad she was talking through her teeth. "Alice Wangera is in jail for driving drunk and killing my son. So. *No*. She isn't here."

As soon as she said it, she was washed in shame. She pushed END and dropped her head to the top of the newel post. She stood like that for a long time.

"Fuck." She smacked her forehead on the post once, twice, a third time. *Fuck. Fuck. Fuck.* She raised her head and pressed redial like the good girl she'd been raised to be. It rang only once before Maggie Wells answered and apologized.

"I'm so sorry."

"Well...me too."

"I'm embarrassed, but I don't remember your name."

"Lily."

"What's your son's name?" Maggie asked softly.

"Adam." She opened the book to her inscription. Was it that same birthday they'd given him his Sherlock Holmes hat?

"How old was Adam?"

"Eight. I mean, 21."

She tucked the book back between its stair bookends.

"I just lost it there for a minute, but it's not your fault. It's been a hard day. And now this, with Kena. She was a Little Sister to him… to Adam…in this program at the university…and he actually felt that way. I mean, like a big brother. I kept putting off meeting her… them…her and her mother. Alice. Because—well, that's neither here nor there. She's just a little girl! But still, Alice Wangera should never have let her come!"

"Come?"

"To the service. Today was our service for Adam."

"Today? Oh, honey…I can't believe you're still standing."

Lily's knees buckled, and she folded onto the bottom step. It was being called honey.

"It's just…it's not *fair*," she blurted. "Everybody's running around because of *her* kid, not Adam. It's snowing! And he loves the snow! And Yule! It's going to be Yule! He's missing everything! And it will keep happening! Being a vet! Homer! Homer only *really* smiles for Adam. And now Homer's gone too, and it's Kena's fault! Her mother takes my son, and then *she* takes my dog!" She stopped, appalled.

She rushed down the hall and into the bathroom, pushing the door shut. She staggered to the toilet and put down the lid and sat. She sobbed, pulling toilet paper, wiping, tearing more off, mopping, blowing, tearing off more. Snot ran down her wrist. Oh, God. Oh, *Adam.*

I wasn't *there*! You didn't *wait*!

Why did you get in the fucking car?

Oliver's pants hung neatly on the towel rack, a sock on either side. One had a hole in the toe. She remembered his phone. It was on her lap. She started to laugh. "Oh, God, are you still there?"

"Oh, my dear."

"It's just so…so *hard*! I don't know how to do this!"

"If anyone tells you there's a way, you tell them to put it where the sun don't shine! It's the hardest thing you'll ever do. There isn't a how-to for what you're going through. You'll just keep living, a day at a time…or an hour, some days, or minutes. Crying helps, but it hurts worse than anything you can imagine. Well, you know that."

How did she know, this Maggie person? And as if she'd asked it out loud, Maggie answered.

"My daughter, and my granddaughter, died."

I'm not the only one, Lily thought. And it felt like gratitude. Her mind stumbled, shocked that she could think such a thing. Her daughter and her granddaughter. Both.

"My granddaughter was 27," Maggie said. "She walked in front of a mail truck. I never did meet the driver. I should have made an effort, at least later, but I was too angry for a long time. It wasn't his fault, not at all. There was a photograph in the paper. He looked like he'd been tortured."

Alice Wangera looked tortured too; that was a good word for it. She'd looked stunned. Crazy. Lily was shocked when she saw the photo but not from the craziness; she'd thought Alice was Black. For the first time, Lily wondered: had Kena seen it?

"I hated him, even his family…*especially* his family…that he got to have a family," Maggie said.

"It's like a worm inside," Lily confessed. "Like she's evil. Even Kena! She's eight-years-old! It makes me feel evil *thinking* like that…

Adam would want me to forgive. No, not forgive. He wouldn't think it needed forgiving in the first place." Lily looked at her sticky, snotty hand. Ugh. "Are you still mad at him?" She turned on the water.

"It usually means I need to cry."

Lily put the phone down and rubbed her hands under the water and took a washcloth from the shelf and soaked it. She wrung it out and washed her face and picked up the phone.

Maggie Wells had kept talking. "…such a relief when I realized it wasn't my *duty* to be mad, like a dog trying to protect…well, nothing…I haven't anything left to protect. Do you know the poet Denise Levertov? She wrote about her grief being a homeless dog under her porch. 'Talking to Grief.' Like that was the dog's name and she needed to invite it inside."

Homer!

"I'm sorry, but I have to go. I'll tell Oliver Wangera you want to talk to him."

"I have a proposal for him. But don't say that. He'll think it's for the orphanage."

Lily had a devastating thought. "Did Kena come from that orphanage?"

AIDS. But wouldn't Adam have said?

"No, from her relatives, when she was a baby."

"So she doesn't have it." Of *course* she doesn't. Just look at her, dancing like that.

"You'll have to ask Oliver about—"

"Wait! She *has* it? AIDS? Her mother? Her birth mother?"

Maggie gave in. "Her parents died from it. But you should ask Oliver."

Oh, Adam, I've messed everything up! "Do you wonder? I mean…" she hesitated. "About souls?"

"Of course. When I was a girl I imagined souls looked like jelly beans with little wings, and we got to pick our flavor. Mine was 'very cherry'. I read somewhere that maybe we're not Earth beings with spirits…we're spirit beings with Earth bodies. Like we *chose* to come here for a while."

Lily gripped Oliver Wangera's phone. She didn't want to hang up. "I have to go."

"Listen, you call me any time! In the middle of the night, tomorrow, in a year, *any time*. I mean it."

Lily stood on shaky legs and went to the hall to zip the phone back into Oliver's pocket with the note. It was still snowing hard. Just a week ago she was wondering if it would snow for Yule and telling Ellie about the year she and Enoch dressed Adam up as a sun god. They'd made a paper crown and drenched the rays in gold glitter. Adam's hair sparkled for days. Enoch would sing "Here Comes the Son."

Lily walked into the living room. Lois and Patrice were sitting on the couch, and Bernie was snoring in the yellow chair. She fell into the other chair and closed her eyes. She just needed a minute. Then she'd go.

"No one's called since the sleeping bag," Lois said softly. "Patrice has been telling me about her foster children. I was just asking her if any of them were Fresh Air children. You know, like the child who stayed at Clare's when Mari was in elementary school. From the city?"

Lily looked at her blankly.

"My kids can't do that," Patrice said.

"They don't let foster kids come?" Lois asked indignantly.

Something in Patrice's voice broke through, and Lily thought she knew why her foster kids couldn't be Fresh Air kids. How could she have forgotten, for even a second? Kena had HIV. "My God!"

"What's wrong?" Lois asked.

"I just realized—*that's* why the mask and gloves! When I saw Kena at the hospital!"

They heard rushing footsteps in the hall. Then Mari was in the doorway, breathing hard, covered with snow, and holding Lily's old phone in her mittened hand as if she had a phone call.

"Gideon's coming. Kena was with Homer. She's pretty sick."

# Chapter 36

## Gideon

Gideon held his aching hands under the warm water. Gauze and tape were on the counter; he hoped it meant someone had taken care of Kena's hand. Lily's bathroom looked like a porch sale. Kena's sweatshirt was draped over the shower rod between tiny pink tights and dirty leggings. Her pink dress hung from a hanger hooked on the shower head. The star-decorated sock she'd worn on her hand was draped over the edge of the bathtub.

There was a scrap of paper on the counter next to the tape. It was damp, and he unfolded it cautiously. Some of the ink had run, but he could make out most of the words.

> *The same stars*
> *The same moon*
> *The same…*sun?
> *Look up, and I—*

The rest was a smudge. He draped it next to the single sock. Stars and stars.

For some reason he felt like bawling.

He stopped outside Adam's door. He could hear Lily's voice and, judging by the accent, Oliver Wangera's. Kena was crying. Then he heard his dad's deep voice.

Okay, then.

The door opened and the "snowballs-to-me" police woman came out. She motioned to the stairs, and he followed her down. She began to zip up her coat and stopped to reach into an inside pocket. She handed him a card.

"Your dad said he was your best friend," she said, and went out the door.

*CompassionateFriends.com.* He felt like he'd been caught out.

And he couldn't hide out in Adam's room; it was taken. What if he just went home? But Lily and his dad were coming down the stairs, so he trailed them into the living room.

"Well?" Clare said.

Lily squeezed Gideon's arm, aimed for the couch, and fell back with a groan. She picked up a pillow and hugged it. Gideon scanned the room; besides his dad and Lily, his mom, Enoch and Khai, Clare, and Adam's grandparents were there.

And Mari.

He walked toward the kitchen.

"Gideon, would you mind getting me a glass of white wine?" Lily called out. "And bring in those blondie things," his mom added. He stood in front of the open refrigerator. He never drank in front of his mom. But Lily was about to, and Enoch and Khai were drinking beer. He brought Lily her wine and handed the tin of bars to his mom. Then he went back for a copper ale, picking up one of the chairs from the kitchen and setting it down next to Mari. Mari raised her eyebrows, and Gideon handed her the bottle. She took a sip, looking over to her mom. Clare frowned, and she gave it back, making a face. With everything that had happened, Gideon had forgotten she was younger than he was. Three years. Was it too much?

It had felt good to escape the house and enter the snowy night with her by his side. Her dark hair swung under her red stocking cap and sparkled from the snow. It had felt good when she grabbed onto him when she slipped. She was so small.

"Homer! Ho-mer!" he'd yelled.

"Kena!" Mari had called. "Kena!"

But when they got to the river, he didn't feel good at all. The beam of his flashlight didn't penetrate the black water. He shook his head, pushing away an image of a little body being carried away in it.

"Ho-mer! Ke-na!" His voice was muffled by the snow. "Let's try the old train track," he finally said. "This was just to make sure, anyway."

Mari tripped. She hung onto his arm to stoop and dig around. She came up with a telephone handset. She wiped the snow off and pressed TALK. Nothing. What in the world? He took it and pressed TALK himself. She gave him a look and he gave it back to her.

"This is so weird," she said. "It's not even a cellphone. Who comes here?"

"Just us." Him and Adam. "And Lily, I guess."

Mari zipped the phone into her pocket. It was colder going the other way, as if the snow had turned to show its real face.

"Where's the track go?"

"What?"

"You said 'old track.'"

"To the station and to an old quarry. Kids used to swim there before they put the fence up."

"Did you and Adam?"

It hurt to hear "you" and "Adam".

"A couple times." He'd been too chicken to jump.

They'd come to the crossing. They looked both ways as if a ghost train might suddenly explode out of the snow. Gideon turned right, toward the station. Kena might not know that was the way to go, but

Homer wouldn't let her go toward the quarry; he'd hated it when Adam jumped in and disappeared under the water.

"Homer!"

"Kena!"

They plowed on, hunched over against the deepening cold, her hand hanging onto the back of his parka. The snow felt like needles. Gideon stopped.

Something.

"Did you…" she began.

He held his hand up. Nothing, just the hissing of the snow. They started to walk again.

Something. He was sure this time. They stopped and listened.

Barking.

"C'mon!"

He kept having to wait for Mari to catch up.

"Go…go!" Mari pushed him. "Don't worry, I can't get lost." She looked up at him. Snowflakes hung on her eyelashes.

He wanted to kiss her. How could he want to kiss her with everything that was happening?

"Gideon! Just go!" She handed him the flashlight and held up her cellphone. "I have a light."

He stepped ahead, picking up his pace.

"Homer!"

Barking. And then, around a curve he hadn't realized he was on, there they were—Kena a dark huddle on the ground and Homer standing over her.

"Kena!"

Her eyelashes were stuck to her cheeks, and snot was frozen on her upper lip. She was cradling one hand in the other. Was that a *sock*? She began to cry.

Mari's light came bobbing toward them.

"Oh God, Kena, thank God!"

"Mari!" Kena cried harder.

"Hey, shh, you'll make it worse," Gideon said. "Mari, shine your light on her."

He peeled the soaking sock from her hand and used it to wipe her eyelashes and nose. He took his glove off and held it open for her other hand, but she was shaking too hard to get her fingers in. He wiggled it up and tugged it over her jacket sleeve.

When he touched the injured hand, she cried out and yanked it away from him. He swallowed. Her palm was swollen to twice its size. He pulled his other glove over it slowly, but she cried out as he tucked her sleeve in. Then he grabbed her under the arms and set her on her feet. Ice chunks clung to her legs.

Gideon slid the backpack off Homer. "Like old times, huh, buddy?" He ran his fingers through Homer's fur, combing the ice and snow off. He picked up each paw and picked the ice out from between Homer's toes. "Good boy. Adam would be proud of you." At Adam's name, Homer made a feeble attempt to wag his tail.

Gideon watched Mari put her lips to Kena's forehead the way his mother did to check for fever. She raised her eyebrows over Kena's head.

"My flashlight!" Kena wailed.

"It's okay," Gideon said. "I have one."

"It's from my *mom!*"

At least she'd stopped crying to yell.

"It's right here," Mari said, reaching down. "The batteries must have died." Reaching for it, Kena swayed.

"Gideon, you'll have to carry her."

But Kena couldn't hold on for piggyback, so Gideon picked her up in his arms. They set off with Mari in the lead, lighting the way, Kena's pack on her back.

Homer limped behind them. He'd done his job, and Adam would be proud.

◊

Gideon took a gulp of the copper ale. It didn't taste as good if Mari couldn't have any of it.

"Well, how is she?" Clare asked Lily again.

"She's a very sick little girl," Abe said from the doorway. "She's spiking a high fever and has pneumonia. She might have a concussion. I'd say the hospital, but it can wait until tomorrow. And she'll have to be in isolation, but those two up there seem to know their stuff, for now. I gave her a shot, and I'll order an antibiotic in case her pneumonia is bacterial."

"Isolation?" Clare asked.

"She's HIV positive," Lily said.

Everything seemed to stutter to a stop.

Gideon felt like he'd been punched. Bodily fluids, isn't that what they said? Snot. Tears. He'd wiped his hands all over that filthy sock. But then he'd run them under water. He held them out. No scratches. It didn't seem possible that someone so little could be dangerous. "What about her hand?"

"Oliver took care of it," Lily said.

"Oh!" Mari said. "She didn't want any Band-Aids."

"What?" Clare asked.

"At the inn. Her hand was bleeding."

"Marisol! Did you touch it?" Clare asked, alarmed.

"No, Mom, that's what I'm saying: she wouldn't let me."

"You should have gotten me," Clare admonished.

"Mom! I *should've* made her put on Band-Aids!"

"It was really something to see, the two of them, Kena and Oliver," Lily said. "He asked me to bring a bunch of stuff. That I had it all is a miracle, even those plastic gloves—who would have thought? First he cleaned the cut on her head while she sat still as a statue. Then he lanced her palm. He just said 'Ready, Kena?' and all this pus came out."

Everyone recoiled.

"Lily!" Enoch said in a covering-his-ears voice.

"Well, if she can take it, you can hear about it! I thought the least I could do was hold her other hand, but she wanted none of that. She just worried her hair." Lily demonstrated, rubbing her own between her fingers.

"Gideon used to do that," Abe said, going over to Rachel on the loveseat. "Shove over. Remember that blanket he had?"

Rachel made room for him. "Fubby," she remembered. Gideon glanced quickly at Mari, who grinned.

"Then Patrice did the bandaging, like they were a team," Lily continued.

"Patrice is a nurse," Lois offered.

"Did she cry?" Mari asked.

"At first. Then she just watched Oliver as if—oh, shit!" Lily flung off the pillow. "I forgot Maggie and the note!" And she left the room.

"Who's Maggie?" Clare asked.

Rachel shook her head. "Who's *Oliver*? It's the same name. Wangera."

"He used to be married to Alice Wangera," Lois said. "Patrice told me. They visit him every summer in Kenya."

"Well, it's not fair, Lily having all this dumped in her lap," Clare said. "Especially today."

"Mom! Do you think it's *fair* to get AIDS?" Mari exclaimed.

"Oh, honey, you know that's not what I mean," Clare said.

"She's so little!" Mari said. "Could she die?"

"No, no, she should be fine with the antibiotics." Abe said. "And being HIV positive isn't the same as having AIDS. They'll have to keep an eye on that hand, but we have the best medicine in the world here. She's lucky she was adopted so young; it would be a different picture if…where's she from?"

"Kenya," Lois said. "Like Oliver."

"It's not just the HIV," Rachel said. "What kind of future does she have with her mother in jail?"

"Who's Alice Wangera's attorney, does anyone know?" Khai asked.

"Someone from the…not the district attorney, the other one," Clare said.

"Public defender. If she's lucky it'll be Abbott, but it's probably some kid fresh out of law school." Khai frowned. "What about this Oliver? Maybe he's the solution."

Lily was back, and with Patrice.

"Oliver's staying with her for the night," Lily said. "Kena is sound asleep, and Homer is too, next to her on the bed. Where he's not allowed, I might add, but I wasn't about to make him leave."

"He's a rescue dog for real now," Mari said.

"I'm headed for bed myself," Bernie said, getting stiffly to his feet. Lois stood to offer her shoulder, but Enoch was there first. Bernie leaned his weight on him over to the door and patted Patrice's arm. "Take my place." He addressed the room. "My bride and I will be leaving in the morning, so I'll say goodbye." There was a chorus of goodbyes.

"I'll be up soon," Lois said.

Enoch followed Bernie out. Gideon leaned back with his chair on two legs, wanting to leave too, except for Mari. He closed his eyes. Patrice perched on the edge of Bernie's vacated chair, as if she might be invited to leave.

"Khai, what were you talking about when I came in, that Oliver might be a solution?" Lily asked, returning to the couch. "Solution to what?"

"For Kena. While Alice Wangera is in prison."

Gideon opened his eyes and put his chair down.

"That office is all about politics, with the DA leaving," Khai shook his head. "And the assistant DA wants the job."

Enoch came into the room. "What are you riled up about?" he asked, going to sit down and taking Khai's hand.

"Little Kena." Rachel looked at Patrice apologetically. "Not that she hasn't been in good hands."

"Well, she got away from them," Patrice said. "And I apologize. Keeping that child from doing what she's bent on doing is like trying to nail Jello to a tree."

Lily nodded. "She was bent on me getting her mother home. I said I couldn't help, of course. I mean, what else—"

"Imagine the courage it took just to talk to you!" Lois interrupted. "And then to *ask*!"

◊

Lily gawked at her. Lois didn't interrupt. And she certainly didn't get angry. Or at least she didn't show it. Who knew what was hidden behind those stiff manners?

Gideon watched the exchange. He'd always felt a little scared of Enoch's mother. She'd never played with them like Adam's other grandma had before she died—Go Fish and Uno, even hide and seek. And now she'd squinched her lips together as if she'd locked herself up and was swallowing the key.

"Well, I felt terrible!" Lily looked at Patrice. "And I didn't just say no, I told her she shouldn't have come. I thought her mother had sent her." She turned to Lois. "And I wish I could go back and fix it." Lois flinched.

"This isn't the time for this," Clare said.

"But does it even matter what we think?" Enoch asked.

"A lot of things will be taken into account," Khai said. "After the DA decides the charges, her attorney—"

"Decides? There are *choices*?" Lily asked.

"Charges stemming from alcohol and drugs are all over the place," Khai explained. "We see them in court—the same people over and over sometimes—until the worst happens."

"But you told me Alice Wangera didn't have a record of driving under the influence," Enoch said.

"She hasn't. But it doesn't mean she never did it before. I've never understood it." Khai grimaced. "I mean alcohol and driving. Putting other people in danger. And their kids! Driving with their kids in the car."

"Well! It could have been me. I drove with the kids," Rachel said.

Gideon stiffened.

"If I'd faced it then, we might still be together," his mother said, looking at his father.

Gideon had always thought the divorce was his father's fault.

Everyone was staring at his mom.

"I can't tell you how many times I've thought about it since June," Rachel went on. "Every day."

"But you stopped, you go to—" Gideon remembered AA was supposed to be anonymous.

"I didn't start AA until after your father left."

"I never knew," Lily said in disbelief. "You drove the kids *all the time*."

"No, I covered my tracks well. My breath, too. I was embarrassed."

Gideon looked sideways at Mari.

"I used to wish you'd get stopped—get at least a warning, or even a DWI. Like a wakeup call," Abe said.

"But how could you even *let* her?" Lily demanded.

Gideon looked at his feet. How many times had he driven David stoned? Lily herself had driven stoned just last night.

Patrice stood up abruptly. "I'd best be on my way. I'll just check on Kena."

"Out in this?" Clare asked. "You can't!"

"Oliver said he'll find a motel near the hospital and bring Kena home as soon as she's well enough. It looks like he knows what's involved." Patrice had been looking at Lily, but now she appealed to Abe. "I know it's a lot to ask, but maybe you could check too, at the hospital?"

"We'll take care of her like she's our own child," Abe said.

Tears began to trickle down Patrice's cheeks.

"You'll stay with us tonight!" Clare was on her feet. "We had two storm cancellations and have rooms to spare, and you can leave in the morning. I'll bet it's been an age since you got to sleep through a night without one ear open."

Patrice wiped her cheeks with her palm. Lois got up and gave her a handkerchief. "I need to call my sister and neighbor, but if they say okay, well, that would be a mercy." She touched Lois's shoulder. "And I won't forget that recipe for your Christmas cookie exchange."

"Christmas!" Lily put her arms up like she was doing the Wave. "That's what Kena asked: would I help them get home for Christmas." She dropped her head into her hands. And she, who tried never to say no to a child, said there was nothing she could do.

After everyone left, Lily and Enoch and Khai began to gather up the glasses and bottles.

"I need to tell you something," Lois said from the couch. But she didn't say anything more.

"Okay, Mom," Enoch finally said. He put two bottles down and sat next to her. Lois straightened the hem of her funeral dress and smoothed the lace collar. She folded her hands in her lap. And still she didn't say anything.

"Mom?"

She sat up straight, her back away from the couch. She spoke to the wall across the room.

"When your father and I were first married and he was stationed in Guam those two years, there were parties every weekend. Something called a sidecar was a popular drink." She looked at Khai, as if he were the judge. "I drank a lot of them. Like they were Kool-Aid." She put her feet together. "One night I went for cigarettes."

She took a breath, and then rushed in. "I hit an old man, a native, with our car. He stepped off the sidewalk, and I hit him."

"Oh, Mom!" Enoch moved to touch her arm, but she swatted him away.

"I was drunk."

Lily's hand went up to her mouth.

Lois looked at Enoch. "I never told your father, and don't you! It will just make him feel bad, and there's nothing to be done about any of it now."

Khai and Lily stood holding glasses and bottles, as if caught in a game of freeze-tag. Enoch put his arm around Lois, but she leaned away, unyielding.

"It seemed like something you should know. Under the circumstances," Lois said softly.

"But, Mom, what happened? How badly was he hurt?"

"I don't know. I don't know! I didn't stop!" And she burst into tears.

It's a wonder this old house doesn't just float off its foundations from sorrow, Lily thought. She was too tired to react anymore. Someone else would have to take care of Lois.

As she pulled herself up the stairs step by step, hanging onto the banister and clutching Adam's book, she couldn't stop "I'll Be Home for Christmas" from playing in her head. She'd ask Abe if Kena Wangera could get "well enough" right where she was. In Adam's room with Homer and Oliver to take care of her.

Oh, Adam, I'm sorry.

# Chapter 37

## Lily

The morning had a lot of distractions, for which Lily was grateful, because she woke up to it thinking "The First Day." Not the day of the accident. Not yesterday, the day of his service. Not even the day after he died. *This* day was the real beginning of her life without Adam. People called it bereavement. Bereave. Root word: reave. Meaning: to rob. Grief. Latin: gravis. Heavy.

She hurt all over like she had the flu. Even her hair hurt. Maybe this was the day she'd chop it off. And rend her clothes. Rend: to tear something apart. Maybe she'd tear the whole house apart and sob and wail and carry on like a crazy person.

Except her house was filled with other people.

Patrice came to check on Kena and drop off her Medicaid card. Enoch and Khai came to pick up Lois and Bernie to take them to the airport, passing Clare and Rachel coming up the driveway to help clean up. It was one of those perfect post-storm days, the rooms bright with snow light, the yard sparkling with smooth snow frosting. It hurt her eyes.

They were an efficient crew: Clare upstairs, Rachel and Lily down, and Oliver doing what he called the washing-up in the kitchen after Kena went back to sleep. He'd emerged earlier to make oatmeal for her. And could Lily show him where the tea was, and a plastic bag for bandages? And did she have any duct tape for the fender on his rental car? Except he said "duck tape," almost making her smile. And where should he go—then Rachel offering—for Kena's prescriptions? Rachel left for the drugstore, dropping Clare off on the way, leaving Lily alone downstairs and acutely aware of the two upstairs in Adam's room. Three, counting Homer, who'd become Kena's nurse, like Nana in *Peter Pan*.

Lily wandered through the clean empty rooms, sat, got up, wandered, and finally gave in and tiptoed up to sit on the top step. Eavesdropping.

"Did you tell that story to the other orphans?" Kena was asking.

"What do you mean, 'other' orphans?" Oliver asked.

"Like me."

"You're not an orphan."

"Keisha said I'm an orphan because my mother's in jail. But Toby said don't listen to her."

"I vote for Toby."

"You never even met him! And besides, he says a *good* father wouldn't live across a whole ocean." Lily leaned closer. But Oliver didn't respond.

Kena began to cough.

"Here, drink."

"It hurts."

"Just a sip."

"You cried when Haron died. Wanja told me."

"I did."

"If I ask something you have to tell the truth."

"I'll do my best."

"Does it hurt when you die?"

Lily strained to hear, as if he might know.

"Haron hurt from being very sick. When he died—"

Lily waited along with Kena for the rest.

"When he died, he didn't hurt anymore. I was holding him and singing."

"You can't sing," Kena said.

"It didn't matter. It was from my heart. And then…well…he left, leaving his body on my lap, like clothes he'd outgrown."

"How did you know?"

"I just did."

"And you were sad."

"I *was* sad."

"Adam died."

Lily jerked.

"I never saw him again!"

"Oh, Kena. I know. I know."

"And Homer! He never did either! And he can't even cry!"

"Oh, kanini…come here."

Lily stayed huddled on the step and listened to Kena cry, and cough, and cry, and cough, and cry. She wrapped her arms around herself. Oh, Homer! She'd read that elephants cry tears; Oliver would probably know. Elephants and people. Built so we can cry, as if whoever designed us knew how much we'd need to. Not that she thought there was a Whoever.

"Here, blow. More. That's good. One more."

"If I die will you sing for me?"

Lily held her breath.

"Do you think you're going to die before me?"

"Haron had the same thing as me."

"Yes, but he didn't get medicine when he was a baby. You can live as long as anybody."

"Promise and cross your heart?"

"Promise and cross my heart. Now slide down and I'll tuck you in for a nap."

"Sing."

"But I 'can't sing'."

"From your heart."

"What shall it be?"

"You know."

"Slide down. 'Little bird, our soft and downy bird, singing in the tree, in the tall tree, sing, sing free, ina amaazo, baba'—"

Kena was right, Lily thought. Oliver *couldn't* sing.

Kena broke in. "I asked Adam's mother if she would help Mama come home, and she said she couldn't do anything! But Toby said when his dad went to jail, the judge asked the family what they wanted. I'm Adam's Little Sister! The judge should ask *me!*" She started crying. "I want my mama!"

Lily suddenly felt ashamed to be listening. She crept back downstairs.

She emptied the dishwasher, words spinning in her head. *Like clothes he'd outgrown.* Like a chrysalis.

*I want my mama.* She was grateful to hear the buzz of the dryer. Something to do. She brought the basket into the living room and dumped the laundry out on the couch. When she shook out the table-cloth, Kena's clown T-shirt clung to it like they were dance part-ners. She began to fold the napkins and stopped. Little girls liked to fold napkins.

But Kena wasn't in kindergarten. And Lily felt shy.

She always enjoyed the sock pairing—sock twins, Adam called them—and folding Kena's leggings and tights into a little stack, and smoothing out her sweatshirt, a miniature of one she had herself, from parents' weekend freshman year, was almost a joy.

A sock was missing. Digging around the cushions, her fingers felt the phone Mari had brought back. She dropped it as if Ellie's words were inside it like poison. She went into the kitchen and stuffed it down low in the garbage.

When she returned, Too was curled on top of the warm clothes and stayed there as she carried the basket upstairs. There was a plastic-wrapped face mask and hand sanitizer in front of Adam's door. Where had they come from?

Maybe she should just leave the laundry outside the door. No. The last thing Kena needed was Adam's mother avoiding her, especially after what she'd said. She put on the facemask, used the hand sanitizer, and knocked.

"Come in," Oliver called out.

"Speedy Delivery." Mr. McFeely's greeting to Mr. Rogers. She hadn't said it for at least a dozen years, but it was right there on the tip of her tongue.

Kena was sitting up in a pink and white flannel nightgown, holding Oliver's cellphone to her ear. Homer was sprawled out next to her and turned his head away so she wouldn't see he was on the bed. Oliver sat in Adam's desk chair, a mask on his face, typing on a laptop. A small plastic Christmas tree blinked on the bedside table.

Lily teetered in the doorway. *Of course* Kena would talk to her mother. Of course, and she *should*.

"You will?" Kena said into the phone. She smiled. "Okay. Afterwhilecrocodile."

Kena looked up at Lily. There were deep circles under her eyes. "That's Toby. He's sending me a Christmas card." Too suddenly leaped from the laundry basket to the bed and began to knead the comforter.

"Too!" Kena leaned forward and rubbed around his ears. "He didn't like me before."

"He likes you now," Lily said, hoping she sounded like a normal person. "I brought your clothes, all except your pretty dress. I didn't know if it could go in the dryer. What did your mother do?" There, that wasn't so hard.

"She never saw it, I just got it Friday. At the Goodwill store, and my boots. It has good prices if you're on a stingy budget."

Goodness.

"But I can't wear it to see Mama because the buttons are metal."

"Buttons can be changed. I have a whole box of buttons if you want to pick some out. I'll leave the basket here, just let me get the sheets." She leaned over and brought them up to her face to smell.

"That's what Mama does! When she grew up, they hung them outside even in winter, and they got stiff as boards, and she had to iron them. Her aunt's underwear, too! Her mother died, so she lived with her Aunt Lena. We went on the train to Wisonscin, and she didn't like me, but Mama said she never liked her either. She wasn't a liking person."

Lily hid her masked face in the sheet. How little she knew. She'd been making Kena and her mother up forever, even before the accident. Wisonscin. For some reason it was reassuring.

"Kena was about to take her pills," Oliver said. "And I was about to get her some water."

"Oh, let me!" Lily said. She stuffed the sheets in the linen closet and went into the bathroom. It was sparkling, with clean towels hanging just so. Clare. She washed her hands, singing the alphabet song under her breath like she taught her students. When she returned with the water, Kena had two and a half pills lined up on top of a book. Seeing Lily look, she went to cover it with her hand.

"Oh, sorry…I'll just…let me know if you need anything else." Flustered, Lily gave the glass to Oliver and turned to go.

"I stole it. I'm sorry," Kena said in a tiny voice.

Lily turned back. "What?"

Kena pointed to Adam's bookcase. "I wanted something to keep. We went to the museum, me and Adam, like in the book."

The book? She looked again. Of course, that book about the two kids.

The Metropolitan Museum. Oh, sweetie.

"I think Adam would like you to have it."

"Really?"

"Really."

If a smile could light the world—

Lily watched Kena put a pill on her tongue and gulp down half the water. Then another, and more water, and the half pill and water. Oliver handed Kena a plate of apple slices.

"Would you like a piece?" Kena asked.

"Oh!" Lily said. "Thank you." A chance to say yes.

"You're welcome."

And that was all she'd seen of Kena. Oliver came down and asked if she'd listen while he moved the car up and taped the bumper. She hovered at the bottom of the stairs, both dreading and hoping that Kena would wake up and need her.

Rachel returned with the pills and indignation.

"Listen to this! If she didn't have Medicaid—" Rachel took out four green pill bottles and lined them up on the hall table. "This one's a dollar a pill. This one is *thirteen dollars* a pill! This one is three dollars a day, and the last one is sixty. *Sixty!* That's a total of one thousand, one hundred, and twenty dollars. For one month! God bless America!" And Rachel stormed out the door.

Lily imagined Rachel doing the math in her head on her drive back, getting madder and madder, like Enoch with the bill from the White Plains hospital. "TV? Did they think he was sneaking in *Jeopardy* between seizures?"

There was still something in the bag. More masks.

So they were staying.

The day went on. Molly Mulligan called. Should Roger Caldwell take the tree to the library? Enoch called. His mother had hugged Khai goodbye. *Hugged.*

She didn't know if Alice Wangera called.

Then, finally, she could take a pill and get into her own fresh-sheeted bed to fall asleep and look for Adam.

*He was on the back porch at The Lake House.*

*"You went swimming alone? What if you got a cramp!"*

*"Mom, it's okay…see, I'm safe and sound."*

*But she couldn't see him; she couldn't see him anywhere. Just his voice.*

*"Mom, if you had your way, I'd go through life inside a bubble."*

*In her heart of hearts, that's exactly what she wanted. We have to let him grow up, Enoch said, and Clare. We have to let them go. She'd made all the motions, she'd tried. It was her guilty secret how she couldn't.*

*She watched two boys hoist themselves up the ladder at the end of the dock, yelling in those pure and heartbreakingly ephemeral little boy voices. They shook their heads like puppies and chased down the dock. She held her breath until they got safely to the sand. They grabbed their towels and snapped them at each other as they dragged their feet along the grass to clean them off. The screen door slammed, and they stopped, surprised to see her there.*

*For a second, they were Adam and Gideon, caught in the act, some act that only they knew about. They probably broke most of her rules at some time or another, wasn't that how it worked? She built fences and Adam jumped them or dug under them like the* Pokey Little Puppy.

*The boys waved and went inside, just nine-year-old boys going in to change for supper, excited about the fireworks later.*

*"It's to keep you safe," she said to Adam. "Not to keep you back."*

*"Remember in* Owls in the Family *when Billy left Wol and Weeps at that farm?"*

*"You cried. He couldn't keep them."*

*"That's not why. I cried because they couldn't go back and be wild. They had to go into another cage."*

*"Well, sweetie, they wouldn't have been able to look out for themselves. And they were fine."*

*"That's the point! They were too tame to even know! It sure was nice of Dr. Rose to come yesterday," he said. "I'd planned to call up to VINS to see how the owl was."*

*She felt a breath on her cheek.*

*"Mom, I gotta go."*

*"No!"*

*"Mom. I gotta go, I'll be in touch."*

*"Wait…Adam! No!"*

*And she saw him.*

*He was at the end of the dock, wearing the swimming trunks he'd bought in Belize, golden cat eyes peering out between fluorescent green leaves. He leaped and became a silhouette, arms and legs stretched out as if to grab the sun and take it with him into the dark water.*

She woke up clenched into a ball, her cheeks wet. He'd been there! She was sure. How else would she know the name of the bird sanctuary—VINS? He'd been there.

Homer was nosing her cheek. He whined. She slid out from the covers and followed him to Adam's room. The little Christmas tree cast light on a striped tail sticking out of a stuffed animal tucked into Kena's neck. The tail had a bald patch. From loving, she thought, slammed with pity for Alice Wangera.

Oliver was asleep in the chair, a blanket pooled at his feet. She lifted it over his knees. Homer was licking Kena's face.

"Homer, no," she whispered.

But Kena's cheek was wet from more than Homer's tongue. She'd been crying in *her* sleep too. Suddenly she opened her eyes and looked at Lily.

"Don't tell Mama."

"Don't tell?"

"I'm sick." She closed her eyes.

Lily put her hand on Kena's forehead. Warm. She didn't think Kena had been all the way awake. She looked around and saw the bag of masks on Adam's dresser. She slipped one on and cocooned the comforter around Kena, kneeling next to the bed. She hummed softly, the words singing in her head: *Daddy's at the engine, Adam rings the bell, Mommy swings the lantern to show that all is well.* She'd been right here, next to Adam's crib, singing until the spaces between her words were so long she'd sing herself to sleep and wake up hours later, stiff and cold, to creep out the door.

She tucked the striped tail in, and Kena pulled it under her cheek. "Mama."

Lily froze. Finally, after what felt like forever, she tiptoed out and Homer followed and led the way down the stairs and back to the kitchen.

Africa. Bush baby?

When Homer saw that his water bowl was empty, he went to Too's and lapped it up. Too slunk through the doorway and nosed it suspiciously.

"Oh, come on, it's all in the family." Lily filled both bowls with fresh water.

Homer left. Back to being Nana.

Lily filled the kettle and put it on the burner. She took down the chamomile. Then she opened the cupboard below and pulled the garbage out. She dug out the phone, and put it to her ear. *I'll be in touch.*

What was she *doing*?

"I'm awake," Oliver said softly from the doorway.

Lily's hand jumped and hit the cupboard, and the phone dropped back into the garbage.

"I'm so sorry."

"It's just…I didn't hear you come."

"Wanja says I'm sneaky. It's from sneaking out with my mates when I was a teen-ager."

Lily shoved the garbage back with her foot and closed the door on it. "You rescued me from serious magical thinking. Would you like some tea?"

"Love some, whatever's going," he said. "Magical thinking has its uses."

"There's milk in the fridge," she said, getting two mugs down and putting a bag and a teaspoon in each. "Honey's on the table."

He took the milk out of the refrigerator. Lily poured the steaming water into the mugs and brought them over. They dipped and stirred and clinked. She remembered what he'd said. "Wanda?"

"Wanja. My sister. She teaches at the orphanage. Clare told me you both teach. Are you on Christmas holiday?"

"I'm on leave," Lily said. "And I need to decide about the rest of the year in the next two weeks, and I haven't a clue about what to do. It's like I don't know who I am anymore. And I dread going back." She covered her mouth as if against blasphemy.

"I expect you need more time. Your son's—"

She interrupted. "I've been thinking about my son and Kena. He'd planned to bring her here this last summer for Fourth of July. Do you think she might like to come next year, after things are settled? It's something I can do for him. And there's Homer and the playhouse and swimming…"

Oliver held up his hand. Stop. "I need to say something." He held the honey bear upside down over his mug and squeezed it. As if *he* needed more time.

"You forgot the top, that little red cap-thing."

"I've made a mess." He rubbed around the bear with his finger and dipped it in his tea to clean it off. He poured in a dollop of milk.

"You needed to say something."

"Right." He hesitated. "It's easy to see you're good with children. And a compassionate person. But it wouldn't be good if Kena thinks you're friends, because you're…" There wasn't an easy way to say it. "You'll be…you're on the other side. The prosecution."

It was like what Rachel had said that morning, standing there with a bulging trash bag hanging from each hand like the balancing scale at school.

"If you embrace that little girl, then you're going to have to find your way to embracing her mother too. You're Adam's mother, and Kena just assumes you'll love them both like he did. They're a package deal, but what about that district attorney?"

Lily realized that she was stirring her tea furiously, making an actual tempest in a teacup. What *about* that district attorney?

"I've been offered a job," Oliver said. "By the woman who called here. Maggie Wells." Lily stopped stirring.

"Based in New York City. I'd be liaisoning with the UN. There'd be some travel, but I'd have people to do most of it. I even know somebody I'd like to have on staff."

"New York City." She looked up toward the ceiling, seeing Kena, watched over by Homer, sleeping in Adam's bed. "What's the job?"

"I'd be helping set up protocols for adoptions of undocumented African children. HIV-positive and AIDS children would have priority." He rubbed the back of his head.

"How do you bear it? Children dying," Lily blurted.

Oliver heaved up and walked to the sink. He looked out the window into the night.

"Too many *kids* have seen someone die." He turned around. "There aren't so many kids dying now from AIDs. But all the kids we've saved, who've lost their parents to it, who are alone in the world—isn't there some idea that if you save somebody's life you're responsible for it?"

He was staring at her, but she didn't think it was her face he saw. He cleared his throat.

"Please forgive me. Your son just died, and here I am blathering about myself. And I spoke out of turn about Kena too. She's not mine to speak about."

"Well, she needs to be someone's! God, I'm *sorry*! I used to be a nice person, but I seem to have lost that quality these days." She put her question to her tea, so he couldn't see that her eyes were brimming with tears. "Is she going to be okay?"

"I think we've turned the corner for now, and we should be out of your hair in a few days."

"That's not what I meant." Oh, God! What a mess. What would Adam want her to do?

And then she knew.

And as she got back into bed, Lily thought about the two calls she needed to make in the morning. One, to that VINS place. And two, to Khai.

It was time to go into the lion's den.

Oh, please. Get over yourself.

# Chapter 38

## Alice

Alice shuffled into line for her tray. Monday breakfasts were seasoned with hopelessness, everyone subdued, another week to be endured. It had been like the sun to hear Kena's voice the night before—and Oliver's in the background. *Oliver.* But today was another Monday, and she felt wretched; it was a week ago that Adam died.

And it was writing day; she'd completely forgotten. It was the last thing she wanted to do. Then, when the CO brought them to the room, only paper and pencils were there. Her books were gone.

"What are we gonna do?" Sylvie asked.

"Well, shit," Keresha said. "Let's just sit here and play duck, duck, goose." Cricket laughed. They looked at Alice.

But Alice felt almost panicky. Her books! Her precious books, almost like a second child. She wanted to send out an alarm—everyone should be looking! There needed to be a BOOK-FIND, and they were staring at her as if she was in charge.

"I know a nursery rhyme," Cricket said. "Baa baa black sheep—"

"That's racist!" Keresha said.

"Oh, get over your sad self!"

"I know a poem." They gaped at the CO as if he'd sprouted horns.

"You know a *poem?*" Keresha asked.

"What do you think, he's some redneck that never read a book?" Cricket asked. The CO blushed bright pink from his tight collar to the top of his bald head.

"I'm sorry, I shouldn't-uv said that," Cricket apologized. Sylvie glowered at her and turned to the CO.

"Thank you. We appreciate your offer," she said in her politest voice.

"Should I say it now?" the CO asked.

"Is it long?" Sylvie asked. "We usually read through them twice."

"I'll do that—say it twice. Should I say it now, then?"

Keresha got a fit of giggles and looked at Cricket. But Cricket wouldn't play. Instead, graciously, like a hostess, she said, "You can say it now. I mean, may."

Alice smiled for the first time that day. The CO clasped his hands and rested them on the top of his belt buckle. He cleared his throat. "'Hiawatha's Childhood,' by Henry Wadsworth Longfellow." He lifted his chin and looked over their heads as if the words were floating in the air.

> "'At the door on summer evenings
> Sat the little Hiawatha;
> Heard the whispering of the pine-trees,
> Sounds of music, words of wonder;
> "Minne-wawa!" said the pine-trees,
> "Mudway-aushka!" said the water.'"

They couldn't take their eyes off him, their taciturn CO—his shoes and belt polished just so, his khaki pants with their perfect crease, his pressed blue shirt, and the shiny badge with his name on it: Phipps.

*Minne-wawa, mudway-aushka*...unlikely and foreign under any circumstances, and they were enchanted, laughing the furthest thing from their minds, even Keresha's.

> "'Saw the fire-fly, Wah-wah-taysee,
> Flitting through the dusk of evening,
> And he sang the song of children,
> Sang the song Nokomis taught him:
> Wah-wah-taysee, little fire-fly,
> Little, flitting, white-fire insect,
> Little, dancing, white-fire creature,
> Light me with your little candle,
> 'Ere upon my bed you lay me,
> Ere in sleep I close my eyelids!'"

They heard the whispering and the lapping; they saw wah-wah-taysee twinkling in the dark.

When they clapped, Phipps turned even a darker pink.

"How'd you learn that?" Cricket asked.

"In sixth grade. We had to pick something to learn by heart. I practiced on the cows."

"Cows?"

"Milking. They like to hear some poetry," he said. "Should I say it again now?"

"Wait…what's the topic?" Sylvie asked. She furrowed her forehead. "How about we choose our own."

As he said it again, Alice closed her eyes. The words washed over her like a remembered lullaby, and with them a wave of intense loneliness. Kena and Oliver were together without her; Adam's dog was there too, in Adam's cozy bedroom, in Adam's wonderful house, with a swing on the porch and another one hanging from a tree in the yard. She'd slept all night under a heavy blanket of grief, not just for Adam and his parents, which was acceptable, but for herself, which wasn't. Her grief was for the life she'd never had, and now never could. And she'd taken away Kena's chance, too.

She sat for a long time, stuck on *"Sang the song Nokomis taught him."* Then she picked up her pencil.

*Lake Superior is between Minnesota, where my mother grew up, and Wisconsin, where my father came from. You can't see across it. We went there a few times a year when I was little. I'd sit on my father's shoulders. The waves would crash on the big rocks, but they couldn't reach me, just the spray on my bare feet. I'd hold onto his hair, the same color as mine. He smelled like butterscotch lifesavers. He'd pretend to drop me and catch me. He'd say, "By the shores of Gitchee Gumee, by the shining big-sea water, stood the wigwam of Nokomis, daughter of the moon." And he'd smile at my mother. The wind blew her black hair behind her like a cape. The lake was the big-sea water. My mother was Nokomis. I was the granddaughter of the moon.*

"I think it's time," the CO said softly.

"Oh! I lost track!" Alice looked at the clock. "I'm sorry! We won't have time for everyone to read. We'll have to finish next week."

"Next Sunday's Christmas," Keresha said. "We can't meet then, we'll be in lockdown."

"What?" Alice asked. "What about visits?"

"There aren't visits on Christmas Day, or any activities either, so more staff can take it off," Sylvie explained.

"But I told Kena we'd be together," Alice protested. She'd *promised.* Christmas, she'd said, over and over.

"The *real* Christmas?" Kena had asked. Over and over.

"The *real* Christmas."

"I'm sorry, but you're going to be out of time," Mr. Phipps reminded them. Keresha held up her paper.

"Mine is short." She twisted around to make sure the CO was listening too.

*"Me and Kenny went to sleep-away camp one time, upstate. We were nine."*

"You're twins?" Cricket asked. "You never said."

*"We lived in a foster home so that was special that we got to go to that camp. It had these cabins with three walls, so you could look out."*

"That's called lean twos," Cricket corrected. "Even if they have three walls, not two."

"They called them cabins," Keresha said. "Mine was Chipmunk Cabin. Girls and boys were in different ones. We had shelves for sleeping on."

"Were there chipmunks?" Cricket asked.

"Cricket, we're going to run out of time!" Sylvie said.

*"One night in bed I was looking out and I saw this little light like someone lit a cigarette which was totally not allowed even with the counslers. But then it moved like it was dancing. Like in the poem. And I wondered if it was the tooth fairy because one of the kids lost her tooth that day. I didn't believe in fairies anymore but it was like Tinkerbell how it danced around. And then there was another one in a different place. And more came, and then more. I wanted to go tell Kenny but was scared they'd fly away if they knew I saw them so I just watched. It was so pretty. It was like magic. Kenny said the next day they were just flies. But that girl got a half-dollar. And I made a wish, and it came true because Mom met our stepdad and we moved into his house that winter. It was our first house, not a apartment. I was glad I didn't go tell Kenny that night, or maybe we wouldn't have gotten to move cause he didn't believe. You gotta be a believer in some situations."*

She looked at Alice.

# Chapter 39

## Lily & Alice

Lily made it all the way to the jail with her banner still flying—her intention, her fantasy, intact: being a forgiving person, a good person, the person Adam would want her to be. The person Kena thought she was.

The night before, she'd sat on Adam's bed looking at a slideshow of the orphanage on Oliver's laptop while Kena kept up a steady narrative.

"That's a papaya tree. They taste good except I don't eat the seeds, ugh! That room, that's where we eat, except I get to choose if I want to eat with the babies and Zari instead." She turned to look at Lily. "That's Oliver's mother, she's not my actual grandmother but she said I can think of her that way." She turned back to the screen. "That's Nia! She follows me around. She has a pet chicken that follows *her* around, even to the toilet!"

A photo of a sad-eyed little boy with sores around his mouth appeared, and Kena got quiet. "I don't know him. I had sores when I was a baby and Mama put socks over my hands so I couldn't scratch. Because I would make scars." She raised her hand toward her eyebrow and dropped it to her lap. "I guess it wouldn't matter now."

Khai had arranged Lily's visit to the jail for Tuesday morning, and she'd lain awake most of the night determined not to be scared.

Then she saw the razor wire.

Khai stayed behind while she placed her bag on a conveyor belt to go through a metal detector. A woman ran a wand up and down her body without looking at her. When Lily said, "How are you doing?" the woman said, "Turn around" and ran the wand up and down her other side. Then she went through her bag for "contraband", and Lily said thank you out of sheer cowardice.

The linoleum gleamed as if it had just been waxed. And maybe it had, because they passed a woman in an orange jumpsuit with a mop and pail. She didn't look at Lily either. Lily followed the CO (*don't call them guards, Kena had warned*) through one metal door after another, each locking firmly and unquestionably behind her with a hard clang that bounced off the cement walls.

"Wait here."

The room was the size of her bathroom. Two stools were screwed to the floor on opposite sides of a table that was screwed to the wall. A ceiling light was locked in a cage. Like her, she thought. Oh, stop! Get over yourself! She sat down facing the door and tried to lower her heartbeat.

Just think of Adam.

◊

Alice made it through breakfast by breathing into her hand to cover the odor of food, then went back to her cell to throw up. She brushed her teeth again and put on another layer of deodorant with a shaking hand, getting the inside of her elbow. Then, too soon, she was walking down the hallway, wishing there was something to hang onto, even the CO's sleeve. Her legs were acting like they didn't want to go either, lagging one foot behind the other.

Thinking of Kena, Alice stiffened her resolve.

◊

"I have to leave the door open."

The CO was speaking to Lily, who was staring at Alice, stunned. A pale stick of a girl who looked about 15 was at the door. Her legs were too long for the awful orange jumpsuit that exposed skinny white ankles above ugly canvas shoes. And did they *make* people cut their hair off like that? Her eyes were huge. She had freckles. And knobby wrists. And hangnails bitten raw. She looked scared to death.

"Don't close the door," the CO said. This time she was speaking to Alice.

Lily met Alice's eyes for a second of us-against-them.

Alice pointed, feeling ashamed, like a hostess who only had bad seating to offer. "I'm supposed to face the door. It's a rule." Her neck and face turned a bright red.

Lily got up and they did an awkward do-si-do, their arms stiff against their sides as they traded places. Alice felt even taller—and uglier—than usual. Lily St. John was small and round and tucked in; her red sweater was buttoned to the top. She reminded Alice of the mother robin in *Are You My Mother?*

"Oh, rules! Kena told me!" Lily pulled her canvas bag from under the table and set it on top.

For a second Alice thought it was hers. It was exactly like the one she'd used for student papers and everything else: Kena's hair ties, Band-Aids, wipes, Neosporin, pads and pencils for drawing, and butterscotch Lifesavers.

"They went through this…" Lily nudged the bag. "…as if I might be smuggling in a bomb! Kena warned me about no metal and no jewelry…not that I wear much, maybe earrings once in a blue moon. But finding out I couldn't made me want to decorate myself like a Christmas tree. Oh, God, I'm babbling!" She took a white envelope from the bag. "I brought you a few photos. At least they let *them* in. Oliver took them. Well, not one; that was me."

Lily held the envelope out. Alice's hand was trembling. Who was more nervous, Lily thought, me or her? "Go ahead and look. I promised Kena I'd give them to you first thing."

Alice took one out. It was of Kena in last year's Christmas nightie with her arms full of a big brown dog. Her skin had the bruised look that meant fever.

"Homer doesn't leave her side."

Alice had resolved not to cry. If anyone got to cry, it wasn't her. She pulled out another picture: Oliver leaning back in a chair, his long legs extended, a laptop open on a desk next to him. Asleep. She'd seen him like that a million times.

"I couldn't resist; he looked so sweet."

Alice felt the hot flush rising again and bent her head down.

"He showed us a slideshow of the orphanage…what's it called?"

"Kirinyaga."

"Those kids!"

Kena with a cat. Holding it up under its front legs the way she did. Alice's lips twitched. Shoes lined up on the end of the bed. Black heels, sandals, shearling slippers, black high-tops, and pink boots.

"She taught me the moccasin game. She said you're part Ojibway?"

Alice half-shook, half-nodded her head. *Half-breed.*

"She didn't have a fever this morning. The doctor, a friend of ours, says she's out of the woods."

"I'm—"

Lily held her hand up. Stop. "I didn't do anything. It's all Oliver."

The next picture was of Homer on the bed with a blanket covering him to his neck.

"She was playing elephant sanctuary. She told me how each baby had a blanket and a person to be its mother or father."

For a second Alice could smell it. The dust. The damp mud and sweat and dung mixed with leaves and grass. The hot breath of an elephant on her face. She felt feverish with longing. She'd never be able to go back.

But Kena could, with Oliver.

In the last photograph Kena was holding a doll. It looked like an American Girl doll. Her skin was white. She wore a red dress and white tights and shiny black shoes. Two of Kena's butterfly barrettes stuck out of her black hair.

"My friend's daughter, Marisol, gave it to her." Lily could see something was wrong. "You'd probably want her to have a Black doll, but it was Mari's. Mari was born in China and she—I mean Kena—she and Mari seem to have a bond, maybe because they're both adopted." Lily was floundering. "But she's obviously your daughter, her way with words." She smiled. "Though I love 'Wisonscin.'"

Alice was reeling. It was too much. Too much, too much. And she was jealous, and had no right to be.

But it was *her* doll to give. It was *her* word to treasure. And Kena this and Kena that, as if Lily St. John had some kind of claim. *But you've lost that privilege.* And she had. She *had.* If she didn't say it now, she never would. And however inadequate, she had to say the actual words.

She swallowed. "I'm sorry. I'm sorry, and…I'm sorry, and I'm guilty."

Lily pulled her bag onto her lap. She fished out a piece of paper.

"Our librarian gave this to me. May I read it?" But she didn't wait for permission.

> "I looked and looked.
> Because they'd never leave me.
> My aunt said They're gone.
> They won't come back.

I got lost, searching.
Hide-and-seek.
Come out, come out.
I lay by the shore like a tossed stone
looking at the sky for heaven to come by
and pick me up too.
Then. Slowly.
My eyes were washed by grief
into seeing the shapes of clouds,
and the birds, and the light.
The light.
Oh God. The light.
Can shards become birthstones
If they're washed enough?"

Don't, don't say anything, Alice begged in her mind. It was a terrible poem, mushy and trite, but still, it was a piece of her. She owed Lily whatever she wanted from her, but please. Not this.

Lily slid the paper across the table. "You wrote it when you were just 17. Oliver said you lost your parents when you were younger than Kena."

Alice shook her head.

"Tell me."

Alice shook her head.

"No, please." Lily felt greedy. She knew she was being pushy. Even rude and hurtful. But she had a terrible hunger for Alice Wangera's story of grief. "Please."

"My parents died in a car accident. There was going to be a funeral. I'd overheard that they'd be there." She'd put on her blue corduroy jumper on which her mother had embroidered a pear cactus, her best blouse, and her white lace-trimmed socks. She'd packed her pajamas and a change of underwear in a paper bag and sat on the edge of her bed to wait. A part of her had been there ever since.

After a long silence, Lily spoke. "Then what happened?"

"I was waiting in my room, and my aunt came in." *Where the hell do you think you're going?* "She said they'd gone to live with God in heaven. She said, the way I acted, I'd never even get to purgatory."

Lily wanted to go back there and grab that little girl and walk out of that house. She wanted to shove that witch of an aunt into the next county. Into purgatory! No, into hell. Shaking with anger, she concentrated on the ceiling.

Square tiles. Six across, eight to the door. Forty-eight. You could stand on the table and push, and pull yourself up, and crawl along a beam to the outside wall and escape through a vent to where the guards—*COs!*—took their breaks and ask for a cigarette. Oh, how she'd love a cigarette!

She looked at Alice. "You were just a little girl!"

"You're like Adam."

"How?" It was a command.

"Generous," Alice blurted.

*Generous.* Lily was suddenly sick of being a good person. In fact, she felt like screaming. She'd spent her *whole life* keeping him safe. *His* whole life! She had a right, a duty, to be angry. Didn't she? She leaned across the table.

"You're a *mother.* How could you be so careless?" Shocked, she slapped her hand over her mouth. "I'm not so generous, as it turns out."

Alice didn't have any defense. "I wish—"

Lily put her hand up to stop her. "I wanted you to be a monster. If Kena hadn't shown up, you still would be." She looked at Alice soberly. "But here you are. A person."

A CO stuck her head in. "You've got five minutes. Sorry."

"She seems nicer than the other one," Lily said, wanting reassurance.

"Some are."

"What about the prisoners? Are they nice?" Lily asked. "I guess that's a stupid thing to ask!"

"We don't say prisoners. It's 'inmates.' Isn't that funny? Like playmates who can't play outside. It's hard for anybody to be nice in here. There's too much fear. I try to remember everyone wants the same things."

"What things?"

"Oh! Well, to have a home to go to. To belong to someone." Alice lifted and dropped her shoulders.

Kena does that, Lily thought. She stood up. "Before I go, I promised to ask if Kena can stay an extra day, for Yule; it's our town solstice celebration. There's fireworks and a bonfire." Should she say the rest? "Adam told Kena he wanted her..." Say the rest. "and you, too, to come to it someday."

*I promised to ask*, Alice thought. Lily had promised Kena. Was she supposed to give Kena to Lily now, in exchange for what she'd destroyed?

"David—that's Gideon's little brother—did you ever meet Gideon?" Lily was still on the solstice. "David's called twice, asking."

Alice touched Kena's picture. Kena with her new doll from her new friend. She looked sick, but she looked happy. The happy one. She gathered the photographs and tucked them into the envelope. She folded the poem.

"She has to go back to her foster home." To no Toby, Alice remembered. And years. Years. YEARS. "She can't be friends with you, or that girl and that boy. Remember what's coming up! She won't understand. Her feelings will be hurt if you're friends."

Lily hadn't a clue what else might happen that day, but she'd imagined getting back and telling Kena she could stay for Yule, and she'd imagined—she'd imagined being the hero. She gestured to the envelope. "Those are for you to keep." She knew she sounded stiff.

Alice pushed the envelope across the table. "They won't let me, but thank you for bringing them," she said. "And please tell that girl thank you from me. For Kena's doll. And thank you for coming. It was brave."

"There's one more thing, if you can say." Lily mustered her courage. "What was the last thing, in the car…before—"

Alice shook her head.

"Please."

Alice closed her eyes.

"Please."

"They were singing along with a song on Kena's CD player."

Lily had to lean in to hear.

"It was the soundtrack from *Oh Brother Where Art Thou.*"

Alice opened her eyes.

"What song? Please."

"I can't."

"Please."

"'I'll Fly Away'. It was 'I'll Fly Away'!" Alice covered her ears.

Lily groped for her bag and stumbled to the door.

Alice stood up. "Adam would want her to stay for it. For the solstice thing."

Lily stopped, but she didn't turn around. "I want us to be on the same side. For our children," she whispered.

But Alice heard her. "How can we?"

Lily turned around. "Grace."

Each of them, being led through their series of locked doors, kept hold, Alice until she got to her cell, and Lily until she got to Khai. And then they sobbed. The envelope stayed on the table until evening, when the inmate who did the cleaning found it there and turned in the photographs.

But she kept the poem.

# Chapter 40

## Gideon

*Restorative justice is an approach that focuses on the healing of victims and offenders rather than on law and punishment. Offenders are helped to take responsibility and make amends as much as possible; victims are helped to express how they've been affected. Everyone must agree to be active and sincere in their participation.*

"So sorry if I've kept you waiting," Oliver said. He handed Lily a small book. "I'll just fetch some tea, won't be a minute."

*He's* right at home, Gideon thought, looking up from reading the description Khai had given him. Lily noticed him watching and held up the book. "It's Alice Wangera's poems. To my surprise, Molly Mulligan had it at the library. I mean, of course, it's a *book*, but at our tiny library…who would have thought!"

Oliver returned with a steaming mug and studied the plate of Saturday's leftover bars on the table. He chose two broken brownies and placed them on a napkin next to his tea. He turned to Gideon and stuck his hand out.

"We didn't meet the other night. I'm Oliver Wangera. Kena told me you and Adam were best friends. I'm very sorry."

Gideon shook his hand, ashamed of his earlier thought.

Oliver picked up the paper listing Alice Wangera's charges and sat down, biting into a brownie piece. He made a face as if it had gone bad.

Gideon looked away, feeling like an intruder. The possible sentence horrified *him*, so what was it like for Oliver Wangera?

"How *is* Kena?" Clare asked. "Mari said she didn't have a fever yesterday." Gideon looked at Lily. Mari was *here*?

Oliver's forehead cleared. "She's at the library. And thrilled to be there. We helped Ms. Mulligan put out a buffet of shiny materials for kids to glue onto cardboard suns. She's got quite a collection. Remember those stars we earned as children for a good result?"

Gideon instantly remembered their taste. And he remembered pawing through Molly Mulligan's treasure box the summer his dad left. He'd found a bag of seashells and she'd let him take it home. They were scattered now in the woods, leavings from fairy houses he and Adam had built. He'd hoped if he made enough fairy houses to put wishes into, his dad would come home. Adam had let him be the boss that whole summer.

"When I left," Oliver continued, "Kena was reading a storybook to a little boy who'd cried when his mother left."

"What story?" Clare asked.

"The one with the moon…"

"*Goodnight, Moon*?" Enoch ventured.

"No, the one with the cow."

"*And the little dog laughed to see such sport and the dish ran away with the spoon*," Enoch chanted. "So, was the dish absconding with the silverware?"

"Of course not! They were eloping!" Lily admonished.

"All right," Khai interjected. "I'd think you were avoiding the subject at hand, except I've been witness to this kind of stuff before."

*With Adam*, Gideon didn't say.

"So, here's the situation," Khai went on. "As you know, Lily visited Alice Wangera Tuesday, and Enoch and Lily want me to feel out the DA to see what influence they can have regarding her sentencing if she pleads guilty. I suggested they take a look at the restorative justice process to see what they thought might be useful."

Gideon stared at Lily. *He* didn't know about any visit. Except for Oliver, he'd been the last one to arrive at the house, and he'd found the others all cozy in the dining room with papers and coffee. Sitting at the table he and Adam had lugged home from a yard sale. That he'd helped sand and refinish.

That they played knock-hockey on. Where he'd eaten too many meals to count.

He used to know everything that happened in this house.

His mom, sitting cozily herself, in their sunroom with newspapers and coffee, and his dad, who'd slept over—said he owed it to Lily to come, but she hadn't said anything about Lily going to visit Alice Wangera in jail. Maybe his mom didn't know either. The thought gave him perverse comfort.

Khai looked over the top of his glasses. "It would be similar to a pre-plea conference, where both parties discuss ways to avoid a trial. A final plea conference is when the prosecutor and the defense attorney meet with the judge to finalize the charges and sentencing. At a restorative justice conference, instead of the attorneys being adversaries working out a deal, their job is to listen while everyone else talks, and then try to agree on the best outcome for both sides. It's not commonly used in cases like this, but could have an influence on the length of Alice Wangera's sentence."

"Who's at the conference?" Clare asked.

"A restorative justice facilitator, the Assistant DA Robin Barker, Alice's attorney from the public defender's office, Brian Abbott, and possibly the judge. Plus Lily and Enoch, me, and Alice Wangera. And any others we, and Alice, decide should be there."

"What about Kena?" Lily asked. "Does someone represent her?"

"Her foster mother?" Enoch suggested.

"Or Oliver," Lily said, looking across the table. Gideon snuck a look at Oliver, silent next to him. His face was impassive.

"A guardian ad litem has been assigned to represent Kena's interests, but she'll need weeks to prepare a report." Khai said.

"How does it work? The restorative justice thing, I mean," Clare asked, frowning. "I mean, I see why it's good for Alice Wangera… but how's it good for Lily and Enoch?"

"First, they can say how they feel to Alice directly. They can ask her questions. Their opinion about what happens to her, and what she might do to make what amends she can, will matter."

And Adam? Gideon wondered. What amends for him?

"Second, Alice Wangera can say she's sorry directly to everyone effected. Of course that's inadequate, but it's not silence, which is… silence is never really silent; it fills with what people imagine, and we usually imagine the worst. We'll be able to express our hurt…or anger. Our grief."

Gideon looked down, horrified at the idea. But Khai went on as if it were not just possible, but a good thing.

"What it comes down to is that, out of this tragedy, the next steps might bring some healing…or at least not more harm. Restorative justice is about healing rather than punishment, about the offender being included in the circle of humanity instead of being banished. As for Kena, just imagine if we, who love Adam, her 'big brother', end up being responsible for her mother being in prison for the rest of her childhood."

Khai cleared his throat. "Anyway, we'd try to reach consensus about sentencing and restitution and ask the judge to take that into account. We might suggest community service, AA, and counseling.

The judge, the DA, and Alice's attorney would then work out the legal plea and sentence."

Gideon picked up the book of poems and opened it blindly. Did he hate Alice Wangera? He saw that he'd opened to her dedication page. *For my mother and father, who gave me the roots I needed when everything fell away.* There was a stick drawing of a tree with roots beneath it. There were two Vs above it. Birds? What fell away? But she'd said. *Everything.*

And now it had again.

There was a tiny V in the tree.

"I'd want you to come," Lily said to Oliver. She leaned his way like a conspirator. "Have you told Alice about the job yet?"

He shook his head. "I need to meet with Maggie Wells first. Even then…I don't know…if Alice would *want* me to take her. I don't know if *Kena* would want it. Or if I can provide what she needs."

Gideon's head jerked up. Kena going to Africa?

"The thing she needs is that you *love* her." Lily said. "But do you *want* to take care of her?"

Gideon's heart began to beat furiously.

Oliver rubbed his face and looked at his palm as if the answer might be written there like a fortune. "Of course I do," he said. "It's just—it's just why would she trust me? I left them before."

Gideon couldn't let it go on. "You can't take Kena away! She needs her mom! Even if it's in a prison! She still needs to see her!"

"What are you talking about?" Lily asked.

"Him taking Kena back there." Gideon glared at Oliver Wangera.

"Back where?"

"To Africa."

"Gideon! He's talking about *here*."

"Here?"

"New York City," Lily said. She hesitated. "But I might go. I've been thinking about it."

"To New York City?" Gideon asked.

"To Kenya, to visit the orphanage." She looked around the table. "I've been thinking I might start a camp. I mean, here. And maybe some of those kids could come to it." Lily's voice got smaller. "What do you think?"

No one said anything.

"It's just awfully early," Clare ventured.

"What's *that* supposed to mean? Am I supposed to sit around and cry for a year wearing black?"

"Oh, Lily—"

"It would be for HIV kids and AIDS kids. Kids from Kenya and Patrice's kids. Like Fresh Air kids, except not one or two…about a dozen. I mean, look how much room there is." She motioned with her arm. "And the barn, and the woods. I'd need to do some renovations. And get a van. I'd have to raise money. Oh! Is it stupid?"

Khai jumped in. "I wasn't going to tell you 'til after tomorrow when we know the amount, but you know how the Yule money goes to a different place each year? Well, this year it's for Adam. They made the decision back in the fall, but they're going ahead…they thought it could go to some place in Adam's memory. Maybe you could use it for your camp. And Adam loved Yule."

Clare looked stricken. "Lily, I just worry. I just don't want you to get even more involved. More hurt. It's just—it's not a normal situation. Kena here, and Oliver—" She looked at him apologetically. "Well, under the circumstances, it just isn't *normal*. And about the restorative justice process…well, what *about* Kena? I mean, she lost Adam *and* her home, and didn't I hear someone say she had to change schools? Doesn't all this make you…well, angry at Alice Wangera? *I'm* angry!"

"Of *course* I'm angry. Of course I am! But I'm more sad than angry." Lily opened her hands on the table. "I never believed in punishment—or prison, God!—before, and now it's harder, of course it is; it's *real*. It's not just some principle anymore. It's not like I can sit around and go through the stages of grief—if grief even *has* stages, which I doubt, now that I'm feeling it—and then decide! Kena needs help *now*, not after some long court thing, and God forbid *any* of us have to go through that. And I'm not helpless! I might not be happy for a long time, or ever, but at least I can do my best for Kena. And that means doing my best for Alice Wangera! And, Clare, nobody feels Kena's feelings more than her mother, nobody could possibly worry more. Just *think* about being in her place! And think of Adam! I couldn't look him in the face if I didn't help."

Lily and Clare looked at each other, exhausted, as if they'd done 10 rounds.

"I think we should go for it," Enoch said. "I mean the justice thing. We can talk about the camp another time." He picked up Khai's pen as if to record their votes. "And Gideon, you'd be valued. I hope you'd be part of it, if we do it. But it's been a horrible week. A horrible *year*. Take your time. Talk to your folks about it. Or me. You can *always* come to me about anything."

Gideon nodded, wishing he were anywhere else.

*Think of Adam. I couldn't look him in the face.*

His phone vibrated. He pried it out of his pocket. Mari. His heart quickened.

*cu2nite?*

He looked to see if Clare was watching. But Clare was talking to Lily.

"Remember, Lily, when you told me to keep a gratitude list? You said I couldn't be scared and grateful at the same time. It was the horrible year when we tried IVF. I kept being scared, then mad, then scared. And *then* I'd get scared that it all was going to make the baby stressed out if I ever *did* get pregnant. Like a vicious circle. Remember?"

"Of course I do."

"I've watched you try to be grateful your whole life. To not chase fear. To say yes to the right things even when they were hard. You said yes to being "best woman" for Enoch and Khai, once you got over the shock of being asked. Actually, I think the hardest part was what to wear!"

She and Lily shared a smile.

"You said yes to changing Jamie Hurd's diapers so he could be in kindergarten. You had to say yes every time you went into Adam's room at the hospital, never knowing what you'd face. It's like your religion." Clare paused.

"You struggle a lot. A *lot*. I know you do, but you come around to it. You know how I am, having to dig and dig for the worst, like if I come up with everything to worry about I'll be armed and ready. But I *promise*—I promise that if you decide to do this, I'll support you. I'll try as hard as I can to help however you want."

Tears were running down Lily's cheeks. "I don't have a however-I-want, not really! I'm trying too! And I don't feel *grateful* at all! I don't feel scared either. I just feel sad!" She turned to Gideon and wailed. "You were there! Where did he *go*? Why didn't he *wait* for me? *Why*?"

"Oh, Lily. Maybe that's the only way he could do it," Clare said softly. "When you weren't there." She got up from her chair and went around the table. Lily stood up, and they put their arms around each other. And they rocked and rocked.

Gideon sat frozen-faced. *Where did you go, Adam?* They were all moving on, even Lily. Lily and her camp. Oliver Wangera and Kena. His mom and dad, cozy in the sunroom. Even David had told on himself. Everybody except him was moving on. But where would he even go?

"I'll call Robin Barker, then," Khai said. "And you should start writing down what you want to say, or want to ask."

"Oh, God," Lily said. "I don't think I can."

"Start with sticky notes. You're the sticky-note queen," Khai said.

*Fuck, fuck, fuck,* Gideon thought. That's what he'd write.

Khai slapped his hands on the table. "So are we good to go?" Lily and Enoch nodded. "Then we are adjourned."

Clare and Lily began to gather up the cups and plates. Lily stopped behind Gideon. "If I do it, I was thinking you might help with the camp. You could make videos with the kids." She swept into the kitchen.

"Lily said you're going to see Alice tomorrow," Khai said to Oliver.

"I'm taking Kena for an early Christmas. Then Saturday, I'll take her to Queens."

"I'll still be here to say goodbye, then," Enoch said. "Khai and I will be staying here through Yule. Adam always made sure to be home for Yule."

"Maybe Kena and I should leave after we visit Alice, before Yule," Oliver worried. Lily had returned.

"What are you talking about? You'll break her heart! The plan is you bring her back here for a nap and then Yule. And that's the end of it." She swept up the spoons and forks and returned to the kitchen; they could hear her indignant voice reporting to Clare.

Enoch held up his hands. "And it shall come to pass." He stood up and looked across the table. "Gideon, don't be a stranger. We don't want to lose you too."

"Enoch, could you fill the bird feeder?" Lily called through the door.

Gideon brought his hand up to cover the tears that sprang to his eyes.

"I'm off to get Kena," Oliver said. He rested his hand on Gideon's shoulder for a moment as he passed behind him.

Gideon looked at his phone again. *cu2nite?* Had he brought his brown sweater, the one his mother said matched his eyes? He'd never unpacked. He'd been pulling clothes out and stuffing them back in like a homeless person. He opened Alice Wangera's book.

> *They drove me away*
> *from the house.*
> *Its eyes were shut tight not to watch.*
> *Was there an echo of an echo in a corner*
> *of my room, the letters of the alphabet song*
> *scattered on the floor?*
> *What was soft was now stone—*
> *no, dust.*
> *Not stone all smoothed and soothed*
> *by stockinged feet, but dust that was once stone.*
> *Life and no life can't meet.*
> *One holds hands and makes memories.*
> *The other is a hole with no bottom.*

The meeting house was dark when he'd passed it coming today. It had been filled with memories. And Kena, her arms raised to play with the wind.

Okay, then. Okay, then, to the fucking justice thing.

Okay, then, to Lily's fucking camp. Okay. *Okay.* Yes.

*Yes.*

He typed in *cu* and stopped, his finger hovering.

# Chapter 41

## Oliver

Oliver watched as Kena broke the rule and ran to Alice. He watched as Alice caught her up and whirled her around. Kena twirled again to show off her pink dress.

"It had metal buttons but Lily changed them so I could wear it here!"

Alice felt Kena's forehead with her lips and examined her bandaged hand.

"Oliver changes it every day." Kena looked at him. "You get two hugs, one at the start and one at the end." And it was her turn to watch, watching them hug. Then, satisfied, she scurried to sit down.

Oliver knew she had a lot to say, having heard most of it coming from the back seat, where she was strapped into a booster seat that came, to his astonishment, built in. Mei—that was her new doll's name—was strapped into the booster on the other side.

"Why Mei?" he'd asked innocently.

"Because it's her name." If a voice could roll its eyes, hers had. "You don't change somebody's name just because they get adopted!"

She'd begged to sit up front after Nigel spoke. That was her lead topic.

"Mama, there's a voice in Oliver's car. He's a computer, and I told him where to go. I said, "PLEASE DIRECT US TO 10 WOODS ROAD, VAL-HAL-LA, NEW YORK. And he told Oliver every direction! Turn right. Turn right. Go straight for twenty-four miles. Go left. Go right. He talked the whole way. His name is Nigel."

"Nigel?" Alice asked Oliver, lifting her eyebrows.

"He wears a waistcoat—that's a vest, if you never heard of it, spelled like waist—" Kena put her hands on hers. "Not like waste basket! And he wears a bowling hat."

"Nigel said that?"

"Oliver said."

"And what's a bowling hat?"

"For bowling!"

"Of course, what was I thinking?" Alice said, giddy with Kena safe and sound and there where she could touch her.

Oliver elaborated. "Nigel lives with his pug…" He looked to Alice, and she took it up like old times.

"…his pug, Clover. He has nyama choma for dinner—"

"Yum!" Oliver smacked his lips.

"Clover licks the plates," Alice finished.

"What is that nya-chom?" Kena eyed them suspiciously.

"It's goat," Alice said. Kena made a face.

"That's mean!"

"You ate goat at Kirinyaga," Oliver said.

"I never did! I threw it up when you weren't looking!"

"Tell your mother about tonight."

"First, Mama, you need to know about Frigga. She was a goddess of love and marriage." Kena slid her eyes from Alice to Oliver meaningfully. "She had a baby named Baldur who's God of the sun. He's the *boss* of the sun. And tonight's his birthday!" She paused to ensure Alice's full attention and raised her arms. "No Baldur, no sun! No plants! No animals! No *people*!"

"I know a story about Frigga and Baldur. Do you want to hear it?" Alice asked. Kena nodded vigorously.

"In Scandinavia, where my father's side of the family came from, the winter solstice—tonight—is called Mother Night to honor Frigga. Frigga helped human spirits go from one place on a life's cycle to the next, like births and deaths. And she was a weaver. She spun her thread from the clouds. Wreaths symbolize her spinning wheel. The Scandinavian word for wheel is J U L, the J pronounced like a Y. So—Yule."

"That's what *we* call it!" Kena exclaimed.

Oliver could see that Kena's *we* jarred Alice. *We* were Adam's people, the people she'd hurt irrevocably.

"The story," Kena prompted.

"Frigga could see the future in her weaving, but she couldn't change it, and one day she saw something terrible. She saw that her beloved Baldur was going to die, though the wheel didn't foretell how it would happen. As you can imagine, she was frantic to save her son, and she begged all living things to take an oath and promise never to hurt him. And they did, out of compassion for her mother-love and their own love for bright Baldur. They even made a game of it, hitting Baldur with spears and arrows that, because of their oath, didn't hurt him." Alice frowned, to warn that the story was about to take a turn for the worse.

"There was a tiny plant called mistletoe. Frigga didn't ask the little mistletoe to promise because she thought it was too young to find out about death. And that was her undoing. When Loki, who liked to do mischief, realized Frigga hadn't asked the mistletoe to promise, he carved a tiny arrow from its stem. He gave it to Baldur's brother Hodor to play the hitting game."

Oliver looked back and forth, enthralled by Alice's voice and the emotions passing over Kena's face.

"Hodor shot his brother in the heart, and Baldur died instantly."

"Oh!" Kena gasped, clapping her hands over her own heart.

"The little mistletoe cried and cried, and its tears turned into berries as they fell. From that time forward the mistletoe has been a symbol of love at Yule time. Frigga was shattered, of course. And Hodor, distraught with guilt and grief that he'd killed his own brother, went to the land of the dead, where Hel reigned, and offered himself in exchange for Baldur. Hel was so moved by Hodor's sacrifice and the little mistletoe's tears that she bestowed an act of grace: Baldur could return to the land of the living, and Hodor need not stay in his place." Alice looked from Oliver to Kena. "But there was one condition."

Alice waited.

"What?" Kena asked. "What condition?"

"That everyone weep for Hodor's release." Alice opened her hands. "And everyone *did*. People and animals and trees and flowers and even rocks, and, of course, water." She closed her hands. "All except one."

"No!" Kena said. "Who?"

"It was Loki."

"Oh, no!"

"So Hodor had to stay with Hel after all. And on the longest night of the year, the winter solstice, some things still cry for Hodor."

Oliver remembered the first time he heard Alice tell a story.

They were in the hills at the weighing station where farmers brought their tea. Alice was there to record a few of the old stories while people waited for their turn. A small boy came to their make-shift table, a board Oliver had put across the back of his father's truck bed. The boy wanted to know how the tape recorder worked, so Alice dictated a story about a muskrat diving to the bottom of the ocean to dig up a pawful of mud. "Then the brave muskrat smeared the mud on the back of a turtle, and it became Turtle Island, the first land!"

But even the smallest child in Kenya knew that Ngai made the first land, which was Mount Kenya, so he could sit at the top and boss everybody below. Oliver grinned at the memory of the little boy's skepticism.

"Some things should cry for Loki," Kena said. "He must feel so bad!" Sadness crossed her face like a shadow. "Is Hodor in the dark?" she whispered.

"That place is made up," Alice said. "And anyway, there's nothing wrong with the dark. If we didn't have it, we couldn't see the stars."

"Or fireworks," Oliver offered.

"And fireflies," Kena said. "They're one of my most magic things. What are yours, Mama? Say two."

"Candlelight, and crocuses in the snow."

"Yours," Kena commanded Oliver.

"You and your mother," he said emphatically. He watched the color rise in Alice's face. He'd always loved that.

"God is great, God is good, let us thank him for our food," Kena said, drawing her eyebrows together.

"What?" Alice asked.

"You said, Mama. Grace. Like before supper."

"*Who* says grace before supper?" Alice asked. She'd never made Kena say any kind of prayer. She never would.

"Patrice and us. 'God is great, God is good'—"

"You say it every day?"

Oliver winced at the sharpness in Alice's voice, as if Kena had done something wrong.

"Hel said grace for Baldur to be alive," Kena defended. "You *said*."

"I think what…" Oliver began. Alice made an infinitesimal, but unequivocal, headshake.

"It's a different meaning," Alice said. "Frigga did it as a favor, like a present."

"I don't believe in it, or God either." Kena said it like a confession, and as if by confessing she was giving up her last hope. "God let Adam die! And you feel so bad, like it's your fault, all the time!" Kena swiped at her cheeks, angry at her tears along with everything else. She began to cry outright. "Doesn't God is good mean you're forgiven?"

Oliver started to put his arm around her, but she pushed him away and wiped her face on her sleeve. Alice got to her feet.

"Wangera!" She sat down.

"There's nobody left to ask!" Kena wailed. "Lily said she can't help!"

Oliver lifted her over to his lap. "Ask what?"

"For us to go home! For Mama not to feel bad!"

Alice looked at Oliver helplessly.

"Kena, listen to me," she finally got out. Kena turned her wet face toward her mother.

"I *need* to feel bad. When you do something wrong, it's *appropriate* to feel sorry, right?"

Kena nodded stiffly.

"I shouldn't have been driving the car. It was dangerous." She grabbed Oliver's outstretched hand like it was the end of a rope that would tow her to safety.

"Remember when I told you about the DWI? Driving while intoxicated? I broke the law, a *good* law to keep people *safe*. And I *didn't*. I didn't keep you and Adam safe."

Tears streamed down Kena's face.

Alice was barely holding it together. "I'm very, very, very sorry I hurt you." She took a deep breath and let it out. "And Adam died."

"But you didn't mean to, Mama!"

"No, I didn't. But still, Adam died. Because of me. You love Adam.

*We* love Adam. But even with all that love, Adam died because I made a terrible mistake. And Kena, trying to find a way we can go home… thank you for trying to do that. And Lily came to see me, that was because of you, and it meant a lot to me. Her too, I hope."

Kena wiped her face on her sleeve. "Now she knows you're not mean, Mama."

"I hope so. But Kena—"

"What, Mama?"

Another deep breath. "About going home. We won't be able to for a while. Maybe a very long time. But when you come here, we *make* home. And on the phone. Home is *us*."

"No, Mama! People need their bed," Kena corrected. "Children need a *place*, with their family."

Oliver felt it in his own body, how Alice folded into herself. He ached for her not being allowed to hold Kena. What kind of world didn't let a mother hold her child! He held Kena more tightly. But Alice straightened up.

"You're *right*, what was I thinking? But Kena, I don't think God is in the business of stopping the painful things that happen in this world. You know how grownups have a hard time seeing fairies? We miss a lot of the grace stuff too. But we can help each other."

Kena sat up straight. "Like Oliver and Patrice. And Lily and Mari. And Molly."

Alice winced. "Yes, everyone there, in Adam's family and town. The world offers us presents. Our job is to accept them and say thank you."

Kena got down, walked over, and climbed onto Alice's lap. Alice wrapped her arms tightly around her and rested her cheek on her hair, not caring that she was breaking the rules. Oliver wanted to put his arms up and yell Alleluia. He looked around. The CO was wringing her hands.

"I think it's present time," Alice said suddenly.

"Presents? *Real* presents?" Kena sat up. "How?"

Alice put Kena gently back on her own stool and walked over to the hand-wringing CO. The CO went behind the desk and handed Alice a paper bag. Alice set the bag in front of Kena and went to her side of the table. Kena got on her knees and looked in. She took out a tube of white paper.

"That's for Oliver," said Alice.

Kena peered in. "It's words. Read it!"

"I'll wait for you."

Kena slid the rest out. There were two presents wrapped in newspaper. One was shaped like books. She looked for tags.

"They're both for you."

Kena tore the paper off the books. One was fat with gold cut-outs down the side. Letters. "*Random House Webster's College Dictionary.* College!"

"Let's try it out," Oliver suggested. But Kena was looking at the other book. There was a golden lion carrying a boy and a girl across the sky. *The Lion, the Witch, and the Wardrobe.*

"It's a series," Alice said. "Seven books, if you like it. They'll be at the library."

Oliver thumbed through the dictionary for the right page.

"See at the top, Kena? These are guide words. Everything on the page fits between them."

"It says hoo-ha!" Kena laughed.

Oliver pointed to the definition.

"An uproarous..."

"Uproar-ee-us," Oliver pronounced.

"...commotion."

"Like fireworks," Oliver said. "Look at the other guide word."

"'*Home.*' Mama! Almost the whole *page* is home words! *Home, home base, home-made,...Homer*! It says Homer!"

Oliver held the dictionary up for Alice to see, following her eyes as they went to where his finger pointed. *A place in which one's affections are centered.* Home is us.

Kena tore the paper off her other present.

"Five minutes!" the CO called out.

"My Christmas nightie!" It was blue with clouds. The clouds were animals! A giraffe, an elephant, a lion. A lion!

"Don't wear it until it's been washed. I couldn't wash it, so you'll have to ask Patrice."

Kena petted the soft flannel. "Okay."

"I'll read my 'words,'" Oliver said. He anchored the curled paper with the books.

> "There's a place, a secret place, in each of us.
> The scoops of regular day-by-day-by-days
> won't find it; you have to suffer a deep wound.
> It's lined with stardust from your birth.
> It's as astonishing as the nest of the eagle
> whose home is the whole sky and maybe more.
> (I don't know. I haven't been one yet.)"

Kena leaned on Oliver. "Adam saw baby ones with his father."

> "The loves from your lives before are there,
> and the wonder of first snows,
> and seeing your shadow that first time.
> Pieces of rainbows drift in the air,
> lit by the glow-spark
> of a flame you'd never see
> except for the dark around it.
> Your gentlest and fiercest ancestors,
> and the ancient beings

from stories someone who loved you
told so long ago you might not remember
(it could have been before you were born),
sit on soft-sprung sofas with their feet out,
warming from that tiny flame,
reminiscing about joys and sorrows.
(and now-and-again, a birthday cake someone made
from scratch)
They make a place for you.
They say all has been forgiven.
They say:
All will be well."

"It's just a rough draft," Alice said, looking at Oliver anxiously.
"Like us," Oliver said, his heart too full to say anything more.

*Yule*

# Chapter 42

## Kena

"Kena!"

It was Clare, calling from the porch of the inn. Small paper bags glowed and flickered along the tops of snowbanks on both sides of the sidewalk where Enoch had dropped them off. Looking into one, Kena saw a fat candle stuck in sand. It was like Cinderella's fairy godmother had swept over Farleys' Dock with her wand, sprinkling magic. She felt proud, as if it were her town. She wished Toby could see.

The stick family was buried in the snow halfway up. But her socks were still there, keeping the littlest one's stick hands warm. She leaned to adjust them, just to have a say.

"There you go."

"Let's go say hello," Oliver said.

The bus driver from Adam's funeral was ladling hot chocolate into green cups. Her hands trembled, but nobody seemed to mind the drips. Clare stood next to her, a row of red bowls in front of her. She had a crown of leaves on her head. A man came through the door bearing a big tray and put it down. He was wearing a white hat like the Swedish Chef on *The Muppet Show*.

"Next batch," he said. "Oliver Wangera! Good to see you found your way. And you're Kena." The man put out his hand. "I'm Charlie Lewis. I'm Mari's dad."

Clare poked him.

"And Clare's better half."

"Kena, I'm so glad you're better!" Clare said. "I hope you brought your sweet tooth because it would be a shame to miss our sun cookies." Clare waved her hand above the line of bowls. "It's do-it-yourself frosting: maple, chocolate, strawberry, peppermint, lemon."

Kena counted. Each cookie had five rays. She could frost each one a different flavor. She gave Lily's mittens to Oliver and got to work.

"I like your wreath." Oliver swirled a finger over his head. He stuck the mittens into his pocket and slathered a cookie with chocolate.

"You can make one over in the gazebo," Clare said, pointing.

As they crossed the street, Kena ate four rays off her cookie until it looked like it was wearing a pink party hat. She grabbed onto Oliver's sleeve.

There was a crowd in the gazebo, everyone gathered around a table stringing green tissue paper leaves along green wire. Like making a shish kabob, one of her favorite words. She put her cookie down and picked up a leaf and a wire.

"Good evening, Makena." It was the principal from David's school. Even with tissue paper on her head, she was dignified. She was fitting a wreath on a boy, twisting the wire ends together.

"Hello," Kena said, feeling shy.

"Are you feeling better?"

"Yes, thank you." How did principals know everything?

"I believe introductions are in order."

What? Oliver's hand squeezed her shoulder. Oh.

"This is Oliver Wangera. And this is Mrs...." But she didn't know.

"I'm Louise Berdick, and this young man is Lucas. I heard you're from Kenya, Mr. Wangera, where Kena was born."

"Yes, Kena and I have known each other since she was a baby."

"I hope you enjoy our Yule festival. I don't suppose it's something you celebrate back home." She made a final twist and adjusted the wreath. Lucas was staring at Kena. At her scar? He smiled, and she saw that he was missing his top front teeth. She smiled back.

"No, but everyone tries to get home for New Year's Day," Oliver said.

"Will you?"

"I expect to be," Oliver said.

Kena abruptly hated Lucas, who probably got star cookies and wreaths his whole life. And Mrs. Berdick too. And Oliver! With his stupid New Year. And Nia and her stupid chicken aunt. She wanted to punch them all in the face.

She'd let herself pretend, but here it was.

"Let's see how this looks." Oliver took her leaf-strung wire. Kena stood stiffly while he curved it to fit, then twisted the ends together and placed it on her head.

"Like Frigga herself!" he said. He twisted his own and offered it to her, bowing down like she was a queen. She crowned him without meeting his eyes.

"If you go to the other end of the green you'll find the wishing trees," Mrs. Berdick said. "It was very nice seeing you again, Makena, and meeting you, Mr. Wangera."

They were silent as they walked. Kena had lost her appetite for her cookie and stuck it in her pocket. The pink party hat had broken off anyway, and she'd left it back on the table. She snuck a glance at Oliver. His wreath looked silly perched on top of his big head. She was too heartsick to smile.

Oliver stopped in the middle of the path.

"Okay, what's got you all twisted up?"

Asking could make it worse.

"Tell me. It's not fair to be mad and not say why. How can I apologize if I need to, or help?"

"I'm not mad." And she wasn't anymore. She was scared. And sad. Oliver was right there, right there next to her, but she was alone, and would be alone forever. Was this how Loki felt?

"Why do your eyebrows look like angry caterpillars, then? They're glaring at me right now."

Kena wouldn't smile.

"Tell me."

"You're leaving."

"And then I'm coming back."

"You *are*?" She examined his face for the truth. "Then why are you going?" She crossed her arms, tucking her bare hands in her armpits.

Oliver held out the mittens. "Because I promised Wanja and my mother and the children at Kirinyaga." He took her bandaged hand and pulled a mitten over it. Then the other. "It doesn't mean I don't love you."

That was better, but it wasn't enough.

"What about Mama?" She studied his eyes. He didn't look away. "Are you sure you're not still married?"

Oliver took her good hand and started walking again. There were gold circles floating in two trees; splinters of light glinted off them. Two people sat at a picnic table, writing with markers. As they approached, a teenage girl came up, two circles dangling from her finger. "The idea is you write a wish on one side, or someone can write for you."

"I know how to write," Kena said. She pulled off her mittens and stuffed them into Oliver's pocket.

"Oh, I didn't mean *you*—just anyone. And on the other side, if you want, you can write the name of someone who died. It can be a pet too. Yule is the most powerful night of the year for wishes, and it's also a night to grieve."

"I know," Kena said. "To honor Hodor."

"What?"

"And Loki. Can…may I start now?"

"Of course. Oh, one more thing. The markers are permanent, so be careful." She caught Kena's look. "Anyway, they're permanent so they won't run if it snows."

Kena picked out a purple marker and hunched over her sun. She knew it was better to have only one wish so the spirits would be working together on the same thing. But how could she choose?

She imagined walking out of the jail between her mother and Oliver.

She'd be wearing a long pink dress and pink shoes with real heels and holding little pink flowers, called a posey, when they got married again. They would live half a year in Kenya and the other half in Farleys' Dock. She'd visit Patrice. No, Patrice would visit her, and Toby would come, and they'd sleep in the playhouse with Homer. Mari and Gideon would take her and David to see Adam's owl. She'd help Molly at story hour.

She sighed. She wrote in capital letters. She drew a heart over each one. H O M E.

Patrice said wishes are like prayers, and if two people pray for the same thing it will be answered. She needed one more person. She turned the circle over. She surrounded Adam's name with as many hearts as she could fit in, like stars in heaven.

Oliver was waiting, his sun swinging from his finger. She wanted to sneak and read it but that wasn't good for wishes. He lifted her up, and she hung hers from a branch. He handed his up. As she hung it, it spun, and she couldn't help seeing: Alice was one of the words!

As they walked away, she saw a man and a girl playing fiddles.

People were dancing right in the street! One couple was an old man and a baby. She saw a boy with a small dog tugging at the end of its leash. Daisy!

She ran into the street. "Daisy!"

"Daisy, stop!" the boy called. "Heel!"

Daisy jumped up to greet Kena and then tried to take the toe of her boot in her mouth.

"She always wants my boots," Kena boasted.

"I'm trying to make her heel."

"She likes toes."

Oliver laughed, but the boy didn't.

Kena rubbed behind Daisy's ears. "You have to have treats."

"I have to get her home. She's scared of fireworks," the boy said. "Come on, Daisy. Heel."

Oliver laughed again when Daisy sat down. Kena held her cookie piece out to the boy. "Try this." The boy, followed by Daisy, crossed the street, and they walked alongside until he veered off toward the school.

The suns that she and the other kids had decorated the day before were strung along the fence in front of the library. Inside, the children's room was noisy with kids and their parents. The stuffed animals were buried under mittens and hats and snowsuits. A woman was changing a baby's diaper on the floor.

"Hi, Kena!" a little girl called out. Adam's tree was next to Molly's desk, a line to the bathroom snaking around it. Kena ran up and straightened Molly's bird. There you go.

They stuck their heads into the other room. A clutch of kids sat on the rug, facing someone with long silver hair topped by a wreath of silver leaves. When the kids looked at the door, she turned around.

"Kena!"

Molly stood up and raised her arms and twirled. She was wearing a long green dress shot through with shimmery silver thread. Silver glitter dotted her cheeks.

"You look like a goddess," Oliver said.

"I *am* a goddess!" Molly said.

Back on the sidewalk, a little boy ran up to Kena and stood in front of her expectantly.

"Hi, Peter."

"You must be Kena," his mother said.

Peter smiled but didn't say a word and kept looking back as he followed his mother into the library.

"Everyone knows you," Oliver said.

Kena smiled in contentment.

There was a sign in front of the drugstore: Face Painting. Tattoos. Kena wasn't allowed to get either, in case she had a reaction, but she wondered if Oliver knew that. Maybe a tiny tattoo on her hand or cheek.

"Where are Lily's mittens?" she remembered. Oliver patted his pocket.

Three girls dashed out the door and rushed past, giggling. They were wearing necklaces that glowed.

A tiny, gnome-like figure tripped on the threshold and fell down. Insulted, he instantly emitted a piercing wail. No one came, so Oliver scooped him up, and when he saw Oliver's face he became just as instantly silent. He put out a fat finger and poked Oliver's cheek. Oliver made a pop! sound. The baby looked startled but poked Oliver's cheek again, and at the second pop! he put his head back and laughed.

"Jackson! Thank God!" A young woman was at the door. "Everyone keeps leaving the door open, and he's getting to be so fast," she apologized. But she was beaming at Jackson, who'd put his arms out. She bounced him on her hip. "Thank you!"

"It was truly my pleasure," Oliver responded.

"Is he dressed as an elf?" Kena asked. "What are the ears?"

"Maybe he's an elf teddy bear?" His mother held him up and pushed her nose into the baby's round tummy. "Are you a little elf teddy bear, Jackson?" Jackson threw his head back again and laughed.

"Do you know where we can find one of those glowing necklaces?" Oliver asked, motioning around his neck.

"At the co-op. It's a fundraiser for the St. Johns. Every year it's different, and this year it's in memory of Adam St. John, a young man from here who died recently. There are buckets around, too, for donations."

She suddenly squeezed Jackson tightly against herself. "It's too sad."

She went back inside and closed the door. Tattoo had flown from Kena's mind when she heard Adam's name. As if he was just a sad story. As if he was a stranger and not her Big Brother.

She carefully didn't touch Oliver, afraid she might cry.

The co-op window was stenciled with a border of holly leaves, a menorah in its center with snow that looked like powdered sugar sprinkled around it. Inside, it was bustling and smelled of pizza. Everyone seemed to be talking at once. Oliver found the line for the glow necklaces, but as they stood there, Kena motioned for him to bend down.

"I have to answer a call of nature," she said in his ear.

"What?"

"The bathroom," she whispered.

To her mortification, he asked the lady in front of them and said "toilet."

"It's down there, by the back door." The lady pointed and smiled at Kena. Everyone was looking at them now, and someone called out "Hi, Kena." Someone she'd never seen in her life.

She threaded her way toward the bathroom. A lady patted her on the head, so she took off her wreath and pulled up her hood. She only had to wait for two people, which was a good thing. And when she came out, Oliver was there with a necklace hanging from his wrist and two cups of cider.

"There's a doughnut in my pocket," he said, pointing with his elbow.

It was a plain one.

"Thank you, but you may have it."

"It's just that you had the cookie."

"I didn't eat it all."

Oliver put the cups down on a stack of boxes and slipped the necklace over Kena's neck, hood and all. Kena bent it, and it went from an ugly plastic ring to a rainbow. Did Oliver know the story about the rainbow and the sunbeam?

"Kena! Hi! Is this your dad? Hi, I'm Morgan, and this is *my* little girl, Steffi." It was one of the mothers from the library.

Kena wanted so much to say, "Yes. This is my dad." For Oliver, just this once, to say "Yes, this is *my* girl, my daughter." One of her unwritten wishes coming true.

The little girl wore a gold crown.

"Hi, Steffi. That's a pretty crown."

Steffi narrowed her eyes. "I'm a pinkess. I'm Ariel! Are you Tiana? Where's your crown?" Kena put her hand up to her head and realized she'd left her wreath on the back of the toilet. "Of course you're Ariel! I'm just surprised to see you so far from the ocean."

"We're going to see a fiah."

Fiah? Fire! "We are too!"

"Come on, Mommy!" Steffi pulled her mother's hand. Morgan shrugged, smiling, and followed her. Oliver and Kena finished their cider and looked for a trash can.

"There's one out back," a man said, passing them. So they followed him. When they got outside, Kena gasped. They weren't even close, but she could feel the bonfire's heat on her face and hear its roar. It towered over the crowd surrounding it. Kena held back. Oliver picked her up to sit on his shoulders so she could see better, holding her legs tightly.

A pine tree blazed at the bonfire's center. As high as she was, the tree was much higher. She flinched when a branch broke off with a *wumph*! Sparks burst out. Ashes bigger than her hand rose into the dark sky and broke into pieces that drifted down and sizzled on the snow. She followed one flame and then another, mesmerized as they shape-shifted like ghosts. Fire-ghosts.

She saw Mari on the other side. She saw Gideon seeing Mari and calling out. Mari turned around. Gideon's smile was so big it seemed to take over his whole face.

Just like that, Kena missed Adam. Her whole body hurt with missing.

"You okay up there?" Oliver squeezed her ankle.

More and more people were coming—from the co-op, from down the beach, from the back of the inn. The circle around the fire got wider and wider until she and Oliver were a part of it. Kids were walking around with buckets, people taking stubby candles out of them. A boy came up, and Kena saw it was Jimmy, David's friend. Not her friend, she thought, remembering that day at Lily's house.

"Hi, Kena!" He grinned and held out the bucket. Oliver swung her to the ground. He took two candles.

"We've been looking for you!" Jimmy said. "David! She's over here!"

She spun around. There was David holding a necklace out. He hesitated when he saw she had one, but she bowed so he could put it over her head.

"Want to pass out candles?"

Kena looked at Oliver.

"I'm easy to see, and I won't move from this spot."

So she went with David, handing out candles. Everyone smiled at her.

When the bucket was empty, Kena ran back to Oliver. But it wasn't just Oliver anymore. It was Oliver and Gideon and Mari. Mari hugged her.

People began lighting each other's candles around the circle, starting on the inside and working out, and as they did, they stopped talking. Then it was their turn. Jimmy to David to Gideon to Mari to her to Oliver. And it kept going until the only sound was the fire's snapping and crackling and its soft whooshes. And then there were two fires: the huge bonfire and the circle of fire.

There was a bell, and then again, and a third time, with spaces between for the sound to fade away. People began to sing.

> "'Tis a gift to be simple, 'tis a gift to be free
> 'Tis a gift to come down where we ought to be
> And when we find ourselves in the place just right
> It will be in a valley of love and delight.'"
>
> Oliver drew Kena inside his jacket. Adam's jacket.
>
> "'When true simplicity is gained
> To bow and to bend we won't be ashamed
> To turn, to turn will be our delight
> 'Til by turning, turning we come 'round right.'"

The song rose above their heads and dissolved into the sky with the ashes. Kena felt hollowed out with missing.

Nothing had ever been so beautiful. Nothing had ever hurt so much. It was awfully hard to have so much beauty when her mother and Adam couldn't have it too. The little candle flames lit the faces staring up at the flames that licked the black sky. Like Aslan, flying, and not tame.

Where was *her* place just right?

People began to blow their candles out.

"Mama," she wished, and blew. She stepped out of Oliver's arms and tipped her face up to the sky. "Adam," she whispered. Oliver hunkered down.

"Let's come back another year with your mother," he said.

Kena turned and pressed her face against him. She could hear people moving away, the scrunch-squeak of boots on the snow. She heard kids shouting in the distance.

"Is she okay?" It was David. She felt Oliver's nod.

"Kena, wanna play freeze-tag while we wait for the fireworks?"

She looked down the beach. Glow necklaces leaped and darted.

"I don't know if that's a good idea. You shouldn't get sweaty and then stand around in the cold," Oliver said.

"I won't! I won't get sweaty!" Kena begged.

"Five minutes," Oliver said. "Keep an eye on her," he added to David.

"Oliver!" Kena said. She gave him a look. She tagged David and ran down the beach toward the inn.

It was a wild game, who's It constantly changing in stumbling exuberance from the sliding and falling and laughing. She turned and turned and was only ever frozen for seconds before being rescued by someone flying by. Rainbow tag! *Turning, turning, we come 'round right.*

She saw Oliver and Clare standing by some chairs. Lawn chairs in the snow! Oliver waved his arm. Time to stop.

She spun around, pretending she didn't see.

◊

"Oliver! Clare!"

Oliver turned around. It was Lily, hanging onto Enoch as they stepped gingerly down the slope. But then Lily ran, clumsy in tall black boots, slipping and catching herself, plunging forward as if getting to them was urgent.

"Khai called!" Lily leaned over, breathing hard. "She said yes, the DA, she said yes! She said she'd meet with us about it!"

"The justice thing?" Clare asked.

Lily stood up straighter. "Yes! She said she was willing to talk about it!" She looked toward the lake and became still.

Oliver swung around too, heart-stunned, working against sudden tears. These good people. These good, *good* people. He found Kena easily again, in her double necklace.

There was a swoosh and a POP and everyone looked up. Bright pink lit up the sky and was mirrored on the lake. Kena burst out of the pack of children and ran to Oliver. She saw Lily.

"You came!"

*Swoosh*. The next rocket popped and streamed and crackled in glorious color. Kena pressed against Oliver's legs and covered her ears as another one boomed and echoed.

"Ohhhh!" everyone said. "Ahhh!"

Hoo-ha!

Star flowers were blooming in the sky.

Then she saw the back of him, sitting on the end of the dock. Adam, come to see the fireworks! *Boom! Boom! Boom!*

It was a triple, green and purple and gold, one after the other after the other, blazing into sizzling streamers that crackled apart and drifted down like snow. Rainbow snow.

Kena looked back to the dock to share it with Adam.

He was gone.

Kena looked up at Oliver. He was smiling. Everyone was smiling at the sky.

Except for Lily.

Kena pulled on Oliver's arm. Lily was crying.

◊

Lily's joy when she'd heard what Khai had to say, her hope for Kena and Oliver, even for Alice—all of the hopes she was working to nurture—drained out of her when she saw the children playing in the snow. Like Adam used to do. Adam and Gideon on this most magical night, year after year after year.

It wasn't *fair*.

There were supposed to be more years after years, until she was an old lady watching Adam's children play in the snow. And even as she knew better, she couldn't help herself. She searched the backs of the people in the crowd, her eyes starved for a glimpse of him.

She wanted to be away. Away and away, *away*. From all the happy people, the happy families. What had she been *thinking*? That she could have a camp, or Kenya, or *Kena*, as if there would ever be room again in her for happiness? She was too filled with sadness. And when all was said and done, or not, what did anything good matter anyway? Adam would never be home again. Not ever.

Forever.

Oh, it hurt. Oh, *Adam*!

Kena let go of Oliver's arm. Lily was crying. Kena plunged through the snow. She squeezed in next to Lily on her chair. What could she do?

What could she do to comfort Lily? What could she *do*?

What would her mother do?

"Mama," she whispered.

She pulled one of her glow necklaces over her head and put it on Lily's lap. And Lily, who couldn't refuse a gift from a child, put it around her own neck and picked up Kena's hand. And when she did, she picked up her life and everything it held.

She held Adam in her heart and picked up Kena and Oliver and

Gideon and Enoch and Khai and Homer and Too. She picked up snowstorms and friends and Charlie Brown trees and orphans whose chickens might be aunts and a sky raining rainbows.

She picked up Alice.

Kena's hand was cold, and Lily nested it in hers.

*'Til by turning, turning, we come 'round right.*

# Acknowledgements

Writing a book is a solitary endeavor, but in the end the hope is that someone will be touched by it. Before that, it needs to be vetted by willing readers. Reading a 400 page novel-in-progress, especially by someone you care about, with the promise that you'll share not just your positive reactions, but negative ones too, is a generous gift. I am deeply grateful to my husband Gerry, my children Poppy and Tor, and my sisters Anna, Jeanie, and Kathy for that gift. Their unwavering encouragement and thoughtful feedback have meant more to me than these words can express. Anna has read *homefree* so many times that its characters—including the dog and cat—have become like a second family to her, as they are to me.

Gerry died in May, 2023. He'd be very happy that this story he loved has made its way into the wider world. Knowing that while doing the final draft and cover have given me purpose during this painful time.

A special thanks goes to my brother-in-law John, who drew and painted Kena in all her pinkness with such care and skill. He sat with me and drew and erased and drew and erased until she came alive as the little girl I'd imagined.

Thank you to David Wang'oo Kimiti and to Laurie Sherman for their invaluable help with specific aspects of the story.

The incarcerated men who were at Washington State Correctional Facility in Comstock, New York, when I led Alternatives to Violence workshops provided inspiration and details for some of the most meaningful parts of the book. Thank you for opening your hearts and sharing your experiences.

Thank you to the team at Onion River Press, especially their designer Sofia Silva Wright, and to my editor Louise Watson.

And finally, it's been a wonderful and amazing experience to meet the characters who lived inside of me. Thank you to Alice, Kena, Lily, Gideon and Oliver—and Homer and Too!—for telling me your stories so I could write them down.

# About the Author

Bobbi Loney lives in Middlebury, Vermont, where she and her husband raised their two children while teaching at the elementary school they co-founded. She retired to spend time with their three wonderful grandchildren and to pursue her dream to write. Her first novel, *Jenny's Law*, came out in 2022.